THE **FOLLOWER**

ALSO BY JASON STARR

THE FOLLOWER

JASON STARR

 ST. MARTIN'S MINOTAUR ⚏ NEW YORK

This is a work of fiction. All of the characters, organizations, and events portrayed in this novel are either products of the author's imagination or are used fictitiously.

THE FOLLOWER. Copyright © 2007 by Jason Starr. All rights reserved. Printed in the United States of America. No part of this book may be used or reproduced in any manner whatsoever without written permission except in the case of brief quotations embodied in critical articles or reviews. For information, address St. Martin's Press, 175 Fifth Avenue, New York, N.Y. 10010.

www.minotaurbooks.com

Library of Congress Cataloging-in-Publication Data

Starr, Jason, 1966–
  The follower / Jason Starr.—1st ed.
    p. cm.
   ISBN-13: 978-0-312-35974-4
   ISBN-10: 0-312-35974-8
  I. Title.

PS3569.T336225 F65 2007
813'.54—dc22
               2007014167

First Edition: August 2007

10 9 8 7 6 5 4 3 2 1

For Sandy and Chynna

It is a truth universally acknowledged,
that a single man in possession of a good fortune,
must be in want of a wife.

—JANE AUSTEN, *Pride and Prejudice*

PART ONE

1

Peter Wells had never been turned down for a job. He didn't have to work very often, thank God, but when he needed work—and he desperately needed the receptionist job at the Metro Sports Club—he always got hired.

The interviewer, a musclehead named Jimmy, seemed like an asshole from the get-go. He told Peter to wait in his office because he was "in the middle of something." Meanwhile, Peter watched through the Plexiglas as Jimmy hung out by the front desk with another musclehead, the two of them hitting on practically every girl who passed by.

Finally, maybe twenty minutes later, Jimmy came into the office and said, "Sorry about that, buddy, it's been crazy here today," and sat at his desk.

"No, problem, man," Peter said, talking the way Jimmy talked, knowing it was a way to instantly connect with an employer.

Jimmy squinted at the résumé for several seconds, and then started looking at Peter's left ear. That was what Peter thought anyway; then he turned and saw what Jimmy was staring at—the skinny dark-haired girl in black bicycle shorts who was bending over doing a hamstring stretch.

"Gotta love Nikki," Jimmy said. "Comes here two times a day—uses machines, does cardio, must spend an hour on the Stairmaster. Phenomenal body but, honestly, she's only average at this place. People say the best-looking girls are in the Village and the Meatpacking District, but I'll take the Upper East Side chicks any day. Watch the advanced step classes sometime. I mean, yeah, you got some girls who need to lose some poundage, but most of them are total babes. They all starve themselves, that's why. They eat salad and Tasti-Delight for dinner every night, then come here to work off the calories. But, trust me, these chicks could be eighty-five pounds and you'd still wanna fuck 'em."

Peter knew Jimmy would be an absolute nightmare to work for, but keeping the act going he said, "Yeah, she's hot all right."

Jimmy, looking at the résumé again, said, "So let's see. You worked at Body Image in Santa Monica?"

"That's right," Peter said.

"How'd that go?"

"It went well. It went really well. But then they closed down so I had to leave."

Actually, Peter had never worked at a health club in Santa Monica. He'd never even been there.

"And you worked in Mexico?" Jimmy asked.

"Yeah," Peter said, "I was traveling a little bit, trying to figure out what to do, you know? I taught ESL."

Another lie, although he'd lived in Mexico for a while.

"At L'Escuela International de Guadalajara?" Jimmy asked.

"*Hablas español?*" Peter said.

"What?" Jimmy waited, then laughed and said, "Just kidding, man. I took it in high school and my dad's half Puerto Rican, but I can't talk for shit. But that's good—you're bilingual. You should talk to Carlos, trainer works on weekends . . . So you got any more gym experience?"

"Sure have," Peter lied. "In college, I worked in the weight room a couple semesters. Volunteered."

Peter hadn't gone to college, but he doubted Jimmy would start checking references.

"Let's see," Jimmy said. "BA in English at the University of Colorado at Boulder. Looks like you've been all over, huh? Where'd you grow up?"

"Massachusetts."

"Boston?"

"Lenox."

"Oh, that's why I didn't hear a Bahston accent." Jimmy laughed. "So you say you want to be a trainer, huh?"

"That's my goal," Peter said, although he didn't care what he did at the gym. He was planning to work there for a couple of weeks, tops, but he knew he had to show ambition.

"Well, this is a good place to work when you're going for your license," Jimmy said. "We're flexible if you wanna go to school, take classes, whatever. We don't give benefits for part-time, but a lot of people who work here start part-time and work their way up to full. But all I've got for you right now is a part-time desk job. You make sure people scan their cards when they come in, hand out towels, answer the phones . . ."

"That sounds good to me," Peter said.

"It only pays nine-fifty an hour."

"Money doesn't matter."

Jimmy looked up, surprised. Peter wished he could take that back.

"I mean, it matters," Peter said. "Of course it matters. I just mean I want to work here to get some more health club experience under my belt so I can become a trainer someday. So it doesn't really matter what I make right now."

"I got ya, I got ya," Jimmy said. "Well, it looks like you've got the credentials and you're a good guy—if you want the job it's yours, man."

"I definitely want it."

"Great. I can only give you part-time—morning shift, six to noon—and you gotta work weekends. I can get you extra hours here and there, but I can't get you benefits and I'm gonna have to ten ninety-nine you."

"That's fine."

"You can work out whenever you want and I'll introduce you to the trainers—Scott, Mike, Carlos, Jenny. Man, wait till you see Jenny."

Trying not to roll his eyes, Peter said, "A babe, huh?"

"Fucking smoking," Jimmy said. "When can you start?"

"How about tomorrow?"

"Tomorrow works. Welcome aboard, my man."

Jimmy and Peter shook hands.

As they left the office and headed along the corridor toward the front of the gym, Jimmy said, "So where do you live?"

"Right around the corner," Peter said, "with my girlfriend."

"Yeah?" Jimmy said.

"Yeah, maybe you know her. Katie. Katie Porter?"

"She's tall, blond, nice shape?"

"Actually she has light brown hair and she's about five three. But, yeah, she has a nice shape."

"Nah, I'm confusing her," Jimmy said, "but if she works out here I'm sure I've seen her around. But that's cool—that's real cool. You got a girlfriend belongs to the gym, you're living close by. So how'd you guys meet?"

"We grew up together."

"High school sweethearts, huh?"

"Yeah, kind of."

The musclehead Jimmy had been hanging out with before was walking by in the other direction.

"Hey, Mike," Jimmy said to the guy. "This is Peter Wells. He's gonna be working at the front desk and he wants to be a trainer."

"Great," Mike said and shook Peter's hand with a very firm grip. "See you around, man."

"Yeah, you, too."

Peter and Jimmy stopped near the entrance to the gym.

"I gotta hit the weights, man," Jimmy said. "When you come in tomorrow you can find me in the office and we'll take care of the paperwork and all that bullshit then. Sound cool?"

"Sounds cool."

"Hey, and you gotta introduce me to your girlfriend sometime."

"I definitely will."

Jimmy went back toward the locker room.

Peter was proud of himself. He'd hung in there, said all the right things, and he'd gotten the job. It was only a first step, but so far everything was going according to plan.

As he zipped his windbreaker, he scanned the main level of the gym. Dozens of overworked-looking twentysomethings were listening to iPods or watching TV while they worked out on the Stairmasters and treadmills. Peter hadn't seen Katie when he arrived for the interview, and he didn't see her now, either. He exited the health club and headed downtown along Third Avenue, walking fast with his hands in his pockets.

2

Andy Barnett was looking at the monitor on his PC, at the little digital clock in the lower-right-hand corner. He had plenty of work to do—a new monthly sales survey for one of the companies he followed was due tomorrow—but it was 4:22 and after four in the afternoon Andy could never deal with work. He wished he could go online—check out his fantasy football team or IM his friends—but the bank's system people monitored everything employees did on the Net and this dude, Justin, who'd worked two cubicles down, had been fired two weeks ago for surfing on company time. So whenever Andy didn't feel like working, he couldn't do anything but zone out, staring at the monitor with an intense, focused expression, as if he were trying to solve some complicated problem, in case his boss or somebody else in management happened to pass by.

At 4:26, Andy's phone rang. He recognized his friend Scott's number on the caller ID. He picked up and said in a low voice, "Dude, what's up?"

"Chilling," Scott said. "Waiting to get the hell outta here."

"Me, too, bro. Me, too. What's going on later?"

"Some guys at work are gonna check out the happy hour at McAleer's."

"McAleer's blew last week, dude."

"Yeah, but it should be pretty cool tonight. My buddy Dave knows a girl there and she's bringing friends."

"Cute?"

"One's a babe, two're borderline, the others I don't know. But, hey, if the talent's lame, we can just hit Fire House. Dave says there was a ton of tuna there last week."

"I don't know, dude," Andy said. "Maybe we should stay east. I mean, I can only stay out till like seven, seven-thirty tonight anyway."

"Don't tell me you're seeing that chick again?"

"Yeah, we're gonna go out to dinner."

"Dude," Scott said. "What's this, like the third time in two weeks?"

It was actually their fourth date.

"She's really cool," Andy said.

"Bro, how many times I gotta tell ya? You can't stick around, begging for it like a dog. If it doesn't happen on the second date you gotta bail."

"What makes you think I didn't get any yet?"

"You? If you got some I would've heard about it the next morning. Hell, you would've jumped out of bed and called me in the middle of the night— *Dude, I just fucked this girl. Really, I did.*"

Scott was laughing.

Andy said, "Look who's talking. When was the last time you had a girl-friend, freakin' sophomore year?"

"Yeah, but I got laid last weekend. I'm tellin' ya, dude—you keep it up with this chick, pretty soon she's gonna wanna take you ring shopping."

Drew Frasier, one of the senior analysts, passed Andy's cubicle.

"I better go," Andy said to Scott, nearly whispering, "before I get busted."

"So what's the deal tonight? You coming out with us or not?"

"I told you, I can meet up if we stay east."

"So let me get this straight," Scott said. "You want me to meet you for a drink at some lame East Side bar and blow off my friends and the hot, fuck-able babes at McAleer's so you can take off at seven o'clock for a date with your future fiancée?"

Andy, used to taking crap from Scott, was shaking his head, smiling.

"Come on, man, blow her off," Scott went on. "You'll probably hook up with one of the chicks at McAleer's. Then, later, we're gonna hit this party on Broadway in the sixties. Cornell dudes are throwing it. It's sup-posed to be hot and you're guaranteed to hook up or at least get some num-bers."

"Sorry, bro, can't make it tonight," Andy said. "But I'll definitely meet up with you guys tomorrow to watch the game."

"Yeah, if you're not engaged by then."

"Later, dude."

Andy clicked off and resumed staring intently at the clock on the moni-tor. At four fifty-nine, he starting putting on his suit jacket. At five, he was leaving his cubicle, heading toward the elevators.

Walking along Park Avenue toward the subway stop on Fifty-first and Lex, Andy checked out every good-looking girl he passed. He couldn't help it. He was a twenty-three-year-old single guy in Manhattan, and as far as he was concerned there were only two types of people in the world—hot girls and everybody else.

As Andy approached the crowded entrance to the subway, he zeroed in on a really cute chick with straight brown hair in black pants and a black suit jacket. The clothes were loose, but it looked like she had a nice body—thin anyway, which was all that really mattered. There were about five people between them as they headed down the stairs, but he kept watching her as the crowd moved toward the turnstiles. She swiped her MetroCard and went down the steps toward the jam-packed platform. He followed her as she wove through the crowd toward the end of the platform where it was slightly less crowded. When she stopped, Andy stopped, right next to her.

Every time Andy rode the subway, he would automatically zero in on the cutest girl on the platform and stand as close to her as possible. Then he would try to get into a conversation, or at least make a lot of eye contact, and then when the train came he would make sure they got on the same car. If things went well, he'd keep the small talk going, hopefully say a couple of clever, witty things to make her laugh—getting a girl to laugh was key—and then ask for her number. He'd gotten a few numbers on the subway, and even went out with this one girl a few times and wound up getting laid. But most of the time, he struck out. The big problem was that a lot of girls were paranoid as hell on the subway and wouldn't talk to guys, even though if they saw the same guys at a bar or a club they'd gladly talk to them then, because *that* was more socially acceptable.

Andy was looking at the brown-haired girl, but she wasn't noticing him, or at least wasn't acting like she did. A train pulled into the station and Andy boarded directly behind her. He followed her to the middle of the car and gripped the same pole she was holding, their hands inches apart. She was staring up ahead, as if she were reading the START AN EXCITING CAREER AS A DENTAL ASSISTANT ad over and over again. Man, she was even better-looking than Andy had thought. She had big green eyes, nice lips, and no zits. Andy always told his friends that the best place to meet girls was the subway because the fluorescent light was so unforgiving. If a girl looked good on the 6 train, she'd look good anywhere.

At the next stop, Fifty-ninth Street, the girl shifted her attention away from the ad toward Andy.

"Hi," Andy said.

"Hi" was by far the best pickup line, much better than, "Have we met?"

The girl hesitated, then smiled and said, "Hi," and looked away again. Andy knew he had his opening; it was just a matter of delivering the perfect follow-up.

People exited and entered the train and Andy and the girl were squeezed even closer together. The train started moving and Andy waited for the girl to look at him again, and then he said, "Now I know what sardines feel like."

"What?" the girl asked.

The line wasn't that funny and he wished he'd said something else. He knew it would sound even less funny when he repeated it, but he did anyway.

The girl smiled and laughed a little, but Andy wasn't sure that she'd even heard him over the noise of the subway. Andy was trying to think of some other clever thing to say, but then the girl moved away toward the door and exited at the Sixty-eighth Street stop.

Andy looked around the train for more talent and saw a good-looking Chinese girl with funky glasses sitting at the far end of the car, reading a thick paperback. There was space in front of her, so, at the next stop, Andy casually moved over there. He tried to make eye contact with the girl but she was too engrossed in her book to notice.

At Ninety-sixth Street—Andy's stop—Andy followed the girl out of the station. Andy was hoping that she lived in his building so he could get onto the elevator with her or follow her to the mailbox area and say, *Hey, didn't I just see you on the subway?* a line that sometimes worked even when he *hadn't* just seen the girl on the subway. But at the corner of Ninety-sixth and Lex, the girl headed uptown, and Andy went in the opposite direction, toward Ninety-fifth Street.

Andy lived in Normandie Court, a complex of three massive apartment buildings that took up an entire square block between Second and Third Avenues and Ninety-fifth and Ninety-sixth Streets. The majority of residents in the building were recent college grads, which was why many people referred to the buildings as Dormandie Court. Andy lived in a three-bedroom apartment with five other guys and shared a room with his buddy Greg, a frat brother from Delta Kappa Epsilon at Michigan. Last year, Andy had had his own room at the frat house and he felt like he was taking a step backward in life, having to share a bedroom again, but he had little choice. Manhattan rents were so out of control that unless he wanted to move into some dive walk-up, or to an outer borough or Jersey, sharing was the only way to go. The rent on the apartment was $3,600 a month so Andy's share came to only $600, which left him with plenty of expendable income for beer and going out.

Andy went through the revolving doors into the lobby, which had the same anonymous, corporate feeling as the lobby in the building where he worked, and rode the elevator to his apartment on the twenty-seventh floor. As usual, the door was unlocked, and when he opened it he saw Chris sprawled on the couch in his boxers, watching porn. Chris worked nights, bartending at Bar East on First, which was very cool because he could sometimes give his roommates free drinks, but it was also very annoying because he worked until four or five in the morning, slept until two or three in the afternoon, and spent most of the rest of his time parked on the couch in his underwear.

"Hey," Andy and Chris said at the same time, and then Andy went down the hallway into his room. He took off his suit, added it to his half of the closet with his nine other suits from Banana Republic, and then went into the kitchen. Every dish and piece of silverware the guys had was dirty and piled in the sink. The counter was covered with pizza boxes, Pringles cans, beer and soda bottles, and Chinese take-out containers, and the garbage can was overflowing. Andy opened the fridge, which contained nothing but beer, soda, and leftover pizza and Chinese—most of which had been there for weeks—and took out a bottle of Lowenbrau. He went into the living room and sat in the red IKEA chair, next to Chris on the couch. On TV, an Asian woman was making out with a blonde. When the camera panned down to the Asian woman's backside, Chris said, "You like that?"

"Nice," Andy said.

"I don't know, she's too bony for me. I like some meat to grab on to, know what I mean?"

Drinking their beers, not talking at all, they watched the girls go at it for several minutes. Then the front door opened and Will entered with a knapsack slung over one shoulder.

"Hey," Andy and Chris said, and Will said, "Hey." Then Will looked at the TV and said, "All right, carpet munching!"

Will was a med student at Mount Sinai and planned to become a pediatrician. He shared a bedroom with Steve, who was working as a paralegal while studying for his LSATs.

Will grabbed a beer, then sat on a chair and started watching the movie. A couple of minutes later, John, who shared a room with Chris, came home. Although Andy had only had a few sips of Lowenbrau, he put the bottle down on the coffee table and announced, "I'm showering," because he knew that John, who was a total metrosexual and took as long as a girl in the bathroom, always hogged the shower when he came home from work.

The bathroom hadn't been cleaned since they'd moved into the apartment five months ago, and there was mildew all over the tiles and the shower curtain, and the drain was clogged—thanks to John and Steve, who were both going prematurely bald—and the tub always filled with about six inches of water during showers. Whoever had used the toilet hadn't bothered to flush and a few turds were floating on top.

"Jesus, you guys are fuckin' disgusting!" Andy shouted.

"Thanks!" Chris, who was always proud of his big dumps, yelled back, and then Andy flushed, drowning out whatever else Chris was saying.

Andy peed—not bothering to flush—and then took a quick shower. After he shaved, he returned to his bedroom with a towel around his waist and discovered that Greg had come home from work. Greg was sitting on his bed with Jessica, a-little-heavy-but-still-kinda-cute curly-haired Italian-looking girl who lived in one of the other buildings at Normandie.

"Sorry," Andy said.

Jessica was looking away, embarrassed.

"It's cool," Greg said. "Want us to go in another room or something?"

Andy knew Greg would've killed him later if he said yes. Greg hadn't hooked up since college, and Andy didn't want to be a dick and take away a chance for his buddy to finally get some.

"No, it's cool," Andy said. "Lemme just grab some clothes. Sorry to interrupt."

"You're not really interrupting anything," Jessica said, obviously trying to protect her dignity.

Greg glared at Andy, as if Andy had blown it for him.

"It's okay," Andy said. "I can get dressed anywhere."

Andy took a pair of socks, boxer briefs, Banana Republic jeans, a navy Banana Republic button-down shirt, and his Banana Republic loafers, then said, "See you guys later," and left the room. Andy went into John and Chris's room, got dressed, and then went into the steamy bathroom—John was showering—and gelled his hair, applied deodorant, and dabbed Lucky You cologne all over, including his pubic hair.

He had some time to kill before he had to leave for his date, so he rejoined Will and Chris in the living room. Chris still had control of the remote and was switching between sports and porn. Watching a red-haired woman having sex with two big black guys, Chris said to Will, "So what happened with you and that girl the other night?"

"Which one?" Will asked.

Chris looked at Andy. "Listen to this guy, 'Which one?'" He turned to Will again. "Short, poodle hair."

"Oh, Lara. She's really cool. She's a speech therapist."

"Did you fuck her?"

"Nah, I like her friend."

Chris said to Andy, "You shoulda seen this guy. He comes into the bar last night at one o'clock. He's in his scrubs, of course, and he's got two girls with him. Not one—*two*. Jen, the red-hot new bartender, goes to me, 'Is your friend single?'"

"The guy's a magnet," Andy said.

"It's because he's a fuckin' doctor," Chris said.

"I'm not a doctor yet," Will said.

"You know what I'm talking about," Chris said. "You wear those scrubs everywhere—supermarket, Blockbuster, running in the park—and babes come up to you like you're fucking fly tape."

"Jealous?" Will asked.

"Of the scrubs, not you," Chris said. "Even Andy could get laid wearing that doctor shit, right, And?"

Andy was staring at the TV. The redhead was in a contorted position on a staircase, between the two guys. Chris used the pause feature on the DVR and then slo-mo'd the scene.

"I saw that chick in this other film the other day," Chris said.

"Listen to this dude—*film*," Will said. "Like it'll win a fuckin' Academy Award."

"Shit, what the hell's her name?" Chris asked.

"Ginger something," Will said.

"No, I know who you're thinking of," Andy said. "This one's Heidi or Hillary or something with an H . . . Holly? . . . Nah, wait a sec, it'll come to me."

Chris continued playing the scene at normal speed and then, just as the guys started to orgasm at the same time—Andy had always wondered how they did that; didn't they, like, get grossed out by each other?—Greg and Jessica came down the hallway. Chris spotted them and flicked the channel back to ESPN, but Greg and Jessica had obviously heard the sex sounds because Jessica was smiling and blushing and Greg looked pissed off.

"Hey, what's up?" Chris said, trying to act casual.

Andy and Will were trying not to crack up.

"You guys going out tonight?" Jessica asked.

"I have to work," Chris said.

"Studying," Will said.

"I have a date," Andy said.

"Cool," Jessica said. "If you guys aren't doing anything tomorrow night, me and my roommates're having a party."

"Thanks," Andy and Will said.

"Yeah, thanks," Chris said.

Greg walked Jessica out to the elevator and returned a couple of minutes later. The guys were watching porn again.

"You're such fuckin' assholes, you know that?" Greg said.

"What?" Chris said innocently.

"Why can't you turn off that shit when I've got a girl in the house?"

"Relax," Will said. "She seems to like you."

"Yeah, she seems chill," Chris said. "What the fuck's she doing with you? Her roommates good-looking or what?"

"I'm serious," Greg said. "First Andy walks in on us—"

"I had to get dressed," Andy said.

"—and then she comes into the living room and it's porn central."

"Somebody sounds like he didn't get any," Chris said.

"Yeah, I guess the drought ain't over yet, huh?" Will said.

"Drought?" Chris said. "It's like the fuckin' Sahara in there."

"I'll be lucky if she even wants to go out with me again," Greg said.

"What're you talking about?" Chris said. "She loved us—she invited us to that party. So what's the deal with the roommates?"

"One's hot as hell," Greg said. "The other one's pretty cute, too."

"Jessica's cute, so that sounds promising," Chris said. "So did you get *anything* off her yet?"

"We got to second base."

The guys laughed.

"Second base!" Chris said. "Listen to this guy. It's like he's back in junior high. So you got in her shirt, huh?"

"I thought second's a hand job," Andy said.

"Bullshit," Chris said. "Second's the shirt. The guy probably didn't get under her bra, either. See, look at him, I can tell he didn't." Chris laughed.

"I have to admit, that's pretty pathetic," Will said.

"You're still the only guy in the apartment who hasn't gotten laid," Chris said to Greg.

"So what?" Greg said. "I don't have to prove anything to you guys."

"You have to prove you know how to get laid," Chris said.

John came into the living room and Chris added, "Even John got some last week."

"What's going on?" John asked.

"Greg's still oh-for-Manhattan," Will said.

"Thanks to these assholes and their fuckin' porn," Greg said.

"Whoa, so now you're antiporn?" Chris said. "How come the *Penthouses* have your name and address on them?"

"And the *Screws*, too," Will said.

"Look who's talking," John said to Chris. "Whenever I come home at night, the TV suddenly goes off and I see you lying on the couch, covering up."

"I gotta agree with that one," Andy said.

"I admit I like to shoot my rod every once in a while," Chris said, "but I think Greg's the official jerk-off king of this apartment." He looked at Greg. "Maybe that's why you're not getting laid—because you're jerking off too much. It's fucking up your sex drive."

"No, I'm not getting laid because I'm living with you guys," Greg said.

"So it's our fault," Chris said as a statement. "Like if you were living in a studio, the chicks would be lining up for you."

"Maybe," Greg said.

"Living here doesn't stop me from getting laid," Chris said. "It doesn't stop John or Doc, and it doesn't stop your own roommate." Chris turned toward Andy. "You've been fucking that chick, right?"

"Yeah," Andy lied.

"See?" Chris said to John.

"Hey, how come we haven't met this girl yet?" John asked Andy.

"Yeah," Will said. "When's the reveal?"

"Maybe she's a pig," Chris said.

"I'm just preparing her," Andy said.

"For what?" Chris asked.

"Yeah, we're nice guys," Will said.

"Yeah," Chris said. "I mean, it's not like we're disgusting porn-watching scumbags or anything like that."

Will and Chris laughed, and then Will took a big gulp of beer.

"Maybe he's talking about the apartment," John said.

"What's wrong with the apartment?" Chris asked.

"It's a fuckin' pigsty," John said. "It's a miracle we don't have mice."

"I think I saw a roach the size of a mouse last week," Will said.

"I'm talking about the apartment *and* you guys," Andy said.

"What?" Chris said. "You're embarrassed?"

"You guys don't exactly make a great first impression," Andy said.

"Whoa, whoa," Chris said. "What do you mean? We got a med student, a law student, a handsome-as-hell bartender . . ."

"He's got a point," Will said. "Ever notice how girls don't wanna go out with us again after they come here?"

"That's what I'm talking about," Greg said.

"No, the problem is *you*," Chris said. "You fuck around, trying to get to second base, when you should be getting laid like your roommate."

Andy got up, then said, "I gotta get going."

"I wanna see a picture of this mystery girl," John said to Andy.

"Or how 'bout you set up a Web cam tonight?" Chris added. "See some filmage."

Andy took his brown leather bomber jacket out of the hallway closet and then said, "Later on, dudes," and left the apartment.

It was a relief to be alone. Andy had nothing against his roommates—they were cool and everything—but this sharing-a-place-with-five-other-guys shit was getting old. He was glad he was taking the GMATs next month and would be in business school next year. He hoped to go to Wharton or Harvard and when he had his MBA and some kick-ass job he'd move back to New York the right way. He'd be working at Lehman Brothers or Morgan Stanley or someplace A-list, and he'd have his *own* three-bedroom. He'd also have a Ferrari, a house in the Hamptons, and everything else he'd always dreamed of.

Heading along Second Avenue, Andy passed a Korean grocery with flowers for sale in front, and he decided to buy a bouquet of pink roses for Katie. He really liked her. She was the first girl he'd met since graduation whom he could see taking home to Pennsylvania to meet his parents. She also was the type of girl he could see being with long-term, even after he got his MBA. He could imagine taking her out to dinner at fancy, trendy restaurants and to work-related parties and feeling proud. The last girl he'd gone out with, Steffi, was cool and everything, but she didn't have class. She was the kind of girl you want to go to bars with but not who you want to marry. Katie was totally different. Andy knew that Katie liked him as much as he liked her, which was why it was starting to frustrate him that he hadn't gotten any yet.

Katie said she wanted to take it slow—which was cool with Andy at first because he didn't want to date a total slut—but he didn't want to wait forever, either. The next time he told his roommates that he and Katie had had sex he wanted it to be the truth, and since they both really liked each other and were perfect for each other and all that, he didn't see why they had to wait any longer.

As he crossed Second Avenue, and continued along East Ninety-third, he knew the roses would help big-time. Last year, in Ann Arbor, he'd gone out with this girl Alison. The first couple of times they were alone together, he didn't get any, and then he went over to her place with a couple of roses and he wound up getting laid.

He went up the stoop of the walk-up apartment where Katie lived, confident that tonight would be his lucky night.

3

Katie Porter was in the bathroom, putting on mascara while holding her cell up to her ear, saying to her friend Amanda, "And then he called me the other day at work, not for any reason—just to say, Hi, what's going on?"

"That's a good sign," Amanda said.

"Isn't it?" Katie said. "And he's a really sweet guy. He always holds the door open for me when I'm getting into cabs, and he helps me put my coat on—"

"That's great."

"And he's not one of those guys you can't hold a conversation with. Like that guy Dave I went out with last month, you know the one who kept going on and on about the Mets. I wanted to strangle myself."

Amanda laughed, then said, "So have you guys . . . ?"

"No, not yet," Katie said. "I mean, I think he wants to, but, I don't know, I just want to wait. But he's really cool about it, you know? He's not pressuring me or anything."

Katie put the mascara in the medicine chest and looked at herself, making sure she looked perfect.

"It's so great you found each other," Amanda said.

Katie was outside the bathroom, looking in the full-length mirror on the back of the door. "Oh, shit."

"What's wrong?"

"I'm wearing jeans and I had sushi with tons of soy sauce for lunch."

"I'm sure you look amazing."

Still thinking her thighs looked bloated, Katie squatted, trying to stretch the jeans out, then said, "But I really want you to meet him. Maybe we can go out next week or something."

"Does he have any single friends?"

"He doesn't talk about his friends that much."

"Oh." Amanda sounded like she thought that was weird.

"It's only been two weeks," Katie said. "I haven't even been to his apartment yet."

"You haven't?"

"No, but I know he has roommates."

"Normandie guys?" Amanda asked warily.

"Andy's a Normandie guy," Katie said.

"I know, but most of those guys are so immature. My friend Jen at work went out with a Normandie guy last year and he was the biggest asshole. They're all, like, frat boys."

"He said one's in med school and one's in law school," Katie said, as if Amanda could be missing out on a major opportunity.

"Have you seen pictures?"

"No, but they could be really good-looking. Andy's adorable."

"I hate being set up," Amanda said. "I mean, maybe if there's, like, a party or something—"

The buzzer rang.

"That's him," Katie said.

"Call me tomorrow and tell me everything."

"I will."

Katie clicked off. She buzzed Andy up, then went into the bathroom and put on some more Tommy Girl perfume. She was slightly pissed off at Amanda for acting so high and mighty and she wondered if Amanda was just jealous. Although Amanda was really sweet—well, sweet most of the time, anyway—she'd been having a hard time meeting guys lately. It wasn't because Amanda wasn't pretty. She was a little on the heavy side, but she had a cute face and great blue eyes and a beautiful smile. Her attitude needed work, though. She was a year older than Katie and had been living in New York since graduating from Wesleyan a year and a half ago. Lots of guys had screwed her over, especially since she'd been living in the city, and she let it show, acting all standoffish and bitchy when guys tried to talk to her at bars.

The doorbell rang. Katie looked in the full-length mirror again, still thinking her legs looked fat, wishing she'd changed into something else. Well, too late now. She opened the door and Andy was there, looking really cute in a Banana Republic shirt and with his hair gelled. They said hi and kissed and then Andy handed her a bouquet of pink roses.

"Oh my God, thank you." She recognized the bouquet and the wrapping from the flowers that were sold at the Korean deli on Second Avenue. She knew these bouquets cost ten dollars and she was disappointed that Andy hadn't sprung for a little more. Then she reminded herself that he was poor—well, maybe not poor, but he was at his first job out of college and was probably paying off student loans—and it was the thought that counted.

"They're so beautiful," she said. "I better go put them in water."

Andy took off his jacket then followed Katie into the kitchen. As Katie filled a vase with water, Andy held her from behind and said, "Hey, where's Susan?"

"Oh, she's sleeping over at Tom's tonight."

"Really? You mean we have the whole place all to ourselves?"

Katie wasn't sure she liked the tone in Andy's voice.

"Yeah," Katie said. "I guess we do."

Andy came over and started kissing Katie's neck.

"You're gonna make me drop the vase," she said.

Katie finished putting the flowers in the water and went toward the small dining area. Andy followed her and kept kissing her.

"Down boy," Katie said.

"I can't help it," Andy said. "You're so beautiful."

Katie put the vase on the table and said, "How do they look?"

"Awesome," Andy said, turning Katie toward him. They started making out, then Andy pulled back and said, "It's so great to see you."

"You, too," Katie said.

Andy kissed her again and steered her backward onto the couch. He was on top of her, pressing down a little too hard, but she didn't say anything. Then his hand slid down her right leg and he started squeezing the side of her thigh and she wondered if he was feeling her fat.

After he undid her bra and started rubbing her breasts, Katie pushed him back gently and said, "We should go to dinner now."

"Why?" Andy said and started kissing her again.

"Because," Katie said, her voice muffled. "I'm starving."

Andy pushed himself up, halfway off her, and said, "How about we just order in?"

"No, I really wanted to go out to that Spanish place."

"Come on, how often do we get the place to ourselves?"

"We can come back later."

Andy started kissing Katie again, feeling her breasts and thighs. As his hands crept closer to between her legs, she squeezed them together and said, "Seriously," and turned away. "I want to go out."

"Whatever," Andy said, sitting up, as if offended.

"It's just that it's Friday night," Katie said. "I hate sitting home Friday nights. It makes me feel like such a loser. I like to get out and—"

"It's no big deal," Andy said coldly. "I just thought it'd be cool to order in and watch a pay-per-view or something. But if you want to go out, let's go out."

Katie got her J. Crew leather jacket from the closet. Although Andy was standing right there, he didn't help her put it on, the way he usually did.

Outside, walking along Second Avenue, they held hands and things seemed normal, but when they got to the restaurant Andy started acting weird again. He kept getting distracted, looking away, and he didn't seem to be having a good time. He said his paella was "too gummy" and wouldn't eat it, and he refused to even try her seviche. At first, Katie thought he was being all moody because he'd wanted to stay in, but then she started wondering if maybe there was more to it. Maybe something had happened at work or something, or maybe something was going on with his family. He didn't talk much about his family, but on their first date he mentioned that his parents had almost gotten divorced last year.

Whatever was going on with Andy, it was annoying Katie, but she didn't feel comfortable enough around him yet to ask him what was wrong, so she tried to ignore it. She kept making small talk—he was barely answering—and by the time the check came, she was so fed up she just wanted to go home and watch TV by herself.

"So what do you want to do now?" Katie asked.

"What do you want to do?" Andy asked.

"I don't know. It's getting kind of late, I guess."

"So you don't wanna go out for a drink or something?"

"I'll go if you want to go," she said, hoping he'd get the hint that she was pissed off.

"No, it's cool," Andy said, not getting the hint at all. "Let's just go hang back at your place."

Katie didn't want to invite Andy back to her apartment, and she tried to think of a way out of it. She figured she'd say she wasn't feeling well, or she was exhausted, or something like that. But then, all of a sudden, Andy was acting like his old self—making jokes and paying a lot of attention to her. She didn't know what was going on with him—if anything was going on; she could've been making it all up—and she decided to let him come back to her place and see how things went. He was really nice and sweet and they wound up on the couch, making out, listening to KT Tunstall. She was going to forget about the way he'd acted at the restaurant, not bring it up anyway, but it was still on her mind, and she blurted out, "So what's up with you to-night anyway?"

"What do you mean?" Andy said, lost, or pretending to be lost.

"In the restaurant," Katie said. "You were so, like, I don't know . . ."

"I'm sorry . . . I guess I just had a long week at work, you know?"

"Oh," she said, thinking, *That's no excuse.*

"Sorry if I was a jerk," Andy said, and kissed her, running his hands gently through her hair. Then, touching noses, he said, "Your eyes are so beautiful."

"Thanks," she said.

They continued kissing. He was on top of her now, in the same position they were in before they went to dinner. He undid her bra and started feeling her breasts and it felt really nice. Then he started grinding up against her and feeling her over her jeans. They were both breathing heavier and she could tell he wanted to do it and she wanted to do it, too.

"Wanna move to the bedroom?" he asked.

"Yeah," she said.

They went into the bedroom and then she said she'd be right back and went into the bathroom. She was going to get a condom, but then decided she wouldn't make love to Andy tonight. Although she liked him a lot and he seemed like a really nice guy, she wanted to wait awhile, at least two more dates. She felt like she'd had sex too quickly with her last couple of boyfriends and she felt bad about it and she wanted to take things slower this time. Maybe she'd do a little more with Andy tonight, but they definitely wouldn't have sex.

Katie returned to the bedroom and Andy was sitting on the edge of the bed. He had taken off his button-down shirt but was still wearing a white V-neck T-shirt. The lamp on the dresser was shining on him, and his skin looked very smooth and tan.

She sat next to him and they started kissing and then he pulled her shirt off over her head and she pulled off his. Then he took off her bra and kissed her breasts in a nice way and then she said, "Wait," and leaned over toward the night table. She flicked on the iPod, which was connected to a docking station. A few seconds later, Norah Jones was into "Come Away with Me."

Sitting up, they continued kissing each other and then they lay down, side by side, and suddenly his hand was under her panties. She was kind of surprised because he hadn't even unsnapped her jeans and because he hadn't asked her if it was okay to do this. They hadn't gone this far before, and the last time he tried, she told him she wanted to wait. But she didn't say any-thing, because it felt good, and she was ready to go further tonight anyway.

After a while, she opened his jeans and started touching him. She'd wondered if, because his hands were kind of small, he'd be small everywhere, and she was glad to feel that it was normal sized, maybe even on the big side. She wanted to make love, but she knew it would be better to wait. They'd fool around tonight and then maybe next time they'd do more. It would be hard for her to finish this way—it was already getting a little uncomfortable—but he'd finish and that would be far enough for tonight.

Then he started pushing her head down with one of his hands. Well, he wasn't really *pushing* it—he was guiding it, with steady pressure. This felt weird because, although she didn't really mind going down on him, and was actually about to do it anyway, she felt it was something *she* should've initiated. She started kissing his chest and his stomach and stopped there. If he kept guiding her head down, she was going to say something, but he stopped doing it so she went down farther on her own.

His balls smelled musky, like *bad* musky, and she couldn't get used to it so she took shallow breaths through her nose and took breaks to take deeper breaths through her mouth. She did it harder and faster and used her hands more than she usually did. It seemed like she was down there for a long time and she was thinking about having sex with him tonight after all. At least she wouldn't have to smell his musky balls anymore or let him come in her mouth.

Then he backed away suddenly. She wondered if she'd done something wrong, maybe bit his dick or squeezed his balls too hard. She was going to ask him, but she thought he was about to say something, so she waited. Then she realized he was putting on a condom. She didn't know where the condom had come from and she figured that he must have gotten one from his wallet, while she was going down on him. She didn't know what to say—it was all happening so fast. He kissed her with a lot of tongue and then suddenly he was on top of her and they were doing it. She was dry and it hurt, but she was too confused to say anything.

He must've at least sensed something was wrong because he stopped thrusting into her and asked, "What's wrong?"

"Nothing."

"You sure?"

"Yeah . . . it feels great."

"Cool."

He was holding her arms down too tight and it still hurt a lot. But she just lay there, ignoring the pain, even saying "Oh my God" a few times, hoping that would make him finish. Finally his noises got louder and he pushed her arms down harder and pounded into her faster, so she knew he was getting close, but it took a long time, maybe another minute, before his face scrunched up and turned sunburn red, and then he said, "Oh, fuck," grunted, got totally still for a good five seconds, and rolled off her.

He was breathing heavily, like he'd just climbed a few flights of stairs carrying heavy packages, but he wasn't touching her at all. Her arms hurt like hell, she was very sore, and she felt like she wanted to cry.

He didn't say anything for a long time, then he said, "Wow." His breathing returned to normal but his eyes were closed and she wondered if he was falling asleep. Then he turned toward her and gazed sensitively into her eyes. She expected him to ask her what was wrong. She'd tell him how upset she was and they'd talk and maybe things would be okay.

"So," he asked, "did you?"

"Did I what?" She couldn't believe this.

"You know," he said, brushing the hair away from her eyes with his fingers. "Did you come?"

4

Katie didn't know what to say—she definitely didn't want to cry—so she said the only thing she could think of that she knew would end the conversation immediately.

"Yeah. It was great."

"I thought so," Andy said and snuggled up next to her, with one arm over her breasts, and after a couple of minutes he started snoring lightly. She didn't want him to touch her; she didn't even want to be near him.

She managed to free herself without waking him. She sat on the edge of the bed and starting bawling, but tried her hardest not to make any noise.

A few minutes later, she was about to tap him on the shoulder to wake him up and tell him to get the hell out of her apartment, but she stopped herself, realizing she could be making a huge mistake. First-time sex always sucked and maybe that was all it was—bad sex. She figured she'd go to sleep and decide how she felt about the whole thing in the morning.

She put on her bra and panties and a long T-shirt and lay on her side, turned away from him. She stirred for a while, unable to stop replaying what had happened. At one point Andy rolled over and his foot touched hers and she jerked away quickly, as if he repulsed her, which he actually did.

When Katie woke up, Andy was trying to have sex with her again. Well, he wasn't really trying, but he was hugging her from behind, breathing into her left ear, and she felt his dick pressing up against her butt.

"No," she said.

"Oh," Andy said. His voice was crackly from sleep and his breath stank. "Sorry."

Katie's heart was throbbing. If Andy tried to touch her again, she was going to turn around and slap him.

"Something wrong?" Andy asked.

She wanted to snap, You mean, except for you trying to stick your dick in me while I was fast asleep? But she didn't want to overreact, sound nuts, so she said as politely as possible, "I'm just not really a morning-type person."

Andy didn't push it. "That's cool. You just looked so good I couldn't resist."

She got out of bed quickly before he could touch her again.

"You sure something isn't wrong?" he asked.

"Positive." She didn't want to talk about it. She just wanted him to go home so she could be alone and try to figure out how she felt.

"That's cool," he said.

She wished he would stop saying that. He was so annoying.

"Hey, I have an idea," he said. "You wanna go to a diner or something?"

"Can't." She thought up an excuse. "I have a lot of work stuff to do."

"On Saturday?"

"Yeah, my boss is making me work on this proposal thing—I have to get it done by Monday morning."

"Can't you work on it later?"

"No . . . I mean, I'm going out shopping later, and tomorrow I'm busy, so I really have to get this out of the way this morning. Sorry."

She got her robe out of the closet and put it on.

"That's cool," Andy said. "I should probably get home, too. I wanna hit the gym and then I'm gonna go watch the Michigan game . . . You sure everything's cool?"

"Yes."

"You sure? Because you sound like—"

"Everything's fine. I have to use the bathroom."

Katie stayed in the bathroom for at least five minutes, hoping Andy would get the hint and be dressed and ready to leave when she came out. The strategy seemed to work because Andy had his jeans and shirt on when she came out. While he went to the bathroom, she turned on her PC and opened an Excel spreadsheet.

Andy came out of the bathroom, saw her, said, "I guess I should get going. So what's up for tonight?"

"I'm not sure," Katie said.

"Well, I'll call you later from my cell. A couple of my roommates are heading out and maybe we can hook up with them. It would be cool for you to meet some of my friends."

"Yeah," Katie said, typing a few random numbers into the spreadsheet. "Okay."

Katie remained at her PC while Andy put on his shoes, then Andy came up behind her and put a hand on her shoulder and her whole body tensed.

"Wanna let me out?" he asked.

She led him to the door and kissed him goodbye quickly, although she didn't really want to. When he was gone, she went right into the bathroom and got into the shower. She scrubbed herself hard for a long time but still felt like she couldn't get clean. Finally, she got out, her fingers pruny, and went into the bedroom and took off the bedsheet and pillowcases and stuffed them into the laundry. She figured she'd wash her blanket later, too, because she didn't want to sleep with anything Andy had slept with. He was such a son of a bitch; she didn't know why she hadn't kicked him out of bed last night. She couldn't understand how she'd let this happen to her.

"Hey."

The voice startled Katie and she turned so fast she strained her neck slightly. It was just Susan, her roommate, standing at the door.

"Sorry," Susan said. "I didn't mean to scare you."

"It's okay,"

"Doing laundry?"

"No, just straightening up." She wanted to change the subject. "So what'd you do last night?"

"We went to this great Japanese place in the West Village, I can't remember the name. The eel rolls were really good and I usually hate eel—it's so gooey. You and Andy should go there sometime."

"I doubt that," Katie said.

"Why?" Susan asked.

Katie paused, considering telling her what had happened. It would be good to get another opinion on the whole thing because she knew she was being very emotional right now and she still wasn't sure whether she was making too big a deal about it—if it was Andy's fault, her fault, or no one's fault. But Katie knew that Susan was the absolute wrong person to get advice from. She'd been with her boyfriend, Tom, since high school and she knew zero about dating and complicated relationships. She was also from Greenwich, went to prep schools, and everything had always been perfect in her life. She sometimes got uptight when Katie talked about anything personal, especially sex, and Katie decided there was no use even bringing it up.

"Andy's just not very into sushi," Katie said.

A few minutes later, Katie went online and did a search for date rape. She didn't find out anything she didn't already know. All the articles and posts talked about guys who keep going even after girls says no, and guys who act much more aggressively than Andy had acted. Katie was starting to feel guilty, wondering if she'd been too harsh with Andy this morning. He'd probably never want to see her again, and last night might've been more her fault than his. If she'd said, "I'm not ready yet," or "I have a headache," or just, "No," he definitely would've stopped and she wouldn't be feeling the way she did right now.

Although it was still very early—not even nine o'clock—Katie decided to call Amanda. Amanda had a lot of dating experience and she'd be able to give solid advice.

But before pressing the last digit to Amanda's number, Katie had second thoughts and clicked off. She remembered how Amanda had acted on the phone yesterday, putting down Andy and his roommates for being frat boys, and Katie knew Amanda would tell her that she had been raped and to never talk to Andy again, and maybe even to call the police and try to press charges. Besides, Katie didn't think Amanda would give her an honest opinion because she had been date-raped in college and she was always "anti-guy" in these types of situations.

Now, even more confused, Katie decided to try to forget about it for a while. She had a quick breakfast of coffee and a slice of raisin bread toast with fat-free cream cheese, and then put on her gym clothes. She needed to de-stress on the treadmill for a while, maybe go to a yoga class.

She left her apartment and crossed Second Avenue, then went up the hill on Ninety-third Street, toward Third Avenue. Her legs felt heavy already and she didn't think she'd have a good workout today. Then she started panicking, remembering how Andy had mentioned that he was going to go to the gym this morning, too. He'd never mentioned which gym he belonged to, and she was pretty sure that there was a gym in Normandie Court, where he lived, but that didn't mean he couldn't have joined an outside gym. The last thing she wanted was to run into Andy at the gym and have to work out next to him.

She entered the gym cautiously, looking around for Andy. If she saw him and he didn't see her she intended to do a one-eighty and hightail it out of there. She didn't see him on any of the machines on the main level, but that didn't mean he wasn't in one of the weight rooms. She headed toward the desk, where she had to scan her membership card, when someone said, "Katie?"

For the second time this morning, she jerked her head quickly, and she felt the strain again in her neck, but she relaxed when she realized it was just the guy at the desk who had spoken to her.

"Yeah?" she said, wondering if something was wrong with her card.

"You don't remember me, do you?"

She took a closer look at him and realized he did look kind of familiar. He was tall, with blond hair and very blue eyes. She wondered if she knew him from college. He seemed several years older than her, maybe twenty-seven or twenty-eight, but maybe he'd been a grad student or an assistant professor or something.

"Did you go to Wesleyan?" she asked.

"Nope."

She racked her brain, but couldn't come up with another guess.

"Come on, I know you didn't forget me."

"I'm sorry."

"Okay, I'll give you a clue . . . Bev's."

Bev's was the ice-cream parlor in Lenox, Massachusetts, where Katie had hung out a lot when she was a teenager. She squinted at the guy for a few more seconds, still lost, then it clicked.

"Oh my God, Peter. Peter Wells!"

"You got it."

"Oh my God, I can't believe this. What're you *doing* here?"

"I work here."

She noticed he was really cute, had dimples. "No way!"

"I just started today."

"This is *so* funny."

"I know—I can't believe it either. When I saw you walk in here I was shocked."

"I live right down the street."

"Really?"

"Where do you live?"

"I just relocated to Manhattan," Peter said. "I'm staying downtown right now."

"Wow. This is so unbelievable."

"I know."

"I mean when you said Bev's I looked at you and I thought, Who is this guy? And then I thought, Wait, that's Peter Wells. I can't believe I didn't recognize you right away. You look so different."

"Really? How's that?"

She wanted to say that he was much better looking than she remembered, but she said, "I don't know. Maybe it's just your hair or something."

"Yeah, I finally got rid of the bangs . . . But I recognized you right away."

"But I was, what, thirteen the last time you saw me?"

"Yeah, but you're just as pretty."

"Thanks." She hoped she wasn't blushing.

"God, I remember all those conversations we used to have."

"You do?"

"Of course. I always got a big kick out of talking to you . . . So how's everything else? How's your sister?"

The muscles in Katie's face tensed and Peter must have noticed.

"I guess you didn't hear," she said.

"Hear what?"

"Heather died."

"Oh, God. When?"

"She committed suicide in college . . . at UMass."

"*What?* Jesus, I had no idea . . . God, that's so awful."

"I know."

"Oh, wow, I'm so sorry. I just can't believe that. Shit."

"I know. It's still, like, really weird for me when I think about it."

A girl came over and asked Peter for a towel. He gave her one, then said to Katie, "I'm really sorry about Heather. I haven't been in touch with anyone from Lenox since my family moved . . . Wow, suicide. I'm still shocked."

Starting to feel sad and wanting to change the subject, Katie said, "But it's really great seeing you again. It's a total blast from the past."

"Isn't it? So when did you move to the city?"

"Like five months ago, after graduation."

"Like it?"

"Yeah. I mean, it takes some getting used to, you know, but it's great."

"Where you working?"

"This financial PR firm in midtown."

"Really? That's great."

"It's not very exciting. I might go back to school, I'm not sure yet. I might be taking the GREs in the spring. What about you? I mean, is this your, like, permanent job?"

"No. Actually, I'm going to be a physical trainer."

"That's cool." Katie remembered Andy saying "That's cool" so many times this morning and how annoying it had been. "I mean, that's great."

A couple of gym members were standing near the desk, waiting to get Peter's attention, so Katie said, "I'll talk to you later."

"Yeah, definitely. And, hey, we should really hang out sometime."

"Yeah, that sounds great. Let's definitely exchange numbers before I go."

"Terrific."

Peter smiled and Katie noticed his high cheekbones and those dimples again, then she walked away toward the treadmills. As she waited for one to become available, she turned on her iPod to the "workout songs" she'd downloaded. As Kelly Clarkson belted out "Walkaway," Katie still couldn't get over running into Peter Wells this way, and she was still surprised how good-looking he was. She didn't remember him being bad-looking, but there used to be something awkward about him. Maybe it was just because he was very thin and his long, grungy bangs used to hang down over his eyes. Now he was in great shape, with nice arms and shoulders, beautiful blond hair, and he seemed like a really great guy, too. He was Heather's age—five years older than Katie, which made him, what, twenty-seven now?—so Katie never knew him very well, but she remembered how she used to see him in the ice-cream parlor. Sometimes he'd have the latest video he'd rented from the video store next door and they'd talk about movies. She saw him around town all the time—riding his bike, skateboarding, or hanging out at the library. He seemed to be alone a lot. She remembered vaguely that his family had moved away—probably when he was about seventeen.

A treadmill freed up. Katie did some light stretches and then started her workout, walking for about a minute before starting to jog. She was still thinking about Peter, about the huge coincidence of running into him in New York City, and how it felt kind of nice and homey to see a familiar face, and then her mood soured as she remembered what had happened to her last night and how Andy could belong to this gym. She looked to her left and right, not seeing Andy anywhere, but then she looked straight ahead, at the mirrored wall, and saw Peter, behind the front desk, watching her. He had a blank, distant expression, and she wondered if he was actually looking at *her,* or at something else in the mirror, and then she smiled and he smiled back, showing off those adorable dimples.

5

Katie was so beautiful, so perfect in every way, that it was hard for Peter to stop staring at her. He loved the way her legs and arms moved as she ran, and the way her ponytail bobbed back and forth against her back. She had a great back—smooth, muscular, and lightly tanned. He forced himself to look away a few times, because he didn't want to make it too obvious, but she was just impossible to resist.

After her workout, she did some more stretches, then went over to the mats to do abs. As she did crunches on the exercise ball, he watched, loving the way her lips parted with each exhale. He was hoping she'd meant what she said about exchanging numbers and getting together sometime, that she wasn't just being nice.

When she finished doing abs, she did some isometric-type exercises, and then came over to him at the desk.

"Good workout?" he asked.

"Yeah . . . not bad."

Even sweaty she looked amazing, much better than in those pictures of her he'd seen on the Internet. Standing next to her he felt a spark between them, an energy that was so intense he knew she must've been feeling it as well. He had an impulse to screw all of his plans, to tell her straight off how he felt about her so that they could start their lives together, but he resisted it. He'd planned everything carefully and knew it would be crazy to try to rush things now.

They chatted for about five minutes about Lenox and about people they both knew—a typical what-ever-happened-to, I-wonder-where, oh-my-God-do-you-remember conversation. Then things progressed even faster than

Peter had anticipated. Instead of having to ask for Katie's number, she spontaneously wrote it on the back of a Metro Sports Club business card and said, "You have to call me so we can hang out sometime." Peter, trying not to let his delight show, but trying not to sound too nonchalant, either, said with the perfect balance, "Yeah, definitely."

The rest of the morning, Peter was so thrilled that he was barely aware of even being at work, at his silly job, and he felt like someone else was going about his duties of handing out towels, answering phone calls, and dealing with whatever mundane questions gym members had, and he was just sitting back, observing it all. At around noon, Jimmy introduced him to a guy named Todd, who relieved Peter at the desk; then Jimmy asked Peter if he could stay late—even though it was his first day on the job—to stand on the street and hand out flyers to passersby. Peter knew that Jimmy was pulling a power trip, telling the new guy to do the dirty work. Jimmy was really getting to Peter. It was so painful, listening to him go on and on about the hot chicks at the club, acting like he was some kind of Casanova or something, when he was obviously the type of guy who couldn't even get a girlfriend.

Normally, Peter wouldn't have had the patience to put up with a guy like Jimmy, but today he was in such a great mood that Jimmy could've asked him to scrub the insides of all the toilets and he would've happily said yes.

Peter stood outside and handed a flyer to almost everyone who passed by, giving the BS sales pitch—"A two-day free trial and initiation fee waived for today only," as if prospective members weren't always offered two free days with no initiation fee. He was so pepped up because of Katie that he managed to convince several people to walk in off the street and talk to the sales rep about a membership, and Dave, the sales rep, even managed to close a sale.

At the end of Peter's workday, Jimmy came over to him and said, "Great going, man. I didn't know you had sales skills."

Peter knew he easily could have felt insulted. It was as if Jimmy was treating him like a five-year-old who'd spelled his first word—*Oh, you made a sale, Peter Weter. I'm so proud of you. You're such a smart little boy.* But since Peter didn't really care about this job and wasn't even planning to keep it for more than a couple of weeks, he smiled and said, "I was just doing my job."

"Maybe you're wasting your time, trying to become a trainer," Jimmy said. "Maybe I should just train you to be a membership consultant."

Again, Peter felt like Jimmy was trying to get a dig in, but he just brushed the whole thing off, making it into a joke, going, "Yeah, maybe that's not such a bad idea."

"Hey, was that your girlfriend you were talking to before?"

"Yeah. Actually it was."

"I've seen her here before. Yeah, she's a babe all right. Well done, my man. Well done."

Jimmy told Peter what a great job he was doing so far and how happy he was to have him on board at the gym and then he finally said, "See ya tomorrow, bright and early," and walked away.

Peter was glad he would be quitting soon because he didn't know how much longer he could stomach working for Jimmy.

At around two P.M., Peter left the health club. Automatically he started toward Katie's apartment, where he'd been hanging out a lot every day for the past few weeks—in a disguise of a Yankees cap and mirrored sunglasses—but then he reminded himself that there was no reason to watch her anymore and, although he really wanted to see her again, going there could be a big mistake. If she spotted him it would ruin everything, and there was no reason to risk that when things were going so well.

Instead, he walked down Third a couple of blocks, then cut over to Lexington and hailed a cab. He had the urge to call Katie from his cell and arrange a time to meet up, but he stopped himself. He knew that getting a girl was just like getting a job—attitude was everything. If he came off as desperate, impulsive, overzealous, it would turn her off and he'd take a major step backward. He had to stay cool, keep telling her what she wanted to hear. Every girl has a fantasy of her perfect guy. The trick was to transform yourself, to become the fantasy.

From observing Katie when she was a teenager and from watching her lately, Peter had figured out a lot about her. He knew that she was a good dresser and cared about her appearance. He also knew that she was very close with her father, and that she was looking for a strong, conservative, good-looking guy to protect her. At the ice-cream parlor in Lenox, she used to talk about her father a lot and Peter used to see her with Mr. Porter all over—at the supermarket, playing tennis, at the beach at Laurel Lake. Sometimes he'd see her walking down one of the side streets in Lenox, holding hands with her dad, or sitting with her arm around his shoulders at the movie theater at the Berkshire Mall.

From watching her in Manhattan, Peter had figured out that not much about her had changed. She wasn't ultrahigh maintenance, but she liked to take care of herself—going to the nail salon on Third Avenue once a week, getting her hair cut and highlighted at Amour de Hair on Madison Avenue, shopping at Bloomingdale's, J. Crew, and Ann Taylor Loft, and, of course, working out at the Metro Sports Club, which cost her seventy-four dollars a month. He knew that with the money she was making at her entry-level job there was no way she could afford this type of lifestyle and that her father, Dick Porter, was probably helping to support her. He was probably paying her rent and perhaps giving her additional money. Peter also got the sense, by Katie's mannerisms, such as the way she twirled her hair self-consciously and occasionally glanced in mirrors in a dissatisfied way, that she was insecure, that despite everything she had, she still felt like something was missing. Whenever she arrived at her apartment building alone, after going out with her friends, or when she came home from work, she'd look around nervously, obviously afraid that someone was going to try to follow her into the vestibule. Peter couldn't help thinking of her as a baby deer, alone in the dark, dangerous woods of Manhattan, desperate for a strong, secure guy, a father figure, to come along and protect her.

Peter knew that he could be that guy, that rock. All he had to do was play up to her fantasy, give her what she wanted. He was five years older than her, which already gave him a big leg up; girls who idolized their fathers were always attracted to older guys. She wanted a guy who was secure, mature, who could take care of her, make her feel safe, like she used to feel safe when she was daddy's little girl. She was probably used to dating guys in their early twenties who went on and on about themselves and treated her like crap, but what she really wanted was a more mature guy who cared about her, who *listened*. As for appearances, she seemed to be attracted to guys who had the same general features as her father. When she was walking along the street, or sitting in a restaurant or at a coffee bar, or that time last Saturday night, when she went out with her friends to that bar in Chelsea, she seemed to notice the clean-cut, conservative-looking guys. When Peter came to New York, his hair was long, almost down to his shoulders, and he had a scraggly beard. But before he interviewed for the job at the gym he got a close-cropped, military-style do and trimmed his beard to a goatee. Afterward, when he looked in the mirror, he was surprised and delighted by how much he resembled Katie's dad, Dick Porter.

When Peter said hi to Katie at the gym he knew right away that his makeover had been successful. He could tell by the way she kept smiling and blushing that she was attracted to him. Because he knew she was insecure and would respond well to compliments, he made sure to tell her, in a very sincere way, how beautiful she looked. That scored a lot of points for him, and he knew he'd also won her over big-time by hanging on her every word, being genuinely interested in what she had to say.

The traffic was stop-and-go in the East Sixties and it probably would have been faster for Peter to get out and walk. But then he had another thought—maybe he should just go for it and tell the driver to make a left at the next corner and head back uptown. Peter imagined going to Katie's building and buzzing her apartment. She'd wonder how he knew where she lived, but he could cover for it easily—tell her that he'd gotten her address from the health club's database. She'd invite him up, and since she'd have just got out of the shower, her hair would be wet. She'd be wearing baggy sweats and a long man's T-shirt, and would look great with no makeup. Although he'd never seen the inside of her apartment, he pictured the whole place being pink and very girly, like a teenager's room. And it would smell flowery, like potpourri or the perfume she was wearing at the gym today. She'd look warm and cuddly and he'd want to give her a big, long hug. He'd look into her eyes, showing her how caring he was, and say, "I figured, why wait? Let's go for that coffee right now." He'd have to deliver that line carefully, so he wouldn't sound too pushy or overanxious, but he was sure he could pull it off. Then they'd go out to a dimly lit coffee bar and sit next to each other on a fluffy couch and talk and laugh and look into each other's eyes for hours. As long as he said the right things, treated her the way she wanted to be treated, she'd start to fall in love with him, and then they'd start seeing each other all the time, become inseparable, and when the time was right, he'd propose, giving her the Tiffany two-carat diamond engagement ring, and it would be the happiest day of their lives.

Beyond Fifty-ninth Street, as the traffic thinned and the cab started moving at a steadier pace, Peter decided to hold off on going over there. It would be better to just relax, to let things take their course. Although he knew he could go over to her place and everything could work out perfectly, there was no reason to rush things. He'd stick to the plan and call her tomorrow night and suggest that they meet for coffee the following day—Monday.

He had taken out the business card with her number on it and now he stared at the handwriting. It was very neat and controlled; every letter in "Katie" and every digit in her number was easily readable. This was another sign that she was into him. If she didn't like him or didn't care if he called her, she would've scribbled her number; obviously she wanted to make sure there was no way for him to dial a wrong number and not be able to get in touch.

Zoning out, thinking of things to say to her on the phone when he called her and when they went out for coffee, he didn't hear what the driver had asked him.

"What?"

"What side?" the driver asked, annoyed. "Right or left?"

"Oh, left," Peter said. "Across the street."

The cab pulled in front of the Ramada Inn on Lexington and Thirtieth. Peter gave the driver a twenty, which was nearly double the fare, and told him to keep the change. The driver seemed surprised and suddenly cheerful and told Peter to have a great day.

Hector, the young Puerto Rican guy, was working at the hotel's front desk. When he saw Peter he cupped a hand over the mouthpiece of the phone and said, "Yo, Peter, I gotta talk to you. Hold up one sec."

"Sure," Peter said.

Peter knew what Hector wanted to talk about. Peter had been giving him advice on how to break up with his current girlfriend so he could get back with his ex. It was a sticky situation because the two girls lived in the same building in the Bronx and Hector didn't want his ex to know that he had been dating the other girl. Peter's advice was for Hector to be honest with the girl he wanted to break up with because when you came right down to it people always appreciated honesty.

Hector hung up and said to Peter, "Yo, you're a genius, man."

"It worked?" Peter asked.

"Hell yeah, man. I mean, I wasn't gonna do it. I went over to Jessica's place last night and I was, like, I gotta be crazy doin' this. She gonna be freakin', know what I'm sayin'? I gotta lie to her, make up somethin'. Then I was like, Naw, maybe Peter's right. So I tried. I mean, I did everything you said I should do, man, said everything you said I should say. I was lookin' into her eyes, being nice and sweet and all that shit, and I just told her, I was like, we gotta break up 'cause I'm in love with Lucy and that's just the way it is. I didn't say it like *that,* but that's kinda like what I was sayin', you know, and she was like, 'Yeah, you wanna break up. That's cool. I just want you to be happy, I wanna be friends.' I'm serious, yo, that's what it was like."

"I'm really happy for you, man," Peter said, consciously trying to talk like Hector, even taking on a bit of a Puerto Rican accent.

"Yo, I owe you, man," Hector said. "Serious. Anything you want's on me. Tonight, do any pay-per-view, take whatever you want from the mini bar, whatever, and you won't get charged for nothing."

"That's okay—I'm just glad I could help you out. I'll talk to you later, all right?"

Peter took the elevator up to the twelfth floor and went into his suite. He was still very excited about how well everything had gone with Katie and he couldn't stop replaying their conversation in his head. There wasn't one thing he'd said that he regretted; if he'd written his lines in advance and read from the script, it couldn't have gone any better. Again, he took out the business card with her name on it and, touching the writing gently with his forefinger, he had to resist calling her. He wanted to hear her voice. He wanted to know if she sounded different on the phone than in person and he wanted to make sure she was okay. Of course, he didn't think anything *bad* had happened to her, but suddenly he felt protective over her, as if she were his child, and he knew it would make him feel better, more relaxed, if he could just talk to her.

But he reminded himself that this was only the beginning. There would be days, months, years, a whole lifetime of talking on the phone. Soon they'd have so many phone conversations that calling her would be something he wouldn't even have to think about or prepare for; it would come as naturally as eating or breathing.

Peter felt grimy from the city, so he took a quick shower. Afterward, he opened the closet, which he had filled with his new wardrobe—upscale, conservative clothes that he knew Katie would like—and picked out beige chinos and a black mock turtleneck. He didn't want to leave anything to chance. If something went wrong between him and Katie and things didn't work out as perfectly as he imagined, he didn't want to look back later and wish he had done something differently. He knew there would be a greater chance of winning Katie over if he looked and acted the right way.

He was planning to have a mellow day alone. He figured he'd take a walk downtown, hang out for a while at a Barnes & Noble or a Starbucks, grab some sushi for dinner, and then maybe go to a movie. He had to go somewhere because if he stayed in his hotel room all day, he knew he wouldn't be able to stop thinking about Katie and he didn't want to do something stupid that he'd regret.

It was a beautiful November afternoon—clear sky, chilly but not too cold, leaves whipping around on the sidewalks. Before heading downtown, Peter decided to stop by the co-op he had purchased in the brownstone on East Thirty-second Street, to see how the renovations were coming along.

He opened the door to the building and went up to the second floor. The door to the apartment was propped open with a piece of wood and a worker was using a power tool in one of the back rooms. Peter checked out the dining room and kitchen, very pleased with how things were progressing. The crown molding was up and all the painting was done and the new Brazilian cherry strip floors had been laid down. The new Silestone breakfast bar had been installed in the kitchen and all of the maple cabinetry was in place and looked great. The stainless steel refrigerator and Viking stove hadn't been delivered yet, but that was scheduled to happen sometime next week.

Peter went down to the main bedroom where two Mexican men were installing shelves in the walk-in closet.

"*Cómo están?*" Peter said to the men.

"*Muy bueno,*" the older man said. "*Gracias.*"

"*Me gustan todos.* Seriously—it really looks great."

"*Gracias.*"

"*Cuándo ustedes acabarán?*"

"*Dos días. Quizás tres días.*"

"*Ah, muy bueno. Muchas gracias. Estoy muy, muy contento.*"

Peter peeked into the master bath, glad to see that the renovations were about halfway done and looked fantastic, and then he went across the hall to one of the bedrooms, which he planned to use for a home theater. The two leather chairs from Restoration Hardware had been delivered and were facing the wall where the sixty-four-inch LCD TV would be placed. He imagined him and Katie, wearing comfy sweaters on a cold winter night, sipping hot chocolate while watching a movie, a love story, and then he peeked into the room across the hallway that would be their first child's room. The room was empty now, but he imagined it filled with toys, a rocking chair, a crib. It was going to feel so great to sit in the rocking chair and rock his child to sleep, knowing that the baby was his *and* Katie's, that they had created a life together.

After spending another several minutes checking out other odds and ends, he left the apartment and headed downtown. He walked around Gramercy Park and then along Twentieth Street for a few blocks before cutting over toward Union Square. Although he'd only been living in New York at the hotel for about a month, and before then had only been to the city several times—a few short trips with his parents when he was very young, and then, more recently, the trips in from Mexico to look at apartments and to close on the co-op—he already felt very comfortable in New York, like a native. This surprised him a lot because when he was growing up he could never have imagined living in Manhattan, or anyplace urban. He always imagined himself living in the mountains, maybe in Vermont or New Hampshire.

A few months ago, he'd been planning to move back to New England, but then, surfing the Net one day in Guadalajara, he decided to Google Katie Porter. He didn't find out much about her, except that she had gone to college at Wesleyan and was living in Manhattan, but he knew he had to be with her, that he couldn't live without her. He also knew that he would have to reinvent himself in many ways to win her over, and becoming a New Yorker was one of them. Since she obviously viewed herself as a city girl nowadays, he figured if he was a city guy she would be much more likely to fall for him, and he also knew it would be nearly impossible for any single girl in Manhattan to resist a guy who owned a huge, spectacular apartment. So Peter shelled out the $975,000 for the co-op, figuring he'd unveil it to her at the perfect time, when all the renovations were complete and their relationship was in full swing.

As Peter walked through the Saturday farmer's market at Union Square, he decided that waiting until tomorrow night to ask her out could be a big mistake or, at the very least, create unnecessary awkwardness. He knew, from following her around, that she usually went to the gym on Saturdays and Sundays. This didn't necessarily mean that she would work out tomorrow, but she was a very regimented person, sticking to a tight routine for most of her activities—leaving for work between eight ten and eight fifteen every morning, stopping at the same coffee cart outside her office for a breakfast of coffee and a raisin bagel, "nothing on it," returning from work every day between five forty-five and six, except that one day last week when she went out to a bar after work with friends and didn't get home until later—so he figured there was a decent chance that she would be going to the gym tomorrow morning. If he saw her tomorrow and hadn't called her yet, she might get the wrong idea, think he wasn't interested in her, and it would put him in an uncomfortable position.

He went to ABC Carpet and did some shopping for the apartment, but then he couldn't take it anymore. He took out his cell and dialed Katie's number, which he had memorized.

"Hello?" God, her voice was amazing.

"Hey, it's me, Peter."

There was a pause. It only lasted a second or two, but it was plenty of time for Peter to get paranoid. He wondered if she wasn't really expecting him to call and was upset that he had, or if she thought it was weird that he was calling so quickly, or if she was with that guy she'd been dating.

But Peter's fears were alleviated when she said, "Oh, wow, Peter. Sorry, I just walked in the door and I didn't check my caller ID. What's up?"

"Not much. I was just wondering if you had any plans for tomorrow afternoon."

Damn, he sounded too pushy. He should've had a short conversation with her first. Why didn't he think all this through?

"No, I don't," she said. "Not really."

"Great," he said, relieved. "So how about we meet for coffee at around two?"

"Yeah, okay. That sounds great."

"Cool. I'll stop by your place after I get off work."

"I better tell you where I live."

"Yeah, that would be a good idea."

She gave him her address and he pretended that he was writing it down somewhere. He was angry at himself for making that slipup, implying that he already knew where she lived. He hoped she hadn't picked up on it.

"You know, I have a better idea," she said. "Since you're gonna be working, how about I just come by the gym and meet you there?"

Peter wasn't crazy about this plan, but didn't want to be difficult.

"Okay," he said. "Whatever works best for you."

They exchanged some small talk about how they were going to spend the rest of their afternoons—she said she was going to do some laundry, which he expected because she'd done laundry on two other Saturdays at around this time, and he said he had to "do some errands around the neighborhood"—and then they said goodbye and clicked off.

Overall, he was happy with how the conversation had gone. He didn't think she was suspicious of anything and he was glad that she seemed excited about him calling and about their date tomorrow. Still, he wished he didn't have to be on eggshells with her, watching every word he said. He wanted to let loose, be natural. He knew that once she got to know the real Peter Wells she'd never even think about another guy again.

6

Michigan was beating the hell out of Michigan State 17–zip midway through the second quarter and Andy, Scott, and Scott's work buddy Dan were on their second pitcher of Heineken. When they arrived at the bar, Andy had noticed a girl with long dark hair and bangs sitting at a table in the corner with two other girls. She'd looked cute but too old about an hour ago, but now, with a few beers in him, she looked a lot younger and a lot cuter.

"Stop staring," Scott said.

"I wasn't staring," Andy said, but he knew he was.

"You practically had your tongue hanging out of your mouth, dude."

"Look who's talking," Andy said. "Whenever a girl walks into a bar you're like . . ." Andy made an exaggerated, deer-in-headlights expression.

"I saw her checking you out before," Dan said to Andy.

"Bullshit," Andy said.

"I'm serious. When Michigan scored that last TD and you cheered, she was looking over at you."

"Yeah," Scott joked. "Probably wondering, Who's that idiot with his tongue hanging out?"

"She's not bad-looking, dude," Scott said. "Got some big tits going on there."

"Age guesses?" Andy asked.

"Twenty-six," Dan said.

"How drunk are you?" Scott said. "Twenty-eight, easy."

"Too old," Andy said.

"She's not exactly your grandmother," Scott said.

Andy looked at her. She was smiling, listening to something one of her friends was saying. She looked pretty good.

"You're staring again," Scott said.

"What do you want me to do?" Andy said. "I have my back to her."

"Why don't you just go talk to her?" Dan said.

"Yeah, what's the matter?" Scott said. "Afraid what your fiancée might say?"

"Fuck you," Andy said.

"Then go over there. She's looking at you again right now . . . Don't turn your head . . . She really wants you, dude. It's like she's in heat or something."

"She's with friends," Andy said.

"So?"

"So why don't you guys come with me?"

"In case you didn't notice, the friends are pigs," Scott said.

"The short one's not bad," Dan said.

"Yeah, if you like 'em shaped like the friggin' Liberty Bell," Scott said. "Her face is cute, but I saw her go to the bathroom before and there were big problems below the waist, dude. Besides, there's nothing stupider than three guys going over to three girls."

"Yeah, you're right; that never works," Dan said and gulped his beer.

"Come on, just go for it, dude," Scott said to Andy.

"Whatever," Andy said, and got up casually. He figured he'd head toward the bathroom and look in the girls' direction—if the cute chick made eye contact with him, he'd go over there; if not, he'd keep going. As he strode by the bar, he realized he was drunker than he thought and tried his hardest to keep his balance and seem sober. Passing the girls' table he glanced at the girl with the bangs, and sure enough she was looking at him, smiling. It was a definite green light.

Weaving by a couple of tables, he headed over there. There was big trouble up close. She was at least twenty-eight, maybe even thirty. There was no way he could ever date an old lady like that—his friends and roommates would never stop making fun of him—but she did seem to have a nice body. He figured he'd work toward getting her number and then decide if he really wanted to call her or not. If he did go out with her, though, she would definitely be one-night-stand material.

"Hey, ladies," he said. "Enjoying the game?"

"Not really," the girl with the bangs said, pointing to the Michigan State logo on her sweatshirt.

"Oh, well, there's always next year," Andy said. "I'm a Michigan man."

The girls moaned.

"Hey, don't hold it against me," Andy said, holding up his hands in a joking way.

"Don't worry, I won't," the girl with the bangs said and, the way she was looking at him, Andy could tell he was in like Flynn.

"I'm Andy."

"Janet."

"Nice to meet you, Janet," Andy said and shook her hand and held it a couple of seconds longer than necessary.

"So when did you graduate?" Janet asked.

"Four years ago," Andy lied, figuring she might get freaked out if she thought he was too young. He could tell she was doing the math in her head, and then he said, "How about you?"

"A lot longer than that," she said.

"How much longer?"

She hesitated, then said, "Eight years ago."

Andy figured she'd probably shaved two years off, meaning she was about thirty-two—way too old to be seen with on a date.

They continued talking and they actually had a lot in common. She worked in bonds at Morgan Stanley, so they discussed stocks and interest rates and the economy—serious shit like that. He didn't want to tell her he hadn't gone to grad school yet, so he lied and told her he was finishing up his MBA at NYU. He thought he was going to get busted when she said she knew one of the economics professors in the grad program there, but he lucked out when Michigan State scored a touchdown on a punt return and everyone at the table started cheering. Janet got distracted and didn't bring up the subject again.

At one point, Andy looked over at his friends at the bar and Scott was smiling, giving Andy the thumbs-up signal. Andy decided it was time to make his move. He knew that one of the tricks for getting girls' numbers at bars was to never give the conversation a chance to get stale. If things were going well—if the girl was laughing and seemed into him—it was time to get the digits and get the hell out of there before something went wrong.

So Andy said, "I really should get back to my buddies over there at the bar but, hey, you wanna hang out sometime?"

"Sure," she said. "Actually, I'm having a party tonight if you wanna come."

This was even better—no phone calls at all. He could go to the party, fuck her, and be done with it.

"That sounds really cool."

She gave him her address—she lived in a high-rise on Eighty-fifth and Lex—and he said he'd swing by at around nine o'clock.

Andy said bye to Janet and her friends and went back to the bar.

"Way to work it, dude," Scott said.

"Yeah, nice," Dan said. "She seemed totally into you."

"She invited me to a party tonight," Andy said.

"Sweet," Scott said.

Andy hung out for a while longer, finishing his beer with his friends, then he announced he was going to take off. Before he left the bar, he went over to Janet and told her how stoked he was about tonight.

On his way home, Andy remembered that he was supposed to go out with Katie later. He figured he'd call her and make up some excuse, tell her he was sick or something, because although he liked her a lot and everything, she was starting to bum him out. It was weird because he usually didn't start getting tired of girls until he'd had sex with them at least ten times, but this morning he already started having that this-is-getting-old feeling. Maybe it was because the sex last night was only so-so. Yeah, it was their first time, and first-time sex always sucked, but it bummed him out the way Katie just seemed to lie there, not making noise or getting into it. She said she came, but he wasn't sure he believed her, and if she *did* come, that was even worse because it meant that she'd always suck in bed. Then, in the morning, she didn't want to do it again and she was acting like something was wrong, like he'd pissed her off somehow, but she wouldn't talk about it at all. Andy had no idea what was going on and didn't want to try to figure it out, either. He'd learned a long time ago, back in college, that it was impossible to figure out what was going on in chicks' heads, so there was no use trying.

As Andy entered his building he started to call Katie on his cell. But then he decided to text-message her instead so he wouldn't have to speak to her.

It definitely wasn't rape," Amanda said to Katie.

They were sitting across from each other at Saigon Grill, at a table near the window facing Second Avenue. Katie had decided to talk to Amanda after all, to get her advice, because she couldn't think of anyone else to talk to.

"Really?" Katie said. "I was, like, so convinced you would think it was."

"You didn't say no and you weren't even sure you wanted to say no. Yeah, he should've communicated with you better, but you never said no, right?"

"Right."

"So you couldn't expect him to read your mind. I mean, yeah, it's a kind of gray area, but I don't think you can say it was date rape. I mean, what happened to me in college was totally different. Brad, that fucking prick, wouldn't stop even though I said no like twenty fucking times. Did you ever say no?"

"No, it was just the opposite. I told him it felt great."

"Yeah, then I don't think you can call it date rape. I mean, what happened definitely wasn't good, because you're not supposed to have negative feelings the next day. That's definitely an indication something's wrong. You should talk to him about it, let him know how you feel."

"I wanted to talk to him about it," Katie said. "I mean, in the morning, but I wasn't sure how to. What was I supposed to say, 'Good morning, I think you date-raped me last night, you son of a bitch?'"

"You could just tell him you felt uncomfortable."

"Yeah," Katie said. "I guess you're right."

Amanda took a bite of her beef cube steak and Katie had some of her spicy green papaya salad. But she couldn't enjoy the food because as she swallowed she started thinking about all the nuoc cham sauce bloating her and how she could barely fit into her jeans yesterday.

She put her chopsticks down, deciding she'd had enough even though the dish was half full, then said, "Oh, something really weird happened at the gym this morning. I walked in and this guy at the desk goes, 'Katie?' and I'm like, 'Yeah?' It turns out the guy's this guy Peter who grew up with me."

"That's so funny."

"I know. I mean, I didn't grow up with him. He was my sister's age, but I used to see him around all the time and everything. Isn't that unbelievable? I mean, I haven't seen the guy in, like, nine years."

"So is he cute?"

"Very," Katie said. "I mean, I never thought of him that way because he was older, and back then he was kind of goofy-looking with these bangs in his face all the time. But, yeah, he's very good-looking now. He's tall, has short hair, dimples, nice eyes. Hey, I should set you guys up."

"But you said he works at the desk, right?" Amanda looked disgusted.

"Yeah," Katie said, "but it's not like that. He just moved to New York. He said he wants to be a trainer."

"That's better," Amanda said, though still not enthused. "How old is he?"

"He must be twenty-seven. He didn't mention a girlfriend and I definitely got a single-guy vibe from him."

"He hit on you?"

"No, he was totally cool. I just didn't get the impression he was with anybody, that's all. But I'll ask him if you want me to—we're supposed to meet for coffee tomorrow afternoon."

Amanda took another bite of the cube steak with some rice and said, "I don't know—a blind date. I hate blind dates."

"Come on, you've met guys online."

"That's different. I mean I, like, e-mail with those guys first."

"It's just one date. If you hate him, don't go out with him again. I mean, it's not like I'm *friends* with this guy. It'd be no big deal."

"What's he like? I mean, he wants to be a trainer. Is he, like, some jerky musclehead guy?"

"No, he's thin. I mean, he has nice shoulders and arms, but he isn't, like, some steroids guy. He seems really nice, too. I think his parents moved when he was seventeen, right after high school. I couldn't believe he recognized me. I mean, when I saw him, I thought he was somebody I knew from college. You know, maybe an RA or something. But I don't want to, like, put pressure on you or anything. I mean, if you don't want me to ask him—"

"No, go ahead," Amanda said. "I mean, why not, right?"

After lunch, they decided to go to Sephora on Third Avenue. In the cab, Katie got a text message from Andy:

hey had really great time last night   just back from watching the game
with my buddies   am feeling kind of sick right now   maybe it s the flu
i think im gonna stay in today but will cal later hope u r having great day
bye

Katie read the message to Amanda, then Amanda said, "God, what an asshole."

"What?" Katie said. "You don't believe he's sick?"

"No, but he's still an asshole. I mean, he spends the night with you for the first time and he can't even call you the next day? He has to, like, text-message you?"

"I guess you're right."

"You *guess?* I mean, it's not like he can't get in touch with you. You know, I think you're giving him way too much credit. Maybe he didn't date-rape you, but that doesn't mean he's not a total dick."

"Whatever," Katie said, changing the subject. "I guess I'll talk to him later."

At Sephora, Amanda sampled bronzers and eyeshadows, and Katie looked for a new mascara. Katie was trying to relax and have a good time, but she couldn't get Andy and last night out of her head. She was convinced that he had just wanted to have sex with her and now was blowing her off like the typical guy. He probably wouldn't call her tomorrow, or the next day, and then finally she'd have to call him. Then he'd blow her off again, with some other excuse, and she'd never hear from him again.

Katie didn't buy anything, but Amanda spent about a hundred dollars. When they left, Amanda said, "Hey, you want to go to Urban Outfitters?" and Katie said, "Yeah, if you want to."

As they walked downtown, Amanda could tell something was bothering Katie and said, "You have to just forget about that loser."

"It's not that," Katie lied. "I'm just feeling kind of out of it, that's all."

The rest of the afternoon, Katie couldn't stop thinking about how Andy had used her for sex and was dumping her and what an idiot she was. She hoped she never had to see his stupid, lying face again.

7

Peter's goal was to make the perfect second impression. He knew he'd already made the perfect first impression, but the second impression was even more important. When someone meets someone for the second time, they either confirm the positive impression that they already have of the person, or realize that their first impression was wrong and they form a new impression. In some ways, the second impression is even more crucial than the first. If you make a bad first impression, you have a chance to redeem yourself, but if you make a bad second impression, you're screwed.

Since Peter was going to meet Katie at the health club at the end of his shift, he knew he couldn't get too dressed up or it would look weird, like he was trying too hard to impress. Still, this would be the first time he'd spent any serious time with her, and he didn't want to look like a slob, either. He put on several outfits and decided to go with jeans, a black T-shirt, and a thin black leather jacket. He'd seen Katie wear a black leather jacket before, and he knew that this would create an instant, subconscious connection with her.

He took a cab uptown and arrived at the health club at Ninety-second Street. All morning he couldn't stop thinking about Katie and he knew exactly what would happen. She'd show up at two o'clock, looking beautiful, and he would tell her how great it was to see her. She would be shy, blushing, and then he'd say, "I thought maybe we could grab some lunch." He'd keep it casual like that, not wanting to seem like he was trying too hard to upgrade the date from coffee to lunch. She'd say, "Yeah, that sounds great," and they'd go to a nearby Japanese restaurant. He would've loved to take her to someplace fancier, but once again it was all about perception, playing his cards right. He didn't want to seem like he was going overboard to win her over; he wanted to keep things cool, relaxed. At the restaurant, they'd hit it off, laughing, having a blast, then, at the appropriate time, they'd hold hands. It would be a beautiful moment, one they'd remember forever, and he'd savor it, gazing into her eyes longingly, but not *too* longingly, just longingly enough. After lunch, they'd take a walk in the park, holding hands, and then they'd have their first kiss on the platform overlooking the duck pond near Belvedere Castle. Then he'd walk her home, to her apartment building, and they'd kiss and tell each other what a perfect day they'd had and how they couldn't wait to see each other again. And then he'd say, "How about we have dinner tonight?" and she'd say, "That sounds like a great idea." Then he'd return to his hotel and, after he showered and changed, he'd pick her up at her place at around eight o'clock. They'd go out to dinner at a nice restaurant; not too nice, but nice enough to show her how much he liked her. Then, after dinner, they'd take a walk and wind up back near the park. He'd suggest taking a horse and buggy ride and she'd say, "I always wanted to do that." Then they'd ride around the park, covered by a fuzzy red blanket, and it would be corny, but good corny, and they'd kiss some more, and by the end of the night, when he dropped her off at her apartment, they'd already be in love.

Peter had the rest of his life with Katie planned out as well. He figured that after a week or two of dating he'd tell her about his money and the apartment he'd bought for them and how he'd only gotten the job at the health club because he wanted to meet her in a romantic way. She'd be flattered and thrilled and tell him how much she loved him, and they'd move into the apartment together. Then, one night, they'd have champagne in front of the fireplace, and he'd get down on one knee and give her the two-carat diamond ring, and she'd be the happiest girl in the world. They'd get married at the Boat House in Central Park and have their children and travel a lot and maybe buy a summer house in the Berkshires, near where they grew up, and someday, maybe when their kids were in college, they'd move up there full-time and keep the place in the city as a pied-à-terre.

At one thirty, Peter started getting nervous. He went to the bathroom three or four times, and each time, at the sink, he looked in the mirror and checked to make sure his hair looked perfect and rehearsed his first words to Katie: "Wow, you look beautiful today." Like an actor, he said the line in different ways, putting the emphasis on different words. He knew he had to be careful with the word "wow." He didn't want to make it sound as if he were too blown away by her appearance, as if he were some desperate guy who'd never gone out for coffee with a beautiful girl before. But, at the same time, he wanted to show her how attracted he was to her and how much he liked her. Finally, he decided that he wouldn't put a lot of emphasis on "wow," but would focus on "beautiful" instead. When he said "beautiful," he wanted her to get the sense that he really thought she was beautiful, that he wasn't just *saying* it.

Two o'clock came and there was no sign of Katie. Peter was disappointed because he'd actually imagined that she would arrive a few minutes early, but he tried to not let it get to him. He hung out at the desk, talking to Jenny, the trainer. Jimmy had been right—Jenny was very good-looking, with long, straight blond hair, and was in near perfect shape. It didn't matter, though, because Peter had no interest in her. At the first opportunity, he made an excuse to get away, telling her there was an important call he had to make, and then he went into the bathroom and rehearsed his line again, deciding to put the emphasis on "wow" after all. When he came out, Katie still wasn't there, and he was starting to wonder whether something was wrong and if he should call her to see if she was okay. But he decided that calling could send out the wrong vibe, and that he'd wait until she was at least twenty minutes late before even contacting her.

"Peter, hey."

He was near the front desk, looking outside, when he heard Katie's voice behind him. He turned around and was disappointed to see that she wasn't dressed up. He didn't expect her to look the way she did when she went to work or on dates with the frat boy, but he'd expected her to at least make an effort to make a good second impression. But she obviously didn't even try. She was in faded jeans, sneakers, and a Wesleyan sweatshirt. She wasn't wearing makeup, her hair was back in a ponytail, and she was wearing glasses instead of contacts. She didn't even look as put together as she did when she went to the gym to work out. She looked the way she did when she did her laundry at that Laundromat on First Avenue.

Peter tried to not let his disappointment show. Forcing a smile he said, "Hey, Katie." Then, just to be polite, he added, "Wow, you look beautiful today."

"Thanks," she said. He expected her to return the compliment but she didn't. "So where are we going?"

"I thought maybe we could grab some lunch. There's this Japanese place I read about in Zagat just up the—"

"Oh, I already had lunch, I'm sorry. I mean, I could sit down with you, but I'm not really dressed for it or anything. Can we just get coffee?"

"Sure," Peter said, struggling to stay upbeat. "Coffee's cool. Actually, I had a late breakfast myself, so that would be great."

He was hoping that they at least could go to a little outdoor café, have cappuccinos or something, but when they left the health club she was quick to say, "There's a Starbucks right across the street," and all he could say was "Great."

As they headed there, they made small talk, mostly about the gym. She was saying that she liked it most of the time, but they didn't have enough machines, which was a pain, especially when she went right after work. She asked him how he liked his job so far and he said it was "all right" and that the people he worked with were "really cool." He noticed that Katie seemed slightly distracted and that she looked tired, as if she hadn't gotten much sleep last night. He was dying to ask her what was wrong, to be a father figure and help her through whatever problem she was having, but he also knew that it took time to build up that kind of trust. He couldn't expect her to open up to him right away. He had to earn her confidence, with body language and by telling her what she wanted to hear. Eventually, she'd realize, unconsciously, *I trust this guy,* and that's when she'd fall in love with him.

At Starbucks, he ordered a triple grande skim latte and he knew what she'd have—a venti coffee—before she asked for it, because he'd seen her buy coffee at Starbucks several times before.

There were no tables, so they had to stand, waiting for one to free up. This definitely wasn't turning into the perfect, romantic afternoon he'd envisioned. Katie still seemed distracted and upset, and he wanted to do whatever he could to change her mood. He knew the most attractive thing about his appearance was his smile, because he had perfect straight white teeth and dimples that girls seemed to like, so he smiled and laughed a lot, trying to get her to notice. Finally, a table became available, near the bathroom, and they sat down.

He thought the conversation was getting better, and her mood was improving, but he'd noticed, a few times, her checking her watch, which kind of irritated him, and then she said, "I'm gonna have to get back in, like, a half hour," which really pissed him off.

Staying totally relaxed, doing a really great job of hiding his emotions, he said, "What's going on?"

"Oh, nothing," she said. "I mean, I have to just do this project for my boss, and it's due tomorrow. It's nothing, but I have to take care of it."

Peter knew she was telling the truth, that she wasn't making up an excuse. Even though something was obviously troubling her, he knew she was very attracted to him, that they'd made a big-time connection yesterday when they'd met, and if she didn't really have work to do, there was no way she'd want to go home and miss out on a chance to spend more time with him.

"That's cool," Peter said. He was going to tell her how disappointed he was, but he didn't feel he had to. She already knew how much he liked her and how badly he wanted to hang out with her, and some things were better left unsaid.

Then, a couple of minutes later, while he was telling her a story about his time in Mexico, she interrupted and said, "Sorry if I seem kind of out of it today. I've just had a really bad night."

Peter was thrilled. She was confiding in him, showing trust in him already. He'd thought it would take at least a few dates to have this kind of breakthrough, and he took this as a surefire sign that she was well on her way to falling in love with him if she wasn't in love with him already.

"Really?" Peter said, relaxed. "Why's that?"

"Nothing," Katie said. "It's just this guy I've been dating."

This was even better. Subliminally, she was telling him that she was through with that frat boy Peter had seen her with a few times, that she was ready to move on. Peter had known she would come to this realization soon anyway, but he didn't expect it to happen *so* soon.

"Yeah," Peter said, leading her on, letting her do the talking the way a shrink would.

"Well, I know I shouldn't be complaining to you about him, but he did this really jerky thing yesterday. We've been seeing each other for, I don't know, like, three weeks? Anyway, we were just starting to get serious—I mean, I thought we were anyway—and then we had plans for last night and he text-messages me and tells me he's sick. I mean, maybe he really is sick, but why couldn't he call me and tell me? . . . I'm sorry, I shouldn't be venting to you about this."

"No, it's all right, really," Peter said. "So have you spoken to him at all since then?"

"No. I mean, I'm not gonna call him, that's for sure. I mean, I was going to call him last night just to see if he was really sick and if he was okay and everything, but I was too pissed off about the text-messaging thing."

Knowing that women always wanted support, not solutions, in situations like these, Peter said, "I don't blame you."

"You really think so?" Katie said.

"Definitely," Peter said. "Text-messaging you was a total assholish thing to do. The guy sounds like a real dick."

"That's exactly what my friend Amanda said."

"Well, you know what they say—if you hear something from one person, forget about it. But if you hear it from two people, start to listen."

"I guess you're right. I was just feeling guilty last night, I mean, for not calling him."

"You have no reason to feel guilty."

"Really?"

"*He's* the one who screwed up."

"You're right. It *is* his fault, isn't it?"

Peter was thrilled with how this was going. He was an ally to her now, someone she could trust, and it was a brilliant move on his part to not go overboard in bashing the guy she'd been dating. If he'd gone on about what an asshole that guy was, it could've turned her off; but he'd played it perfectly, badmouthing him just enough. Now Peter noticed how Katie's attitude toward him had taken a total one-eighty. She was making more eye contact with him, paying more attention to what he was saying. At one point, when they were talking about the Bryants, an eccentric family in Lenox whom they both knew from their childhood, she laughed, and it was such an irresistible, spontaneous, childlike laugh that he wanted to lean over the table and kiss her. He actually started to lean forward, but then managed to stop himself. He knew she probably wouldn't have minded if he kissed her because it was obvious in the way she was acting that she wanted to kiss him, too. But a spontaneous first kiss was way too big a risk at this stage in the game, especially when things were going so well.

He was imagining kissing her, thinking about how amazing it would be to feel her lips against his, when she said, "You know, I think you'd really love my friend, Amanda. You want to meet her sometime?"

He was so surprised by the question he had to ask her to repeat it.

"My friend Amanda," she said. "You wanna meet her?"

He was still pretty sure she was trying to set him up with her friend, but he decided not to rush to judgment. Maybe this wasn't her intention at all. Maybe she just wanted him to meet one of her friends, to hang out with her and get to know her. Maybe it was another sign that Katie was starting to feel closer to him.

"Yeah, I'd love that," he said. "Maybe the three of us could get together sometime?"

"Wow, that'd be cool," she said. "Yeah, I think you'll really like her. I mean, she's really cute and smart and fun to be around. She might be a little young for you, though."

Trying his hardest to not let his irritation show, Peter said, "I'm sorry. Were you talking about setting me up on a *date* with your friend?"

"Yeah," Katie said. "I mean, only if you—"

"Not interested." He realized that might've sounded a little curt, even nasty, so he added, "I mean, the truth is I'm involved with someone else right now."

"Oh, sorry," Katie said. "I had no idea. You didn't mention a girlfriend, or at least I didn't think you did."

"No, it's my fault for not saying anything." Peter realized he was grinding his back teeth so hard his jaw hurt, and he had to force himself to stop doing it.

"Well, I'd love to meet your girlfriend sometime," Katie said. "What's her name?"

"Cleara."

"Wow, that's great. Where'd you guys meet?"

"Mexico."

Before she could ask another question, Peter changed the subject, asking her about her job. As the conversation continued, he noticed that, surprisingly, there was no difference in her body language. She still seemed to be into him, leaning toward him slightly as he spoke, making plenty of eye contact. Women sometimes became even more attracted to men when they found out they were unavailable, and the Cleara story seemed to be working big-time. It still disturbed Peter, though, that Katie had tried to set him up, and he wondered if Katie had only done that as a roundabout way of finding out if he was single. Or maybe it was his fault for not giving off a strong enough vibe that he was interested in her.

They drank their coffee and continued chatting for longer than the half hour Katie had allotted—forty-nine minutes to be exact—and then Katie said, "I guess I really should be getting back."

She seemed disappointed, which Peter took as another positive sign. He considered asking her if she wanted to take a walk in the park, but quickly decided against it. The romance would have to wait till their next date.

They left Starbucks and Peter said, "Can I walk you home?"

"Oh, you don't have to."

"It's okay. I'd love to see where you live."

She said, "Okay, great," and Peter realized that she wouldn't be nearly so comfortable, so natural around him right now if she thought he was single.

As they approached her building, a modest tenement, Peter, who had to act as if he were seeing it for the first time, said, "Hey, this is pretty cool. Nice location."

"It's okay," Katie said. "I mean, it's kind of small and not-so-nice inside, and the walk to the subway's a pain. I have to go to the subway on Eighty-sixth."

Peter, of course, had already followed her along that route several times. He knew exactly which side streets she took to get there, and had even ridden the subway with her to work a few times. He was dying to tell her about the apartment he was renovating for them, about how great her new life with him would be.

"Yeah, that is a long walk," he said. "But I guess you have to start somewhere, right?"

"Right . . . So are you looking for a place?"

"I already found one."

"Really? Where?"

"It's downtown. I'll have to show it to you sometime."

"That would be great . . . Hey, you want to come up and see my place?"

God, he wanted to say yes. He would've loved to spend the whole day with her.

"I should probably be getting back, too," he said. "But, hey, how about we have lunch sometime?"

"Yeah, that would be great."

"How about tomorrow? I could meet you for lunch near your office." He had to be careful, he realized, because she hadn't mentioned where her office was located.

"Um, I'm not sure if I can tomorrow. But lemme give you my cell number. Later in the week might be better for me."

She told Peter the number and he punched the digits directly into his phone. Then she looked at him expectantly and lovingly. He knew she wanted to be kissed on the lips, but he left her wanting more and gave her a peck on the cheek instead.

Walking away, Peter decided that, all in all, he was pleased with the way his first date with his future wife had gone. Although it would've been nice to spend the day with her in the park and have dinner and the carriage ride, it was probably better to hold off, to let their love simmer. And he was glad he'd told her he had a girlfriend. People always want most what they think they can't have, and now he had Katie right where he wanted her.

8

Andy didn't want to have to wait for the party to end to get laid, but it seemed like there was no way around it. It was a two-bedroom apartment, but there were people hanging out everywhere, so there was no place to go with Janet where they could be alone. At one point, at around eleven o'clock, Andy thought, *Fuck it; it's not happening,* and he was about to bail, but just then Janet came over to talk to him, even held his hand for a few seconds, and told him how glad she was that he'd showed up. He had to admit, she looked a lot better than she had at the bar in the afternoon. She was wearing more makeup and some perfume that reminded him of a girl he once hooked up with junior year at Michigan, and her body looked hot in tight jeans and a low-cut black V-neck top. He'd already spent an hour at the party, and he figured it was worth hanging around an hour or two longer if it meant that he would score.

The problem was it was so freakin' painful. When he arrived, he knew he was in trouble when he heard the jazz playing and saw the dim lighting and saw all the people sitting down on couches and chairs instead of standing around. It was like a party his parents would have; there were even hors d'oeuvres, for chrissake. He was definitely the youngest one there. Most people looked like they were Janet's age or older, and they all seemed like uptight, artsy, downtown types. They were dressed in black, and a few of the guys were wearing geeky, rectangular black-rimmed glasses, like the ones the film students at Michigan used to wear. Andy was surprised because he figured that since Janet worked in finance, her friends would be more normal-type people. But Janet had explained that most of the geeks were friends of her roommate Elizabeth, who worked at the goddamn *New Yorker.*

Although Andy had spent most of the time at the party by himself or talking to Janet, he'd managed to get into a few conversations. One weird-looking bearded guy with glasses came over to him while he was pouring himself a glass of wine and introduced himself. His name was Jerry, and he was a freelance writer. To Andy, "freelance" sounded like another name for "unemployed," and when Andy told the guy he was working as a junior analyst at a Park Avenue bank the guy seemed equally unimpressed. The conversations with the others went just as badly. Everyone was a writer or an editor or reviewer of some kind. Andy felt out of place around all these artsy-fartsy wannabes, and they seemed to think something was wrong with him because he actually had a real job and was on track to be rich and successful someday. Fucking losers.

One girl—Sharon or Shannon—seemed cooler than the others. Although she was really old, at least thirty-five, she didn't have that annoying, pretentious, I'm-so-much-better-than-you-because-I-live-in-Alphafuck-City attitude the others had. She said she had a cousin who worked at Smith Barney and seemed impressed with Andy's lie that he was currently going for his MBA at NYU. Her cousin had gone to Wharton and they talked about different business schools for a while, then Andy asked what she did. She said she was a film critic for some newspaper or magazine Andy had never heard of, but he figured, films, he could bullshit about that. He told her how much he loved the *Lord of the Rings* movies and knew most of the lines by heart, and he knew he was in for a buzz kill when she didn't seem at all impressed or interested. He asked her what kind of stuff she liked and she went off, talking about all these obscure movies with weird foreign titles. She went on and on, wouldn't shut up, and Andy just had to stand there, totally trapped, nodding his head, saying things like "Wow" and "Cool" and "I definitely gotta check that one out," as his eyes darted back and forth, trying to get someone to come over to save him from this boring-as-hell conversation.

When she started talking about how there was going to be this great Goddard festival next month at Lincoln Center, Andy had had enough. He interrupted whatever she was saying and said, "Excuse me," and went to the bathroom. When he came out, he went right into the bedroom and stayed there for a while so he wouldn't have to keep talking to her. There were two large built-in bookshelves in the bedroom—it looked like a freaking library. Andy browsed the titles, just to have something to do because there was nothing that bored him more than books.

After a while, he went back out to the living room and hung out around the food and drink table most of the time. He wouldn't've minded being by himself, if there was some good music cranking, but they kept playing shitty jazz-type stuff.

Finally, around midnight, people started to leave. Andy made a point of having another conversation with Janet and holding her hand longer this time, and tickling the inside of her wrist. He wanted to make his move on her right then, but the problem was that several people wouldn't leave the party. They were sitting around in a small group, some Indian style, and then they started passing around a joint. Andy liked getting high, but by the time the joint reached him it was a soggy stump and he said, "No thanks." Janet was smoking, giggling with her friends, and Andy had to sit there, breathing in the secondhand pot smoke. If he hadn't invested so much time in trying to score with Janet he probably would've taken off, but he figured he'd done the dirty work, so he might as well stick around to fuck her, or at least get a blow job.

But when it got to be past one in the morning he knew the odds of having any type of hookup tonight were getting slimmer and slimmer. All guys knew that late-night hookups were almost impossible unless the girl was really drunk, and Andy was out of luck there. Janet had stopped drinking a long time ago—switching to club soda, for chrissake—and the pot had given her the munchies. She seemed a lot more interested in stuffing her face with Pringles than in getting laid. When she went into the kitchen and got into a long, intense conversation with one of the black-rimmed-glasses guys, Andy decided it was time to motor.

He got his jacket from the bed in Janet's room and then announced to her, "Hey, I'm gonna take off."

Janet came over to him, acting all concerned, going, "Why're you leaving? Is something wrong?"

Andy wanted to say, You mean except for you getting wasted and blowing me off when you know I just want to get you in bed and fuck you stupid? But he went with "No, it's just getting kind of late."

"Oh, come on, stay," Janet said.

Andy didn't like this whole sudden turnaround routine; after what had happened with Katie, he definitely wasn't in the mood for any head games with girls. Besides, he wasn't lying—he *was* ready to crash—and the way Janet was starting to look her age in the bright fluorescent kitchen light, with all the laugh lines around her eyes, was another buzz kill.

"Sorry, I really gotta go," Andy said.

"Well, I'm so glad you came."

Thinking, *Sure you are,* Andy said, "Yeah, me, too."

"Wait, let me give you my number. We're gonna have to go out sometime."

Andy, knowing he'd never call her, said, "That's okay," and left.

Man, what a waste of a fucking night, Andy thought as he walked uptown along Third Avenue. The sidewalk was empty except for an occasional drunk guy, or group of drunk guys, stumbling home. It was a Saturday night and Andy wasn't even buzzed. How fucked up was that?

Andy wished he'd just gone out with Scott and the guys, or hung with his roommates, maybe gone to some party in his building. Or maybe he should've just gone out with Katie again. At least if he was with Katie he would've gotten laid tonight. Yeah, the way she'd freaked out, getting all weird on him and shit when he was leaving her place, was a pain, but maybe it was just that time of the month or something. Or maybe she had other problems. On one of their dates, she'd mentioned that her sister had committed suicide in college, so who knew what other kind of personal, messed-up family-type shit she had going on in her life? Girls always went on about how guys shut down, they don't communicate, they keep things to themselves. Meanwhile, Andy had never met a girl who didn't have baggage and kept shit to herself.

Continuing up Third, he thought about stopping at the bar at Brother Jimmy's or Parrot Bay or swinging over to Blondie's on Second. Andy had hooked up at Blondie's a few times, including with one girl, Lara, the actress, who was superhot, but scamming a girl from scratch at two in the morning was a tall order. Besides, there wouldn't be any serious talent there at this time of night.

He stopped at a Korean deli and bought a three-pack of fig cookies, a couple of Slim Jims, and a can of Yoo-hoo, and then headed home.

When he opened the door to his apartment, the TV suddenly switched to a different channel and Chris pulled a blanket up over his lap.

"It's okay, you can jerk off in peace," Andy said. "I'm gonna go crash."

"What're you talking about?" Chris said. "I wasn't jerking off, I was watching a movie."

Andy didn't understand why Chris bothered denying it. Who'd he think he was kidding, especially with the box of Kleenex right there next to him?

"Whatever," Andy said, and went through the living room, toward his room. He was about to open the door, when he noticed the tie hanging from the doorknob, meaning that Greg was hooking up. Andy was glad that the drought was over for his roommate, that he was finally getting some, but it made him feel like more of a loser for his own wasted night.

The TV in the living room had already switched back to porn, and Andy could hear the grunting and moaning that he hoped was coming from one of the guys in the movie and not Chris. John and Chris's room also had a tie on the doorknob, so Andy went into Steve and Will's room. Will was passed out, still fully clothed—in his scrubs, of course—but Steve's bed was free. Andy had a couple of bites of a Slim Jim and the whole can of Yoo-hoo. Then, after jerking off quickly, imagining the blow job he should've been getting from Janet, he fell asleep without bothering to pull up his boxers.

9

Katie had a quiet Sunday morning at her apartment. Susan's boyfriend Tom had spent the night and gone out early in the morning and brought back bagels, a few different types of cream cheese, whitefish salad, and the Sunday *Times*. Katie hung out with them in the living room for a while, having a bagel—scooped out—with a little sun-dried tomato spread and a cup of coffee, skimming the Sunday Styles section. After breakfast, Katie went into her room and made the bed and did some straightening up. Feeling fat from the bagel, she played Kelly Clarkson and did some Pilates and several sets of crunches. The phone rang and Susan came in and told her it was her mother, and Katie sat on the bed, talking to her mom for a while. Katie and her mother had a surfacey relationship. They rarely fought about anything and they laughed a lot, but they usually didn't talk about anything serious. Their main topics of conversation were shopping, diets, and family gossip. Katie had always felt that she had to hold back with her mom, that she couldn't express herself fully.

Her mother asked her what was going on and she told her that the apartment was fine and she was starting to like her job a little more lately, but was still thinking about trying to find something else. Then her mother reminded her that Katie's father's birthday was coming up next month and that she was planning a surprise party. They discussed where to have the party—in a restaurant or at home—and then her mother asked her how things were going with Andy.

The last time Katie had talked to her mom, she'd raved about Andy, about what a great guy he was. Now she wished she could tell her the truth about what was going on, but she knew it would be pointless. Her mom would just say, "That's too bad," or "Oh, well, there are a lot of fish in the sea," or some other cliché, but wouldn't offer any real support.

To avoid all that, Katie said, "Andy's fine," then quickly changed the subject, asking her mother how the construction on the new deck in the backyard was coming along.

A few minutes later, as Katie finished her exercises, she realized she had the same sad, distant, empty feeling she always had after talking to her mother. She wished they were closer, that she was like some of her friends who were best friends with their moms. But there was no way that was ever happening. It was even worse with her father. At least she could talk about mundane things with her mother, but since Heather died she and her father had absolutely nothing to say to each other. They used to be very close, but now when she went home for a visit, she'd say hello and goodbye to him and that was practically it.

Katie hung out for the rest of the morning, talking to Susan and Tom some more, and listening to music in her room. She ordered in a Greek salad for lunch and watched some TV. At two o'clock she remembered she'd arranged to meet Peter Wells for coffee and she rushed over to meet him at the gym. They went to Starbucks and she had a pretty good time—he was a really nice guy, was easy to talk to—and around three o'clock he walked her back to her apartment. She went online and read a few e-mails, including one from her gay friend Mark, whom she went to college with and who now lived in Vermont. Mark's message about how during his first, and last, white-water rafting trip he'd capsized dozens of times made Katie laugh out loud. But then, as she was typing a response, her PC made a beeping noise and an instant message from Andy appeared on the screen:

ABARNETT007: hey

Katie's whole body tensed. She wished she'd changed her Yahoo! messenger settings so she didn't log on to IM whenever she got online, or she should've at least blocked Andy's IMs. But she knew he knew she was online and that totally ignoring him could make things more awkward if she ran into him on the street or something. It would be better to answer back and just tell him she wasn't interested if he tried to ask her out again.

LENOXGIRL: Hey, can't talk now I'm doing something online

She hoped that would be enough to get rid of him, but then the message flashed that he was typing a response. Hopefully he was writing "bye" and she'd never hear from him again.

ABARNETT007: cool what did you do last night?

"Shit," she said. What a jerk. Couldn't he just get the message? She hoped she didn't have to tell him to leave her alone, but she would if she had to.

LENOXGIRL: Not much

There was a pause, then he started typing.

ABARNETT007: i was really sick last night   throwing up and everything

He inserted a symbol of a green sick face.

ABARNETT007: but I'm a lot better now

Katie didn't know if he was lying, but if he wasn't, she realized she could be making a mistake by blowing him off. If he didn't lie to her and he didn't date rape her, what exactly had he done wrong?

She typed "great" then, thinking that sounded too upbeat, deleted it and typed:

LENOXGIRL: I'm glad

Andy started typing right away.

ABARNETT007: i had a great time the other night

Then a smiley face appeared.

She didn't know how to respond. She still felt weird about what had happened and didn't want to tell him she had a great time, too. She didn't see any point in creating drama about it, either.

But she didn't have to write anything because Andy wrote:

ABARNETT007: hey, wanna see a movie tonight?

Her first thought was, Yes. But then she reminded herself that he was a loser and that she'd been planning to dump him.

She was trying to decide what to do and a lot of time must've gone by, maybe thirty seconds, because Andy typed:

ABARNETT007: you still there?

She lied:

LENOXGIRL: Yeah phone just rang   one sec

She thought it over some more, finally deciding that she might as well go out with him. A movie was innocent. She could see how it went. If he acted like an asshole, she could just break up with him and that would be that. It seemed like a mature way to do it. More mature than lying to him, blocking his IMs and e-mails anyway.

LENOXGIRL: A movie sounds cool
ABARNETT007: cool!!!!!
LENOXGIRL: Okay but r you sure you're feeling up to it?
ABARNETT007: yeah yeah, I'm fine
ABARNETT007: totally fine
LENOXGIRL: i mean if you're sick it's cool
ABARNETT007: i mean
ABARNETT007: i was still feeling kinda sick this morning
ABARNETT007: but I'm better now
ABARNETT007: all better
ABARNETT007: i'm psyched!!!!

They spent a few minutes, going back and forth, trying to decide which movie to see. She thought that, like most guys, he'd suggest a horror or action movie, but instead he suggested seeing the new Lindsay Lohan comedy. She knew he was just doing this to score points, but there was something nice and considerate about it, too.

After she finished the e-mail to her friend Mark, she put on jeans and a sweatshirt and a full face of makeup—just in case she ran into somebody she knew—and then went out to do some chores. She dropped off her dry cleaning and then went to Key Food to do her grocery shopping for the week. Carrying three heavy bags back to her apartment, she had to stop every half block or so to take a break. She wished she could afford to use Fresh Direct to buy her groceries over the Internet like a lot of other Upper East Siders did, but her credit cards were already nearly maxed out. Although she was getting financial support from her parents—they direct-deposited a thousand dollars into her bank account every month—it wasn't nearly enough to help her live the way she wanted to. She didn't think she was living excessively, either. She had half the clothes most girls she knew had and she only had three or four pairs of shoes to last the whole season. But New York was so expensive it was ridiculous, and she didn't know how she'd ever be able to afford it. She had to get a better job, that was for sure. She was only making forty-four a year and that was nothing in the city. She had to make double or triple that to live the way she wanted to.

When she returned to her apartment, exhausted from carrying the shopping bags up the stairs, she checked her mailbox on the phone and listened to a message from Peter Wells:

"Hello, it's, um, Peter. How're you doing? Just wanted to say I had a really great time at coffee and I, uh, just wish we had a little more time to catch up. I'm really looking forward to lunch next week. I'm around tonight, so give me a call when you get in and hopefully we can set something up . . . Alrighty, talk soon. Bye-bye."

Katie smiled, listening to the message, thinking how glad she was that she and Peter were back in touch. Sometimes—well, a lot of the time—she felt lonely in the city and it was nice to know that there was someone she knew so close by, working right at the health club. She deleted the message, figuring she'd call him tomorrow, or maybe just run into him again sometime.

In her bedroom, she opened the closet, trying to figure out what to wear on her date with Andy.

10

Peter couldn't understand why Katie wasn't returning his call. He'd left the message two hours ago and she must've gotten it by now. She didn't mention having any major plans for tonight, and she'd even said something about how she had to finish some project for work. Even if she went out for a while, shopping or to do whatever, she had to be home by now.

Lying in bed in his hotel room, watching *Sleepless in Seattle* on mute, he wanted to call again, or try her on her cell phone, but he knew a second call would be very tricky to pull off. If he called again and she picked up, he could have an excuse ready, like, *The machine made a funny sound before—I wasn't sure it was working.* That could come off as natural, but if it didn't, if she saw through it, it could backfire big-time. She could think he was desperate or, even worse, obsessed. He didn't want to risk blowing it now, especially when everything was going so well.

He hated that it had come to this, spending the whole goddamn night waiting for his phone to ring. Left with two options—call her again right now or wait to call her at work sometime during the week, he chose option number one. He'd already shown his hand by calling her earlier, and if he waited another day or two to call her again, she might think he'd lost interest.

So he called her landline again, and when her voice mail answered, he had no choice but to leave another message. Shit, why didn't he try her cell? Now he was stuck with nothing to do except wait for her to call back. If he called her cell now and then she came home and found the message *and* the missed call on her phone's log, she'd think he was some kind of nutcase.

He continued watching the movie. Although he'd seen *Sleepless* more times than he could count, he never got tired of it. The first time he'd seen it, he was sixteen. He'd rented it from the video store in Lenox and loved it so much that he spent a whole weekend watching it again and again. He couldn't help crying during the scene at the end when Tom Hanks met Meg Ryan for the first time at the Empire State Building. It was the way he looked at her, with all his longing for her finally realized, that always got to Peter. There were other movies like that, ones he never got tired of watching. It was mainly the classic love stories from the eighties and nineties, like *Pretty Woman, Dirty Dancing,* and *When Harry Met Sally,* that did it for him. He liked the predictability of watching movies he'd already seen, of knowing exactly what was coming next. But it had to be a love story or a movie with romance in it. He hated violence. Seeing blood—even fake blood—was way too disturbing.

Peter couldn't wait to move into the new apartment and watch movies with Katie on their home theater. Maybe, for old times' sake, he'd christen the new TV set with *Sleepless in Seattle.* He knew Katie would love the movie because she'd love all the things he loved. Maybe he'd even pop the question to her on top of the Empire State Building. She'd appreciate the thoughtfulness of it, and it would be a special moment she'd cherish forever.

It must've been a romantic comedy marathon or something, because *Till There Was You,* another of Peter's all-time favorites, came on next. Another hour went by and he realized he hadn't eaten since a bran muffin for breakfast, so he decided to go out to have some dinner. He went across the street to a decent Japanese place he'd eaten at several times since he'd been in New York. He sat at the sushi bar and ordered the chirashi, but he was so distracted, thinking about Katie, that he could only manage a few bites. It frustrated him that he couldn't remember everything Katie had said to him earlier. He could recall most of the conversation, but there were gaps. Next time he saw her he was going to bring a digital recorder so he could record everything to play back later. Although he was happy with most of what he thought he'd said to her, he wished he hadn't acted so harshly when she offered to set him up with her friend. He thought he'd covered for it well afterward, but his initial reaction might have turned her off. Maybe she thought he was weird, or had a temper, and that's why she wasn't returning his call.

He felt queasy, as if his stomach wasn't handling the food. He left a twenty-dollar bill next to his plate and rushed back to the hotel across the street, just making it into the bathroom in time. Sitting there, staring at his cell phone, he wondered if it was possible that she somehow didn't get the message. Maybe the answering system on her phone was broken, or maybe her roommate had played the message and deleted it without telling Katie.

Or maybe Katie was just playing games. Some girls didn't like calling back guys too quickly, thinking it made them seem too desperate.

No, Katie wasn't the game-playing type. She didn't get the message—Peter was convinced of it. He left the bathroom and sat at the foot of the bed. After rehearsing possible conversations in his head for several minutes, he called her cell. Her voice mail picked up right away, meaning the phone was probably off. He ended the call and tried her home number.

"Hello."

"Katie?" He was sweating.

"No, it's Susan. Katie's not here. Can I take a message?"

She didn't sound at all like Katie. What was he thinking?

"Um, no." Shit, he hadn't prepared for this. He'd have to wing it and he *hated* winging it. "This is her, um, friend, Peter. Do you know, uh, when she'll be back?"

"She didn't say. I think she went to a movie or something. Can I take a message, or do you want to call back and leave one on her voice mail?"

Peter didn't want there to be two messages from him on her voice mail, and a voice mail and written message would be even worse.

"Oh no, that's okay, I'll just talk to her later," he said. "Thanks."

He ended the call and threw his cell phone onto an armchair and watched it bounce onto the rug. What the hell was he thinking, calling her? Now her roommate would tell her that some guy named Peter called but didn't leave a message and then, when Katie listened to her voice mail, she'd either think it was strange that he'd called twice, or she might think that there was no urgent reason to call back because he'd said he'd "talk to her later." Peter slapped the top of his head a few times, then realized what he was doing and stopped. He had to come up with a plan, some way out of this. He couldn't take not hearing from her today, or even tomorrow. He had to hear her voice, talk to her, at least see her.

He opened a drawer, took out his Yankees cap and cheap sunglasses, and went down to the street and hailed a cab. He knew he might regret this, but he didn't care.

He had the driver drop him off on Second and Ninetieth, a few blocks from Katie's apartment. He walked up the avenue toward her block, looking around to make sure she wasn't nearby. It pissed him off that he had to do all this sneaking around crap again. After he'd "met her" at the health club, he thought he was done with all that. He thought they could have a normal re-lationship from then on, be like any other two people falling in love. But he knew he had to wear the disguise tonight. He was planning to wait across the street from her apartment, to watch her when she came home from the movie. He couldn't actually *say* anything to her, though, or let her see him, because he knew she wouldn't believe that he had just run into her by accident on a side street where there wasn't much pedestrian traffic.

He found a good spot, near a parked SUV, directly across the street from her apartment. He'd be able to see her perfectly, and if she saw him he could duck and hide behind the car.

It was past ten o'clock. After waiting awhile longer, Peter started to wonder if it was possible he'd missed her, if she'd already returned from the movie and gone into her apartment. It had taken him about twenty minutes to get from his hotel room to where he stood now, and it was very possible that she had come home while he was on his way over. But there was no way he was leaving now. He'd rather stay where he was all night just for the chance of seeing her than go back to the hotel and have to sit there, waiting for the goddamn phone to ring.

He waited another hour or so. He had to pee badly and was about to go between an SUV and another car when he saw Katie walking up the block on the opposite side of the street. He was so excited to see her that he almost shouted her name and he didn't notice right away that she was with that guy again, the frat boy.

Peter was shocked. He didn't understand how, after she had met him, she could want to be with anyone else. He was especially surprised to see her with Frat Boy again. He knew she was an intelligent, sensible girl and he would have expected her to have better judgment than to go out with a guy who had absolutely no respect for her, who had treated her like dirt.

He slipped behind the SUV for better cover, and then he peered out slightly and watched them stop in front of her building. If they went inside, he didn't know what he'd do. Maybe he'd go after them and try to stop them somehow. Who knows? Maybe he'd even fight the guy. Girls always loved that, when guys fought over them, and Peter knew he could whip the skinny frat boy, especially if he took him by surprise.

But they weren't going inside—not yet anyway. They were talking, and although Peter couldn't hear what they were saying, they seemed to be having a serious conversation, probably about the state of their relationship. Frat Boy was doing most of the talking, using a lot of hand gestures to help plead his case, as Katie stood there with her arms crossed, looking unconvinced. Peter had read a lot of books on body language and knew that excessive hand gestures were a telltale sign of insincerity and he hoped that, if Katie didn't know this, too, she at least sensed it and wouldn't fall for his crap.

But then Katie's arms relaxed at her sides and she smiled a few times at whatever Frat Boy was saying to her. He was so phony, such a bullshit artist. Couldn't she see it?

Then Peter read her lips as she said good night and backed away a couple of steps toward her building's doors. Maybe she'd blow him off after all, but no, Frat Boy followed her and she stopped. They talked for another minute or so and she seemed into the conversation, smiling, and even laughing once, and when he reached out to hold her hand, she let him. All of it was making Peter nauseous. Then they kissed good night. It wasn't a peck good night on the cheek. It was a real kiss, a long kiss—it seemed practically endless. Peter felt acid rising through his throat, stinging his tonsils.

This was all wrong. This wasn't the way it was supposed to go at all. In all the hours he'd spent, working out scenarios in his head, rehearsing lines, he hadn't even contemplated this possibility. *They* were supposed to be kissing right now, not *them*. They were supposed to be in love already, starting the rest of their lives together. He didn't know how things had gotten so screwed up so quickly.

Finally the kiss ended. Peter read Katie's lips, *Call me,* and heard Frat Boy say, "I definitely will." Then Katie went into the vestibule of her building. Frat Boy remained standing there, watching her, and after Katie opened the inner door she turned back to look at him. He made a gesture with his hand of sipping a drink from a glass—probably some inside joke between them because it made her laugh—and then she waved goodbye and went upstairs.

Peter remained behind the SUV, watching Frat Boy walk up the block toward Second Avenue. It took awhile for Peter to get hold of himself. He couldn't believe that Katie was still with that loser and he wasn't exactly sure how to handle it. He knew he had to adjust his plan, the same way a general needs to adjust his army's tactics after a sneak attack by the enemy. The problem was he didn't know what adjustments to make because he hadn't even contemplated the possibility of failure.

He went across the street, into the vestibule of her building. Her name wasn't posted, but the buzzer of Apartment 10 had a label S. Roberts above it. He remembered Katie's roommate saying her name was Susan, so Peter figured that this was the right apartment. He knew if he buzzed right now, Katie probably wouldn't even ask who it was. She'd think it was Frat Boy and let him right up. When she opened her door and saw him there instead, she'd be surprised. But then they'd sit down and he'd explain everything, lay it all on the table. He'd tell her that he was in love with her and that he wanted to spend the rest of his life with her. Then she'd start to cry and admit that she was in love with him, too. Then the music would swell up and they'd kiss.

Although Peter knew he could win her over tonight very easily, he decided to do the smart thing and play it safe. In all love stories, things work out, the hero gets the girl in the end—it was guaranteed. The competition—if you could call it that—from Frat Boy was actually a *good* thing. Compared to that slimeball, Peter knew he would come off as an even better catch. Besides, there's always "the other guy" who seems right for the girl, who seems like he might get her, but who really has no chance at all. The other guy is just a plot device, an obstacle, and in the end his only purpose is to make the victory for the hero even sweeter.

11

Another Monday morning, another day Katie didn't want to get out of bed. After hitting the snooze button three times she finally dragged herself into the shower. A cup of coffee with Splenda barely had any effect. She felt like she could crawl back under the covers and sleep till noon.

She had some good days, when the city didn't seem so bad—maybe when she was having a nice day in the park or was out with her friends—but, all in all, life in New York was burning her out big-time. She was sick of the grind, of the same routine day after miserable day, of always being exhausted and stressed out. It seemed like she worried and obsessed all the time these days, and she never used to be that way. Once in a while, she'd catch a glimpse of herself in a mirror and wonder, *God, is that what I really look like?*

She never would've believed New York could do this to her. When she was growing up in Massachusetts, she used to dream about living in the city someday. Yeah, Lenox was beautiful, with all the mountains and trees and lakes and everything, but it was boring as hell, especially at night. There were no bars or clubs to go to—even the nearest city, Pittsfield, was dead at night. The most exciting event of the year was on Fourth of July weekend, when Peter, Paul, and Mary, or some other old-fart band, played at Tanglewood. Movies and TV shows set in New York always made big-city life seem hip and exciting, and she wanted to be like one of the Friends, and hang out at coffee bars with cool, interesting people. When she was in college, she and her friends took day trips into the city sometimes, to go shopping or to have lunch; she always had a great time and she decided she'd move to Manhattan the first opportunity she got. When she graduated last May, a friend told her about how this girl Susan, who'd gone to Brown, was renting an apartment on the Upper East Side and was looking for a roommate, and Katie jumped at the chance. After she got her first job, as an assistant at Hamilton & Forster, a financial PR agency, she was looking forward to living out her dream.

But, pretty much from the start, New York had been a disappointment. Her job sucked, definitely not worth all the stress, and she wasn't crazy about any of the people she worked with. Most of them were from New Jersey or Long Island and she felt like she couldn't connect. A few friends of hers from college lived in the city, but she didn't see them as much as she would've liked because they were busy at their jobs. The times she went out she had fun and she met a few guys, but no one she really liked or who really liked her. She wound up spending most of her nights alone, which was unusual for her because she'd always been a very social person. Making things worse, it had been a hot, miserable summer in New York, and all her friends had weekend shares at houses in the Hamptons. She couldn't afford her own share and didn't want to ask her parents for any more money. A couple of weekends, she went out as a guest, but she felt like she was freeloading and she didn't have such a great time anyway—the people out there had way too much attitude. So she spent most of the summer by herself, having some good days—shopping, hanging out in the park, going to movies—but most of the time she felt lonely and depressed in the sweltering, half-deserted city.

In the fall, her friends were in town more often and the weather improved, but her rut continued. Her job wasn't getting any better, and whenever she went out she seemed to attract the world's biggest assholes. If she was at a bar and noticed a cute guy, she'd do everything she could to let him know she was interested—making a lot of eye contact, smiling, even winking at this guy one time when she had a little too much to drink. But at the end of the night only the assholes wanted her number, and because her social calendar wasn't exactly filled, she usually gave it to them.

She finished doing her hair and makeup and then got dressed, putting on the gray pin-striped pants suit she'd bought last week. It had looked so good on her in the store, but now she felt like it made her look dumpy. She tried on a couple of other outfits but didn't like them, either. Searching her closet she couldn't find anything else decent to wear. All of her work clothes that she liked were dirty and she'd been putting off getting them cleaned because she couldn't afford the ridiculous dry-cleaning prices in Manhattan—like, eight dollars to clean a fucking skirt; were they serious? She tried on another outfit, hated it, and started to cry. This had been happening a lot lately—little things that she used to brush off and barely think about overwhelmed her. She'd had a meltdown at a store recently when she found out they didn't have a jacket in her size, and the other day when she got her hair highlighted and didn't like the way it came out, she had a brat fit. It seemed like anytime something minor went wrong she was suddenly on the verge of tears.

Realizing that if she procrastinated any longer she'd be late for work, she put on the navy-pants-with-navy-jacket outfit that she'd worn on Friday, figuring she'd just have to hope no one noticed.

Although her commute only took about twenty minutes door to door, it always drained her. As she headed toward the Eighty-sixth Street station, she was already dreading having to pack into the subway, like she was a fucking cow or something. Then, realizing that she was taking the same route to the subway that she took every morning, she said, "No, I'm not a fucking cow, I'm a fucking rat." She realized she'd spoken out loud when some guy passing by gave her a look like, *Wow, that chick's nuts,* and she wondered if she was. You live in New York long enough, you start to lose it. Whenever she walked around on the Upper West Side, on Broadway, she witnessed the city's effect firsthand. It seemed like every other person—especially the ones over sixty— was mentally ill, or searching garbage cans, or walking around mumbling to themselves about socialism or whatever. But Katie had no idea that it could happen so fast, that she could start going crazy in just five months.

In the subway station, she made her way through the crowd to the stair- well and went down halfway so she could watch for an express train on the lower level and a local train on the upper. The local came first so she had to rush upstairs with the other commuters who'd been waiting at the halfway point, and when the doors opened she had to force her way inside, with the other people who had been waiting, five or six deep, on the platform. When Katie reached the door, there was no more room in the car. The last person in, a guy in his forties, had backed his way in and was standing facing the platform, holding his briefcase in front of him as if somebody was shooting at him and he was trying to block the bullets. Katie heard the beeping sound, indicating the doors were about to close, but then the doors kept closing partway and reopening because somebody was blocking the doorway. Katie glanced at her watch: 8:41. She had plenty of time to get to work if she got on this train; but if she didn't and another train didn't come right away she'd be a few minutes late. Today was the Monday morning staff meeting and she'd been late last Monday and didn't want to hear it from her boss again.

"Move in, please," she said, in a bitchy, impatient tone she wouldn't have recognized as her own before she moved to Manhattan.

The guy with the briefcase managed to move a couple of inches to his left and Katie had an opening. She backed partway into the car, wriggling her ass to try to create more room, getting groans from everyone around her, and one guy with a Spanish accent said, "Damn bitch." Now Katie was preventing the door from closing. They closed against her arms a couple of times and Katie said, "Move in, please. Can you please move in?" The doors closed against Katie's arms again and the conductor over the PA system ordered, "Stop blocking the doors!" Somebody told Katie to just get off the train and Katie found herself muttering, "Shut up," as she continued to wriggle and twist her way farther into the car. Finally, she got far enough in that the doors could close, but she was pretty sandwiched between people, her face maybe a half inch away from the door.

Looking at her reflection in the dirty Plexiglas, she thought, *God, I look like dogshit.* She appeared bitter, worn, as if she'd aged five years since college. She used to be such a happy, positive person; she didn't know how she'd turned into *this*.

At the next stop, Katie managed to maneuver her way farther into the car. She put in her ear buds, turned on her iPod, and closed her eyes, trying to block out the world. Coldplay was into "A Rush of Blood to the Head," and she decided enough was enough with all this bullshit—today was a wake-up call; it was time to make some serious changes in her life. Last night, on the way to the movie theater, Andy had been talking about studying for the GMATs and applying to business schools, and she decided she was going to start studying for the GREs, maybe even take a course at Kaplan. Deadlines for next fall probably weren't due till January and February, so she still had time to apply. She was going to start doing research online, to try to figure out where to apply and what she wanted to study. She knew she wanted to work with people, so maybe she'd go for a master's in communication or education. She wasn't sure how she'd pay for grad school, though. She already owed something like twenty thousand dollars in student loans, which she knew she wouldn't be able to pay off for twenty years, unless she won the lottery or married a rich guy. But she figured she'd find some way to make it work—take out more loans, get some aid or a scholarship, do something. The key was that things would eventually change; this nightmare she was trapped in now couldn't go on forever. She wasn't going along some dark road that led to nowhere. There had to be a finish line ahead, a bright light at the end of the tunnel, even though she couldn't see it right now.

She was jolted from her thoughts when the old, sickly guy next to her started having a coughing fit. As she turned away and started breathing through a tiny space in the left corner of her mouth because she was convinced the guy had TB or something deadly, she thought, *I am so moving out of this city.*

At Fifty-first Street, she got off the train, moving toward the exit in shuffle steps with the rest of the crowd. There were four sets of stairs leading up to the street and, as always, she took the one at the far right because it let her out practically right in front of the doughnut cart where she bought her coffee and raisin bagel every morning. She felt like a rat again, but this time she didn't bitch about it out loud. Now that she knew her time as a New Yorker had an expiration date, she felt more removed from everything.

There were five people on line ahead of Katie at the cart. In Lenox, it might've taken ten minutes but in New York everyone moved quickly and in less than a minute it was her turn. The very-gross-looking-but-very-nice guy at the cart started pouring her coffee, knowing exactly how she took it, and said, "Hi, sweetheart, how're you today?"

"Fine, thanks," Katie said.

As she was digging into her purse, looking for money to give the guy, she looked up for a moment and saw a guy in a Yankees cap and dark sunglasses on the corner of Fifty-first and Lexington. He was about thirty yards away and she couldn't see his face very clearly but he looked a lot like Peter Wells.

The guy at the cart plopped the bag with the bagel and the coffee onto the counter and Katie handed him the five. He gave her the change and said, "Have a good day," and Katie said, "Thanks." Then Katie looked toward the corner again, but the guy with the sunglasses was gone. Katie was usually good with faces and had thought the guy looked exactly like Peter, but it didn't make sense that he'd be just standing there at nine in the morning. She figured she must've made a mistake.

"Excuse me," the woman behind Katie on line said in a bitchy tone because Katie had blocked her from the cart for, like, two seconds.

Katie gave the woman a dirty look, then made an annoyed *tsk* sound and walked away.

Although Katie wasn't late for the staff meeting—actually, she arrived a few minutes early—Mitchell, her boss, still found something to get on her case about. After the meeting he complained that she hadn't e-mailed a press release to somebody-or-other at so-and-so, even though Katie was positive that Mitchell had never told her to send the stupid e-mail. Katie wanted to tell him to go to hell, but she'd worked at her job long enough to learn that arguing with her boss was pointless. It was much better to swallow her pride and spew all of the usual, *Oh, I'm so sorry, my mistake* crap, than to get into an argument and feel shitty about it for the rest of the day.

Katie didn't know what Mitchell's fucking problem was, why he seemed to have it in for her, but she thought it might've been because he was attracted to her. Although he was in his forties and married, he had definitely been flirting with her at the job interview. He hadn't come on to her or anything, but she noticed him checking out her legs and breasts a few times, and he'd said, "It'll be a lot of fun working together," in a very suggestive way. Of course there was no way Katie would ever get involved with a married guy even if she was attracted to him, and she was not, in any way, attracted to Mitchell. He was old, and old guys always grossed her out. He also had a fake tan that was too dark and fake teeth that were too white. He looked like a sleazy game-show host.

The first few days at the job, he was very nice to her; then, probably when he started catching on that she wasn't interested, he changed. He snapped at her a lot—not yelling or even raising his voice, but just acting irritated. He nitpicked her work to death, never satisfied with anything she did, always telling her she needed to do more of this or less of that. Sometimes he put her down in front of other people, embarrassing the hell out of her and making her feel like an idiot. She couldn't believe he was acting like such an immature jerk. He was like a boy in grade school who likes a girl but, because she doesn't like him back, he starts hitting her and treating her like crap.

Katie complained to her friends about the Mitchell situation all the time. Amanda told her to just ignore it, that things would get better. Katie tried to take the advice, but nothing seemed to change. She felt more like a gofer than an assistant. She'd wanted to work in PR to interact with people, to use her communication skills, but it seemed like all Mitchell did was have her run errands and do clerical work. And whenever he asked her to do something, it was always with that *tone* in his voice. Everything he told her to do was a command, with never a please or thank-you. It got to the point that Katie couldn't even stand looking at him anymore. The tan, the teeth, the Rolex, the pinky ring—the guy was a total Mr. Smarmy. And his cologne! Katie didn't know the name of it, but he must've used half a bottle of the stuff every day. The whole office reeked of it, even the women's bathroom. Katie wondered if he wore all that cologne as some kind of sick power trip—he wanted people to smell him, like a cat that craps all over a house to mark its territory. One night at a bar, a guy came up to Katie, wearing the same cologne as Mitchell, and even though she thought the guy was kind of cute, she blew him off. She just couldn't deal with any guy who smelled like her creep boss.

Things got so bad, Katie even tried to talk to her mother about it, but of course she didn't have any real advice. She just said, "If you're unhappy, quit," and then started talking about pruning the rosebushes or whatever. Katie was like, *Gee, thanks for the great advice, Mom. Well, it was really great talking to you, too.* Of course, Katie had been thinking about quitting. She would've loved to work someplace else, anyplace else, but she was afraid that leaving her first job out of college so soon would look bad on her résumé. She wanted to get at least a year in and then move on.

But now that she'd made the decision to go back to school, and knew that she'd be leaving her job by next September, it made it much easier to brush Mitchell's comments aside, to not take the things he said so seriously.

She was going about her workday, having one of the better mornings she'd had in a long time. She managed to finish all her work without getting overly stressed or pissed off, and had some time to look into some grad schools on the Web. She requested applications from several schools, including Berkeley and the University of Washington.

Mitchell was in and out of meetings most of the morning and she barely even spoke to him. Then, around eleven thirty, Katie was getting a cup of coffee in the kitchen, making small talk with Rachel, an assistant, and JoAnne, an intern, when Mitchell came by and said, "You can stop talking about me now."

"Sshh, everybody, Mitchell's here; be quiet," JoAnne said, playing along.

"It's okay, I don't mind," Mitchell said, starting to pour himself a cup of coffee. "As long as it's only good stuff."

"Of course it's good stuff," JoAnne said. "Right, girls?"

"Yeah, it was all good," Rachel said. "Definitely."

They were beating the joke to death, but everyone was smiling anyway. Mitchell was smiling because he always seemed to be smiling, probably because he thought his choppers were so great and he wanted to show them off to the world. JoAnne and Rachel were doing major ass kissing. Rachel was up for a promotion, which Mitchell would have input in, and she'd been joking around with him, doing blatant brownnosing for weeks. JoAnne was trying to kiss up to Mitchell, too, trying to position herself for a possible full-time job at the company after graduation. Katie was smiling, not because she thought anything was funny or even amusing, but because she felt above it all, like she knew what was really going on and everyone else didn't.

Then, maybe Mitchell saw Katie smiling and wanted to put her back in her usual, miserable place, because he said, "Katie, I meant to say something to you before, but I really like that outfit you're wearing."

Katie knew some zinger was coming. After all, Mitchell wasn't exactly the type who dished out compliments, and straight guys didn't normally comment on women's clothing.

"Yeah, I love it, too," JoAnne said, naturally agreeing with whatever Mitchell said. Why didn't she just get it over with and blow him already?

"Me, too," Rachel said, also sounding totally fake. "Where'd you get it?"

"Oh, Ann Taylor," Katie said.

"It's great," Mitchell said, pouring it on, sounding like freaking Isaac Mizrahi. "But didn't I see you in one just like it the other day?"

It was a typical passive-aggressive Mitchell comment. He had the uncanny ability to zero in on the thing Katie was the most sensitive about, the thing she was praying no one would notice. There was no reason for him to mention anything about her clothing except to be cruel and to embarrass the hell out of her. And, as usual, it worked. Katie's face was burning up and she wanted to run out of the office and never come back. She could tell that JoAnne and Rachel knew what Mitchell had done to her, but they were too wimpy to come to her aid. Katie thought, Couldn't one of them even, like, change the subject or something?

Then Katie realized everyone was staring at her, waiting for her to answer. It felt like a full minute had gone by but it had probably only been a few seconds. She could tell that Mitchell, that prick, was enjoying watching her squirm.

Finally, she heard herself say, "I have two of them."

She knew the excuse sounded very lame, like an obvious cover-up.

"So you were wearing the *other* one the other day," Mitchell said, as if he bought the explanation even though it was obvious he didn't. "I get it now."

Katie returned to her desk with her coffee. She felt, strangely, the way she had after having sex with Andy the other night. Then, in one of those weird moments of kismet that always made Katie think that there had to be a God, an e-mail from Andy arrived in her in-box.

> Hey,
> Just wanted to say, I had a great time last night. I'm really looking
> forward to seeing you again. Will call you later!
> XOXO Andy

The note upset Katie and she didn't know if she had the right to feel upset about it, which made it even more upsetting. There was nothing really *wrong* with the message. If it weren't for what had happened between them, she might have thought the note was sweet and thoughtful. Making things even weirder and more confusing, she'd had a pretty good time with Andy on their date last night. At first, when they'd met in front of the movie theater on First and Sixty-second, she'd regretted agreeing to go out with him. She felt uncomfortable and couldn't even make eye contact. She kept replaying that night in bed, remembering how he'd pinned her arms down and forced himself on her. Although she kept reminding herself that he hadn't actually pinned her down, that he hadn't used any force at all, actually, it didn't matter, because this was how she kept remembering it.

In the movie theater, during the previews, her whole body had tensed when he rested his hand on her knee for a couple of seconds. She shifted away but wanted to move to another seat or, better yet, leave. But then the movie started. It was okay, not great, but Andy laughed a lot, even at the jokes that weren't very funny. Katie wasn't sure, but she got the sense that Andy's laughing was part of a strategy for getting laid, that he was trying to show her that he was a fun guy, that he could let loose. After the movie, Katie wanted to get into a cab alone and go home, but she didn't want to be rude, so she walked with Andy uptown along First Avenue. He was acting very polite, asking her a lot of questions about high school and college. She hated admitting it, but he seemed as charming as he had on their first few dates and she was starting to feel more comfortable around him.

When they reached American Trash, a bar near Seventy-sixth, Andy asked Katie if she wanted to have a drink and she said okay. He was the perfect gentleman, helping her on and off with her coat and even pushing the bar stool in for her after she sat down. He didn't try to come on to her at all in the bar, maybe because he sensed the tension in the movie theater. But then he told her that he wanted to talk to her about something.

"What?" she asked, although she knew from his tone that it had to do with the night they had sex and the awkwardness afterward.

"I just want you to know," he said. "I mean, I hope you know that . . . I mean . . . God, how do I say this?"

He sipped his beer. She thought it was cute, the way he seemed nervous, struggling to find the right words. He was showing a sensitive, vulnerable side to himself that he hadn't let her see before.

"What I mean is, I like you a lot," he said. "And I hope the other night was cool with you. I mean, the last thing I wanted to do was rush you or make you feel . . . I mean, I just want everything to be cool with us, you know?"

"Yeah, I know." She was relieved that he'd brought this up, put it out in the open.

He smiled, looking into her eyes, and said, "Cool. That's very cool."

They finished their drinks and walked back to her place. She was glad they'd talked and she felt a little better about everything. When they got to her building he was very polite and didn't suggest going up to her place or anything like that. He was backing off, taking it slower. Then he kissed her good night and it was a nice kiss—not too long or with too much tongue. Later on, when she was alone in her apartment, she felt very good about the way the date had gone and she was even looking forward to going out with him again.

But now, as she read the e-mail for the fifth or sixth time, she wasn't so sure. She still couldn't get Friday night completely out of her head, and she didn't know if that was the real Andy or if last night was the real Andy. On the one hand, she felt like he was Jekyll-and-Hyde-ing her, playing head games, and she wasn't sure if she wanted to deal with that crap anymore. On the other hand, she wasn't sure that he'd done anything wrong in the first place. Bottom line, she was very confused and didn't know whether she should dump him or keep on dating him. In college, she never used to obsess this way, especially about guys. If a guy treated her like shit, she dumped him, and that was that, end of story. She'd had good judgment, too, what she liked to call "asshole radar." Her friends used to be amazed by how quickly she could tell whether a guy was a jerk. She could tell just by looking at the way a guy dressed, or the way he smiled. But in New York she was clueless. There was no black or white in the city—everything was gray, blurry. When she met Andy she thought he was the greatest guy in the world, and she'd even thought Mitchell was okay. But now she knew Mitchell was a dick, and the jury was still out on Andy.

She decided that she was too caught up, that she needed another opinion about all this. She e-mailed Andy back, asking him if he wanted to go out on a double date with Amanda and one of his roommates. The question wasn't out of the blue because Katie had already told Andy that she wanted to set Amanda up sometime. A few minutes later, Andy wrote back that that sounded like a great idea and that he'd ask his roommate Will, who was a med student at Mount Sinai Hospital, if he was into it. Meanwhile, Katie e-mailed Amanda, and Amanda said she could go out Wednesday or Thursday night, and Katie e-mailed the info to Andy. Then Andy e-mailed back that Will was into it, and after another couple of e-mails they set up the date for Wednesday night.

Katie was relieved. Although the situation hadn't been resolved, she felt like it would be soon.

After lunch at the rip-off salad bar across the street—they charged by the pound and weighed everything down with so much dressing that she always wound up paying like eight dollars for a salad of mostly lettuce—she returned to the office. Finally, five o'clock came—time for another trip through subway hell. The ride itself was okay, but when she got out at Eighty-sixth Street some black guy hanging out near the stairwell said, "Shake that big ass, baby. Yeah, shake that big ass." She gave him the finger and he shouted, "Yeah, I like that! You a dirty bitch, too." Although she didn't want to let the words of some sicko in the subway get to her, she couldn't help it. When she got home, she stared in the full-length mirror, convinced that her ass *did* look pretty big and that she had to lose five pounds, maybe ten. She changed into yoga pants and a tank top and went to the gym for the six o'clock advanced step class.

As she was on a mat, stretching her hamstrings, someone said, "You need to get some more extension," and she looked up and saw Peter Wells standing there.

"Oh my God," she said. "Hi, how are you?"

"Pretty good," he said. "Here, lemme help." As she lay on her back, he held her right leg by the calf and pushed it back with gentle force. "Keep your knee straight. Yeah, just like that. You feel it now?"

"Yeah," Katie said, cringing.

"Hold, five, six, seven, eight, nine, ten . . . and relax. How's that?"

"Great, thanks."

Looking down at her, Peter smiled for a couple of seconds—she noticed that he had really nice-looking white teeth, not obviously fake-looking ones like Mitchell—then he said, "So how're you doing?"

"Okay," she said. "Tough day."

"Sorry to hear that."

"What can you do? That's New York, right?" Katie squinted. "Wait, I thought you work mornings?"

"I do," Peter said. "I was just here working out myself, actually."

"Oh, that's cool. Hey, you want to hear something really weird? I saw somebody who looked just like you before."

"When?"

"Today. This morning."

"Really?"

"Yeah, I was buying my coffee outside work and I could've sworn it was you. He had these sunglasses on and a baseball cap, I think."

"Maybe I have a twin."

Katie laughed, then said, "Yeah, maybe."

"Actually, today's my day off," Peter said. "I just came here to work out. I woke up at around noon."

"Late night last night, huh?"

"Yeah, kind of."

"Out with your girlfriend?"

"No. Actually we broke up."

"Really?"

"Yeah, but it's not as sudden as it sounds. We were just kind of incompatible. We've barely been together anyway."

"What do you mean? I thought she was in New York."

"No, no, she lives in Mexico. It was a long-distance relationship and we drifted apart, you know?"

"Yeah, that's hard. When I was in college I was dating this guy for a while. He was going to Penn and, yeah, it was tough. Why does life have to be such a bitch?"

"Your life's a bitch?"

"It's just an expression but, yeah, things have been kind of . . . stressful lately."

"It doesn't have to be that way."

He was looking into her eyes intensely. She had to look away.

"Yeah, I know," she said, "but sometimes things seem so . . . I don't know . . . out of control."

"Trust me," Peter said. "Everything's going to be okay."

The instructor was getting ready to start the step class, and Katie said, "Well, better go. It was really nice talking to you."

"Would you like to have dinner with me tomorrow night?"

"Oh, shoot, you called me, didn't you?" Katie said. "I got your message, but I didn't have a chance to call you back. I'm really sorry."

"That's fine, I understand. So I was thinking I can make a reservation for around seven. There's this great French place between Madis—"

"Sorry, did you say tomorrow? I can't make it. I have so much stuff to do for work, and I have a Pilates class."

He waited a couple of seconds, then said, "Oh, okay. How about Wednesday?"

"Can't make that, either," she said. "I have to go on this double date. Remember that guy I told you about, the one I've kind of been seeing? Well, I'm setting his roommate up with one of my friends. Not sure how that's gonna go but—"

"I thought you were breaking up with that guy."

"Yeah, I know, I know. I'm such a loser, right? I'm not sure what's going on with us. I mean I still like him, he's not a bad guy. Or maybe he is a bad guy. I don't know. I'm just kind of confused . . . obviously."

"I know it's not my place to get involved, but can I give you some advice?"

"Sure," Katie said. "Help me, please. God knows I need it."

"I don't think you should go out with this guy anymore," Peter said. "He's not good enough for you. You deserve better. A lot better."

"Yeah, but—"

"He's a jerk. He text messaged you."

"That turned out to be a misunderstanding—he really was sick. I think he was anyway. I mean, we went out again and had a good time."

Looking at her in that intense way, Peter said, "Are you happy, Katie?"

"What do you mean?"

"I'm just asking, Are you happy? If the answer's yes, then go out with him, I hope it works out for you guys. But I asked myself the same question, I mean about my girlfriend. The answer was no, so that was it—I broke up with her. I know I made the right decision, too. Life's too short to waste time being unhappy."

Katie was suddenly teary-eyed. Embarrassed, she said, "Sorry, it has nothing to do with any of this. It's just stuff building up. Other stuff." She dabbed her cheeks with the back of her hand, then forced a smile and said, "What is it with you men anyway?"

Maybe something was off in her delivery, because Peter didn't take it as a joke. He said seriously, "Not all guys are assholes."

"Okay," Katie said, "then what is it with ninety-nine point nine nine percent of you men?"

Peter still wasn't smiling.

The step class had started.

"I really have to go before all the spots're gone," Katie said.

"So are we on for Wednesday?" Peter asked.

"I can't cancel. How about Thursday?"

"Thursday's great. So I guess I'll pick you up at your place and I'll make a reservation for seven. Do you like French food?"

Suddenly there was something in Peter's tone that hadn't been there before, or at least Katie hadn't noticed it before. It sounded like he had . . . expectations.

"Yeah," she said, "I mean—"

"Great," he said. "Zagat's gave this place a great rating. There's garden seating so if the weather's nice we can eat outside."

"That sounds really cool," Katie said. "But . . . I mean, this is going to be, like, casual, right?"

Katie thought she saw the letdown in Peter's eyes. But it only lasted a second or two because then he just seemed confused and said, "What do you mean?"

"I mean, going out to dinner. I just want to be sure . . . I mean, I want it to be, you know . . . I mean, I don't want it to be—"

"Don't worry, it'll be casual."

"Cool," Katie said. "Yeah, this is gonna be a lot of fun. I'm really looking forward to it."

She said goodbye and joined the step class, which had started. They were just doing warm-ups, but Katie was having trouble following the instructor. She was distracted, worrying about Peter. She was afraid she'd hurt him or something. He was a nice guy, but she just couldn't see dating him. But she definitely wanted to be friends with him and she was afraid things were going to get weird between them now.

She looked over her shoulder, toward the Plexiglas partition and in the mirrors where she could see more of the gym, but didn't see Peter anywhere. She hoped he didn't leave because he was pissed off at her. Maybe he wasn't asking her out at all. Maybe he just wanted to have a friendly dinner and she'd jumped to the wrong conclusion, creating all this tension for no reason. She could've had another friend in the city, somebody who she could've hung out with and talked to, and now she'd blown it.

Then she realized she was still doing the previous exercise.

"I hate this," she said, louder than she intended.

The instructor and a few other people had heard her and were staring. She glared back at them until they looked away.

12

In his senior year at Michigan, Andy went out with this chick Mindy Somethingorother. He'd actually met her during freshman year—she lived in his dorm and had a super hot roommate—and although he knew she was into him and he could've scored with her at any time, he never tried. She had a nice ass, but needed serious help in the face department, and he didn't like her personality either. She talked way too much. He didn't mind girls who talked a lot—it wasn't like he had to dominate every conversation or anything—but Mindy just never shut up.

Then he was leaving an economics lecture one day, walking with this dude, Cory, when they passed Mindy. Cory gave Mindy a big hug and started talking to her for a while and Andy hung back. Andy said hi to her but not much else. Then when Mindy left and Andy started walking with Cory again, Cory told him about how one of his friends had just broken up with Mindy and she was available.

"I wouldn't waste my time with that," Andy said.

"I don't know," Cory said. "I heard she's pretty nasty."

"How nasty?"

"Really nasty. I heard she does everything."

"We talking anal?"

"We're talking anal."

Suddenly Andy saw Mindy in a new light. Anal sex was the only type of sex he hadn't had yet and it was starting to get embarrassing. He liked to think of himself as a stud. Maybe he didn't do as well as some guys in his frat who seemed to hook up with a new girl every week, but he didn't have a problem meeting girls. He'd had a Chinese girl, a black girl, and a Puerto

Rican girl, and he'd gone short, tall, skinny, and fat. He'd done all the positions he knew about—he learned most of them from watching pornos—and although the sex never lasted very long he knew he was good in bed. He'd gotten a ton of blow jobs and he even did tantric sex one time. But whenever he tried to have anal sex with a girl, it never worked out. Most of the time the girls just weren't into it, acting like he was some big perv or something for even suggesting it. Meanwhile, all the guys in the frat—the major studs anyway—claimed they'd done it with practically every girl they went out with.

So, figuring he'd finally fill the last gap on his sexual résumé, Andy looked up Mindy's schedule and then casually ran into her a couple of days later in the hallway outside of her art history class.

"Mindy, wow. We have to stop running into each other this way."

Mindy seemed a little standoffish at first—well, pissed-offish was more like it. Andy realized he must've acted pretty harshly toward her in freshman year when he blew her off, and that it would be an uphill battle to get her to like him, much less to get her to want to have anal sex with him.

But Andy went to work, telling Mindy how great she looked—even though she'd put on some weight and still had a kinda big nose and double chin—and how cool it was to see her for the second time in a week. Mindy, standing with her arms crossed in front of her chest, was friendly, but not superfriendly. Andy could tell she was still into him, even if she wasn't really showing it, so he asked her out for that Friday night. Mindy acted surprised, wanting to know why Andy was suddenly interested in her, out of the blue, when he didn't give her the time of day freshman year. It was weird, but Andy wondered if Mindy was reading his mind, if she knew he was just after her for anal sex, and she was just trying to give him a hard time about it. But Andy, keeping his cool, laid on the bull nice and thick. He told her how he'd been really shy freshman year and how he'd always had a big crush on her but never had the guts to ask her out. He managed to say all of this with a straight face, even putting on his vulnerable, sincere, sad-eyed puppy-dog look that chicks always seemed to dig, and Mindy was no exception. She admitted that she'd always had a crush on Andy, too—big surprise there!—and she gave Andy her address and phone number and arranged to meet at her place, Friday at eight.

Andy took her out to dinner at Uno and then they hit a couple of parties. She'd started drinking beer with her pizza and by the time they got to the second party she was nice and toasted. Meanwhile, Andy had been nursing his beers all night and had been drinking lots of water so he was ready to rumble. They went back to her place, started going at it in the living room, then moved to the bedroom. Everything was right on schedge. She was a good kisser—she moved her tongue around a lot and she made squeaky orgasmic-like noises—and Andy hoped this meant she would be a nasty dynamo, just like Cory had promised.

But then, when he tried to reach into her shirt, she kept pushing his hand away, and he thought, *Houston, we have a problem.* Finally he got her shirt off and was playing with her big, heavy tits, and then she said something about how "we shouldn't." Andy came back with "Yeah, we should," and a few minutes later her jeans and panties were off. She went down on him for a while—he didn't like her technique; too much hand—and then he sat up and, from a jeans pocket, took out a little tube of Vaseline. He dangled it in front of her face, expecting her to get the hint, but instead she said, "What's that for?" sounding confused.

"You know . . ." Andy said.

"No, I don't know."

She really didn't seem to understand.

"Oh, I get it," Andy said. "You put some in already, right?"

Mindy was silent for a few seconds, then she started laughing. Andy had no idea what was so funny.

"Come on," Mindy said. "That was a joke, right?"

"What was a joke?"

Now Mindy got serious and said, "What exactly did you think we were gonna do tonight?"

Andy recognized Mindy's shocked, suddenly offended tone because he'd gotten similar reactions from other girls after he'd reached for the Vaseline. He knew Cory must've gotten some bad information because there was no way Mindy was going anal tonight, or any other night.

Andy could've stuck around for the regular sex, but he couldn't deal. He told Mindy he had to use the bathroom and then he just bailed.

After the Mindy screw-up, Andy continued to try to have anal sex with every girl he went out with, but he took a more subtle approach. Instead of going for it right away, he waited until the second or third time, but he still couldn't pull it off. He realized that in the age of AIDS it was very unlikely for a girl to be willing to have anal sex with a guy she hardly knew. He needed more time, maybe a month of dating, to make a girl feel comfortable enough to do it with him. The problem was most of his relationships lasted less than two weeks. Another hurdle was that, when he met a girl, it was impossible to tell whether she'd be into it or not. With oral sex, it was a lot easier.

If a girl bit on a pen a lot or ate bananas or licked ice-cream cones in an erotic way, the odds were pretty good that she liked to give blow jobs. But there were no obvious tip-offs for anal sex. It wasn't like you could look at a girl's ass, watch the way she walked, and think, Yeah, she'd take it in the caboose. Some girls who looked like the biggest sluts in the world thought Andy was nuts when he even brought up the idea. But from what Andy had heard, some of the sweetest-looking girls, the girl-next-door types, were totally into it. He figured he just had to keep trying and eventually he'd get lucky.

Andy had no clue whether Katie would be into it or not, but he planned to find out. Actually, it was the only reason why he'd asked her out again. He'd decided that having any kind of long-term thing with her—any longer than a month anyway—was out. She was nice and pretty and all that, but she just wasn't Andy-Barnett-serious-relationship material after all. She was too boring, too moody, too melodramatic, too intense. And he noticed that she had a couple of zits on her forehead. He knew he couldn't blame her for that, but he couldn't understand why she didn't cover them up better with makeup. At the very least, he felt it was an *indication*. If a girl didn't tend to herself, what would happen when she started getting older? Would she put on a ton of weight? Would she just let herself go? These were serious questions guys had to ask themselves.

But it was Katie's attitude that really turned Andy off. At the movie theater, it annoyed him how, when he touched her knee, she acted like he had cooties. They'd already had sex, so what the hell was her problem? What, he wasn't allowed to *touch* her now? Andy was sick of all this game-playing shit. Sitting next to her during the Lindsay Lohan flick, Andy felt like he was in a prison cell. He regretted even asking her out again. He could've been out with his buddies, searching for his next victim, but then, when the movie ended, he reminded himself what the ultimate goal was. He'd already put in some time with Katie, gone on a bunch of dates, and it would've sucked to break up with her before he even had a chance to *try* for anal sex.

So Andy acted like Mr. Gentleman at the bar, telling her that crap she seemed to eat right up, about how he just wanted things to "be cool" between them, and then, when he walked her home, he didn't try to get any. Figuring he'd build up some more trust, he slipped her some tongue, and then, leaving her wanting more, he walked away. In the morning, at work, he decided to put some more points up on the scoreboard, and he e-mailed her some crap about how he'd had a great time with her and he was looking forward to seeing her again. He was bummed when she wrote back suggesting a double date. She obviously wanted her friend to check him out, and he didn't feel like going on a fucking audition, especially with a girl he'd already cleared the bases with. He felt like if she had a problem with him, she thought he wasn't good enough for her, then fuck her—let her find some dork who was willing to put up with that shit. But then, thinking about anal sex again, he sucked it up and wrote back that a double date sounded like a great idea. Then, figuring he might as well use this to his advantage, he decided to set her friend up with his roommate, Will the doctor. Girls always thought Will was really good-looking and if her friend liked Will it would score points for himself, increasing his chances for anal sex. Hey, it was worth a shot anyway.

Andy came up with a new Katie Porter game plan. He decided he'd keep up the act and go out with her for another two weeks, tops. If he didn't score through the back door by then it would be sayonara, baby.

On Monday he sent her an I-can't-wait-to-see-you-again e-mail. Then, on Tuesday, he IM'd with her for a while, telling her how psyched he was about the double date and more bull like that. On Wednesday, Andy and Will—who was wearing his doctor's scrubs—met Katie and Amanda at Katie's place. Andy couldn't believe how hot Amanda was. Katie had said, "She's really cute," but she was fucking smoking. She had a hot body, a pretty face, and had highlighted dirty-blond fuck-me hair. She was wearing a sleeveless low-cut top, exposing her muscular back, but it wasn't *too* muscular. It showed she was nice and toned and was an indication that she definitely took care of herself. When Andy introduced himself and shook her hand, she smiled—she was wearing that shiny-type lipstick and her mouth was really sexy—and it bummed Andy out that she wasn't his date, that he was stuck with nice, wholesome, boring Katie. He could tell that Will was into Amanda, too, just by the way he was acting, but when Andy and Will were alone in the kitchen, Will whispered, "Bro, she is so fucking hot," and Andy said, "Yeah, don't expect a birthday present from me this year, dude."

They went to Mustang on Second and Eighty-fifth and sat outside. Andy had been on some shitty double dates where the two people who knew each other had to carry all the conversation and it was awkward and painful for everybody. But Amanda and Will hit it off right out of the blocks and actually did most of the talking. Andy, trying not to stare too much at Amanda's great tits, was still jealous as hell. Meanwhile, Katie seemed pleased that Amanda and Will seemed so into each other. At one point, Katie and Amanda went to the bathroom together. When they returned, Katie held Andy's hand and started rubbing her leg up against his and making goo-goo eyes at him. It was a total switch from the way she'd acted at the movie theater the other night. Andy figured that he must've gotten a good review from

Amanda and, while if he could've pressed a button and turned Katie into Amanda he would've with no hesitation, he was glad that at least his strategy seemed to be working—Katie seemed to be totally into him now.

Like typical girls on dates, Katie and Amanda left their dishes—Santa Fe Chicken Salads—about three-quarters uneaten, while, like typical guys, Andy and Will wolfed down their burgers. Then, after splitting the check, they took the girls across the street for drinks at Molly Pitchers. They were still having their first round when Amanda and Will started sucking face. Katie was all over Andy, too. When Amanda and Katie took another bathroom trip, Andy and Will conferenced, deciding that the best move would be to get the girls back to their place ASAP. It was already past nine o'clock, and it was Wednesday, a work night. If they stayed at the bar much longer, the girls would start checking their watches or one of them would go, *I have to get up early tomorrow,* and the chances for getting laid would be KO'd.

Then Katie and Amanda came back and Katie said, "So how much longer do you guys want to stay here?" and Will gave Andy a look like, fuck, we blew it.

But then Andy said, "Come on, the night's young, ladies," and Katie said, "We know it is. But this place is kind of boring. Want to, like, go back to your place or something?"

A minute later, they were in a cab, heading uptown. Thank God, Andy's other roommates were either out or in their rooms and the living room was empty. Of course the place was a wreck and Andy and Will made phoney excuses about how "it's usually not like this" and said things like "sorry, our roommates are such fuckin' slobs," as they went around brushing crumbs off the couches and picking up as much garbage and as many beer bottles and soda cans as they could. The girls didn't seem to mind the mess, though, and they started talking about how jealous they were that the guys had so much space and lived in such a nice, luxury building. Andy put on some Green Day and cracked open some brews while Will took Amanda for "the tour" of the rest of the apartment. Andy knew that once Will got Amanda into his room they wouldn't come out, and they didn't. Andy and Katie didn't bother drinking their beers, either, and Andy led her into his room, winding a tie around the outside knob to let Greg know that he was hooking up and to spend the night someplace else.

Andy just wanted to rip Katie's clothes off and get to it and it was annoying as hell that she wanted to talk, going on and on about how great Amanda and Will were together and how glad she was that they had set them up. Andy tried not to let on how pissed off he was, smiling a lot and saying things like, "Yeah, it's great," and "Yeah, I know," while waiting for her to shut the hell up and take her clothes off. Finally, she stopped talking and they were making out and he had her top and bra off and he was about to unsnap her jeans, when she said, "Wait, I want to tell you something else." This time it was hard to hold back and he let out a frustrated breath and rolled his eyes a little.

"What's wrong?" she asked.

"Nothing."

"You just rolled your eyes."

"No, I didn't."

"I saw you."

"I didn't."

"Am I, like, boring you?"

"What? Of course not."

She seemed unconvinced, but after he insisted that nothing was wrong, that of course he wanted to hear whatever she had to say, she started telling him some dumb story that Andy couldn't really follow about how her boss had said something insulting about an outfit she'd worn to work the other day, and how she couldn't stop obsessing about it. The whole thing sounded really stupid to Andy, like typical neurotic, insecure girl shit. Her boss, who was probably a cool dude, had made some passing comment and Katie was blowing it up, getting all melodramatic. But Andy knew he couldn't *tell* Katie this. There was no faster way to put a bullet in a relationship—and to not get laid—than to not take a girl's side in a fight. So Andy told Katie exactly what he knew she wanted to hear, that her boss was a jerk, an asshole, a fucking moron. "That's great, tell me more," Katie said, and Andy called her boss a prick, a jackass, a dickbag, a motherfucking shitface, and Katie was loving it.

"Thank you so much, I feel so much better now," she said, and then she finally stopped jabbering and they started doing it. She got on top but was taking forever. Finally, she made some noise that sounded like she might've come, and that was good enough for him. He was kind of tired and was thinking about just coming quickly and trying for anal sex some other time, but then he figured he was here, he might as well give it a shot. He was going to suggest getting some Vaseline but, remembering all the times that had backfired for him in the past, he decided to try a different approach. Yeah, the Vaseline would make it more comfortable, but mentioning that word "Vaseline" always seemed to do more harm than good. Maybe anal sex was something that girls liked to do, but didn't like to discuss, and the less attention the guy brought to it the better. Seemed logical anyway. So when they were about to do it doggy style, he figured he'd try to slip it in the other way, hoping she'd be totally into it. Although he wasn't religious at all he thought, *Please, God, just this one time,* and looked up toward the ceiling before he tried to enter her.

"Hey," she said.

Fuck.

"What?" he said innocently.

"What're you doing?"

He couldn't tell—was she being, like, *playful?*

He decided to cut his losses, not take any chances, going, "Sorry," like it had been an accident.

Later, while she was sleeping next to him, he regretted not trying to push the issue any farther. Maybe if he'd been playful back, said something like, What do you want me to do? she would've come back with, Whatever you feel like doing. Damn, he was such an idiot. Tonight might've been the night and he'd blown it.

Around sunrise, Katie woke him up. She told him how great last night had been and he told her he'd had a great time, too. He offered to walk her back to her place but she insisted on going alone, which was cool with him because he wanted to grab some more shut-eye.

"When can I see you again?" she asked at the door to the apartment.

"How 'bout tonight?" he said, thinking that there was no way he wasn't going to at least try to do her up the ass next time.

"Yeah, tonight sounds great . . . oh, shoot, I'm supposed to have dinner with a friend."

"Oh, okay."

"But it's no big deal, I can cancel. I'd love to see you again."

They kissed goodbye. Andy tried to fall back asleep, but couldn't. He kept hearing Katie say, *What're you doing?* Who was he kidding? There'd been no playfulness at all in her tone. She might as well have said, *What the fuck're you doing?* He was just dreaming, thinking she'd ever be into having any anal action. The odds of that happening tonight, or any night, were slim to none.

Andy showered and got dressed. When he went out to the living room area he saw Will in the kitchen making coffee. He was wearing boxers and nothing else.

"Amanda here?" Andy asked.

"Nah, she just left," Will said, smiling the way guys smile after they've gotten laid. "Bro, you'll never have to get me a birthday present ever again."

"How was it?"

"Awesome, dude. We were going at it all night. When we went into my room, I swear to God, she gave me one of the best blow jobs I've ever had. You know how some girls try to, like, rush through it? Like it's a race or something?"

"Yeah," Andy said, jealous as hell. Katie hadn't even blown him yet. And *why* was he dating her?

"Well, Amanda was the total opposite, man," Will went on. "She took her sweet time. It was like she was, like, worshiping my manhood. I mean, she'd take breaks, you know, and, like, admire it. It was like she was Picasso and my dick was the clay. She was molding me, using her fingers to—"

"All right, I get the picture," Andy said.

"Then came the Oprah moment, the moment of truth—"

"And the answer is . . ."

"Wanna give me the drumroll?"

Andy rolled his eyes, then started patting his hands against the counter-top dividing the living room and kitchen.

"Swallow, baby," Will said.

Andy shook his head, smiling. He was jealous, but he was also imagining Will as a pediatrician someday. He knew one thing—he was keeping his own kids far, far away from Will.

"But I didn't even get to the best part," Will said.

Andy knew what Will would say, but he prayed he was wrong. There was only so much jealousy a man could handle.

"What?" Andy asked cautiously.

"We did it twice. It was really good. Then, it must've been three, four in the morning, and we're starting to go at it again. I swear, at this point, it felt like my dick would fall off. Then she says, I'm kind of sore, why don't we do something else? So I thought she was gonna go down on me again, but instead she—"

"No way."

"Way."

"Come on."

"Yep, on the first date! Can you believe that?"

Actually, Andy couldn't believe it. He felt like God was playing some kind of cruel joke on him. Was he the only guy in New York not getting any anal sex?

"Man," Andy said, "you better pay me back for this. I'm serious. You better set me up with some nurse at the hospital or something. Someone super slutty."

"Don't worry, you're in, bro, you're in," Will said. "But why do you need somebody else? Katie seems really cool."

"Not so cool."

"What do you mean? She seems totally into you. She's really cute, too, and she probably does everything, right?"

There was no way Andy could tell the truth, that he'd barely fucked Katie after dating her all those times. He'd never live it down with the guys.

"Yeah, she is pretty wild," Andy lied.

"Figured," Will said. "If a girl's good in bed, her friends are always good, too. It's because girls talk about it, you know? I mean about technique. They share trade secrets. So what's wrong with her then?"

"Nothing," Andy said. "I just want to change things up, not get too, you know, intense. And she's kind of a little *too* slutty, you know? I mean to, like, date. I mean, like, seriously date."

"Yeah, I know," Will said. "I like Amanda, too, but I can't see going out with her more than another few times. When a girl does everything on the first date, you gotta wonder, you know? But I won't dump her for a week or two at least. Last night was way too much fun."

Later on, at work, Andy was still trying to get over his jealousy, when he got an e-mail from Katie, telling him how much she was looking forward to tonight. Suddenly Andy felt like he was trapped in boyfriend land. He and Katie had been seeing way too much of each other—what had it been, four dates in the last *week?*—and for what, some just-okay sex? It was time to back off, become more distant, or, better yet, dump her.

He was about to delete her e-mail and forget all about her, but then, remembering what Will had said about girls exchanging trade secrets, he decided he'd go out with her one more time. But if he didn't score anally tonight she'd be history.

At eight o'clock, he went to pick her up at her place. It was raining, which turned out to be key. He was psyched when she said she didn't feel like going out in the bad weather and suggested ordering in Chinese instead. They'd finished their hot and sour soups and were into their steamed shrimp dumplings when Andy leaned over the table and kissed her. They moved to the couch and he could tell she was really getting into it. Then she looked at him, smiling, and said, "Wanna build up an appetite?"

A minute later, they were in her bedroom, getting naked, then they started doing it. He got on top for a while, then she took over. She was bouncing around really hard, making a lot of noise, then she stopped. She bent over, kissed him, and said, "I like you so much," and he said, "I like you so much, too." He could tell this made her really happy because she started bouncing on him even harder. Then she came, her face turning pink and getting all scrunched up, so he knew she wasn't faking.

Afterward, she collapsed onto her back, catching her breath, then said, "God, that felt great." Then, a few seconds later, "How do you want me?"

Andy knew this was code. She wouldn't come out and *say* she wanted to be fucked up the ass. No, no nice, normal girl would ever say something like that. But after last night, she knew what he wanted to do, and she wouldn't've said, How do you want me? leaving the ball in his court, if she wasn't ready for it. Yep, this was it all right—his lucky day. Someday he'd look back on this, the way he looked back on the day he lost his virginity. He wanted to savor every second of this so he'd remember it clearly forever.

"From behind," he said.

She turned over quickly, onto all fours.

"I mean with you flat on your stomach."

She collapsed onto the bed, lying there, waiting for him. He knelt on top of her, knowing that in a few seconds everything would be different. From now on, his life would be divided into two parts—BAS (before anal sex), and AAS (after anal sex). He parted her butt cheeks carefully, but before he could do anything, Katie jerked forward, as if he'd tried to stab her, and said, "Hey."

He was so caught up in trying to savor the moment that he didn't even realize she'd said this, and continued what he was doing, until she said "Hey" again, almost yelling.

Then he stopped and said, "What's wrong?" He wasn't playing dumb. He'd been so convinced that they were on the same page that he honestly didn't know what was the matter.

"I think you lost your sense of direction there for a second," she said.

He wondered if she was being sarcastic, if she really wanted him to continue.

He decided to roll the dice.

"No, I didn't," he said.

He was about to try again but she squirmed away and said, "Come on. Stop kidding around."

"What do you mean? I thought it was cool with you."

"What was cool with me?"

"You never did it that way before?"

"No. Of course not."

"Oh, I just thought . . ."

"That's disgusting."

It definitely didn't sound like sarcasm anymore.

"Oh," he said. "I just thought it'd be cool to try it one time."

"Sorry. I'm just afraid it'll hurt too much."

"I promise I'll be gentle."

"I'm really not into it."

"Oh, that's cool," he said, but couldn't've been telling a bigger lie.

They had sex the normal way, but he was so distracted and angry he almost lost his hard-on. He had to concentrate really hard, pretending she was one of the porn stars he'd seen on TV the other day, that Chinese one, in order to keep it up. Then, finally, after about five minutes, he finished. It was probably the lamest sex he'd ever had.

But by the way she cuddled up to him afterward and started kissing his face and neck, she didn't seem to have any clue that all he wanted, more than anything in the world, was to get the hell out of there. He would've left right away, but he knew that would mess things up for Will and Amanda big-time, so he figured he wouldn't let on that anything was wrong tonight, but then he'd break up with her the way he usually broke up with girls, by e-mail or with a text message. He'd tell Katie he got back with his old girlfriend, or that he wasn't ready for a relationship, or some crap like that.

He stayed for another hour or so, finishing dinner, and then he made up an excuse, telling her he had to go back home to do some stuff for work tomorrow.

"You know what would be cool?" she said. "If we could start leaving clothes at each other's apartments. I mean, so we can stay over sometimes."

"Yeah, that's a really great idea," he said, then he looked away, rolling his eyes, but making sure she didn't see.

He kissed her goodbye, telling her he had a great time and couldn't wait to see her again.

"Hey, you wanna go out tomorrow night?" she asked.

"Yeah, I'll definitely call you," he said, thinking, Yeah, like that was happening.

Finally, he was out of her apartment, by himself, a free man again. It had almost stopped raining. He wanted to find a girl, any girl to make him forget about the whole Katie debacle. Blondie's on Second Avenue looked lame, so he went next door to the Big Easy and hit on the hot bartender. No luck there, so he positioned himself at the bar next to two girls. One of them was cute, one wasn't. Most guys, in this situation, went after the cute one. Big mistake. The cute one usually had a boyfriend and was on a "mercy night out" with her single, not-as-cute friend. Andy knew if he started talking to the cute one he'd wind up buying drinks for her and her friend, and get absolutely nothing, not even a phone number. So Andy started talking to the so-so looking one—her name was Lynn—and things looked great for a while. She seemed really desperate and into him and he thought he was a shoo-in for at least a blow job. The problem was, the good-looking friend was just sitting there by herself. There must've been ten other single guys in the bar, and Andy couldn't believe no one was coming over to help him out. Naturally, the pretty one felt uncomfortable alone and started pressuring the friend to leave with her. Andy could tell the friend wanted to stay, but the pretty one kept bitching, and the friend finally gave in. Andy got the friend's number, but he doubted he'd actually call her. He wasn't looking for a date; he was looking to get laid.

He ordered another beer and scanned the bar. The ratio sucked. There were only two girls in the whole place and they were both on the fat side and they were both with guys. He figured he'd down his beer, then check out a couple of other bars on his way home or maybe just call it a night—he'd see how he felt—when he noticed a dark-haired guy with a goatee standing near the door. It was hard to tell for sure, but the guy seemed to be staring at him. Andy looked away a couple of times, then checked back, and the guy still seemed to be looking right at him.

Starting to get seriously pissed off, Andy glared at the guy, as if saying, *Stop staring at me, asshole.* The guy must've noticed, because he came over to Andy and, smiling widely, said, "Hi, don't you remember me? Joe. Joe the Yankees fan."

13

Andy squinted at the guy but he didn't look any more familiar.

"No, actually I don't remember you."

"Come on," the guy said. "We met a couple of months ago at that bar on Third Avenue. Your name's Andy, right?"

"Yeah," Andy said, looking at the guy closely again, trying to see if something rang a bell.

"And you're a big Phillies fan, right?"

"Yeah, that's right."

"Come on, you remember me. It was late, we were talking near the bathroom. We were both pretty drunk, too."

"Oh, yeah, yeah, I think I remember now." Actually, the guy only looked slightly more familiar, but Andy figured he must've met him before and was just blanking. "What'd you say your name was?"

"Joe."

"Joe?"

"Yeah, Joe."

Now that they were talking Andy didn't get the weird vibe so much anymore; actually Joe seemed like a pretty cool dude. "So how's it going, man?"

"Pretty good, pretty good," Joe said. "So you got that girl's number, huh?"

"You mean the ugly one?"

"She didn't seem so ugly."

"You were twenty feet away, dude. Trust me, there were big problems up close."

"Then why'd you get her number?"

"You mean this?" Andy took out the little piece of paper with her number on it, crumpled it into a ball, and tossed it away over his shoulder. "I'm not gonna waste my time with that shit." He sipped his beer, then looked around. "Man, I can't believe how lame the talent is here tonight. There's usually a ton of tuna here, you know?"

"You're looking to get laid tonight, huh?"

"I already got laid," Andy said. "Now I wanna get fucked."

Andy was trying to be funny and expected Joe to laugh, but Joe didn't have any reaction. Andy thought maybe the guy didn't hear him—the music was kind of loud—but then Joe said, "Why's that?"

"Because it sucked, that's why," Andy said.

"Why did it suck?"

The Q and A was becoming a bummer.

"It's a long story, you know? This girl . . . she's just been stringing me along, you know, wasting my time."

Joe stared, then said, "Yeah, don't you hate that?"

"Yeah, it fuckin' sucks, dude." Andy downed some more beer then put the bottle down hard on the bar. "Well, it's time to blow this place. I'm gonna see if there's any talent at Brother Jimmy's. Nice running into you again, bro."

Andy was about to get up when Joe said, "If you really want to get fucked tonight, I can help you out."

Andy looked at him, wondering, *Whoa, is this guy an ass bandit or what?*

But then, thinking Joe didn't *seem* like the fudgepacking type, Andy said, "Yeah, how're you gonna do that?"

"This might come out the wrong way—"

"As long as it doesn't go in the wrong way."

The guy was staring at Andy, didn't seem to get it.

"I'm not gay, dude," Andy said.

Joe smiled, then said, "No, I didn't think you were. Here's the deal—I'm married, okay. To a beautiful woman. A model, actually. You might've seen her before. You heard of Cleara?"

"No."

"Well, she's a very famous model. She was on the cover of German *Vogue* last month. She's Brazilian, but she's really big in Europe. She was in the *SI* swimsuit issue last year."

"I have that issue at home. Was she on the cover?"

"No, she didn't make the cover . . . unfortunately. There was a shot of her on the beach, near some rocks. She was wearing a skimpy thong bathing suit, but it was coming off, so she had her hands over her breasts like this."

Joe demonstrated.

"She sounds hot," Andy said.

"Yeah, she's *very* hot," Joe said. "Anyway, we don't have the—it's always hard for me to say this—the most typical marriage in the world. See, she likes it when I, like, bring guys home for her."

"You're shitting me."

"No, I swear to God. It's a big turn on for her. That's why I go to bars. Not to try to pick up girls, but to pick up guys."

Andy had heard about shit like this. A buddy of his in high school claimed he'd met a woman in the mall one day who used to invite him over to her place to fuck while her husband watched.

"Don't you get jealous?" Andy asked.

"No, I actually enjoy it."

"You enjoy watching guys fuck your wife?"

"No, no, I'm never in the room. She tells me all about it later. Anyway, if you're interested you're exactly her type. How old are you?"

"Twenty-three, but—"

"Yeah, that's perfect. She's twenty-eight, but she loves young, clean-cut guys. Were you in a fraternity in college?"

"Yeah, Delta Kappa Epsilon, but I—"

"Yeah, she's gonna love you. So what do you say? We live right over on East End Avenue, in a penthouse overlooking the river. We can be there in five minutes."

"Sorry, dude," Andy said. "I mean, it sounds great and everything, but—"

"I know this might sound weird to you, but I'm telling you, it's the truth. I wish I had a picture with me to show you, but trust me, she's unbelievably good-looking. And all the guys I bring back for her leave very, very satisfied."

"I believe you, dude," Andy said. "But, I don't know—"

"Hey, if you're not interested, you're not interested. I don't think you realize what you're missing, but I'm not gonna push it. But, hey, it was nice running into you again. See you around, I guess."

Andy watched Joe go over to two guys sitting at a table and start talking to them. The guys seemed into what Joe was saying and Andy figured he was giving them the same offer. Usually, if a guy came up to him at a bar and told him about his beautiful Brazilian model wife who liked to screw other guys, Andy would've thought the guy was full of shit, but Joe seemed for real. Then Andy wondered what the hell he was doing, letting this major opportunity pass him by. Shit, this could've been one of those once-in-a-lifetime type things, something that fell from the sky right into his lap, and if he let it get away he might spend the rest of his life wondering *What if?* Maybe things not working out tonight with Katie was the best thing that could've happened. Maybe he was meant to run into Joe and go have sex with the model. Maybe she was wild in bed and would do everything, even have anal sex with him. He would have to be out of his mind to not at least check this thing out.

Andy went over to Joe, tapped him on the shoulder, and said, "Okay, I'll go."

"You sure?" Joe asked. "Because these guys—"

"No, I'm in," Andy said.

They went outside.

"So where did you say you live?" Andy asked.

"East End Avenue, right near Carl Schurz Park," Joe said. "It's not far."

"There won't be any cameras there, right?"

"No, it's not like that at all. I mean, you can look around if you want, but I promise you—this is just good clean fun."

They made a left on the next corner and continued along the dark side street. A cold front must've come through because the temperature felt like it had dropped ten degrees. For a while it was awkward, and they didn't talk much, and Andy was starting to feel weird about the whole thing, wondering if this was such a great idea after all. Then they started talking about baseball, about how steroids had ruined the game and tarnished all the records, and Andy started feeling okay about it again. He hoped Joe wasn't bullshitting, that his wife—Cara?—was really some superhot model. But if it turned out she was really ugly or whatever, it would be no big deal, either. He'd just say, "No thanks, see ya," and bail. He had zero to lose, so why not go for it?

When he reached East End Avenue, Joe started crossing the street, heading toward Carl Schurz Park. All the apartment buildings were on the other side of the street so Andy wondered where Joe was going.

"Where's your building?" Andy asked, slowing down, lagging a few feet behind.

"Oh, right over there," Joe said, pointing downtown on East End. "I just have to make a little pit stop first."

"What kind of pit stop?"

"Well, Cleara likes to get high, to get in the mood, and I don't have any shit on me."

"Oh," Andy said, "so where're you going?"

"My dealer hangs out on the promenade," Andy said. "It'll take two secs and we can smoke a little, too. You like to get high?"

Andy hadn't smoked pot since college, but he used to get wasted all the time.

"Yeah," he said. "Sometimes."

"So come on, let's go."

Andy hesitated, worrying about the random drug tests at work. But if he said he was afraid he'd feel like a wimp, and he hated feeling like a wimp. He wanted to be a risk taker, the type of guy who could do something crazy like this, meet a guy in a bar and get high and go to fuck his wife, without getting nervous about it.

"All right," Andy said and followed the guy into the park.

They walked in silence for a while, then Joe asked, "You ever been in this park before?"

"No," Andy said. "I mean, I passed it when I went running once, but I never went in."

"I love it here. It's really quiet, really peaceful. It's like a slice of the country in the middle of the city. You can come here with a book, sit on the grass, and nobody bothers you. Cleara and I have picnics here all the time. Yeah, we really love it."

They continued along the path, stepping around puddles. There was some light from the small, old-style lampposts, but it was still dark and hard to see too far ahead.

"Listen," Joe said. "You can hardly hear anything, right? You wouldn't even know you're in Manhattan."

There were heading toward the stairs leading downward when Joe suddenly started sneezing. He bent over to get a hold of himself then straightened up, smiling, and said, "Allergies."

Squinting, Andy said, "So where does your . . . dealer hang out?"

"Not far from here," Joe said.

They went down the steps, toward an underpass. There was a nice cool breeze coming through the tunnel, pushing back Andy's hair. Then, at the bottom of the stairs, Joe grabbed Andy, forced him back against the concrete wall, and started squeezing his neck.

Andy tried to grab Joe's arms, push him away, but he couldn't get anywhere. He felt pressure building in his head.

"You shoulda left her alone, Frat Boy," Joe said. "You shoulda left her alone."

What the hell was he talking about? What the fuck was wrong with him? Andy tried to suck some air through his throat, any air, but couldn't.

Then he thought, *This isn't happening. I'm not even here.* But, fuck, he still couldn't breathe, and Joe, with his face all red and bulging veins in his forehead, looked totally insane. Andy thought, *If I could just get one breath, one fucking breath.* He struggled, trying desperately to pry away Joe's fingers. But the fucking guy seemed to be wearing gloves or something and Andy couldn't get the fingers loose. He tried to kick Joe but couldn't get any force into it. He was weak, everything spinning, then he couldn't fight back. He didn't know where he was anymore, or who he was. He was looking at Joe's face, but it wasn't even a face. It was nothing at all.

PART TWO

14

When Peter Wells was nine years old he asked his mother if she would marry him someday. His mother didn't take it seriously, acting like it was a big joke—maybe her son was going through some sort of romance period, a phase—but Peter was dead serious. He told his mother again and again how much he loved her and how he wanted to spend the rest of his life with her. Finally, she told him that it was getting to be too much, that he was starting to upset her, and that he had to stop it. Although Peter knew that his mother really was in love with him and just didn't want to admit it, he stopped expressing his feelings because the last thing he wanted was for the woman he loved more than anything to be mad at him.

For the next few years, Peter continued to pine, in secret, for his mom. Most kids his age tried to spend as little time with their mothers as possible, feeling embarrassed to be around them, but not Peter. He loved doing things with his mother. He went everywhere with her—to the Pittsfield Mall, to Price Chopper; he even waited at the salon while she got her hair done. To impress her, he got interested in the things she was interested in—classical music, old movies—and he rushed home every day to listen to NPR. When he wasn't with her, like at school, he'd sit in the back of the class, gazing out the window, thinking about her. After school, at night, he'd tell his mother he needed help with his homework just so he could spend more time with her. Although she'd never admit it, Peter knew his mother enjoyed his company, too, and not only in the usual way mothers enjoys their sons' company. There was definitely an unspoken bond between them, a special connection that other mothers and sons didn't have.

When Peter reached puberty, naturally his mother was the star of most of his masturbation fantasies. He imagined many scenarios, but his favorite was their wedding night. They were in the honeymoon suite and it was their first time together. He imagined taking off her dress, what her breasts would look like, what they'd feel like. He enjoyed the buildup, but tried not to ejaculate, and it annoyed him whenever he accidentally did. He felt like ejaculating degraded his mother, made her into one of the slutty women in a copy of *Hustler* he'd once seen.

Peter became a master at hiding his emotions. No one had any idea that he had a thing for his mother—his father was probably the most clueless of all. As far as his old man was concerned, yeah, maybe Peter was more of a momma's boy than most kids, but there wasn't anything abnormal going on. And the thing was there *wasn't* anything abnormal going on. Of course, Peter knew that most boys didn't fall in love with their mothers and want to marry them, but his situation was different. His mother wasn't even his mother. He'd been adopted and his real parents were Canadian, lived somewhere near Montreal. And there wasn't a huge age difference between him and his adoptive mother either. They were only twenty-seven years apart so when he was twenty she'd be forty-seven, when he was twenty-five she'd be fifty-two, et cetera, et cetera. It seemed like the older they got the less of a big deal it would become. Yeah, some people would think it was weird, a mother marrying her adopted son, but what difference would it make? They would be in love and that's all that would matter.

Peter's plan was to propose to his mother for real on his eighteenth birthday. He figured his father would probably be dead by then anyway. His father was sixty-four, had a heart condition, and had already undergone a quadruple bypass. He was in such bad shape that there was even talk of attempting a transplant at some point. Even if the old man somehow managed to survive, Peter didn't think he would be much of an obstacle. He knew his mother and father weren't really in love and that his mother would divorce him in a second to marry her son, as soon as it became legally possible.

Then, the summer after ninth grade, everything suddenly changed. It was funny because it started as a typical Saturday morning in July—very harmless. Peter and his mother and father had breakfast on the screened-in porch and then his mother announced she was taking a shower. Peter and his father remained at the table, his father reading the *Berkshire Eagle*. Peter waited a couple of minutes, taking the last few bites of his French toast, then said he was going up to his room. Instead, he went to the bathroom door in his parents' bedroom and carefully opened it, just an inch or two. His mother never locked the door while she showered and Peter had always assumed that she did this on purpose, because she expected him to look in, because she *wanted* him to.

As usual the sliding shower door was only halfway shut, so whenever his mother reached for the soap or shampoo, or stepped away from the spray to scrub herself, Peter had a great view of her full breasts, wide hips, and the wet dark hair between her legs. The house was old, built in the nineteenth century, and the stairs and floorboards always creaked in advance of anyone approaching. But because of the noise of the shower, it wasn't as easy to hear, and Peter had to listen closely for any noise of his father. Meanwhile, he unsnapped his shorts and reached into his boxer briefs and started playing with himself. He got hard right away and the sight of his mother, reaching up to massage shampoo into her hair, her breasts becoming higher and firmer, made him even more excited. He had to squeeze himself to prevent an orgasm and then something happened that had never happened before.

Whenever Peter watched his mother in the shower, they never made eye contact, even though he knew she knew she was being watched. Although the bathroom door was always cracked open very slightly, if she wanted privacy she could have simply locked it. Peter had always assumed that his mother never looked in his direction because she wanted him to watch her, but didn't want to admit to it, or at least didn't want to bring any attention to it.

This was why Peter was surprised when his mother looked right at him. It was such a big change from the norm that Peter didn't know how to react. He froze for a couple of seconds, his left hand still gripping his cock, then smiled. He expected his mother to smile back, maybe invite him to come into the shower with her. But his mother wasn't smiling. She had a look of shock, horror, repulsion, and then she was screaming at him, storming out of the shower, grabbing a towel from the rack and fumbling to wrap herself with it. Peter was very confused, unable to understand what he'd done to make her so upset. Before he could say anything, his mother opened the door fully, came over, and grabbed him. She screamed, "You bastard! You disgusting fucking bastard!" and slapped him across the face as hard as she could.

Peter hadn't thought about that slap, how devastating it had been, in a long time, but as he was squeezing Frat Boy's neck, waiting for him to hurry up and die already, it all came back to him—the way his mother had suddenly turned on him, how she'd called him "a disgusting fucking bastard," how in that instant his total love for her turned to total hatred. But he really had no idea why he was thinking about all this now, at this moment, when he should've been concentrating on getting Frat Boy dead. He started squeezing the bastard's neck with even more force, feeling like he was compressing the neck to nothing, that his hands would soon meet in a mess of blood, broken bones, and flesh.

Although Frat Boy's eyes looked frozen and lifeless and his body was limp, Peter didn't let up for another minute or two. Finally, he released his grip and let Frat Boy crumple onto the concrete. Peter's hands hurt and his fingers were so tense that it was difficult to straighten them out of their curled positions. But looking down at the body, he was pleased that problem numero uno was officially out of the way. Not wasting a second, he kneeled, removed Frat Boy's wallet, took all the money, then left the wallet next to the body. Then he took off the gloves and calmly stuffed them in the back left pocket of his jeans while looking toward the stairs to his right and to his left. There was no one in either direction and it was quiet except for the sound of water falling from the ceiling of the tunnel in a steady drip. Peter doubted anyone in the park could have heard anything anyway. Except for a weak gasp when Peter had made his move, pushing him up against the wall, Frat Boy hadn't made a peep.

Peter wanted to leave the tunnel and the park as fast as possible, but he knew running away would be the absolute wrong thing to do. If someone saw him and then discovered the body he would be an obvious suspect. So he left the park calmly, walking with his head down just in case, and made it out to East End Avenue without passing a single person. East End was pretty empty as well. Across the street, up the block, a man was walking his dog but he was facing the other direction and was too far away to get a good look at Peter anyway. Toward Gracie Mansion, a few kids were walking uptown, but they were a block or two away. As Peter crossed the street, a cab was waiting at the red light. Peter purposely didn't look in the driver's direction, but it didn't matter anyway. Why would a cab driver care about some random guy on the street?

Walking along Eighty-sixth Street, toward York Avenue, Peter passed a couple of people. He kept his head down slightly, avoiding eye contact. He didn't care if people noticed his dark hair—he just didn't want anyone to get a good look at his face. Approaching First Avenue, the sidewalks became more populated, and he must've passed dozens of people by the time he reached Third. But Peter wasn't concerned about being noticed anymore. He was too far from the murder scene for anyone to make a connection. But, just to play it safe, rather than taking a cab, he took a subway. While there were many more chances of being noticed on a subway, it seemed more likely that a cabdriver would take a close look at him, and he wanted to stay as anonymous as possible. He also wanted to get back to his hotel room quickly and was worried that he'd have to wait a long time for a train to come. But someone upstairs must've been watching over him tonight, making sure everything went his way, because moments after he arrived on the platform a train pulled into the station. He got on one of the cars toward the back of the train and sat at the far end, near the door leading to the next car. There were several other people in the car, but they didn't even seem to notice Peter was there.

Twenty or so minutes later, the train pulled into the Twenty-third Street station. Peter walked several blocks back uptown to Rocky Sullivan's, a bar on Lexington. Although it was nearly one o'clock there were a mix of twenty-somethings and older alcoholic types, enjoying themselves, and most of them would still be there drinking at three or four in the morning. Sets of eyes shifted toward him as he walked in, the way people always, instinctively, check out fresh meat entering a bar, but no one seemed to take any great notice of him. It helped that the crowd was mostly guys and couples. Peter continued toward the back area, where some more people were seated, and went straight to the men's room. He went in, locked the door, and started washing the color out of his hair, eyebrows, and goatee.

It was temporary spray-in color and the dark brown rinsed out easily with soap and water. In a few minutes, he was a blond again. With some paper towels, he dried himself, and then he left the bathroom. As he walked back through the bar no one even looked at him. He exited and headed downtown on Lexington.

At the corner of Twenty-eighth and Lex, Peter reached into his back pocket, figuring he'd drop the gloves into the garbage can as soon as he passed by, or maybe bury them under the top layer of garbage, but right away he knew something was wrong. The bulge in his pocket seemed smaller than it was the last time he'd felt it, when he was leaving the park. Then he took out one glove from the pocket, not two. He felt his other pocket, but he knew it was pointless. He'd put both of the gloves in his back left pocket and one of them had fallen out.

He started back toward the bar, in case he'd lost it there, but then he turned around and continued downtown again. Going back to the bar would've been a mistake. If he started looking around for something people might've noticed. Besides, he knew the glove wasn't in the bathroom because he remembered checking before he left to make sure he hadn't left anything behind. The last time he recalled actually feeling his back pocket to assure himself the gloves were still there was when he was leaving the park. The most likely possibility was that the glove had fallen out while he was walking on the street or—even more likely—while he was sitting on the subway. If he'd lost the glove on the subway it wasn't a big deal. It was an inconspicuous latex glove that would probably be picked up and thrown away by a sanitation worker. But if he'd dropped the glove on the street, especially anywhere near the park, it would be a major problem.

Peter considered retracing his steps, taking the subway back uptown and walking toward the park along Eighty-sixth Street, then he realized how insane that would be. It was too late to do anything about it now. For all he knew the body had already been discovered. Someone walking their dog late at night might've realized that the guy curled up in the tunnel near the wall hadn't OD'd and wasn't asleep, and the person might've called the police. The entire park could be a crime scene now, with cops searching the nearby streets as well. If he'd dropped the glove anywhere between the park and the Eighty-sixth Street subway station and the police found it, it would be held as possible evidence.

Peter felt like an idiot for not putting the gloves away more securely. Even if he'd put a glove in each back pocket instead of stuffing both of them into one, he probably wouldn't be in this position. He tried to remember if he'd felt the pocket to make sure the gloves were there at any point between leaving the park and leaving the bar, but he couldn't remember for sure. He was certain that if he had dropped the glove on the way to the subway he would've noticed because he'd been so hyperaware of everything at that point. But he was sure that he hadn't looked back when he left the subway so he very well could've left the glove on the seat.

Continuing uptown along Lexington, he decided that in all likelihood he had no reason to stress. Even if the police found the glove, what would they do with it? Peter had no connection to Frat Boy; there would be no reason to even question him. If someone at the Big Easy on Second Avenue came forward, the police would be searching for a dark-haired guy. How would the glove help them one way or another?

Peter became even more convinced that the second glove was insignificant. Everything was going perfectly—he had zero chance of getting caught. At the next corner, he buried the other glove in a garbage can, under some newspapers. Then, casually, he continued toward his hotel.

Hector was working at the desk. There was no way to enter unseen or to avoid a conversation with him, nor was there a reason to. Peter had been staying out late a lot recently so there was nothing unusual about him returning past one A.M. Besides, the police wouldn't be asking.

"Hey, man," Hector said. "Yo, hold up, I got something for you." He opened a drawer, took out an envelope, and said, "Knicks tickets."

"Wow," Peter said. "Why're you—"

" 'Cause you been so cool to me, man, giving me such good advice and shit, I wanted to give you something. It's Knicks-Golden State, a week from Saturday. They're green seats, behind the basket. You won't be sittin' next to Spike Lee, but at least you can see the whole game from there."

"This is really cool, but you didn't have to buy me tickets."

"I didn't buy 'em, man. My cousin got season tickets and he couldn't use them and he was like, You wanna go? So I took 'em, figured I give 'em to you instead."

"You sure? Why don't you take Lucy?"

"She don't like basketball and I been to two games already this year and they lost both times. I'm a bad luck charm and shit. I want you to have 'em, man. You can go, right? You can take your woman, what's her name again?"

"Katie."

"Katie, that's right. She like basketball?"

Peter had no idea, which irritated him. He felt like he should know everything about her, that he should know her as well and he knew himself.

"Yeah, she loves it," he said.

"Cool. So you guys go, have a good time, on me. And maybe the Knicks'll win too, 'cause my ass ain't there."

Peter laughed then said, "Well, thanks."

"I should be thankin' you, man. If it wasn't for you, me and Lucy wouldn't be talkin' about gettin' married and shit."

"Wow, you guys are seriously talking about marriage?"

"Yeah, soon as we get the money we're gonna do it. I figure, Why not? Everybody else gettin' married, right?"

"That's wonderful," Peter said, proud of himself for helping to bring two people in love together. "I'm glad to be of service."

"So when're you gonna bring Katie around here so I can meet her?" Hector asked.

Peter realized it would probably seem weird to admit that Katie had never been to the hotel, so he said, "She was here yesterday afternoon. You weren't working."

"Oh, man, can't believe I missed that shit," Hector said. "Definitely bring her around when I'm working so I can say hey. Or, yo, I got an idea. How 'bout you, me, Lucy, Katie, go out to dinner sometime? You know, a double date."

Peter remembered the double date that Katie, Katie's friend Amanda, Frat Boy, and Frat Boy's friend had been on the other night. Peter had watched them from across the street while the two couples ate outside at

Mustang. They all looked like they were having such a great time, but Peter knew that Katie was just faking it, that she was really miserable as hell and desperately needed to be rescued.

"A double date sounds like a great idea," Peter said. "Let's definitely do that."

After thanking Hector again for the tickets, Peter said good night and took the elevator up to his room. He wanted to call Katie right away. He wanted to tell her that Frat Boy was gone forever, that there were no obstacles in their way anymore, that they could spend the rest of their lives together. But as badly as he wanted to hear her voice and jump-start their future, he knew he had to let things take their own course and unfold naturally.

He went into the bathroom and shaved his goatee. He realized he hadn't been clean-shaven in a long time, in about five years, and he felt like the change in his appearance was appropriate, symbolic. He was looking in the mirror at the new Peter Wells. Tonight marked a fresh start for him; he had taken his first big step toward happily-ever-after.

In the shower, he luxuriated, letting the hot stream relax his neck and shoulders. Aside from the lost glove he was pleased with how well everything had gone. If the body wasn't discovered tonight it would definitely be by sometime in the morning. The police would canvass the Upper East Side, interviewing everyone, and maybe a few suspicious dark-haired guys with goatees and criminal records would be taken in for questioning. But eventually, maybe in a month or two, the police would stop looking and the incident would become just another unsolved New York City homicide.

Peter was proud of himself for handling the situation so well. If he hadn't gotten rid of Frat Boy, Katie could've stayed with him, deluding herself into believing he was a nice guy; or worse, she might've discovered that Peter was following her and misunderstood why he was doing it. She might have freaked, panicked, and then everything would've been shot to hell.

Four days ago, on Monday morning, Peter had decided to resolve the Frat Boy situation. The night before had been total misery. Peter couldn't sleep at all, thinking about Katie, wanting to go over to her place and be with her so badly. In the morning, he couldn't resist. He put on his Yankees cap and sunglasses and went to her block, standing about fifty yards away across the street. When she left for work he felt like he was in a movie, like when the guy looks at the girl everyone knows he's going to get in the end, and you can tell how pained the guy is that he doesn't have the girl yet because there are still obstacles in the way. Keeping a safe distance of about a half block between them, he followed her to the subway. She took her usual route. As she waited to cross Third Avenue, he approached on the other side of the street and he saw her face, how distraught she looked, and it was hard to tell, but was she talking to herself? It sickened him to see her so unhappy, and it was also frustrating as hell. If she only knew that her ticket to happiness was right across the street!

She went down to the subway at Eighty-sixth Street and he followed. He stood on the platform a safe distance away, but it hardly mattered. She looked so pissed off and preoccupied that Tom Cruise could've been standing on the platform and she wouldn't have noticed. When a train arrived, he got onto the same car as her, but went in through a different door. The train was jam-packed and Katie was causing a delay, trying to squeeze in. A few nasty-looking people were complaining and Peter felt protective. He wanted to strangle all of those assholes who were being cruel to his woman, and he might've done it if the train wasn't so crowded.

During the ride to Fifty-first Street, he couldn't stop staring at her. When she got off the train and went up the narrow stairs, he was several people behind her. It was agonizingly hard to be so close yet so far away. He almost went over to her and confessed his undying love. He knew if he did they would've kissed, and then it would've been roll credits, the end. But he managed to rein it in, reminding himself that they were actors in a great romance, and that there was always pain in love stories before pleasure.

As she went to the cart to buy her bagel and coffee, he stood on the corner of Fifty-first and Lexington, watching her. Then, while she was paying, she suddenly turned and looked right at him. He reacted quickly, immediately walking away, and he wasn't sure if she recognized him or not. He was disappointed with himself for not sticking to the plan, for being so impulsive, so careless. He never should've gotten so close to her.

He walked the streets for most of the morning, deciding that it might not be as bad as it seemed. If she'd noticed him, he could simply say she'd made a mistake, that he wasn't there. But the entire morning had been a major wake-up call. He knew if he needed to follow her again, he'd have to get a better disguise.

Meanwhile, his desire to be with her, to talk to her, didn't let up. Although it was his day off, after a nap he went into work to lift weights. Katie usually worked out in the early evening on weekdays and he hoped she'd show up. If she didn't, he had no idea how he'd make it through the night.

When he saw her arrive at the gym for the advanced step class, it was a huge relief. He coolly offered to help her with a hamstring stretch. Touching her skin for the first time was incredible. He'd been imagining what it would feel like and it was even warmer and softer than he'd expected. He couldn't wait until she was *his* and he could touch all of her whenever he wanted to.

Then he told her that he broke up with his girlfriend and he could tell that this pleased her. Everything was going great until she started talking about Frat Boy again.

Peter couldn't believe she still liked that loser. When she said she was going on a double date on Wednesday night with him and another couple, Peter felt like somebody had ripped a hole through his gut. He fought through it, figuring, *Okay, I'll go out with her the night after and then she'll forget all about fucking Frat Boy.* The crushing blow came when she agreed to go out to dinner with him on Thursday but said that it had to be "casual." He was surprised he was even able to speak afterward, but he managed to control himself, telling her that he had no problem with that at all. Meanwhile, he was already thinking about ways to get rid of the little scumbag.

He didn't want to deviate from the script so drastically, but he knew he had no choice. Frat Boy had become more than an obstacle; suddenly he was a major problem. She was spending way too much time with him. He realized he might have misjudged the Frat Boy thing from the beginning. For all he knew *they* would fall in love and there was no way Peter was going to let that happen.

That night, after he left the gym, he wandered around the Upper East Side. Like a soldier on a reconnaissance mission, he knew he had to familiarize himself with the area and find the perfect method and location for an attack. After all, he couldn't go up to Frat Boy on a crowded street and stick a knife in his back. He had to find a place where they'd be alone, and then he had to figure out a way to get him there. He also had to find a better disguise because the Yankees cap and sunglasses weren't hacking it.

He liked the idea of doing it in a park at night, but he thought it would be easier to follow him into the vestibule of his building and take care of him there. If Frat Boy lived in a place like Katie's, in a walk-up apartment on a dark side street, it would be perfect. As for a disguise, Peter decided he'd have to change his hair color, so he went to a drugstore and bought a can of dark brown temporary spray-in hair color. When he colored his hair, goatee, and eyebrows, he barely recognized himself. He still didn't know exactly how he'd get rid of Frat Boy, but he knew that he wanted to strangle him rather than stab him—the less blood the better—so he went to a medical supply store and bought latex gloves to make sure he didn't leave any DNA or whatever from his nails on Frat Boy's neck.

To test his disguise, he waited for Katie outside her office and followed her home. Although he stayed a safe distance away from her, she turned and looked in his direction one time and obviously had no idea who he was. He followed her home and then waited across the street from her building. It was the night of the double date and Frat Boy and his friend arrived at around seven o'clock. It was painful watching Frat Boy go into the building. Peter wanted to run across the street and take care of him right there, but he managed to control himself. Later, when the two couples left the building and headed toward Second Avenue, Peter followed.

While the foursome dined outside at Mustang on Eighty-fifth and Second, Peter was watching from the other side of the avenue. Although Katie laughed occasionally, he could tell she was unhappy, that she didn't want to be there. After dinner, the group went to a bar. Peter went in, too, hanging out near the front, and the disguise worked because Katie had no idea he was there. Then the couples left the bar and got into a cab. Peter didn't know where they were going and was afraid he'd lose them, but he managed to hail another taxi. He felt like he was in some corny crime movie when he shouted, "Follow that cab!" He trailed them into the wraparound drive of a very large apartment complex off Third Avenue. He figured this was where one of the Frat Boys lived, or maybe they were roommates. The building had a concierge and doormen, and there were security cameras everywhere, so Peter couldn't get too close.

He hung out in the public space, near Third Avenue, waiting for Katie to exit the building, but when it got to be one A.M. on the night before a workday, he realized that this wasn't happening. The images in Peter's head of what was going on in that apartment were nearly unbearable. But he couldn't hate Katie for it. She was a victim, that was all. She was vulnerable, naive, lonely. Besides, how could he hate someone who was so perfect in every possible way?

Peter stood outside the apartment building the entire night. If he had to go to the bathroom, he didn't notice. Finally, at around six A.M., Katie left. What kind of asshole was Frat Boy, not even taking her home or putting her in a cab? But standing off to the side, watching her hail a cab, Peter still couldn't hate her. He was disappointed in her, for sure, but he blamed Frat Boy. When that asshole was gone, everything would be different.

At around eight o'clock, Frat Boy left the building, wearing a suit. Peter followed him down to the subway at Ninety-sixth Street and onto the platform. Then Peter couldn't believe it when Frat Boy started hitting on the girl next to him. Was he the biggest scumbag of all time or what? The girl didn't seem at all interested, but he kept smiling, staring at her even when she was looking away. He reminded Peter of the jerks he used to see on spring break in Mexico. Assholes who went around, thinking with their dicks, whose lives revolved around drinking and getting laid. There were so many empty, meaningless people like that in the world—who would care if one of them disappeared? As a train arrived at the station, Peter wanted to push Frat Boy off the platform. But with the girl and other people right there he decided it would be way too risky.

During the ride to Grand Central, Peter watched Frat Boy hit on and strike out with two other girls. At Grand Central, he followed him out of the station, out to Park Avenue. Then he watched him enter an office building. He hung around for a while, then realized that he'd been so preoccupied that he'd completely forgotten about his date later on with Katie.

Figuring he'd better get some sleep or he'd be exhausted, he rushed back to his hotel room. He was lying in bed, imagining every detail of how the date would go with Katie, when she called. He felt like he'd willed it to happen. He was so excited to hear her voice that he didn't realize she was canceling the date with him until after he heard it for the third time. He was too stunned to plead with her. He might've said something like "Okay, well maybe I'll see you some other time," but he wasn't sure. He might've just hung up on her.

The whole thing was crumbling—all the dreams, all the planning had gone to shit. When he got ahold of himself, maybe an hour, two hours later, he decided he had to do something immediately.

Peter showered and sprayed fresh brown color into his hair, eyebrows, and goatee. He had no idea when he'd have the opportunity to do it, but he wanted to be prepared. He put his latex gloves in his pocket and left the hotel room.

At a few minutes after five o'clock, Frat Boy left his office building and Peter followed. Grand Central Station was too mobbed to try anything, and the train uptown was packed as well. Peter felt good, though, knowing he was within striking distance.

Leaving the subway at Ninety-sixth Street, Peter got more brazen. As they went up the stairs, he was right behind Frat Boy, and he stayed just several feet away as he followed him around the corner, to Ninety-fifth Street. He noticed that Frat Boy's neck wasn't very thick. It would be easy to fit his hands around it, and he had to resist the impulse to just reach out and do it.

Peter stopped at the corner of Ninety-fifth and Third and watched Frat Boy head along the brick drive toward the building's entrance. Although Katie didn't say why she was canceling the date, Peter was certain it had to do with fucking Frat Boy. After all, they'd spent the night together last night so it figured that they'd made plans to see each other again. Yeah, like that was going to happen.

It started drizzling. Afraid about his hair color running, Peter jogged to

Duane Reade, a block away, and bought an umbrella. It was a good thing because when he left the store the rain was coming down harder. He returned to
the building, standing under an overhang where he was sheltered from the
rain. But he realized that this could be a big waste of time. The building was
part of a huge complex; there were probably several entrances and it would
be easy to miss someone coming or going.

Then Peter had a much better idea. He walked to Katie's block and
waited across from her building. Hopefully Frat Boy would arrive to pick her
up, or she would go to meet him somewhere, and Peter would follow.

Peter waited in the rain near Katie's building for about two hours. At
around eight o'clock, Frat Boy came walking down the block. He looked so
cookie-cutter, like any Frat Boy in the world going on a date, wearing a dark
green button-down shirt tucked into jeans and his hair gelled back. Again, Peter realized how irrelevant, how inconsequential this guy was. There were so
many in the world just like him that killing him would be like squashing an ant.

As Frat Boy approached the building, Peter looked around in every direction and saw that no one was around. He put on the gloves quickly, then
crossed the street. Frat Boy was heading up the stoop to the building and Peter wanted to get to him before he had a chance to buzz Katie. He put one
foot on the stoop when he noticed the curly-haired girl entering the vestibule,
on her way out of the building. Of course Frat Boy smiled at her and said
something and Peter knew his opportunity was gone. He made a U-turn and
went back across the street.

He waited in the rain, staring at the building. At some point, a Chinese
delivery guy arrived. Peter knew the food was being delivered to Katie's
apartment. They'd probably spend another fucking night together.

Peter didn't care if he had to spend the whole night in the rain, without
food, pissing in the street; he wasn't going anywhere. He felt like he had to
at least be near Katie—if not emotionally, then physically.

Then, at about eleven-thirty, like a prayer answered, Frat Boy left the
building. The rain had diminished to a drizzle. Peter followed him down the
block, then uptown to Second Avenue. He was probably going back to his
building. There were plenty of other people around, so Peter knew he couldn't
try anything. He thought he'd have to wait for another night to do it, then Frat
Boy went into a bar. Peter looked around for security cameras. He only spotted one, outside an apartment building to the left of the bar, and was sure to
avoid it. Then, standing outside, he formed a plan.

When Peter entered the bar, he saw that Frat Boy, that slimeball, had already struck up a conversation with a girl—like Katie wasn't enough for

him. If he left with the girl, the plan would've been shot to hell, but Peter thought, *Blow him off, blow him off,* and she did—well, giving him her number first, but there was no hook-up.

Feeling all-powerful, Peter sidled up to Frat Boy at the bar and started reeling him in. One time a couple of weeks ago, Peter had seen Katie with Frat Boy, and he remembered that Frat Boy had been wearing a Phillies cap. Using baseball as an entree, Peter was easily able to make the idiot believe they had met before. The tough part was segueing to the story about his wife, Cleara, the horny Brazilian model. As Peter was laying it on, he realized how ridiculous it probably sounded, and he didn't think there was any way in hell that even a moron like Frat Boy would go for it. But the guy must've been even more of a walking hard-on than Peter had thought, because he bought the whole thing, hook, line, and sinker.

They left the bar together. The only remaining question was whether Frat Boy would fall for the drug-dealer story, or would Peter have to drag him into the park by force and strangle him in the bushes? Frat Boy bit again and Peter was able to lure him toward the underpass. As they approached the stairs, Peter faked a sneezing fit and was able to put on the large latex gloves. Then, in the tunnel, when he attacked, Peter was surprised that the bastard didn't put up much of a fight. It was like he knew that his fate was to die, and he just gave in to it.

15

Katie entered the deli on Lexington and Forty-eighth and saw Amanda waving to her at a table off to the left. Katie made a salad at the salad bar, then sat down across from Amanda and said, "I want to hear everything."

"No," Amanda said. "I want to hear everything about you guys."

"You first."

"I told you on the phone—it was nice."

"Details, girl, I want details."

"I don't know what to say," Amanda said. "He's a great guy. He called me last night and we talked for, like, an hour."

"Really?"

"Yeah, and we're going out tomorrow night."

"I'm so happy for you."

"Thanks."

Amanda blushed, seeming in love. Katie hadn't seen her get like this about a guy in a long time and it was great to see.

"So," Katie said. "How was it?"

Smiling, Amanda said, "There's not much to say."

"Did you guys—"

"No, we just kissed and stuff then went to sleep. He was a total gentleman."

"That's very cool," Katie said, remembering how Andy had been the opposite last Friday night.

"So what about you guys?" Amanda asked.

"It's a lot better," Katie said. "He was great the other night and he was great last night, too."

"Two nights in a row?"

"I know, right? But, yeah, he was really sweet. I mean, he didn't stay last night, but he said he had to get up early so . . ."

"I guess that's excusable."

"There was one weird thing." Katie looked around then whispered, "It's kind of graphic but, did a guy ever try to, like . . . put his, you know . . . into your . . ."

"He tried that?"

"Two times. I mean, both nights."

Now Amanda looked concerned. "Did he—?"

"No, no, not at all. He just, like . . . tried."

"Wait, let me guess. Did he say, 'If it hurts, I promise I'll stop?' "

"Almost. He said, 'I promise I'll be gentle.' "

Katie and Amanda laughed so hard people started looking over.

Then Amanda said, "Do they honestly think that'll work? A girl'll go, 'Oh, you'll stop if it hurts. That's so nice of you. So if your dick starts tearing into me you'll stop. That's good to know—thank you so much.' "

Katie was laughing.

"So he's into anal sex, huh?" Amanda continued. "So I guess if I see you walking funny one day I'll know why."

"Shut up!"

"I'm surprised you can sit down now. Doesn't it hurt?"

Katie and Amanda laughed even harder, trying to catch their breath.

"But, seriously," Amanda said, "I have to admit, Andy seemed like a really nice guy and you two seem great together."

"Thank you."

"Isn't it amazing? A few weeks ago, we were complaining, thinking there were no nice guys in this city. I was joking with my friend Meg the other day, going, I'm ready to throw in the towel, explore my lesbian tendencies. But now look at us."

"Will's so cute."

"I know, isn't he? When I first saw him I was like, Uh-oh, he's so good-looking and he's wearing scrubs on a first date. I thought he'd be really self-centered, just talking about himself all night, like that. But he was the total opposite. And I have to admit, I was definitely wrong about Andy."

"You think?"

"Definitely. You have chemistry."

"Yeah," Katie said. "I guess we do."

Smiling, Amanda said, "So what'd you think of their apartment?"

"Gross."

"Disgusting, right?"

"I saw something moving in the bathroom garbage."

"Oh my God, what was it?"

"I have no idea. But I got out of there fast."

They started laughing hysterically again. Later, when they were leaving the deli, they talked about going on another double date, maybe even this weekend. Katie said she would talk to Andy and Amanda planned to ask Will.

Heading back toward her office, Katie thought about her conversation with Amanda and laughed out loud. She felt lucky to have such a great friend. The last couple of days, as things in her life had started turning around, she'd been realizing that she'd been so down about everything that she didn't appreciate what she had. It was time to start focusing on the positive. She had lots of great friends, supportive parents, and a really cool boyfriend. Even her job didn't seem so bad. Yeah, Mitchell acted like a dick sometimes—well, a lot of the time—but everything that had gotten her so down before suddenly seemed so petty, even silly.

When she got to her desk, she logged onto her Yahoo! mail account and was disappointed to not see a message from Andy. He'd e-mailed her yesterday morning, so she expected one today. Trying to not make a big deal about who e-mailed whom, she sent him a short message:

Had a great time last night! What's up?

The rest of the afternoon, she went about her work, checking her e-mail every now and then. Each time she saw the 0 MESSAGES display she got a little more pissed off. Although she wanted to give him the benefit of the doubt, she couldn't help wondering if he was playing head games with her.

By five o'clock she felt officially blown off. Deciding that she deserved to pamper herself, she walked to Sephora on Third and bought the Duwop Lip Venom and the Nars blush in Orgasm she'd tried the other day. She still felt like shit. She went to a Ray's Pizza and bought a salad to take home. A few minutes later, crossing Seventy-ninth Street, she felt the oily dressing leaking through the bag, then, as she looked inside, the bag broke and the container fell onto the street. Salad spilled everywhere. She cursed, on the verge of tears. Then, as she bent down to clean up the mess, a cab turned sharply toward her and had to brake. The cabby honked and she stood up, gave him the finger, and walked away, leaving the spilled salad, the bag, and the container on the street.

Figuring that she'd order in Chinese for dinner and they'd better leave the fucking MSG out this time, she continued home. As she was entering the vestibule a man came up quickly behind her. Wishing she'd listened to her father and was carrying pepper spray, she jerked around and may have even started to scream. Then she relaxed, seeing that the guy seemed nonthreatening. He was older, Japanese, in a gray suit.

"Excuse me, miss. Is your name, by any chance, Katie?"

It was weird, hearing that heavy New York accent coming from a guy who looked like him.

"Yeah," she said.

The guy swallowed a couple of times, had to look away for a few seconds, then collected himself. He flashed a badge and said, "John Himoto, Nineteenth Precinct. I'm afraid I have some terrible news."

16

Telling people that their loved ones had been murdered was the worst part of John Himoto's job. The only saving grace was that he didn't have to do it very often. The Nineteenth Precinct encompassed the entire Upper East Side and had one of the lowest violent crime rates in the city. Although they got a fair share of burglaries, assaults, and a handful of rapes, if they got two murders a year it was a lot.

But even though John didn't have to deliver devastating news very often, it didn't make doing it any easier. It always gave him flashbacks to when he was nine years old, living in Flushing, and he and his old man were out shoveling snow after a nor'easter. At first, John thought his father was kidding around, making a snow angel or something; then he saw his tongue hanging out of his mouth. The weird thing was that, as the years went by, the memory of watching his father die didn't seem nearly as traumatic as having to go inside and tell his mother.

Now, as he tried to maintain eye contact with the young, attractive girl, he remembered how he had stood in front of his mother, frozen, unable to speak, for what seemed like minutes, as she said, "What's wrong? What happened? Where's your father?" That last one—Where's your father?—always resonated loudest.

"Your boyfriend, Andrew Barnett, was murdered."

John managed to get the words out matter-of-factly, professionally—nineteen years on the force, seven as a detective, had taught him that much. But Katie, who seemed to have a deer-in-the-headlights way about her to begin with, seemed confused.

"I don't have a boyfriend named Andrew. My boyfriend's name is Andy."

Denial—typical first reaction. When John had been finally able to get those two words out—"Dad died"—his mother had even started laughing. She was convinced that John was playing a joke on her until she went outside and saw for herself.

"It's the same person, miss. He was killed late last night in Carl Schurz Park."

"What do you mean? Why're you telling me this?"

Now the rage. It was all so painfully predictable.

"I really have to ask you some questions right now," John said. "Do you want to sit on the stoop? Or we can go upstairs—you can sit down, have something—"

"What the fuck're you talking about?"

"Your boyfriend was murdered." Himoto was trying to speak as calmly as possible. "It happened last night. He was strangled. Right now that's just about all we know. I spoke to a few of his roommates already—that's how I found out about you. William Bahner said that you live at this address. Believe me, I understand how difficult this is for you to—"

"I can't believe this is happening."

"Maybe we can go upstairs?"

"Who would mur—I mean, why would . . . How?"

"Let's talk about it upstairs. I promise, this will only take a few minutes."

Katie managed a nod and John followed her up the two flights to her apartment.

"Can we sit down?" John asked.

Katie seemed lost, dazed, and the question took a couple of seconds to register.

"Yeah, sit, sit," she said weakly.

John sat at the small dining table. Katie slowly joined him.

"I understand you were with Andy yesterday evening," John said.

"He was here."

John opened a pad and said, "When did you see him last?"

"He came over, then he left. I guess it was around eleven, eleven thirty."

Writing, John said, "Did he say where he was going?"

"He said he was going home. He said he had to get up early."

"Well, he didn't go home," John said. "He went to the park. You have any idea why he would've gone to the park?"

Katie shook her head.

"Think about it for a second. Did he like to take walks at night? Did he like to look at the river? Was he into drugs?"

Shaking her head more emphatically, Katie said, "No, nothing like that. He was . . . God, I can't believe this is happening." She started crying. After a while, she managed, "He was just a really nice, normal guy. He was great . . ." Her voice faded into tears.

John went to the bathroom, came back with some tissues, and gave them to Katie.

"It's good to get it out," he said.

He wanted to say more supportive stuff, but he couldn't think of anything else to say, so he said nothing. He always felt awkward in situations like this, even with his own son, Blake. John's wife, Geraldine, had handled all of the gushy-type talks. Then, when Geraldine died, things got even more uncomfortable. When Blake was a teenager he was out all the time, doing God knows what with God knows who. He and John were like two strangers. They still were. Blake lived in Chelsea now with his boyfriend, Mark. John saw him once in a while, on holidays mostly. He supported his son's sexuality—didn't give him as hard a time about it as some fathers would, anyway—but being a New York City cop with a gay son wasn't exactly easy.

After letting Katie cry it out for a while, John said, "Feeling better?"

Not exactly brilliant words of wisdom, but they were the best he could come up with.

"How much longer is this gonna take?" Katie asked.

"Just a few minutes. I was just wondering—how long had you two been dating?"

"Two . . . no, three weeks."

"Is that all? I had the impression it was longer than that."

"It wasn't."

"Andrew ever mention anything about having any enemies?"

Kate shook her head.

"Someone who wanted to hurt him," Himoto pressed. "Maybe at work. An argument with a friend . . ."

"No, nothing like that. Everything was normal. Very normal."

"What about his family? Any issues there?"

"He didn't talk about his family very much. But no."

Himoto wanted to be careful with his next question. He knew Katie was in a fragile state and he didn't want it to upset her too much.

"And if I can ask," Himoto said, "what did you do after he left here last night?"

"What do you mean?"

"I mean, did you leave the apartment?"

"I went to sleep. Why?"

John knew it was a hell of a long shot that this girl had anything to do with the murder. The full ME report wasn't in yet, but it seemed like Andrew Barnett had died quickly and that whoever did it was strong, probably male, and knew what he was doing. But it was a fact that most murderers know their victims, so the subject had to be broached.

"Well, right now it seems like you were the last one seen with him," John said. He added quickly, "Not that I think you had anything to do with it. I'm not saying that at all. But something you may have done or said, that you don't think is important, might turn out to be very important. You know what I'm saying?"

"We had Chinese food, we had sex, then he said he had to go home and get up early and he left. That's all I know."

John was a little surprised that she'd mentioned the sex part like that. He felt sorry for her, a girl losing a guy she might've been falling in love with. This was rough.

"Look," John said, "the bottom line is that we think he knew his killer. Maybe he wasn't friends with him, but he knew him. His wallet was empty and not next to his body, which is neither here nor there. Maybe he had more money and spent it, or maybe he was robbed, but we don't think so. The way he was killed, strangulation, doesn't fit with some random mugging. But, hey, I have a question for you. You said you had Chinese food last night, right?"

"Yeah," Katie said. "So?"

"Who paid?"

"He did."

"Did you see his wallet? How much money he had inside it?"

Katie thought about it and said, "He had money—twenties. I remember because he asked me if I had any singles for a tip."

"Do you know how many twenties?"

"I'm not sure. At least a few."

"Did he have any other bills?"

"Yeah, I think he did."

John wrote in his pad and said, "That might help us. If he had money, that tells us that the killer might've wanted to make it look like a robbery. Yeah, that could be very helpful."

"Is that all?" Katie asked. "Sorry, but I really just want to be alone right now."

"I understand," John said, getting up. "Yeah, that should do it. Here's my card. If you think of anything else about last night you might've forgotten, anything at all, just give me a call. I'll probably want to talk to you again anyway, just to run some more info by you as the investigation proceeds. Can I have your phone numbers?"

Katie gave him her cell and home numbers, then he apologized to her for her loss again and left. It was a relief to get out of there. Days like this made John want to go for the early retirement plan that had been offered to him a few months ago. Instead of spending his days having to tell girls that their boyfriends had been strangled, he could be sitting at home, watching the Knicks on his big-screen TV. Or, shit, he could be out on a fishing boat, or at the racetrack, or just hanging out around the house, doing nothing.

Although the idea of an early retirement appealed to John, he'd decided he wasn't going anywhere until he turned his career around. Over the last several years he'd been lead detective on four murder cases and hadn't solved any of them. In fact, he had some of the worst stats of any detective in the city. John knew that finding Andrew Barnett's killer could give his career the boost it needed; the problem was the investigation seemed to be stalling. The body had been discovered early this morning and in a little over twelve hours he'd gotten next to nowhere. All they had was the preliminary report from the medical examiner. No usable fingerprints had been recovered from the victim's wallet or from anything else on his person. Although the story was already all over the news—a murder about two blocks from Gracie Mansion was going to get attention—no witnesses had come forward. The talk with Andrew's roommates had yielded zippo. Andrew's parents were planning to come to the city tomorrow, but John had already had a brief phone conversation with them earlier today—that hadn't been exactly pleasant—and they couldn't supply any possible motives for the murder within their family. In Andrew's room, investigators had found a recent photo of the young man. They had started circulating photocopies of it around the neighborhood, focusing on the area between Katie Porter's apartment and Carl Schurz Park, but so far this had led to nothing.

John entered the Nineteenth Precinct on Sixty-seventh Street ready to be humiliated. Other detectives and cops had been getting on him about his bad stats for months—hell, years. Most of it was playful, good-natured ribbing, like the time somebody left a magnifying glass on his desk, as if using a Sherlock Holmes prop might help him solve a case. Yeah, John had a good laugh over that one. But sometimes they went too far, like a few months ago when Tom Delaney, an officer with two years on the job, said to him, "No collars again this month, huh, sushi man?"

Some guys might've let that slide, but John, whose grandparents and father had been forced to live in an internment camp in California during the Second World War, didn't put up with any racist shit. He went after Delaney, decking him, and got suspended for a month.

A few cops and detectives smirked at John as he passed by, but no one said anything until Rich Parkins, who had one year as a detective, came up to him in the corridor and said, "Hey, John, how's it going?"

"Pretty good," John said, knowing Rich meant the case.

"It's getting a shitload of media, huh?"

"To be expected."

John kept walking, hoping Rich wouldn't keep up with him but he did.

Rich said, "Hey, if you wanna talk it out, you know, do a little brainstorming, whatever, I'm available."

John got the hidden implication loud and clear: He was so helpless at his job that he needed advice from some kid. John was forty-seven, Rich was thirty-two, but still.

John glared at Rich and said, "Thanks for the offer. I'll seriously consider that," then continued through the precinct.

John was glad that the door to the office of the precinct's commanding officer, Detective Inspector Louis Morales, was shut and the lights were off. John knew if nothing popped in a day or two, Manhattan North would take over. Given the fairly high profile of the case, he was actually surprised they hadn't tried already.

Sitting at his desk, John made some callbacks to Andrew Barnett's work friends and talked to a couple of Barnett's acquaintances from college, including an ex-roommate. Then, around eight thirty, an updated report from the medical examiner's office arrived. Unfortunately it didn't tell him anything he didn't already know.

17

Peter was having a very normal day at work. He'd arrived at six o'clock and had spent the morning answering phones and handing out towels and standing outside, giving flyers to passersby. The latest promotion was a membership of sixty-nine dollars a month, guaranteed for life for the first fifty people to sign up. Peter was in such an upbeat mood that he managed to convince seven people to come inside to talk to the membership consultant, and four of the meetings led to sales.

"Man, you're really on a hot streak," Jimmy said.

"It's just luck," Peter said.

"Luck, my ass. You know how many people we had handing out flyers? Too many to count. And you know how many times we ran that sixty-nine-dollars-a-month-for-life bullshit? But nobody ever got us four sales in one day off the street—that's unbelievable. You got the knack, man, I'm serious. So what do you say? You ready to move up or what?"

"Move up?"

"To a full-time sales job, baby. It's nine to five but you don't gotta wear a suit. And we pay base plus commission. Big commission, you keep doing what you've been doing on the street. You know Sal? You know how much he made last year?"

"Fifty grand?"

"Seventy-five. And wanna know the truth, he doesn't have half the skills you have. I watch you out there, the way you go up to people. You know how to relate, know what I'm saying? Even some stranger on the street—man, woman, it doesn't matter. They like you right away, and when they like you they trust you. That's the whole key with sales."

"I am pretty good at it, huh?"

"Good? You're freakin' awesome, man. You can start tomorrow, you want, or next week if you need more time. I mean not start start. I'm gonna have to train you and shit, but it's nothing too complicated. Just how to use the software and get you familiar with some of the packages we offer and shit like that. But I'm not gonna tell you how to sell people. I think you got that part all figured out."

Peter didn't hesitate. He told Jimmy that he'd love to be a membership consultant and the sooner he started the better. The truth was, of course, that he didn't care one way or another. He'd just been working at the health club as a natural way to be around Katie and he was planning to quit as soon as they were officially together. But, in the meantime, he figured getting the promotion might help him win Katie over. Maybe it would give her the impression that he was a successful guy, a go-getter, a catch. Not that she didn't have that impression already, but he figured it couldn't hurt.

At noon, Peter left for the day. Clean-shaven, with his natural blond hair, Peter felt completely comfortable walking around the Upper East Side. Earlier, on his way to work, and now as he walked downtown, he noticed cops in the area. He had no idea whether this had anything to do with the murder, but he was pleased that the officers took no special notice of him.

It was a beautiful fall day. After the rain last night, the humidity had dropped and the sky was clear and the temperature was in the low sixties. He stopped at a little Italian restaurant on Second Avenue and sat outside and had penne with vodka sauce, a salad of arugula and shaved Parmesan, and a decent merlot. Then he took a cab downtown to his hotel. He was getting very tired of living at a place he didn't own, of being in this constant state of limbo. Although the remodeling of his apartment wasn't completed yet, he was planning to check out of the hotel over the weekend and move into his new home. He didn't plan to tell Katie about the apartment, though, until they had gone on at least a few real dates.

Peter plopped onto the bed and turned the TV on to NY1 News. Earlier in the day, at the health club, he'd seen a couple of TV news reports about the murder. It was a much bigger news story than he had expected it to be. He knew it would get attention because it wasn't every day that someone got strangled to death near Gracie Mansion, but he had no idea it would be the top local news story. It probably was a racial thing. If Frat Boy had been black, the killing would've gotten attention because of the Grace Mansion angle. But a clean-cut white guy being murdered was always juicy for the media.

Peter waited for the story to come on, and when it did there seemed to be nothing new going on in the case. There was the same videotaped segment of a NYPD detective, John Himoto, giving a report of how the body had been discovered early this morning and how the police were conducting a thorough investigation. Then the anchorman talked about how Frat Boy had worked as a junior analyst at some major investment banking firm and had graduated from the University of Michigan last spring. Frat Boy's friend from the double date was near tears as he talked about how Frat Boy was a great guy and how he couldn't believe this had happened to him. Peter wondered why people always said that, that they couldn't believe this had happened. People died. It happened suddenly and it happened every day. Deal with it.

When the report ended, Peter flicked off the TV. He was glad that there'd still been no mention about a latex glove being discovered, though he wasn't sure the police would reveal this even if it had been. For what seemed like the hundredth time, Peter replayed the events of last night in his head and he still couldn't think of any possible way he had slipped up except, maybe, for the glove.

"Good luck, Himoto," Peter said, smiling, then he checked his cell phone to see if he had missed a call from Katie. He hadn't. He figured she was at work and might not've even found out about the murder yet. Maybe the police would come to her office to tell her, or maybe she wouldn't find out until the evening. When she did, she'd probably be very upset and look for support from someone close to her. It would likely be someone familiar to her, who she felt safe with, who reminded her of her father. Peter smiled again, thrilled with how well everything was working out so far.

Feeling cooped up in the hotel room, Peter went out for a walk. He went across town to Broadway, then all the way downtown to SoHo. He browsed in art galleries and stopped for a glass of Prosecco at a wine bar. Then he headed back uptown, through the East Village. He was in the mood to escape his life for a while, to see a good movie, but there was nothing playing in the multiplex on Third Avenue and Eleventh Street except horror, action, and comic book-based movies. He wondered why Hollywood rarely seemed to produce straight love stories anymore. What was the world coming to?

It was six o'clock when Peter reached Kips Bay, the neighborhood where his hotel was located. He still hadn't heard anything from Katie, and he was starting to wonder why she hadn't contacted him yet. She must've gotten home from work by now and it was highly likely that she had found out about the murder. The police had probably met with her, because she'd been with Frat Boy the night he was killed, and they'd want to see if she knew anything. Of course, she'd be totally clueless.

Peter picked up some Indian food to go and took it back to the hotel room. As he ate the chicken tikka masala right out of the aluminum container, he had a horrible thought. He remembered how, in college, Katie's sister Heather had killed herself. Suicidal tendencies sometimes ran in families, so Peter wondered if it was possible that Katie had become so distraught about Frat Boy's death that she'd tried to kill herself. It was hard to imagine her caring so much about that fucking loser that she'd inflict harm on herself, but sometimes people did irrational things.

He desperately wanted to call her to make sure she was all right. He could say he was just watching the news and didn't she mention she had a friend, Andrew? But he decided against it, figuring she'd call him on her own; it was only a matter of time.

The rest of the evening, waiting for the phone to ring, was torture. Maybe twenty times he started dialing her number, then flipped his cell phone closed. He couldn't stop thinking of her in the bathtub, slitting her wrists, or going to the top of a building and jumping. He tried to assure himself that she was okay; she had her roommate with her and if the police thought she was suicidal they'd get her medical attention, but he couldn't stop imagining the worst.

He was still confident that she'd call eventually—she had to; it didn't make any sense that she wouldn't—but he realized that the call might not come until tomorrow, or the next day, or even later. She might go to her parents for support first, maybe even go to Massachusetts for the weekend to be with them. If that happened, he might not hear from her until next week.

Then, around midnight, Peter was starting to doze when his phone started ringing.

"Peter."

Her voice was the most amazing sound in the world. He was suddenly wide awake.

"Hey, how are you?"

This wasn't acting, pretending he didn't know what was going on. His only actual concern was how she was.

"I'm in a really bad way."

"What happened?"

"Something bad." She was crying, could barely get the words out. "Something really, really bad."

"I'll be right over," Peter said.

As he raced out of the hotel and hailed a cab on Lex he couldn't stop smiling.

Katie had been in bed crying since Detective Himoto had left. Susan sat with her for a while and tried her best to console her. Reporters from the *Post, News,* and other papers buzzed the apartment, and Katie went down and answered their questions, telling them how she couldn't believe this had happened and how shocked she was. The whole thing felt surreal.

At one point in the evening, Katie called home. But as soon as she started to tell her mother what had happened she knew she'd made a mistake. Her mother was upset, of course, but wasn't capable of offering any real support. She went on about how horrible it was and then she suggested coming to New York, with Katie's father, in the morning. Katie agreed to let them come, but later, as she continued to sob, she realized her parents visiting wouldn't accomplish anything. They would have no idea how to handle the way she was feeling right now, and she planned to call them later or first thing in the morning to tell them not to bother.

But she had to talk to someone to get her feelings out, someone mature, someone who "got it." She thought about calling a friend, maybe Amanda, but then she had a better idea and called Peter. He was mature, had a sensitive nature, and she felt like she could talk to him.

When the buzzer rang she dragged herself out of bed and let him up. She stood partway in the hallway, propping the door open with her foot. She heard him racing up the stairs, probably taking them two at a time. Then he appeared on the landing, rushed over, and hugged her and assured her that everything was going to be okay. She felt safe in his strong arms and she knew she'd done the right thing by calling him.

She started crying again and he consoled her, telling her everything was going to be okay.

Then, after maybe ten minutes, he asked, "What happened?"

She couldn't say it at first, then she said, "Andy . . . that guy I . . . was . . . ," really struggling with the last word, "m . . . m . . . murd . . . murdered."

"Jesus," Peter said. His voice cracked as though he might start to cry himself, but he didn't.

He sat next to her on the couch, with his arm around her. She explained that Andy had been strangled and that his body had been discovered early this morning.

"Do the cops have any idea who could've done it?" Peter asked, squinting hard, showing real concern.

Katie shook her head.

"Fuck," Peter said. "I'm so sorry, Katie. I'm so, so sorry."

After hugging her for a while longer, he asked her if she wanted something to eat or drink. She shook her head, but when she admitted she felt a little weak, he insisted. He went into the kitchen and made her tea and brought her out some chips and salsa as well. She noticed he'd shaved his goatee and told him that it looked good, that she liked seeing more of his face. The food and the tea made her feel a lot better and she was able to relax a little—enough to talk anyway.

She told Peter about how Andy had been over at her place yesterday evening and how everything had seemed so normal, more normal than it ever had before. Then she told him about how she'd first met Andy, at Brother Jimmy's on Third Avenue, and how he was a great guy and didn't deserve to die so young. Peter was such a great listener. He looked into her eyes the whole time and really seemed to care about what she was saying.

They started talking about other stuff—deep, philosophical stuff like life and death, God, religion. Katie said that sometimes she believed that God existed, sometimes she didn't, but that days like today she definitely didn't.

"I go back and forth myself," Peter said. "After my parents died—"

"They died?"

"Yeah, six years ago."

"I had no idea. I'm so sorry."

"Thanks." Peter needed a moment to get hold of himself, then said, "Anyway, a few years ago, when I was living in Mexico, I went to a psychic. The first thing the psychic said was, 'Who's Clea?' Cleara was my girlfriend's name. Close, right?"

"Oh my God, yeah."

"She got all this other stuff dead on, too. She said, 'Why's she talking about Florida?' Cleara had just been to Florida to visit some relatives."

"Wow."

"It freaked me out, too, but it made me realize that if there are really spirits out there, then anything's possible, even God, you know?"

"I totally agree," Katie said. "The same thing happened with me with my sister."

"You're kidding me."

"The psychic didn't know her name, but one of the first things she said is, 'your sister died and it wasn't of natural causes. She's saying she's to blame.' "

"Holy shit."

"You should've seen the tears gushing down my cheeks. I said, 'Tell her it's not her fault. Tell her it's no one's fault.' And the psychic said, 'She wants you to know she's okay.' Hearing those words meant so much to me."

They continued talking about their visits to psychics and other psychic experiences they'd had. It occurred to Katie that she never could've had this type of conversation with Andy.

Katie was getting very tired and she asked Peter if he wanted to go home. He insisted on staying, and she was glad because she didn't really want him to go. Eventually she fell asleep on the couch, leaning against him. Around dawn, she woke up, covered with the blanket from her bedroom, and Peter was asleep on the floor. She smiled for a moment, then remembered what had happened to Andy and why Peter was here.

She couldn't fall back asleep. Around seven thirty Peter woke up.

"Hey, how are you?" he asked.

"A little better," she said. "Thanks so much for taking care of me."

"Are you kidding? Why wouldn't I take care of you?"

"Oh my God, shouldn't you be at work?"

"I'm taking the day off to hang out with you."

"You don't have to—"

"I want to. You shouldn't be alone."

Peter went out to Yura on Third and came back with muffins and coffee.

"Are you sure you want to miss work?" Katie asked.

"Positive," he said. "It was supposed to be my first day at my new job, but I'd rather be with you."

"New job?" she asked.

"Oh, I didn't tell you? I was promoted. I'm a membership consultant now."

"Really?"

"Yeah, my supervisor was very impressed with my sales skills, so he hired me for a full-time position."

"That's great." She squinted. "But I thought you wanted to be a trainer?"

Peter hesitated, then said, "I do, but I also love sales, so I took the job."

Katie still didn't get it, but decided not to push it further.

"Well, congratulations," she said.

They hung out in the living room, talking about growing up in Lenox, their parents, and other stuff. Usually when she was with a guy she had to strain to think of things to talk about, but with Peter there were never any lulls.

At one point, he said, "It looks like a beautiful day out there. I was thinking, maybe we could walk around the park, maybe pick up some stuff for a picnic? Keep it mellow, you know. But if you're not up for it . . ."

"I'm definitely up for it. It would probably be good for me to get out of the apartment, to get some air. I think I'm going to call the detective who was here yesterday to see what's going on."

"He'd probably call you if something happens."

"Yeah, I just want to see, though. I mean, it would make me feel better, I think."

"Just don't get your hopes up."

"What do you mean?"

"I mean, you have to prepare yourself, that's all. The sad truth is that a lot of murders don't get solved."

"I know, I'm just scared. I mean, what if he comes after me next?"

"What're you talking about?"

"He could've seen me with Andy, think I can recognize him or something, and—"

"Come on." Peter put his arm around her shoulders and pulled her closer. "I really think you're getting carried away now, don't you think? Maybe the police'll catch the guy, maybe they won't, but it's highly unlikely that this has anything to do with you."

"I know, I know, I'm just being paranoid. I always get like that."

"You have to just deal with things like this the best you can and go on with your life. I mean, you've had some tragedy in your life before and you got through it, right?"

Katie knew Peter was talking about her sister. She said, "I don't think I ever *got through* that."

"Yeah, but you did the best you could, right?" Peter said. "I've had shit happen in my life that I'm still dealing with. It takes awhile, but after time things always start to get better. Baby steps, you know?"

Katie started to cry, thinking about her sister and how much she still missed her. Then she said, "I know, I know."

Peter held Katie, gently rubbing her back. When she started to feel better, he said that he would go back to his place to shower and change and give her some time to herself, but that he would return to pick her up at around noon.

Then, at the door, he said, "So you'll be okay while I'm gone?"

"Why wouldn't I be okay?"

"I just want to make sure. I mean, I don't know why Heather . . . you know . . . But I don't want you—"

"God, no, I'd never do anything to hurt myself. Jesus."

"Just checking," Peter said.

Katie could tell he wanted to kiss her. If he'd tried she would've let him, but instead he hesitated, then gave her a peck on the cheek.

"See you in a bit," he said, and left.

Later, while she was showering and getting dressed, Katie thought about how nice it was of Peter to drop everything to go spend time with a girl he hardly knew. And the thing was, he didn't do it to *get* anything. There were no hidden agendas, no mind games; he didn't expect anything in return. He was just a genuinely good person.

There was no doubt that Peter was one of the greatest guys Katie had ever met. Before last night, she didn't think their relationship would ever go anywhere past friendship, but now she was starting to see it as something more. She couldn't remember this ever happening, where someone she'd seen as an older-brother type at first, turned into someone she could see herself dating.

She opened her closet, trying to decide what to wear. Peter seemed like a casual guy so she decided that simple was the way to go. She picked out jeans and a black top and black boots. After she got dressed, she looked in the full-length mirror, pleased with how she looked older, but in a good way.

After she did her makeup, she sat on the couch in the living room. She still had nearly an hour to kill before Peter was supposed to return. She tried to distract herself, watching TV, but she couldn't stop checking the time. She couldn't remember the last time she was so excited about seeing a guy. And she'd just seen him, which made it even more unusual.

Peter Wells was the kind of guy you would have expected your mother or grandmother to date in the 1950s. He'd show up at your front door in a suit and holding flowers and he'd say "please" and "thank you" and compliment you all night long. He was sexy, too. She liked his cologne and the way his hair looked and his lips were amazing. She loved the way the lower one stuck out slightly farther than the upper and wondered what it would be like to kiss him. She imagined he would do it slowly and romantically. She couldn't imagine he'd be like Andy, who'd always tried to ram his tongue into her mouth.

Katie felt a pang of guilt over thinking about another guy so soon after Andy's death, but the feeling didn't last long. She checked herself in the mirror again, then remembered to call her parents and tell them not to come to New York. She hoped they weren't on their way. She called her mom's cell and her mom said that she and her dad were in the car in Hillsdale, New York, about forty minutes outside of Lenox.

"Go home," Katie said.

"What do you mean?" her mom said. "We'll be there by two, two thirty."

"No, I don't need you. It's not as big a deal as I made it last night. I didn't know the guy for very long. I have friends here taking care of me."

"We're coming anyway," her mom insisted.

"No, go back. Please."

What the hell had she been thinking? Being around her parents always made things worse. She had no idea why she'd agreed to let them come to the city.

Her father, driving, said something Katie couldn't make out and her mother said angrily, "Will you be quiet? I'm talking." Katie could hear her father saying, "Why doesn't she want us there?" and then her mother going, "You want to talk to her? . . . Then stop interrupting."

Katie rolled her eyes. God, she hated this.

Then she said, "I really don't want you here, Mother." *Mother.* Did she really say that? She hadn't called her mom "mother" since she was a teenager.

"We'll just stay for one night," her mother said.

"I don't want you here at all," Katie said. "Just turn around and go home."

The argument with her parents lasted for about twenty minutes. Katie started screaming at her mother, and then her father got on the phone and she had to scream at him, too. Finally, sounding like a melodramatic sixteen-year-old, she told them that if they came to New York she'd never talk to them again and would hate them forever. She knew she was manipulating the hell out of them, that after losing Heather the thought of losing another daughter, in any way, terrified them more than anything. Katie didn't want to make her parents feel bad, but she didn't want the stress of having them in New York, either, and the strategy worked. Her parents agreed to return to Lenox.

Katie was relieved that she didn't have to deal with the hassle of having her parents in town, but then she felt guilty. She was going to call them back, to tell them to come after all, but better sense prevailed. Instead, she called the detective, to see what was going on with the case. She found the business card he'd given her, but when she called she got his voice mail. She left a message with her phone number, and about five minutes later Detective Himoto returned the call.

"How are you today?" he asked.

"Okay," she said. "I mean, I'm dealing, you know?"

"I think I mentioned this yesterday, but if you want me to get you some psychological counseling I'd—"

"That's okay. I think I just need some time."

"Well, if you change your mind you let me know. And I have some news that might make you feel a little better about things."

"Really?"

"Maybe better's the wrong word. Relieved's more like it. We had a break in the case this morning. Looks like we got the guy."

18

"Wow, that's incredible," Katie said. "Who? Where? What happened?"

John Himoto, sitting at his desk, which was covered with stacks of papers and files, said, "Jesus, so many questions, I don't know which one to answer first. I can't tell you the details right now, but a man walked into a precinct in midtown this morning and confessed."

"Who was he?"

"I really can't divulge that information. As soon as I can I'll give you a call and let you know, okay? I know how important it is for you to have closure."

"Is it somebody Andy knew?"

"Apparently not. Sorry, I really can't tell you anything else at this point, okay?"

"Okay, I understand. Wow, this is such a huge relief. I mean, to know this guy isn't out there anymore."

"That's why I wanted to let you know about it. And I'll be back in touch shortly—I promise. You take care of yourself now, okay?"

As John continued eating his breakfast—two eggs with ham on a roll and a black coffee—he felt relieved. It was nice to give someone good news for a change, and he was genuinely happy that Katie seemed to be handling things well.

Then John's commanding officer, Louis Morales, poked his head into John's office and said, "What's this? We get a confession, you go on vacation?"

"What, I can't have some breakfast?" John said.

"In my office, right now."

Louis closed the door and John watched Louis's shadow pass along the clouded glass as he walked away.

John took another bite of the sandwich then flung the rest toward the waste basket. It missed, hitting the wall and rebounding away. "Goddamn it," he said, and shoved a pile of papers off his desk, onto the floor.

When John entered Louis's office Louis was on the phone and motioned with his jaw toward the chair in front of his desk. John couldn't help smiling and shaking his head as he sat down. Louis had made it sound as if the meeting was urgent, but now John had to overhear a conversation between Louis and his wife, discussing repairs on her car.

Finally Louis ended the call and said to John in a no-bullshit tone, "What the fuck is going on?"

"With what?" John had no idea what all the attitude was about.

"The procrastinating breakfast shit. You know how much heat's on this case?"

"I slept two fuckin' hours last night."

"Then go home and take a nap. You're hungry, you're tired. I'm horny, you see me sitting at my desk jerking off? I'll make somebody else lead detective on this case. Fuckin' lucky I didn't do that already, wanna know the truth."

"So what do you want me to do, kiss your ass?"

"No, I want you to cross every t and dot every i and make sure this is the guy."

"What makes you think I'm not?"

"Did you even talk to him?"

"No, I figured, What's the point?"

"Stop fucking with me."

"I interrogated him this morning, was there for the polygraph. Look, the guy's not playing with a full deck—that's obvious. We know he's been on the street for a long time, lately spending some nights at the shelter on Seventy-seventh. Tell you the truth, when I saw him, I wasn't very optimistic. But he passed the polygraph and now we're doing a psych eval."

Louis, still seeming unimpressed, said, "What's his story?"

"He said he was sleeping in the underpass in Carl Schurz Park the other night when Barnett came walking by. He said he was hungry, asked Barnett for money. Barnett was rude to him, so he got pissed off and strangled him."

"What's the guy's name?"

"Franco. Franky Franco."

"Cute."

"Yeah, sounded like bullshit to me, too. He had no ID on him, but that's the name he's been using at the shelters. He said he's from Argentina."

Louis rolled his eyes.

"Hey, I'm right with you, man," Himoto said. "He has no priors, at least no priors under the name Franky Franco, or Frank Franco, or anything fuckin' Franco. I'm waiting for a callback from Immigration, see if they got anything. He said he lived in Califormia for a while, so I got calls in, checking with the DMV, but got *nada* so far. Thing is, the guy doesn't have a hint of an accent, speaks better English than I do."

"So why the fuck do you believe his story? You don't even know who he fuckin' is."

"Because right now there's no reason not to believe him, that's why. A guy walks in, confesses, I'm supposed to ignore it?"

"He's schizo."

"So schizos don't kill people? David Berkowitz. Should've let him walk too?"

Louis rolled his eyes, then said, "Why do you believe this guy killed Barnett?"

"He gave me details. Gave a time of attack that fit with the ME's—"

"So? That was on the news."

"There were other details. Like I asked how much money he took from Barnett, right? And he said one hundred dollars. Barnett's girlfriend told me she saw at least a few bills in Barnett's wallet, so Franco's story might hold up."

"Yeah, and it might not," Louis said. "What else?"

"He described how he killed him," John said, "how long it took Barnett to die, and it all meshed. And the biggest thing—he passed the polygraph. Look, you asking me if I have my doubts? You bet your ass I do. I want the final report from the ME, I want to talk to people who know Franco and hear what they have to say, and I want to get the results of the psych eval. I also want to make sure Franky Franco is who he says he is. If the story still washes, I want to go public with it, see if we can get a witness who puts Franco at the scene."

"Your case is still thin," Louis said. "I mean, what do you got? A confession from a nutjob, that's it. You got no physical evidence, no witnesses. You got zero, zilch."

"That's why I'm not going public with any of this yet." John hated how Louis was laying into him. "I'm still looking into Barnett's background, maybe there's something there. But Franco passed the polygraph—what am I supposed to do, ignore that?"

"Psychos pass polygraphs all the time."

"But you gotta think about motive. Guy can confess to anything, why this?"

"Crazy people do crazy shit," Louis said. "Maybe he just wants to see his name in the newspaper."

"You might be right, but it's not like killing JFK. You think anybody's gonna remember this case next year?"

"You will if you fuck it up," Louis said.

John glared at Louis, then said, "Look, you want to take me off this thing that badly, go ahead. But if you think I'm gonna get on my knees and lick the shit off the bottoms of your shoes, you're out of your mind."

"I'm thinking about you, you stupid fuck," Louis said. "You didn't know this, but I was supposed to demote your ass last month. But I put my *cojones* on the line for you, and you better fuckin' come through for me. I don't know what's going on lately, but you better get your shit together."

Someone knocked and Louis shouted, "What?!"

Mike Grissom, a detective, opened the door and said, "The guy who was whacked in Carl Schurz—his parents are here."

"I'll be right there," John said.

"He's going now," Louis said.

Grissom left.

As John got up, Louis added, "And next time you're eating breakfast in your office I want to see you doing something else at the same time. Multitasking. That's what being a good cop's all about."

John wanted to tell Louis to go fuck himself, but managed to leave without saying anything. Man, though, reining it in around Louis and the other boneheads at the precinct was taking its toll. No wonder his doctor had him on pressure pills.

Heading toward his office, he braced himself, preparing what to say to Barnett's parents. He'd talked to mothers and fathers who'd lost children before, and it was never pretty. They usually took their anger and frustration out on him, and getting ripped apart by grieving parents was about the last thing he needed right now.

In front of his office, John stopped and took a couple of breaths when a stocky man with messy gray hair came out and said, "You Detective Himoto?"

Boy, John wanted to say no. The guy was unshaven, wearing a wrinkled suit, and looked angry as hell.

"Yeah," John said. "You must be—"

"Where is he? Where's the son of a bitch who killed my son?"

"He's not here. He's downtown."

Why am I here? John wondered. *How come I'm not out on a fishing boat, going for fluke, or playing blackjack at goddamn Foxwoods?*

Mrs. Barnett, looking like she'd had zero sleep, with streaks of mascara on her cheeks, came out of the office and said, "Where's the killer? Where is he?"

"He's not here," John said.

"I want to see him, goddamn it," Mr. Barnett said.

A few cops were looking over, including Delaney, the guy John had decked for making the sushi comment.

"Let's talk in my office," John said to the Barnetts.

"I don't want to talk," Mr. Barnett said. "I want to see the man who killed my son."

"I understand your frustration."

"Like hell you do."

"Did he do it or not?" Mrs. Barnett asked.

John went by the Barnetts, into his office, figuring they'd follow him, and they did.

Mr. Barnett said, "Why won't you tell us what the hell's—"

"Look," John said, cutting him off, "the investigation's ongoing. The suspect's undergoing a psych eval; he hasn't even been booked. So both of you need to be patient . . . as patient as possible."

"They told us he confessed," Mrs. Barnett said. "That's what they told us."

"Who told you?" John said. "That information isn't supposed to be public."

"We're not the public; we're the fucking parents," Mr. Barnett said. "I don't have a right to know who killed my fucking son? Are you guys fucking kidding me?"

"The investigation's ongoing," John said again. "It's true we have a confession, but we haven't confirmed the suspect's identity yet."

"And why the fuck is that?"

"You're really going to have to calm down, sir."

"He's not calming down," Mrs. Barnett said.

"I know how you must feel," Himoto said, straining to get the right tone.

"Oh, really?" Mrs. Barnett said. "Was your son murdered?"

Although John's son was alive and well and living with his boyfriend in Chelsea, he had felt sonless for years.

"Of course I don't know how you feel," John said. "It was wrong of me to say that. But I sympathize with you and I want you to know I'm going to do everything I possibly can to solve this case as quickly as possible."

"Yeah?" Mr. Barnett said. "Well, we want a real detective working on this."

John glared at him and said, "What do you mean by that?"

"We understand that you're not exactly the best detective in the New York City Police Department," Mrs. Barnett said.

"Where'd you hear that?" John asked, trying to stay calm, but he was seething, ready to explode.

"An officer at the desk told us," Mrs. Barnett said.

Fucking Delaney. John was going to kick the living shit out of that racist scumbag.

After taking a moment to collect himself, John said, "I'm on top of this case. I'm going to do everything in my power to bring the person or persons who committed this crime to justice. But you have to understand, it's a process."

"So it's true then," Mrs. Barnett said. "You *are* the worst detective in New York."

"As I said," John said, "I'm going to do everything in my pow—"

"We want someone else on this case," Mr. Barnett said. "I want to speak to your supervisor."

"Be my guest," John said. "His name's Deputy Inspector Louis Morales—his office is down the hall. But, trust me, he won't take me off the case. He put me on it because he knows I'm the best man for the job. I've been working my ass off for nearly twenty-four hours straight and, trust me, I'm not gonna stop working till there's a resolution. We have a suspect in custody right now and there's a strong possibility that he killed your son. If we can confirm this, you'll be the first to know. If not, I won't stop searching until I find the guy. That I can promise you."

John managed to keep his cool; he was good all right. He had to be, because he knew if the Barnetts went to Louis and complained loud enough there was an excellent chance that he *would* be taken off the case.

The Barnetts held John's serious gaze for a few seconds, then exchanged looks. John wasn't sure he'd won them over until Mr. Barnett said, "We want to be kept in the loop. Last night, driving here, we had no idea what the hell was going on. That's not gonna happen again."

"I apologize for that," John said. "Take my card. Call whenever you like or call Alyssa Hernandez, the woman at the desk right outside, and she can give you the latest."

"Who's the suspect you have in custody?" Mrs. Barnett asked. "Why hasn't he been arrested?"

John didn't tell them the suspect's name, but he told them most of the other information he'd told Louis. When he was through, he could tell that he'd gained more of their confidence. Then he told them that he needed to get back to work and suggested that they check into a hotel and try to get some rest, if at all possible. Mr. Barnett even shook John's hand before he and his wife left.

John immediately put in a call to Milton Friedman, the forensic psychologist who was interviewing Franky Franco. While he was waiting for the callback he got a call from Immigration, from an officer who had dealt with Franco. The guy didn't supply any eye-opening info, but said as far as he recalled it was a very run-of-the-mill case. He did, however, give John the number of a woman, Carlita Wilkinson, Franco's sister, who lived in Fort Myers, Florida. John was able to reach Carlita on the phone. She confirmed that she was Franco's sister, but was uncooperative. She said Franco had been estranged from the family for years. She said she wasn't surprised to hear he was in trouble and didn't give "a flying fuck" what happened to him.

John immediately called Louis and told him the news.

"So he is who he says he is," Louis said.

"Looks that way," John said. "Of course, there's the possibility that his sister's covering for him. Then again, I doubt it. I mean, if what Franco says is true and he killed Barnett impulsively, it's doubtful he let his sister know about it."

"Gotta agree with you there," Louis said.

"Still waiting for Psych to get back to me, but it looks like he's been giving us nothing but the truth so far."

"Hey, let's hope so."

John hung up, feeling antsy. Something about all this still didn't feel right. If Franco did it, there had to be more to the story. Strangulation was typically a sexual, intimate way to kill somebody, and was usually associated with crimes of passion. John had worked on two cases in his career where people had been strangled—and one attempted strangulation—and they'd all had sexual components. During the interrogation, Franco had claimed to be straight, but he could've lied about his sexuality and there could've been a homoerotic motive for the killing.

The phone rang and John saw Dr. Milton Friedman on the caller ID.

"Hey, Milt, what you got for me?"

"Well, this guy's a character, that's for sure. Big talker. I think I was in there two hours."

"What's your take on him?"

"He's delusional, John. And going by his behavior I'd say he's been off his meds for a long time. He claims he was institutionalized at Patton in California. Have you been in contact with them?"

"No, but I will be."

"Yeah, anyway, he has a very strong conviction about everything he says and presents himself in a very self-assured manner that can be very convincing. I'm not surprised that he was able to pass the lie detector because he really does believe that he's being truthful. But he has a very limited sense of reality. I should say extremely limited."

"So do you think he has any credibility?"

"Not much, I'm afraid. Unless you have some solid evidence against this guy I wouldn't pay much attention to anything he tells you."

Himoto thanked Milton for the info, then slammed the phone down. He would've loved to wrap up this case quickly, but apparently that wasn't going to happen. He either needed something on Franco or he had to continue looking in other directions.

Leaving the precinct, John made sure not to run into Louis. The last thing he needed was to have to tell his boss that they could be back to square one. He wanted to put off that conversation for as long as possible.

19

On his way to Katie's, Peter stopped at a florist's and bought a bouquet of sterling silver roses, the same kind that Christian Slater gave Mary Stuart Masterson in *Bed of Roses*. He'd already stopped at Eli's on Third Avenue and bought truffle mousse and duck liver patés, water crackers, prosciutto, seafood salad, red and green grapes, several varieties of olives, a nice ripe brie, baguettes, and an expensive bottle of chardonnay.

When he arrived at Katie's and she saw him holding the flowers at his side, her eyes widened and she covered her mouth with her hand.

"My God," she said. "They're so amazing. You didn't have to do this."

"I wanted to," Peter said. "You've been through so much lately, I wanted to do something nice for you. They're very rare roses. Notice how they have no thorns."

She felt the stems and said, "Wow, they're beautiful," and he said, "A beautiful girl deserves beautiful flowers."

He hadn't planned to say this last line and he hoped he'd pulled it off. He wanted to impress her, but he didn't want her to think he was trying too hard.

"Thank you," she said, blushing, and he took this as another sign that he was totally in. He could tell she wanted to kiss him, but he didn't want to go there—not yet. They would only have one first kiss together and it had to happen at the right time or he'd regret it forever.

After giving him a peck on the cheek, she said, "Hey, what's that?"

"Oh, just some stuff for a picnic."

"Wow, I can't believe you did all of this. You're so incredibly nice."

She took the roses and said she was going to put them in water. But as she approached the dining room table, and the vase holding a dozen wilted, browning roses, she stopped suddenly.

"What is it?"

"Andy bought me those."

Figured Frat Boy would cheap out. He'd probably spent less than ten bucks on her. If that wasn't an indication of the guy's character, what was?

"If you want to keep them in there, I totally understand."

"No, it's no big deal," Katie said. "I just won't throw them out yet, that's all. Bad karma."

While Katie was replacing the old flowers with the new, Peter wandered into the living room. He'd been so involved in dealing with her grief last night that he hadn't taken a good look around the apartment. He browsed the books on the shelves—mostly self-help, pop psychology stuff, and beach novels. On the CD rack, he noticed the expected Norah Jones, Josh Grobin, and KT Tunstall, mixed in with the more surprising Ja Rule, the Killers, and the Damien Rice album, which included the theme from the movie *Closer*. The DVDs were mostly recent Academy Award winners, but surprisingly no chick flicks. All of this information was good to know. Any details that he could file away about Katie—and even her roommate—could be useful later on.

Looking toward the kitchen, watching Katie fill the vase with water, Peter smiled. He felt a lightness inside, a pure happiness that he hadn't experienced in a very long time. It was in sharp contrast to how he'd felt a couple of days ago, when he thought he'd lost her forever. It amazed him the way one simple event had changed everything, and if he wasn't an atheist—that stuff he'd told Katie had been total crap—he would've thanked God for giving him the strength to do what he'd done.

Katie looked over and saw him smiling at her and she smiled back, blushing. Peter was aware that they were experiencing one of those great moments people have when they're falling in love. While they were looking at each other, the water in the vase started overflowing onto Katie's arm. They both started laughing and Peter came over with some paper towels.

"Thanks," Katie said. Then, as she dabbed her arms, she said, "Oh, I called the police before. You won't believe it—they got the guy."

She was right: He didn't believe it. He thought he must've misheard her. "Guy?"

"Who killed Andy. He came into the police station and confessed. At least that's what the detective told me."

Peter had to resist the temptation to jump up and down. Maybe he was wrong about God because *somebody* was answering his prayers.

"Wow," he said in an interested yet not overly excited way. "That's—that's great."

"I know, isn't it? I was so relieved, you know?" Katie put the vase with the sterling silver roses on the table. "They're beautiful. Thanks again for getting them."

"You're welcome." Peter was desperate to know what was going on. He wondered if this was getting news coverage; he assumed it was. "So did they say, uh, who the guy was?"

"No, he said he couldn't tell me that yet. I mean, he didn't say it was definitely the guy, but he seemed pretty confident."

It was impossible for Peter to feel any anger toward Katie, but his frustration was building.

"I thought you said they got him?"

"They did. I mean, he's in custody. But for some reason the detective said they weren't sure yet or something."

Peter didn't want to press too hard, but he had to know more.

"So did he tell you anything about the guy? What his motive was?"

"No, he didn't tell me anything. I was like, 'Did Andy know him?' and he was like, 'I'm sorry, we can't tell you anything right now, we're still conducting the investigation.' Stuff like that. But he seemed very confident."

"Is that what he said? That he's confident?"

"I don't know if he actually *said* it. But it was definitely the vibe I got."

Peter knew it would start seeming weird if he kept grilling her and seemed overinterested so he said, "Well, it sounds very hopeful anyway. Let's just pray it's the right guy."

Katie started taking about something else, but Peter wasn't paying attention. He was too absorbed in wondering who this guy was and why he'd confessed. There had to be something wrong with the guy, that was for sure. Then Peter caught on that Katie had asked him something about the picnic.

"Yeah, it's going to be great," he said.

"I asked where in the park do you want to go?"

"Oh, don't worry about that. I know the perfect spot."

They left the apartment and headed toward Central Park. It was an ideal day for a picnic—bright sunshine, a cool breeze. Now that the police had a suspect in custody Peter felt even more at ease walking along the Upper East Side streets. As he talked to Katie about her job and traveling and people in common they knew from growing up in Lenox and anything else that came to mind, he felt extremely close to her and had an urge to hold her hand. He was positive she would've let him, but he resisted. He had a plan for how this day would go, and he wanted to follow it to a T.

At Fifth Avenue and Eighty-fifth Street, near the Metropolitan Museum of Art, they entered the park. Katie asked where they were going and Peter playfully said that it was a surprise and that they were almost there. He led her around the Great Lawn and onto the grass near the pond. There were other people around, but they had a nice-sized area to themselves.

"Right here," he said, and he spread the picnic blanket along the grass, about ten feet away from the pond. They sat next to each other and he opened the picnic basket and took out two wineglasses and the chardonnay. He uncorked the bottle, poured two glasses, and said, "To the future."

It was the perfect toast because it had a double meaning. It could mean, To getting on with life after Frat Boy's death. If she took it to mean that, it would've been fine, because it would've been another example of how sensitive he was. But the toast could also allude to the future, as in *their* future. By the way she'd smiled after he said it, he was certain that to her it clearly meant the latter.

The wine was outstanding. He'd studied wines while he was living in Mexico and he commented to her about its oakiness. Again, his delivery was perfect. He'd impressed her without going overboard, sending her the message that she was with a mature, cultured guy, unlike any guy she'd been with before, and that he was much better for her than a dolt like Frat Boy.

Katie gushed about how much she loved the food and the wine and, overall, the conversation remained lively. Then, after she swallowed a cracker with paté, she said, "I'm stuffed. That was so delicious, thank you again." Smiling, she looked at him in a way that told him it was time to hold hands for the first time. This moment wouldn't stick in their memories the way their first kiss would, but it was still important.

Maintaining eye contact, Peter moved his right hand slowly yet steadily toward her left. He could tell that she'd been wanting to touch him as badly as he'd been wanting to touch her. Her hand turned to meet his, and then their fingers squeezed softly. To say it was amazing would be an understatement. It was so much more than holding hands. In that moment they formed a bond that they both knew would last forever.

He could tell that she desperately wanted him to kiss her, but he resisted. The first kiss couldn't happen here.

After maybe ten minutes of hand holding, he said, "Hey, do you want to go look at the ducks?" and she said, "I'd love to."

They had to let go of each other's hands to pack up the picnic stuff and his hand felt naked without hers and he knew she felt the same way. When they had everything packed and were heading away, they immediately held hands again.

They went around to the platform overlooking the pond. Peter had been worried that there would be other people there—if there were kids around, it would've been especially annoying and he might have had to bail on his plan—but the timing was perfect because they had the platform to themselves.

After feeding some crackers to the ducks, Katie went on about what a great time she was having and Peter knew that was his signal. He held both of her hands, looked at her head-on, and told her he was having a great time, too. Then, hearing the romantic music swelling, he leaned in and kissed her. It would've been exactly as he'd imagined except for the raw onion in the seafood salad they'd eaten. He was angry at himself for not thinking about this earlier—after all, he'd been planning the menu for their first picnic for weeks. He could've packed mints or onionless food. He tried to forget about the taste of the kiss and just enjoy it, but the more he tried to forget, the more he thought about it, until it was *all* he could think about. Then she pulled away and the first kiss was over.

He was devastated. There would be no way to get those moments back. For the rest of his life whenever he thought about his first kiss with Katie Porter he would think about the taste of raw onions.

Still, he covered well, with a smile, and said, "Wow," and rubbed noses with her gently, the way lovers in movies always did.

They decided to take a walk in the park. For most of the afternoon, he was able to maintain his charm, and he was certain that she had no idea anything was wrong, but inside he was a mess. They went to the Sheep Meadow and then farther down to the carousel. She said she'd always wanted to go on it, so they did, and he was glad because it was romantic, in a Parisian kind of way, and it distracted him—for a little while anyway—from how badly he felt about the botched kiss.

Afterward, they walked some more, to Wollman Rink, and then they sat on a large rock nearby. She asked him if something was wrong and he said absolutely not.

"Are you sure?" she said. "Because I know you and your girlfriend just broke up and it makes sense that you're thinking—"

"I'm not thinking about her at all—I've just been thinking about this," he said, and leaned in for another kiss. Although the onion taste wasn't as strong, he still couldn't lose himself in the moment the way he wanted to, and now he was angry about their second kiss being forever marred.

They strolled some more, holding hands—at least the first-time holding hands memory was intact—and wandered back uptown along a path on the east side of the park. It was nearly five thirty when they exited at

Seventy-second Street. Peter had been so preoccupied he had no idea how much time had gone by.

As they headed toward Madison Avenue, Katie started talking about how she'd been planning to work out this evening, but might skip it now because she was tired after all the walking she'd done. Peter sensed the date was ending, and he didn't want it to, not without some more romance. Although they weren't dressed up enough to go to Café Boulud, he suggested that they go out to dinner at a more casual Italian place he knew on Lexington.

"You mean right now?" she asked.

"Yeah. Why not? It's not even six o'clock yet. You're having a good time, aren't you?"

"You kidding? I'm having an amazing time."

"Then why not have dinner with me?"

He hadn't anticipated or rehearsed for any of this conversation and was proud of himself for ad-libbing so effortlessly.

"That's a good point," she said. "Why not?"

The restaurant was nearly empty and they got a nice table near a window. She had the eggplant rollatini, he had the portabello ravioli, and they drank from a carafe of very good chianti. It turned out they both loved biking and they planned to go one day over the weekend. They also talked about "doing a movie" sometime. At one point, as they held hands across the table, Peter felt so close to her that he was tempted to come clean to her about a lot of things. He was going to tell her that he only started working at the health club because he wanted to meet her in a natural way, and about the apartment he'd bought for them, and about how even after buying the apartment he had over two million dollars in the bank for them to live on, and how she never had to work again, and how he wanted to have kids with her. But after he said, "I have to tell you something," his better sense prevailed. He decided to stick with his original plan and tell her all this after they knew each other better, maybe next week, after they'd gone on a few more great dates.

"What?" she asked.

He hesitated then said, "You're incredible."

She tried not to blush, but couldn't help it.

"Thank you."

After dinner, the waiter brought mints, thank God. Katie didn't want hers, but Peter went on about how great they were—even though they were very average chocolate-covered after-dinner mints—and Katie gave in and had a bite. Peter figured it would be enough to cleanse her breath.

Leaving the restaurant, Peter said, "I want to take you someplace special."

"Now?"

"It's not far from here."

Katie looked at her watch, then said, "Okay. Whatever."

Peter loved how carefree, adventurous, and easy to please she was. There were never any battles with her. He could say let's go on a plane right now and go to Paris and she'd probably say yes. She was so trustful—that was the best part.

As they headed back toward the park, Katie asked, "Looks like we're going to the park, huh?" Said it just like that, as an observation, with no suspicion or impatience.

They didn't enter the park. They went downtown, along Fifth Avenue, to the area near the Plaza Hotel where the horse-drawn carriages were.

"Come on, we're not," Katie said, but Peter could tell she really loved the idea.

As he made the arrangements with one of the drivers, she went on about how she'd been wanting to go on a carriage ride in the park for years and how excited she was. But then, when he held out a hand to help her get in, he could tell something was bothering her.

"What is it?" He was afraid he'd done something wrong, or said something he shouldn't have.

"It's just—" She looked away, trying not to cry.

"One sec," Peter said to the driver. Then to Katie, "What's the matter? Was it something I—"

"No, no, it has nothing to do with you. It's just . . . I mean, it's just . . . I mean, Andy just . . ."

Peter was relieved that it had nothing to do with him.

"Hey, I totally understand," Peter said, although he absolutely did not understand. "I mean, if you don't feel comfortable—"

"No, no, that's stupid, right? I mean, one thing has nothing to do with the other, right? I mean, it's just a carriage ride."

Peter didn't like the way she'd said *just* a carriage ride when it was so much more than that. He also didn't want her to be preoccupied with something and the experience to be spoiled, the way the kiss had been spoiled for him.

"If you want to go home, we can," he said. "We can do this over the weekend or—"

"No, I'm being stupid. Let's just go. It'll be fun."

They got on and the carriage started away. Somehow it didn't seem as romantic as he'd imagined. There was a lot of street and people noise, and the smell of manure was a big distraction. As they got deeper into the park and after they covered their laps with the fuzzy red blanket, the mood improved, but she was looking away a lot and wasn't very talkative. He wondered if she was still hung up about Frat Boy. He hoped he hadn't made a mistake, pushing for too much romance, too fast. He knew from past experiences how tenuous love was, how quickly things could go to pot, and the last thing he wanted to do was scare her off.

"Is everything okay?" he asked.

"Yeah," she said, "fine."

He wanted to change the mood fast, get rid of the negativity. He leaned in. There was the sound of the horse's hooves against the asphalt and the taste of mint in their mouths and a breeze blowing back their hair. Finally, they had a perfect kiss.

20

It had been the longest, weirdest first date Katie had ever had. The strangest thing was it had started so normally. On the way to the park, the conversation was good and she thought it had been very thoughtful and generous of him to buy her flowers and pack the picnic. It must've cost him a fortune for the patés and the seafood salad and all the other food and for that expensive wine, Jesus. But when he held her hand, near the pond, she started getting weird vibes. He built up to it so slowly, sliding his hand along the blanket and getting this intense look in his eyes, that she almost started to laugh. She managed not to and was glad because she'd had the feeling that would've offended him big-time. But then he wouldn't let go, even when their hands started to sweat. A few times, she tried to wriggle free, and he squeezed harder. She didn't want to say anything, though, because it was only slightly uncomfortable and she kind of liked how seriously he was taking everything. Yeah, it was a little over the top, but there was a sincerity about it that she thought was kind of charming.

Their first kiss, near the ducks, seemed way too planned, as if the only reason he'd asked her to look at the ducks was to have an opportunity to kiss her, but it was still a nice kiss—*she* thought so anyway. Afterward he started acting weird again. She had no idea what was wrong. She wondered if she'd said something to offend him. She didn't think she had, but he seemed distracted and angry. Then she decided it must have to do with his old girlfriend. He'd said they'd broken up, what, a few days ago? She wondered if he was just rebounding and felt guilty about kissing someone else. Then her guilt, for getting so close with another guy so soon after Andy was killed, set in again. She thought, *What kind of person am I? Can't I even, like, let his body get cold?* She was going to make up an excuse, say she was tired and wanted to go home, but she was afraid if she left it would ruin things with Peter, and she definitely didn't want to end the date on that kind of note.

They went on the carousel, which she had to admit was a lot of fun. Later, when they were sitting on the rocks near Wollman Rink, she decided to bring up the ex-girlfriend issue. She knew she'd hit on something, because he seemed evasive and guarded. She didn't press him on it, but felt good that at least she'd gotten an inkling of what was going on in his head.

When they left the park, she was looking forward to getting home and relaxing in front of the TV, but then he suggested going out to dinner. She didn't know how to say no without sounding rude; besides, she was hungry and it was a free meal. The food was excellent again, and she was impressed that he was spending so much money on her. She didn't know how much he was making at his job at the health club, but it couldn't be much. She wanted to offer to pay half, but she didn't, getting the vibe that he'd take that as an insult. Then he kept insisting that she have a chocolate mint. She didn't want to because she already felt guilty about all the calories she'd had today—she was going to have to go to the gym every day next week—but she felt self-conscious, like he thought something was wrong with her breath or something, so she had some of it.

After dinner, she was *really* ready to go home and crash, but he wanted to take her to some surprise place. Although her feet killed from all the walking she'd done, she didn't complain, and even acted like she was into it. But, at the same time, she felt bad for not asserting herself. She'd done that a lot in other relationships, and she vowed to not let the pattern continue.

When they got to the horse-drawn carriages, she decided this was way too much for her. She liked Peter a lot, but going on a carriage ride in the park was something you did when the guy proposed, not on the first date. But, again, she didn't speak up, and instead made up the excuse that she felt guilty about Andy and got into the carriage. She didn't know what was wrong with her, why it was so hard for her to tell guys what she was really feeling. Then, in the carriage, Peter started kissing her again. She totally wasn't into it, but she didn't pull away, afraid it would hurt him if she did, and afterward he rubbed noses with her and smiled, unaware that anything was wrong.

As she finished her nightly routine of exfoliating and moisturizing her face, she wasn't sure how she felt about the date. Mostly, it had been a lot of fun; but, at times, Peter had made her uncomfortable. She felt like he wanted to get into a relationship right away, and while she liked him, she couldn't even think about getting serious with someone right now.

But she didn't want to be too hard on Peter, either. Maybe he'd been nervous and had overdone it, trying to impress her. And maybe this was actually a good sign because it showed he actually liked her. Yeah, he'd gone way overboard, but what if he *hadn't* done all of the romantic stuff? What if he took her to a cheap restaurant, like Pasta Under Five on Second Avenue? Some stockbroker, must've been making two hundred a year, had once taken her there and splurged on pasta primavera for $4.95, the cheap bastard. Or what if Peter's MO was to get her drunk, then go back to her place for sex? There was no doubt he was a caring, generous guy, a perfect gentleman—she just hoped he toned it down the next time they went out, on Monday night. He'd asked her to go to dinner with him tomorrow, Sunday, but she'd lied and said she had plans. After spending two nights in a row with him, she felt like they needed a break, and she was glad she'd finally asserted herself.

In her bedroom, she went online to check her e-mail. She opened a message from her friend Jane from high school. Jane, who lived in Berkeley now, had gone on an awful blind date with a guy who had a really greasy forehead—it looked like an "oil field"—and she described how during dinner a zit on his forehead had started bleeding. Katie laughed out loud several times as she read the message, and then wrote back, laughing again as she asked Jane if she was going to go on another date with Oily Man. Then she told Jane all about her date with Peter. She wasn't sure if Jane even knew Peter from Lenox, because she was Katie's age and she didn't have any older brothers or sisters who would've been friends with him. Katie loved Jane, but in high school Jane had gone out with a guy, Christopher, who Katie had had a big crush on, and Katie had never gotten over it completely. So Katie didn't tell Jane about the weird stuff with Peter, only about the good stuff. She even laid it on, telling Jane that Peter could even be the one, knowing that Jane would feel bad, especially coming off her awful date with Oily Man.

Katie felt good after she clicked send, but several minutes later, when she was lying in bed, trying to concentrate on reading the latest Harry Potter novel, she regretted sending the e-mail. It was mean to do something like that, especially to a good friend, and she wished there was a way she could unsend the message. She was obsessing so much that she kept losing her place in the book and finally closed it in frustration.

She couldn't sleep. At first, repetitive thoughts about Jane kept her awake, and then she started thinking about Peter. She replayed the date a bunch of times and then rehashed older memories, like the times in Lenox that they'd talked to each other at the ice-cream parlor and the video store. It seemed like it was always that way with her memories—she could remember unimportant things with total clarity, but major events, like prom night, the first time she had sex, or even the day Heather died, were blurred.

But then she remembered something else about Peter from years ago. He was in her house—she must've been, what, twelve years old? Heather's hair was shoulder length with bangs, her high school do, so she must've been about fifteen. Peter had come for dinner. He and Heather were in the same grade and she'd had other friends over before, so it wasn't weird that he was there. Katie couldn't remember anything in particular that had happened that night; like the other memories of Peter, it seemed random, uneventful. Still, she wondered why she hadn't thought of it until now. Also, she had a feeling that Peter had been over to the house several times, but she wasn't sure. She knew that he and Heather were, at least for a while, pretty good friends. Because Katie was very young, wasn't even a teenager yet, she might've missed some of the signals, but it was possible, even likely, that Peter had a crush on Heather. Heather was very cute and a lot of guys had liked her.

Lying on her side, Katie was uncomfortable, and turned fully onto her stomach. For some reason—and she wasn't sure why—the idea that Peter and Heather may've been together in some way kept nagging at Katie. Maybe she'd ask Peter if he'd ever had a crush on Heather, or if he'd kissed her. Or maybe she wouldn't. What was the point in causing drama when things were going so well?

Franky Franco looked like the textbook schizo—wide-eyed, fidgety, long messy hair, a scraggly, graying beard. Actually, he seemed so wacko that John Himoto wondered why he'd believed a word the guy had said, despite the polygraph.

Franco stuck to the story he'd told John earlier, that he'd stumbled upon Andrew Barnett in the underpass at Carl Schurz Park and murdered him. He answered every question John asked in a dead serious tone, without cracking a smile, and even started to cry several times. He seemed to believe that what he was saying was the absolute truth. Unfortunately, he didn't create any new holes in his story and didn't give any new details, so the forty-five minute talk with him accomplished absolutely nothing.

After some callbacks that went nowhere, John went to the church on Seventy-ninth Street near First Avenue. He'd been there several times before. Every day the church offered free meals for the homeless, and one morning, about two years ago, a stabbing had taken place. There had been several witnesses to the crime, but no one talked, and the case went unsolved. A minor blotch on John's otherwise stellar record. Yeah, right.

John talked to the administrator of the food program, Helena Adams, a nearly anorexic redhead in a black dress and an expensive-looking pearl necklace who seemed surprisingly uppity to have the job she had. She knew Franky Franco, said he'd been having meals at the church for the past couple of months.

"Has he ever been involved in any disputes?" Himoto asked.

"None that I know of," she said. "But you're aware of his psychiatric history, aren't you?"

She couldn't've sounded snootier.

"Yes, I am."

"He often talks to himself, and seems, well, I guess paranoid is the word. But, no, I haven't seen him become violent and, frankly, I've never felt threatened by him, either. God knows I can't say the same about some of the others who come here. By the way, we had an incident last month, a man was urinating inside the church, and we called the police and it took nearly an hour for someone to get here."

John apologized and explained that he had nothing to do with that and gave her a number where she could file a complaint. She mouthed off at him anyway about how important the church was to the community and how neglectful the police department was. John wanted to leave, but he also wanted more information from her, so he had to stand there, nodding with fake sincerity while the uppity biddy shit all over him.

Finally she finished and John asked her if there was anyone else at the church who knew Franco.

"Maybe one of the volunteers who serves meals could help you."

"You have the same volunteers each day?"

"No, it varies."

"What about friends or acquaintances?"

She let out an annoyed breath and crossed her arms in front of her chest, a not-so-subtle signal that as far as she was concerned the conversation was over.

"I have no idea who knows him and who doesn't know him. We finished serving lunch a little while ago. If anyone's still around, why don't you ask them?"

John watched her walk away, the two-inch heels of her designer shoes clickity-clacking along the floor.

Outside, a small group of homeless people were loitering in front of the church. John asked them if they knew a guy named Franky Franco. Although he hadn't flashed his badge or announced he was a cop, they all seemed naturally suspicious. He sensed that at least two of the guys knew Franco, but no one cooperated.

"All right, I'm a detective, like that surprises any of you," John said. Then, figuring he'd pull the sympathy card, he added, "Look, so here's the deal. Franco's missing; he could be hurt or in trouble and his family's worried. I need to know if anyone was with him on or around Thursday night. I'm talking about yesterday, all day. Did anyone see him or talk to him or does anyone know who saw him or who could've talked to him?"

"Sorry," an older black guy said, "we don't know nothing."

John knew the guy was full of shit, that he probably had a long rap sheet—actually, he was starting to look familiar—and there was no way he'd ever help a cop.

Then an old white guy, who looked homeless in a dirty old suit jacket and jeans, and who had awful BO, came over. He claimed he was a friend of Franco's.

"What happened to him?" the man asked, seeming genuinely concerned. "Is he okay?"

John stuck to the story that Franco was missing, figuring this was his best bet to get the guy to be forthcoming.

"When was the last time you saw him?" John asked.

"The other night," the man said. "What was it? Thursday. I slept next to him at the shelter on Seventy-seventh."

"You sure?"

"Yeah, I'm sure. Then he was here in the afternoon the next day— yesterday. But at night he didn't show."

"So you're positive you were with him all of Thursday night?"

"I wasn't with him—I'm not a faggot. But I slept on a cot next to him, yeah. Why? Wait, let me guess. He said he killed somebody."

"How'd you know that?" As far as John knew, Franco's confession still hadn't been made public.

The man laughed. "He does it all the time, that's why. I guess he started telling you guys the same crap he's been telling me. Last week, some guy in the Bronx got shot—he told me he did it. One time, some husband killed his wife in Brooklyn, he told me the cops got it all wrong—he did it. He tells me he killed somebody new almost every time I see him. Funny thing is, at first I believed him . . . I mean, he seemed for real . . . then I figured out he was taking it straight from the papers. So who'd he say he killed this time?"

Trying to put his embarrassment on the back burner, John said, "A guy—the other night in Carl Schurz Park."

The old guy and the black guy started laughing.

"You mean the guy who got it near Gracie Mansion?" the old guy said. "Yeah, that's just like Franky. I bet he really thinks he did it, too."

"You're sure he didn't leave the shelter Thursday night?"

"Franky's not a killer," the old guy said. "He's crazy as hell, yeah, but he's no killer. What, don't tell me you believed him?"

The old guy and the black guy laughed again, louder than before.

John returned to his car. Maybe some new information would come out on Franco, but John knew that the odds that the nut had killed Barnett were almost zilch. John sat there for a few minutes, with his forehead resting on the steering wheel, trying to think about his next move. It was hard to focus, though, when so many negative thoughts were swirling around in his brain. This case wasn't getting solved. In forty-eight hours he'd accomplished absolutely nothing. Worse, he had no idea where a break would come from. He was so fucking incompetent he wondered if he should take himself off the case—do the public a favor.

"Fuck me," he said, and pounded the dashboard with his fist.

He was sick of this shit but, one way or another, this case was going to get solved. He remembered telling Andrew Barnett's parents that he was the best man for the job and, beneath all the self-doubt, he knew this was the truth. He'd catch a break eventually, but it wouldn't happen sitting on his ass.

He felt like he was missing something very obvious. He had to go back to the basics, the crime itself. It was a strangulation, most likely a crime of passion. Maybe there was jealousy, an affair, a love triangle. He remembered one of Barnett's roommates, William Bahner, telling him about the double date he'd been on the night before the murder with Andrew Barnett, Katie Porter, and a friend of Katie's. John had a feeling Bahner was hiding something. Maybe Bahner had a thing for Katie and bumped off Barnett to get him out of the way. It was worth looking into anyway.

Bahner had given John his cell number. John called, left a message to get back in touch with him as soon as possible. Then he called Louis and gave him the news. Louis told him that he better make some headway fast, the clock was ticking.

John dreaded making the next call, to Mr. Barnett. He was hoping to get his voice mail, but no such luck.

"So?" Mr. Barnett asked.

"We don't think he did it," John said.

Dead silence, then Mr. Barnett said, "Why's that?"

He sounded too calm, as if he were ready to blow.

John explained about Franco's schizophrenia and affinity for taking credit for murders.

"So what the fuck're you gonna do now?" Mr. Barnett asked.

"We have many other leads that we're following up as we speak," John lied. "I guarantee you that we'll do everything possible to catch the son of a bitch who killed your son."

"Everything possible," Mr. Barnett said. "That's not saying a hell of a lot, since so far you've done total bullshit."

Mr. Barnett continued his tirade and John kept saying "Yes," "Yes," "I understand," "Absolutely," until he was able to get off the phone.

Suddenly John had a pounding headache. He was exhausted, too, the sleepless night catching up with him big-time. He pulled over at the Starbucks on First and Eighty-fifth for a double espresso. While he was on line, William Bahner called and John arranged to meet him in the cafeteria at Mount Sinai Hospital in twenty minutes.

Back in his car, John felt like shit for stringing Mr. Barnett along. His son had been killed and he had a right to yell and he had a right to demand results. Then John thought about his own son, who was alive and well, but whom John hadn't seen in, Jesus, over a year.

John wished he could understand what the Barnetts were going through, but the sad truth was he had no fucking clue.

21

Sunday morning, at the gym, Peter looked at his watch for what must've been the hundredth time and said to himself, "Where the hell is she?" Yesterday, in the park, she must've mentioned three times that she was planning to go to the gym in the morning and yet it was almost noon and there was no sign of her. Peter feared that something was wrong—she was sick or something. She'd seemed perfectly healthy all day yesterday, but he couldn't think of any other logical explanation. She had a great opportunity to spend more time with him today and he knew she wouldn't willingly miss out on it.

He resisted calling her. He wanted to, desperately, but his discipline was being tested. He had to stay cool, in control.

But as noon approached it was getting harder and harder to not do *something*. He had started his training for the membership consultant position but was barely listening to Jimmy. He took several breaks, to get water and go to the bathroom, but they were really just excuses to walk around the gym to see if he'd possibly missed Katie.

His agitation must've become very noticeable because during one of the breaks Jimmy came over to him and said, "You feeling okay, guy?"

"Yeah, my back's a little tight," Peter said. "Must've pulled it doing abs yesterday."

"You should ice it, bro."

"Yeah, good idea."

They continued the training but, for Peter, focusing on anything other than Katie had become impossible.

"Sorry, my back's spasming," Peter said. "Can we pick this up tomorrow?"

"Yeah, *no problema,* man," Jimmy said. "But I can't pay you for the time you'll miss today."

Peter, thinking, *Yeah, like I care about your nine fifty an hour,* said, "I totally understand. That's cool."

Working at the health club was getting to be a pain. He couldn't wait to quit and start his new life with Katie.

He took a long time leaving the gym—going to the bathroom again, striking up mundane conversations with a couple of trainers. He was hoping Katie would eventually show, but she didn't. He remembered how she'd said she couldn't go out with him tonight, and instead she suggested going out to dinner on Monday. At the time, he'd thought she was just trying to avoid going out two nights in a row with a new boyfriend—very typical dating behavior—but now he wondered if it was because she had other plans—ie, she was dating someone else. She'd never mentioned a guy in her life other than Andy, but that didn't mean there wasn't anyone. Many girls dated more than one guy at a time so there could be "another Andy" in her life, some other Frat Boy she'd met somewhere, or maybe she was seeing someone at her office. The only guy at her job who she talked about was her boss, Mitchell. It sounded like she hated him, but anything was possible. Maybe the tension meant something was going on.

Or maybe she had guy friends—you always had to look out for them. Girls always naively assumed that guys they were involved with platonically didn't want anything from them, but that was never the case. Peter knew that all guys—himself excluded—were pigs. They hung around, waiting until their female friends got into vulnerable positions, and then they went in for the kill. Peter had no idea how many guy friends Katie had—it worried him how little he knew about her—but he assumed there were some. If not friends, then acquaintances—pigs waiting in the wings for the going to get rough, for her to need a shoulder to cry on, so they could swoop in and take advantage of her.

Peter couldn't let this happen. He had to prevent it. He didn't care if he had to kill a hundred Frat Boys. He'd do whatever he had to do to keep Katie safe with him.

Leaving the gym, Peter's heart was beating wildly. He started walking, then running toward Katie's. Then a voice in his head screamed, *Don't do it!* and he turned around. He sat on a ledge outside a building and tried to settle down. While his first instinct was to get rid of whoever was in his way, he knew if he went over there and demanded to get into her apartment, it would lead to disaster. If she was with a guy, what would he do, kill him in front of her? He had to be a lot more clever about it than that. And what if he was wrong and there was no other guy? She'd think he was a lunatic and would never forgive him.

Rushing over there like a maniac would've been the biggest mistake of his life, and he was glad he'd had the wherewithal to talk himself out of it. He had to bide his time, keep watching her and gathering as much information as he could, and proceed from there. But, from now on, hanging out across the street from her building was out of the question. Although Katie had claimed that someone had confessed to the murder, Peter didn't believe it. There had been nothing on the news or in the papers about a confession. For all Peter knew, the police had found a witness from the Big Easy who had seen him talking to Frat Boy the other night, and maybe his disguise hadn't worked as well as he'd thought. Even going over with a different look could be a mistake if the police were watching Katie for some reason.

Peter racked his brain, trying to figure out what to do, and it didn't take long for the answer to come to him. Suddenly feeling back in the driver's seat, he walked down Second Avenue to a coffee shop that had Internet terminals. He purchased a half hour of time, then went online and searched for private detectives in New York City. He avoided the large companies, figuring they wouldn't answer the phones on a Sunday or wouldn't be willing to start immediately. Instead, on a piece of scrap paper, he made a list of ten or so independent investigators. Then, on the street outside the café, he started making calls on his cell.

A couple of the numbers were disconnected and he reached the answering services of several others. He was beginning to think it would be impossible to reach a PI today when Stanley Ross answered his phone. Peter explained that he suspected his girlfriend was having an affair and wanted Ross to follow her. Ross, an arrogant, gruff-sounding guy, said he was currently working on two other cases and couldn't start until sometime next week.

Peter reached a couple more answering services and was losing hope again. Then, on his second-to-last call, to Hillary Morgan Investigations, Hillary herself picked up. She lived across town, on West Seventy-seventh, worked out of a home office, and seemed interested in taking on the case. She said her speciality was infidelity.

"You sound perfect," Peter said. "The thing is, I think my fiancée's cheating on me right now. Can you start immediately?"

"I'm sorry, I have a personal commitment today," she explained, "but I can start first thing tomorrow."

She sounded tough, competent, and Peter wanted to use her. Besides, he didn't know if he could even reach another PI who was willing to start immediately, so for all he knew she could be his only possibility.

"Look, I really need you to start today. Whatever your fee is I'll pay double."

"I'm sorry, but—"

"Triple."

She paused, not for long, then said, "Well, I guess I can rearrange my schedule."

While he was talking to her, giving her basic information about Katie, he hailed a cab and headed toward her place. When he clicked off, he was riding through the park, halfway there. When he arrived at her apartment, a brownstone, she was amazed that he'd gotten there so fast.

She looked younger and less competent than Peter had expected. She had short dark hair and wore glossy lipstick. She had a raspy, smoker's voice, which was probably why she'd sounded older on the phone. The small one-bedroom apartment was cramped and dingy. She led him into a small alcove, her home-office area. She had a Jack Russell terrier, which kept yapping at Peter, trying to climb his legs.

"Stop it, Duncan," she said, and the dog scampered away. Then she said to Peter, "Sorry—he hates new people. Would you like a cup of coffee?"

"I'm fine," Peter said. "Actually, I was hoping you could go over to her place right now. Here, I can give you some money. I'll give you more tomorrow, or even tonight if you want to meet then."

Peter opened his wallet and took out several hundred-dollar bills and said, "This enough for now?"

Without taking the money, Hillary said, "Why do you think she's with someone right now?"

The questions were getting to be a pain. "Look," Peter said, "you said you can start immediately. That's why I'm giving you all this money."

"I'll take the job," she said. "I'm just trying to find out as much background as possible."

"This isn't that type of job," Peter said. "I just need to know if she's seeing someone else. If she is, some pictures of the guy would be great. But I think what I'm asking for is pretty simple."

"Do you have a photo of her?"

Shit, Peter hadn't thought of that.

"I can describe her. She's short to average height. Medium length straight brown hair. Wait a second."

He asked her if he could go online for a second, and she said that was fine, to go right ahead. He sat at her desk and did a Google image search for Katie Porter and scrolled down to one of the photos he'd found on the Internet while he was in Mexico. It had been taken a couple of years ago, while she was in college and was working as a career resource assistant. It wasn't the best picture of her—no photo did her justice—but it would do.

After printing out the photo on a regular piece of paper, Peter wrote her address below it, along with his cell number.

"This is all the information you need," he said. "Just watch her all day today and tonight and if we could talk this evening, maybe around ten or eleven, that would be perfect."

Hillary seemed hesitant—Peter couldn't tell if she was suspicious of something or not—but agreed to get to work immediately.

Peter took a cab to his hotel. He was relieved that the problem had been taken care of, that Katie was being watched.

Last night and early this morning, Peter had packed all his belongings into two suitcases. After he took a last look around in the closet and under the bed, he wheeled the suitcases onto the elevator and went down to the lobby.

Hector saw him and said, "Say it ain't so, man."

"It's so," Peter said.

"Yo, it won't be the same here," Hector said. "Serious. Who'm I gonna talk to?"

"You have Lucy."

"That's true, but she ain't here at night and I can't talk on my cell all the time, know what I'm saying? Yo, where's your new apartment at again?"

"Thirty-second Street."

"Yo, that shit's close by. You can still come by here and hang sometimes, right?"

"Of course."

"That's cool, yo. And we're gonna go out with our girls sometime, right?"

"Yeah, let's definitely do that."

Hector gave Peter a printout of his bill. Peter signed it without bothering to even glance at the total. Then Hector came around the counter and gave Peter a big hug goodbye.

"I'm gonna miss you, man," Hector said.

Peter told Hector he would miss him, too. But then, walking down Lexington, pulling his luggage behind him, he doubted he would ever talk to Hector again. He had nothing against the guy—he'd actually enjoyed all of their conversations and the guy couldn't have been nicer to him—but he didn't expect his future with Katie to include interacting with many other people outside their marriage. Once they settled down and quit their jobs, the world would be about them and them alone. He couldn't see them as one of those couples that socialized a lot. They'd definitely be homebodies.

It was Sunday, so the workers at Peter's apartment had the day off. When he arrived, he took a look around, delighted with the progress that had been made since his last visit. The final coat of paint in the master bedroom had been applied and Peter was relieved that the Martha Stewart delicious melon looked as good on the walls as it had on the color palette. More furniture had arrived—the Crate & Barrel maple coffee table, the Charles P. Rodgers wrought-iron canopy bed, the dining room table and chair set from Domain. The sixty-four-inch wide-screen LCD TV had arrived and the home theater system was all hooked up. Considering he had only hired a contractor and not a decorator, Peter was very pleased with how well everything went together. He had purchased most of the stuff from catalogs, wanting to get the place together as quickly as possible. If Katie had other ideas, he'd let her redecorate however she wanted to. Hell, if she didn't like the apartment, they could sell it and buy a different one, or buy a house in the country. Peter had only bought the apartment because he wanted to show Katie he was serious about starting a life with her. When he'd arrived in New York from Mexico, he'd immediately gone to several real estate agents and told them that he only wanted to see apartments that he could close on quickly, where the sellers were desperate to make deals. On the second day of looking, he'd found the apartment he ended up buying. He paid for it in cash and was able to close within three weeks.

Settling down on the leather couch, Peter imagined that Katie was next to him. It was a normal weekday night. They'd just had dinner and now they were cuddling. He was looking intensely into her eyes, hanging on every word she said. Then they started talking about the future, about the kids they'd have. They would make great parents, and Katie especially would make a great mother.

Instead of ordering in for dinner, Peter decided to christen the kitchen and the new stainless steel appliances. He could never even imagine trying to cook without following a recipe, so he walked to the Border's on Second Avenue and bought a cookbook by Jamie Oliver, which had a recipe for pot-roasted pork with fennel and rosemary. Then he cabbed it to a Bed Bath and Beyond across town and bought the utensils he needed, and on the way back to his apartment he stopped at a gourmet grocery and bought all the ingredients, and went to a wine store and bought a nice California zinfandel. He wished his stereo was connected so he could play some music to help put him in the mood, but he had to make do by singing an off-key version of "You Light Up My Life." Although he had an awful voice, he loved to sing, especially while cooking or showering, and as far as he was concerned the love ballads from the seventies were where it was at. He also liked seventies and eighties soft rock and as a teenager lived on Barry Manilow, Air Supply, and REO Speedwagon. As with movies, he only liked music that was uplifting, that made him happy. He could never understand how people could listen to stuff like grunge or metal or—the worst—the blues. Wasn't life depressing enough?

Although he made sure to measure all the ingredients precisely and he worked slowly, following every instruction, he must've done something wrong somewhere, because the food came out awful. The pork was too dry, the rosemary was bitter, and the fennel made the whole dish taste like licorice. Even the arugula salad disappointed. Although he'd washed it carefully, he bit down on a pebble and nearly cracked a tooth, and the vinaigrette was too garlicky. He trusted that Jamie Oliver knew what he was doing and the food wasn't supposed to taste like this, so the only explanation was that somewhere along the way he had screwed up. Furious with himself, he slapped his head a couple of times and said, "You fuckin' moron." Then he sat at the dining room table and poured a glass of wine and tried to enjoy the meal, but he couldn't even stomach the first bite. He spit the food out and, in total disgust, flung the plate across the room and swatted away the glass and the bottle of wine.

He cleaned up the mess, but decided not to order in any dinner or cook an alternate meal. Maybe if he went to bed hungry, it would teach him to cook his food properly next time.

As nine o'clock approached, he started worrying about the detective. Not about her doing her job properly—he assumed she was qualified—but about what she might find. Peter had no idea how he'd react if it turned out there was some other guy in the picture. While he couldn't imagine Katie deceiving him in that way, he had to prepare himself for the possibility. He knew what he'd do—get rid of the guy as quickly as possible—but he just hoped that his emotions didn't get the best of him, and that he was able to deal with the situation in a rational, controlled way.

At a little before ten, his cell rang. He was disappointed to see Hillary Morgan's number on the display rather than Katie's. Still, he answered eagerly, saying, "Hey, what's going on?"

"I've been doing a surveillance since a little after you left this afternoon."

"And? What'd you find out?"

"Not much—fortunately for you, I suppose. I didn't see her leave the building with anyone except a girl with curly blond hair. But you feared she was having another heterosexual relationship, right?"

"That sounds like it was her roommate," Peter said. "Where'd they go?"

"To a falafel place on Second Avenue."

"Did they meet anyone there?"

"No, they dined alone. Then, on the way home, they stopped at a grocery store. I'm in front of the building now, and they're still there. I was planning to stay till around midnight, and then I can pick up tomorrow morning if you—"

"No, that's okay," Peter said, smiling, relieved. "If you can stay till midnight, that would be great. But there's no need to watch her tomorrow. If I need your services again, I'll call you. And I'll bring you the balance of what I owe you tomorrow morning, okay?"

Hillary hesitated then said, "Oh . . . Okay," and Peter clicked off.

He went around the apartment, shouting, "Yes! Baby!" and pumping his fist in the air. His prayers had been answered. Katie had been faithful to him; they could start their lives together without any lingering doubts.

Peter felt like he was back in control of everything, and he planned to keep it that way.

22

When Katie woke up on Sunday morning she decided not to go to the gym. She knew Peter would be there, and she felt like they needed a little break from each other and it would be better to spend the day apart.

She still wanted to get some exercise, though, so she went running in the park, around the reservoir. She was in the middle of her second lap when her cell rang. She didn't recognize the number on the display and let her voice mail pick up. When she finished her run and did her stretching near the Ninetieth Street entrance to the park, she played the message from Detective Himoto. He didn't say much, just asked her to call him back as soon as possible. It was hard to read his tone because she'd only spoken to him that one time, but he didn't seem very happy.

She returned the call right away and he said, "Thanks for getting back to me so quickly."

"Is something wrong?" she asked.

"I'm afraid I'm going to have to ask you a few more questions," he said.

"About what?"

"About the murder."

"I thought you caught the guy."

"We had a confession, but it's doubtful the guy did it."

"What're you talking about? Yesterday you—"

"He was the wrong guy." Himoto sounded impatient. "I really need to talk to you again. How's right now?"

Katie explained that she'd just finished a run and needed to go home and shower, but arranged for Himoto to come by her place in forty-five minutes.

Walking home, Katie felt very unsettled. She'd been starting to accept

Andy's death; now it was like she had to deal with the shock all over again. She also felt guilty as hell for going on a date with Peter, for enjoying herself so soon after Andy was killed.

Then the fear kicked in.

The killer was still out there, and for all she knew he'd come after her next. She knew she was being irrational, that the murder was random and had absolutely nothing to do with her, but on the way home from the park she found herself walking much faster than normal and looking around a lot.

At her apartment, she showered, and while she was still rinsing the shampoo out of her hair Susan started knocking on the door.

"What is it?" Katie shouted to be heard over the rushing water.

"A detective's coming up to see you."

Katie cursed Himoto. It couldn't have been forty-five minutes already. God, this was so fucking annoying.

She hurried to finish showering and when she came out of the bathroom, wrapped in a towel, Himoto was sitting on the couch in the living room. He looked over at her, his eyes widening for a moment, then looked away quickly and apologized. Maybe this wouldn't have been a big deal for some girls, but Katie didn't have the greatest body image in the world and she couldn't help feeling embarrassed.

"Give me a couple of minutes," she said, and then she took a good fifteen, wanting to make him wait as punishment for his rudeness.

When she came out, Himoto said, "Sorry about before. Your roommate let me in and—"

"It's fine," Katie said, still embarrassed and wanting to get this over with as quickly as possible. "So what do you want from me? I already told you everything I know the other day."

"Your cooperation is very much appreciated. Unfortunately, these situations often require repeated questioning, especially from those closely associated with the victim."

The formal cop-speak was frustrating, and Katie wished he'd get to the point. She rolled her eyes slightly and said, "I understand."

"Great," he said. "I want to know more about your relationship with William Bahner."

"Who?"

"Andrew Barnett's roommate."

Katie needed a few more seconds, then said, "Oh, Will. What about him?"

"How well do you know him?"

"I barely know him at all. Why? Wait, you don't think—"

"When was the last time you spoke to him?"

"Spoke to him?" Katie was freaking out, imagining having to tell Amanda that the guy she'd set her up with was a killer. "The other day. I mean, Wednesday, when we all went out. Me, Andy, Will, my friend Amanda."

"Did you notice any antagonism between Andy and Will?"

"Antagonism? No, of course not. They're, like, best friends. At least I thought they were. Why are you asking me this?"

"I had a talk with Will yesterday afternoon. Then we did a little research. Did you know he was once arrested for assault?"

"I don't know anything about him. We met the other night and I didn't even talk to him that much."

God, this was the last time she was ever setting anybody up, no matter what. How was she going to tell Amanda?

"His senior year of high school," Himoto went on. "He apparently hit a classmate with a baseball bat at a party, broke the guy's arm. There had been a dispute, apparently over a girl."

"Oh, God, I can't believe that," Katie said. "But why would he kill Andy? That's what you're trying to say, right?"

"Right now it's still in the theory stage."

"Theory? But you can have a theory about anyone, right? How about a theory about me, or *my* roommate? Why Will?"

"I'm asking the questions."

"If you want me to answer them, I want to know why you think a guy I set up one of my best friends with may've killed my boyfriend. I think I have a right to know that."

"He's only a suspect," Himoto said, overly calm, trying to placate her. "For all I know, he has absolutely nothing to do with any of this. But there were some things that intrigued me."

"Like?"

"Like he seemed evasive when I questioned him for the first time, the day the body was discovered."

"Maybe he seemed evasive because he was worried. You said he was arrested before. He's a doctor, or trying to be one. He probably doesn't want stuff like that getting out."

"You know, you're very bright. You should think about being a lawyer."

Kate thought he was being sarcastic but said, "You sound like my father."

"Actually, I learned about William's past partly from Mount Sinai," Himoto said. "They ran a background check on him before he was admitted to med school. So he was forthcoming about the incident, but, yeah, you're right, he'd probably like to keep it as quiet as possible. Anyway, he says he has an alibi for Thursday night—claims he was in his room studying. He also said he was talking to a friend of yours on the phone."

"Amanda?"

"I have a call in to her, but she hasn't gotten back to me yet. Do you have another number for her? I think I have her cell."

"Yeah, I have her home number, but if he has an alibi, why do you think he—"

"I don't think anything. I'm just trying to rule things out. The call to Amanda was placed on his cell—he says at around ten P.M. That doesn't mean he was home. He could've been anywhere when he made that call, and he could've killed Andrew Barnett after he made it, since the Medical Examiner thinks the murder took place between midnight and two A.M."

"What about his roommates? Didn't they see him?"

"His roommate, Steven Walsh, confirms that he was in his room at around ten thirty. But Steven went to sleep at eleven that night, so it's possible that William left while he was asleep."

"I'm sorry," Katie said. "I mean, I know you said he beat up that guy in high school, but that was high school. He's in med school now. And there was no tension at all between him and Andy the other night. They seemed like best friends."

"How'd you get that impression?"

"It was just the whole vibe I got."

"Actually, that's not what I heard. Their roommates said they'd had some friction from time to time. William was against Andy moving in in the first place and tried to convince the other guys to get him to move out."

Katie wasn't sure what she thought anymore. For all she knew, she was in total denial. How did she know what Will was or wasn't capable of?

"But, you have to understand, our investigation isn't focused entirely on William," Himoto went on. "We just believe that there's a personal connection to this, that it wasn't a random event."

"How do you know that?" Katie was feeling paranoid again, like someone was out to get her.

"The main thing is the method of the murder—strangulation. That's often associated with crimes of passion. So we've been looking into Andrew's past, trying to find out if someone had a vendetta against him. Just so you know—we're not only talking to you. We're looking at his other relationships as well."

"What other relationships?"

Himoto took a moment then said, "I don't want you to feel insulted or hurt, but Andy seemed to have a reputation as a . . . well, as a womanizer."

"That doesn't surprise me," Katie said, stone-faced, but she felt like an idiot. She remembered going on to Amanda about what a great guy Andy was, how special he was. What was wrong with her?

"His friends and family say there are a few angry ex-girlfriends from college, and his roommates say he had several relationships in New York that ended bitterly. It's likely a man killed him, however, so I'm interested in any love triangle situations or . . ."

Katie zoned out, thinking about the night they had sex for the first time. Now that she knew Andy had been a womanizer, she felt like it had definitely been rape. There was no ambiguity anymore.

"What?" Katie asked, lost.

"Did Andy tell you about any past girlfriends?"

"No. I mean, nothing specific. No names or anything like that. But I knew he'd dated people in the city."

She was thinking, *How could I have been so fucking stupid?*

Himoto, looking at a notepad, rattled off the names of about ten girls. The only one Katie had heard of was Jen, but she didn't know any details about Andy's relationship with her.

"Let me throw an idea out at you," Himoto said. "Is it possible that Will had a thing for you and didn't like the idea that you were with Andy?"

"I told you, I barely know Will and, besides, he's been dating Amanda."

Himoto seemed very frustrated, and Katie noticed how exhausted he looked.

"Can you give me Amanda's home number?" he asked.

Katie gave it to him, then he said, "I'll let you know how things progress," and he left.

Susan came into the living room and asked what was going on.

"Nothing new," Katie said. "Just more questions. I'm so sick of it I don't even care anymore."

Katie got dressed and went out shopping. She needed to distract herself, to forget about everything, and she couldn't think of anything better to do. She wound up at Bloomingdale's, where she overpaid for a pair of strappy sandals she knew she'd never wear.

When she returned to the apartment, she felt a little better. Susan asked her if she wanted to go out for some dinner. Katie felt like she was too upset to eat, but knew she probably should.

They went to the falafel place on Second Avenue. Although Susan had her limitations—she was very white bread, anal retentive, and closed-minded—and Katie couldn't imagine ever being close friends with her, she was also a truly sweet person. She had a good soul and genuinely felt bad about what

Katie was going through and wanted to help her get through it. Peter had been the same way, and Katie decided that from now on she was going to make a concerted effort to spend more time with people who had a positive effect on her life, and to stop hanging out with toxic, damaging people.

During the meal Katie got a call from her friend Jane, but she let her voice mail pick up. When she returned to her apartment she lay on her bed and returned the call.

"Hey, Jane Blaine," Katie said, using the nickname they'd made up as kids.

"Hey," Jane said flatly.

Katie could tell something was wrong. Then she remembered the e-mail she'd sent.

"Oh, my God, I'm sorry," she said. "I didn't mean anything by that. I felt so bad after I clicked send."

"Bad about what?"

"You're upset about the e-mail I sent, right?"

"Well, yeah. Kind of."

"I didn't mean to rub it in. I mean, I hope you didn't think I was bragging about Peter Wells. I was just—"

"I didn't think that at all. I was just concerned, that's all."

Katie, totally confused, said, "Concerned about what?"

"About you and Peter being together."

Katie remembered telling Jane in the e-mail that Peter "could be the one."

"Oh, that was an exaggeration," she said. "We're not together like that or anything. We just went on one date."

"Oh, because when you told me you were going out with Peter Wells I was like, the weird guy?"

"Who called him that?"

"Everybody. My brother was in his class in junior high and used to talk about how creepy he was."

"Creepy how?"

"He was alone all the time; he didn't have any friends. I just remember he used to go on about what a freak and a weirdo he was."

"He's changed a lot," Katie said. "He's more outgoing now. He's cute, too. And he's a really nice guy. The other day I was going through a crisis and he rushed right over to be with me."

"Well, I just wanted to tell you to be careful. I mean, I wasn't sure how well you knew him in Lenox."

Katie was starting to sense a jealousy vibe from Jane and wondered if that was why she was trying to turn her against Peter.

"I didn't know him very well at all," Katie said. "I mean, I knew him from around town and because my sister knew him. . . .Wait, he wasn't a total loner. My sister was friends with him."

"It's no big deal," Jane said. "I mean, if you say he's changed, I guess he's changed."

"He has. I mean, I'm not in love with him or anything. Honestly, I like him, but I don't like-him like him, I don't think. We'll probably end up as just friends. It's hard because I'm coming out of this relationship with this other guy."

"What other guy?"

Katie didn't feel like telling her about Andy. She would eventually, but right now it was too much of a downer and she didn't feel like getting into it.

"Just a guy I was kind of seeing for a couple of weeks. Anyway, I'm probably just rebounding or something and it'll end up being nothing. So what's up with you? Tell me more about Oily Man."

As soon as the conversation switched away from Peter, Jane became her normal self and Katie was able to relax as well. Lounging in bed, having a meaningless, gossipy teenager-like conversation, reminded Katie of when she was in junior high and would call Jane and say, "Let's talk about people," and they'd stay on the phone practically all night.

This time they yapped away for almost two hours, taking advantage of the weekend minutes on their cell phones. They decided that it had been way too long since they'd last seen each other, and Katie said she would start looking into flights to San Francisco, to see if she could afford to visit.

After she hung up, Katie went online to research flights. She was still smiling, thinking about some of the things Jane had said on the phone. But her mood darkened when she remembered the stuff that Jane had said about Peter. It seemed like Jane was jealous; what other motive could she have for badmouthing him so much? This was a guy she'd barely known as a kid and whom she hadn't seen in years. What right did she have to warn Katie about him?

There was a good fare on JetBlue, but Katie wasn't sure she wanted to go anymore. Jane was a good friend, although maybe she was the type of friend who was great to talk to on the phone once in a while, but who was better off three thousand miles away.

Katie still couldn't shake what Jane had said, about how Peter used to be known as "the weird guy." Katie couldn't remember anything weird about him. True, he always seemed to be alone as a teenager, and he probably got picked on a lot, but what did that mean? Teenagers can be incredibly cruel, and Peter, with his awkward looks, was probably an easy target.

Later on, Amanda called. Detective Himoto had come to talk to her earlier and she was still very upset.

"He was asking me all these questions about Will and I kept telling him that I was only with him that one night and I haven't even heard from him since."

"I thought you guys were going out again."

"We were supposed to—he cancelled on me. He said it was because of what happened to Andy, but I think he was blowing me off. What did he say? Oh, yeah—'My schedule's kinda tight the next couple of weeks, I'll have to get back to you.' Can you believe that? Treating me like I'm a freaking patient or something. He's such an asshole. I'm so glad I didn't sleep with him."

"Just forget about him and move on."

"Trust me, I will. But why is Himoto suddenly asking about Will? Does he really think Will killed Andy? I mean, I can't possibly see Will as a killer, can you?"

"I hope not," Katie said. "If I set you up with a killer, that would be pretty bad."

"Yeah," Amanda said, "it doesn't get much more fucked-up than that."

They were quiet for a few seconds and then started laughing. Katie felt like she hadn't laughed so hard in ages, and it felt really good.

23

On Monday morning Peter called Jimmy at the health club to tell him he wouldn't be coming in to work anymore. Naturally Jimmy was surprised.

"Hey, man, if you don't like the sales gig and you wanna go back to the desk job, that's cool. I mean—"

"Yeah, it has nothing to do with that. I'm just moving on, okay?"

"What happened? You found something else?"

Could the guy be any more unclassy?

"Yeah, another opportunity came along," Peter lied. "But I really enjoyed working for—"

"Because you know I think you've got great sales skills, man," Jimmy wouldn't let up. "You could make a thousand a week here easy. But if you want to be a trainer, you can still do that. I mean—"

"I'm sorry," Peter said. "And you don't have to send me my last check, either. Goodbye."

Jimmy was talking when Peter hung up.

It felt good to be done with his job. He certainly had no need for it anymore. Later on, when he saw Katie for dinner, he would tell her how he'd only been working at the health club to meet her there, and he would tell her about the apartment he'd gotten for them. Their connection had been so strong on their first date that he didn't see any reason to postpone the future any longer. And he couldn't wait to see her reaction. She would have to think that the things he'd done were the most romantic things any guy had ever done to meet any woman. She'd probably even cry.

He had arranged to meet her after work in the lobby of her office building. He spent the entire day preparing for the date, coming up with clever things to say and planning what to wear. He must've tried on ten outfits and didn't like any of them. He wanted to look preppy, but not college preppy—he was striving for an older, more mature preppiness. At around three o'clock, less than two hours before he had to leave to meet Katie, he went into a panic and dashed to Eddie Bauer on Third Avenue and had a salesperson bring him about a dozen different possibilities before he found a black sports jacket, beige chinos, and a black linen shirt that he was pleased with. But he'd spent so much time stressing over what to wear that when he got back to his apartment he barely had time to shower and get dressed. When he arrived at the Lexington Avenue office building, his hair was still damp and he felt unprepared.

Then the doors to one of the elevators opened and Katie appeared and everything was suddenly okay. He remembered about the connection they'd made the other day, and knew that he didn't have to win her over or try to impress her anymore. All the games were over. She was his now.

She was with a woman, one of her colleagues from work. She introduced Peter to her, but he was only concerned with Katie and barely even looked at the other woman.

When the woman left, Peter and Katie kissed each other's cheeks and went outside. The narrow sidewalk was crowded with people rushing by in each direction. As Katie was telling him a story about something that had happened at work, Peter was looking for the right time to hold her hand. He wanted to do it sooner rather than later, but he didn't want to rush it either.

At the corner, Katie said, "So where are we going?" It was a chilly night, and Katie, in a thin suit jacket, seemed cold.

"I thought we'd go to that French place I told you about."

"Oh," Katie said.

"Something wrong?"

"No, it's just, I was hoping to have something lighter tonight. Just a salad or something like that. The food the other night was great, but I gained weight from it."

"Your body's beautiful," Peter said.

Katie waited a moment—she probably wasn't used to guys saying such nice things to her—then said, "Thank you. Well, I guess French food's okay. I mean, there should be something low-cal I could order, right?"

Peter was glad Katie changed her mind. He didn't have a backup plan and had his heart set on going to Café Boulud. He'd even called earlier in the day to make sure that they'd have the most romantic table in the restaurant waiting for them.

Peter figured they'd take a cab uptown, but he hadn't anticipated how hard it would be to hail one on Lexington Avenue during rush hour. They walked over to Park, but every cab was either off duty or filled or there were a few people on each corner, competing, trying to get in the best positions to hail cabs for themselves.

After a few minutes, Katie, who was shivering, with her arms crossed in front of her chest, suggested, "We can take the subway."

"That's okay," Peter said. The subway wouldn't be romantic at all and he wanted this night to go exactly the way he'd planned it.

A few more occupied cabs passed by, then Katie said, "Or maybe we can walk. I mean, it's getting kind of cold, but you said it's right up on Madison and—"

"No," Peter snapped. But he covered well, with a smile, and said, "We'll get a cab in another minute or two. I see a bunch of them coming. Don't worry."

The next wave of cabs came by, but they were all taken and it was getting harder for Peter not to show his frustration. He cursed a few times and didn't even want to look in Katie's direction. He just prayed a cab would come soon so they could get on with their date.

A navy sedan with a cab label on the windshield came by and there was no passenger inside. Peter had to practically leap in front of it to get the driver to stop. When he went to the door a young Asian woman arrived at the same time.

"Sorry, this is my cab," the woman said.

"I've been waiting here fifteen minutes," Peter said.

"So have I and I was here first."

The woman tried to get to the passenger door but Peter moved in front, blocking her, and said, "You're not getting in this cab, okay?"

"Yes, I am," she said.

She wouldn't give in, and the last thing Peter wanted to do was cause a big scene.

"Get away, you fucking bitch," he said.

Peter didn't know why he'd said this. He hadn't meant to. It had somehow slipped out.

He looked over his shoulder and, thank God, Katie was still on the sidewalk, arms still crossed in front of her chest, and hadn't overheard.

The tone in Peter's voice must've frightened the woman, or at least let her know that Peter wasn't the type of guy to get into a fight over a cab with, because she left. Peter motioned with his hand for Katie to come over.

They got in and Peter gave the driver the address. As the cab pulled away, Katie was looking straight ahead and seemed upset, or at least distracted.

"Well, that wasn't so hard," Peter said, hoping the sarcasm would break the ice.

Katie smiled for a moment, but still seemed preoccupied.

"Are you cold?" Peter asked. "Should I tell the driver to put on the heat?"

"No, I'm fine."

"I didn't have a chance to tell you this yet, but you look absolutely gorgeous today."

"Thank you," she said, obviously appreciating the compliment. She was used to going out with young, immature, self-centered guys who never commented positively on her appearance. Or, if they did, it was only as manipulation to help them get laid. She definitely wasn't used to compliments that were heartfelt.

The romantic mood firmly restored, they continued to Café Boulud on Seventy-sixth Street. When the cab pulled in front, Katie's eyes widened—the look was priceless—and she said, "*This* is where we're going?"

"Happy?" Peter asked.

"This is gonna cost a fortune," she said, "and I'm not dressed up enough."

"Stop it," Peter said. "You look perfect."

He took her by the hand and led her inside. The maître d' led them to the candlelit table toward the back. Peter ordered a bottle of chardonnay and Katie said, "How do you afford all this?"

"It's just a bottle of wine."

"But the restaurant Saturday night wasn't cheap, either. I don't want you to spend all your money on me."

"Why shouldn't I?"

"Come on, you don't have to do this. We can go to some Mexican restaurant or something on Second Avenue. I don't want you to go broke."

"That won't happen."

"Why won't it happen?"

"I'll explain it all to you later."

"Why do you have to keep it such a mystery?"

"Don't worry, I won't. Not for much longer anyway. Tonight's the night that all the mysteries will be solved." He smiled, lifting his glass. "To the most beautiful woman in New York."

Katie made it into a joke, looking around, as if wondering where the woman was. Peter was annoyed. This was the time for romance, not for joking around.

"I'm serious, you are."

"Thank you," she said. They clinked glasses and drank, and then she added, "But you don't have to keep complimenting me all the time."

"Why not?" He wanted to hold her hand, but hers were at her sides. Damn it.

"I mean, it's nice and everything," she said. "I don't know. It just makes me a little uncomfortable."

He understood. It was because of her low self-esteem.

"You *are* beautiful," he said. "It's the truth. I was outside today, walking around, and I compared every woman I passed to you, and you know what? It was no contest. You're the best-looking woman in the whole city."

"Okay, enough, enough," Katie said, smiling.

They ordered their dinners. Katie wanted to have just a salad appetizer, but Peter talked her into having the fennel risotto as well. He had the terrine of rabbit and the beef royale.

When the waiter left, Katie said, "Oh, I forgot to tell you—I got some bad news yesterday. They don't have the guy who killed Andy."

"They don't? But I thought you said—"

"They made a mistake. It was the wrong guy."

"Jeez, I'm sorry." Peter shook his head in sympathy—that was a nice touch. "How'd you find all this out?"

"That detective called and then he came over to talk to me again."

"What about?" He wasn't crazy about the detective having so much contact with Katie, but it was to be expected. She'd been Frat Boy's girlfriend after all.

"Pretty much the same stuff he asked me the first time. I mean, I had nothing new to tell him."

Peter took a sip of wine, enjoying its complexity, then said, "I guess that's true."

"But," Katie continued, "he kept asking me questions about Andy's roommate, Will. I mean, I barely know Will—I met him, like, one time. I went on a double date with him and Andy and my friend Amanda and he seemed like a really nice guy. The detective said he has some past record, that he assaulted some guy in high school, but it sounds crazy to me."

Peter hoped they pinned it on Will. That would be a very, very convenient development.

Doing whatever he could to get the idea into Katie's head that Will could've done it, Peter said, "You never know. Sometimes the nice guys are the ones you have to look out for."

Suddenly Katie seemed upset.

"What is it?" Peter asked.

She was starting to cry.

"I didn't tell you something," she said.

"Something about what?" He was worried it had to do with him, that he'd let something slip.

"About . . . about what he did to me."

"What who did to you?"

"Who do you think? Andy."

She'd snapped, but Peter wasn't offended. She was upset and he wanted to be there for her. Her hands were on the table and he reached across and held them. They were warm and soft and perfect.

"Tell me," he said.

She couldn't right away. But after crying for a little while longer, then collecting herself, she said, "I think he date-raped me."

Every muscle in Peter's body seemed to tense.

"Ow," Katie said.

He realized he was squeezing her hands too tightly.

"Sorry." He relaxed his grip but didn't let go. "Why do you say 'think'? I mean, did he or didn't he?"

She explained what had happened the first time they had sex. Hearing about Katie being intimate with someone else, especially that scumbag, was disturbing in itself, but as far as Peter was concerned there was no ambiguity about any of it—the slimy little cocksucking Frat Boy had raped the woman of his dreams. He was so glad he'd gotten rid of him when he did; if there was a way to kill a person twice he would've done it all over again. God knows how many other women Frat Boy had raped. Peter felt like he'd done the world a service by getting rid of him. He'd certainly made Manhattan a safer place for women.

"It's not your fault," he said, trying to soothe her.

"I know," she said.

"You didn't do anything wrong. He was the one who had some very serious problems. You were a victim."

"I know, and thank you for saying that. But now, with everything that's happened, you can understand why this is so hard for me."

"What do you mean?"

She had to struggle to keep her composure. He continued holding her hands and looked into her eyes as sensitively as he could, because that was what she wanted right now, what she needed.

"With Andy dying and everything," she said. "I mean, I feel bad; of course I feel bad. But when I think about what he did to me, and what effect it might have on me for the rest of my life even, I can't help feeling . . . happy. God, I can't believe I just said that. What's wrong with me?"

"Nothing's wrong with you."

"What he did to me was bad, but he didn't deserve to be killed. No one deserves to be killed."

Peter couldn't have disagreed with this more, but he said, "It's natural to feel the way you feel. Anyone in your situation would feel exactly the same way."

"You really think so?"

"Of course. He did something bad to you. Just because he got killed doesn't change that, and it doesn't mean you don't have a right to feel angry about it."

"Wow, you're good. You should think about being a therapist."

Peter wanted to kiss her, but it would've been too awkward, leaning all the way across the table.

"You should think about going to a therapist if you think it'll help," Peter said.

"No, thanks," Katie said. "I saw a therapist once in college. I hated it."

"I've never been a big fan of therapy myself. I went after my parents died."

"How did they die?"

He hadn't planned to tell her a lot of details—not yet anyway—but he realized it could be a great way to get sympathy from her, and he decided to go with it.

"I didn't tell you?" he said. "It happened after we moved from Lenox to upstate New York. There was a fire in our house and . . . it was pretty awful."

"They were killed in the fire?"

Peter nodded then said, "Check this out," and he shifted in his chair, extended his leg so Katie could see. Then he rolled up several inches of his right pants leg, exposing part of a large area of bubbly white scar tissue.

"My God," Katie said. "You mean you were in the fire, too?"

"I was sleeping when it started."

"Jesus."

"That's why I wear sweats in the gym all the time." Peter sat normally in the chair and said, "I woke up in time. Unfortunately, my parents didn't."

"I'm so sorry."

This time Katie reached across and held his hands. This was working out perfectly. If he'd known it would have this effect, he would've told her about the fire days ago.

"I tried to save them," he said, "but it was impossible. I had nightmares about it for months. I still do."

"I can imagine."

"So that's when I saw the therapist. I didn't really get much out of it. What helped me more was eastern philosophy. You know, Buddhism."

"Does that work?"

"It did for me. Hey, if you want to meditate with me sometime, there's this place I go in the Village. It's very relaxing."

"God knows I need to relax," she said. "That sounds great. Yeah, I'd love to."

Peter smiled, happy with himself for pulling the Buddhism card. He'd had a feeling it would impress Katie, make him seem deep, and it worked.

The rest of the meal couldn't have gone better. Opening up to her about his mother's death had created an even greater closeness between them. There was no awkwardness in their conversation. He didn't have to think of things to say and he knew it was the same for her. He could tell she was starting to realize that she was falling in love with him, and he knew it was almost time to tell her the truth about everything.

After dinner, when the check arrived, Katie thanked Peter for the meal, then looked at her watch and said, "Well, I guess I should be getting home soon."

"I want to take you someplace first," Peter said.

"Where?"

"It's a surprise."

"Not another carriage ride."

"No, nothing like that. I want to show you something."

"What is it with you and your surprises?"

"Trust me, you're going to love this one."

"I don't know. Tomorrow's a workday and I have—"

"I promise you'll be home before ten o'clock." He put his hand over one of hers. "Come on, what do you say?"

She smiled, then said, "Well, all right."

Holding hands, they walked to Fifth and he had no trouble hailing a cab this time. There was such a strong connection between them and the conversation was so lively that the fifteen-minute cab ride to East Thirty-second Street seemed to take only a few minutes.

When the cab came to a stop in front of the brownstone, Peter said, "This is it."

"This is what?" Katie asked.

"You'll see."

Peter gave the cabbie a twenty, letting him keep the ten-plus dollars change. Then Peter took Katie's hand and led her up the stoop.

"Whose apartment is this?" Katie asked.

Peter didn't answer, just took out a set of keys. He opened the door, flicked on a light and watched Katie's expression. He'd expected to see a combination of shock, awe, and disbelief, but she seemed more confused than anything. But this was okay—she didn't know that the place was hers yet.

"So what do you think?" Peter asked.

"Where are we?" she said.

"Your future home."

She looked at him seriously and said, "My future what?"

"This is where you're going to live," Peter said. "Where *we're* going to live, I mean. So what do you think? It's not fully renovated yet, and, don't worry, you can make whatever changes you want. We can throw everything out if you hate it, start over from scratch. The important thing is that you're comfortable, that it's a place you can call home."

"Wha-what?" Katie stammered. "Wait, what're you talking about?"

"This is our apartment," Peter said. "I bought it for us."

Katie stared at him, probably in shock, then said, "You bought an apartment for us. Come on, this is, like, a joke, right?"

"I know it's a lot for you to handle all at once, but I wasn't really working at the health club. Well, of course I was working there, but I only got the job so I could meet you. I thought it would be romantic if we met like that, like something in a movie. And it was, wasn't it? I mean, the way we met. Wasn't it perfect?"

She still didn't seem very happy. It was okay. She needed a little more time to digest everything, that was all. The joy would come soon.

"Look, I have no idea what you're talking about," she said. "You got the job to meet me? Why did you have to meet me?"

"Because I was in love with you," Peter said. "I've always been in love with you, Katie. I want to spend the rest of my life with you." He dropped to one knee, took out the ring box from the inside pocket of his jacket, opened it to reveal the sparkling two-carat diamond, and said, "Will you be my wife, Katie?"

He'd been planning for this moment for weeks—hell, in a way, for years. He knew she would look at him with shock at first, and then the smile would come and she'd be so excited that she'd probably start shaking. It might take her awhile to be able to speak, but at least she'd start nodding and eventually she'd say, *Yes. Yes, of course I will. Yes.*"

"What the fuck're you doing?" Katie said.

The response was such a surprise, such a total shock, that Peter continued looking up at her, smiling expectantly for several seconds, before the words registered.

Wondering if it was possible that she actually didn't get what was happening—maybe it was too overwhelming for her—he proposed again.

"I want you to be my wife, Katie. Will you marry me?"

"Can you just get up, please?" she demanded.

He didn't understand.

"But why—"

"Just fucking stop it, okay?" she said.

He stood up and tried to hold her hand, but she wouldn't let him.

"Come on, seriously," Katie said. "Whose apartment is this?"

"Ours."

"Oh, I forgot. Because you're so rich, right?"

"Right," Peter said.

"Oh, yeah. Where'd you get the money?"

"When my parents died. There were insurance policies."

"And you spent all this money on me, why? Because you're so in love with me?"

"Exactly," Peter said.

"I don't even know you." Katie was nearly screaming. "We just met. I mean, met again. I mean, please, *please* tell me this is all a joke."

"It's not a joke, Katie. I'm in love with you. Always have been, always will."

He didn't understand why she wasn't hugging and kissing him and telling him how much she loved him. She was looking at him like she hated him. This was all wrong. How had this happened?

"I'm sorry I proposed," he said. "It was too much, too fast, wasn't it? I should've showed you around the apartment. Wait till you see the bedroom. I got us a Charles P. Rogers bed."

"You're out of your mind."

"If you don't like it, we can exchange it. We can exchange everything."

"Just shut up!"

Why was she yelling?

"I know this all must seem sudden," he said.

"Sudden? This is absolutely fucking nuts."

She left the apartment and hurried down the stoop. He followed her, not bothering to close the door.

"Wait, where are you going?"

She didn't answer, just kept walking. This wasn't like a love story at all, or was it? The guy tells the girl he loves her, the girl panics, the guy stops her and convinces her he really does love her, the girl realizes she does love the guy, and the guy and the girl live happily ever after, the end.

"Katie, come on. I really do love you. Everything I said is true."

"Please just leave me alone."

"You're supposed to stop now."

She shot him a look, then walked faster, nearly at a jogging pace, and he reached out and grabbed her. He meant to do it gently, just to get her attention, but he yanked too hard and spun her around back toward him and she nearly fell down.

"Sorry," he said. "I didn't mean that. Are you okay?"

"I'm going home," she said and marched away toward the corner of Third Avenue.

Following her, Peter said, "Let me take you home at least. I want to make sure you get there safely."

At the corner, Katie signaled for a cab and one zigzagged across the avenue and pulled up next to her.

"I'm going with you," Peter said.

"Don't touch me," she said.

He backed away and she got in the cab and slammed the door.

"I'll call you tomorrow!" he screamed as the cab sped away.

24

Staring out the cab window, past her blurred reflection, Katie's thoughts were swirling and she was getting a migraine. It seemed like her life was getting crazier every day. She had no idea what she'd done to deserve all this crap, or what she had to do to get things back to normal.

In her apartment, she popped two Advils, washed up quickly, and got into bed, waiting for her headache to subside. Finally it did. She still couldn't believe that what had happened tonight had actually happened. Had Peter really *proposed* to her? Did he really say that he'd bought an apartment for them? Up until the apartment thing, she'd been having a pretty good time. It had been annoying that he'd made her wait in the cold while he tried to hail a cab, and all the over-the-top romance crap, with that ridiculously expensive French restaurant and all the gushy hand-holding, was too much for her. Still, he'd seemed like a nice, considerate guy who'd survived an awful tragedy. She couldn't see going out with him, though, and she'd been planning to tell him at the end of the night that she wasn't looking to get into a relationship right now and that she just wanted to be friends. Then, next thing she knew, he was kneeling down, asking her to fucking marry him.

She had to tell someone about what had happened. This was way too nutty to keep to herself.

She called Amanda and said, "You won't believe what just happened to me."

"What?" Amanda sounded bored, uninterested.

"Did I get you at a bad time?"

"No," she said, like her mind was still elsewhere. "What's up?"

Katie told her the whole story, expecting her to be floored. But when she was through, Amanda just said flatly, "Wow, that's pretty weird."

"*Pretty* weird? Are you fucking kidding me? It's beyond weird, it's ridiculously weird. But it's funny you said weird because my friend Jane was telling me just yesterday that when Peter was growing up he was known as the weird guy and I was, like, defending him. And then I go out with him tonight and all this shit happens. I mean, he actually bought an apartment for me. You should've seen this place. It was spectacular. It must've cost him, like, a million dollars. He said he got his money from some insurance policy. I thought he was this poor guy, working at a health club, and he turns out to be Mr. Moneybags."

"That's funny," Amanda said, but she seemed very distracted.

Amanda's lack of interest was really starting to piss Katie off.

"Are you even listening to me?" Katie asked.

"What? Hey, I'm watching *Lost*. Can I call you back in about an hour? Or maybe tomorrow?"

Katie couldn't believe how rude and self-centered Amanda was being. Last night, when Amanda was upset about Will, Katie had stayed on the phone with her for a half hour, letting her vent. But now that there was a crisis in someone else's life, she couldn't even pause her stupid show to give some support. Bitch.

"Whatever," Katie said, and hung up.

Katie went out to the living room to see if Susan was around. The door to Susan's room had been closed earlier, and it was still closed. Tom was probably over and they were probably doing it. Susan had such a perfect, stable little life. Katie couldn't imagine what it would be like to have a steady, reliable boyfriend, to not have some new crazy thing happen to her every fucking day.

Back in her room, Katie's head was throbbing—though it wasn't nearly as bad as before. She went online and checked her e-mail, and then she mindlessly surfed the Net, going on craigslist for a while, and then visiting friends' blogs. It was too hard to concentrate because she was distracted, replaying stuff Peter had said to her. She didn't know if that apartment really belonged to him, and he really was rich, or if he was just fucking with her head. And, God, had he really said that he'd "always" loved her? Growing up, she'd never had a clue that he was in love with her, or that he even had a crush on her. And it was kind of disgusting, considering she'd only been thirteen when he'd moved from Lenox to upstate New York. What was he, some kind of pedophile?

Then she remembered how he'd pulled up his pants at the restaurant to show her that scar on his leg. When he'd told her about the fire and what had happened to his parents, she'd felt sorry for him. But wasn't it weird that he'd never mentioned the fire before? Maybe he was self-conscious about the scar or didn't like talking about his past—a lot of guys were like that. That made some sense, but the other day he'd talked about how his parents had died, but said nothing about a fire.

Katie realized she hadn't Googled Peter at all yet. This was unusual for her because she routinely did Web research on every guy she went out with. Most of the time she couldn't find a lot of information online, but any little tidbits were nice to know and helped to make her feel secure that the guy she'd met at a bar or wherever wasn't some lunatic. Although Googling guys sometimes gave a false impression and worked to her disadvantage. Before she'd gone out with Andy, she discovered that he'd graduated with honors from Michigan and had been in a fraternity. She'd thought he was an all-American, clean-cut, nice guy. Nothing she'd learned online indicated he was a raping misogynist.

"Idiot," she said. "You're such a fucking idiot."

The searching was getting her nowhere. There were too many Peter Wellses in the world, and none of the results seemed to relate to the one she knew. Then she remembered him saying that he'd moved from Lenox to Colonie, New York, which was very close to Albany. It figured that a fire that had killed two people and seriously injured another would have been a major local story.

She went to the Albany *Times Union*'s Web site and did an advanced search in the newspaper's archives. She thought he'd mentioned that his parents had died six years ago and she hoped the stories were still available online. She did a search for the past seven years and was discouraged when she went through several pages of recent results that yielded nothing. But the newspaper's database seemed to be large, going back at least several years, so she continued searching. After a couple of minutes, she was getting tired and was ready to give up when a headline caught her eye:

COLONIE MAN NO LONGER SUSPECT IN ARSON INVESTIGATION

The Albany County District Attorney's office has announced that charges will not be filed against Peter Wells, the twenty-one-year

Suddenly Katie was a frantic wreck. She had to read the entire article immediately but, damn it, she had to register and pay two dollars. She went to her purse and fumbled for a credit card. Typing her personal information into the registration form, she was so frazzled that she made several mistakes, even misspelling her own last name. Finally she finished the process, entered the password that had been e-mailed to her, and was able to read the rest of the story.

It was pretty much what she'd expected. Peter had been the focus of an investigation into the cause of the fire when it was discovered that he was the recipient of two one-million-dollar insurance policies. But officials had concluded that he was innocent of any wrongdoing and an investigator was quoted as saying, "There is no evidence to show that Mr. Wells was responsible, nor that he acted in any way other than heroically."

Katie read the article three or four times. The brief description of the fire—"rapidly spreading"—and mention of what had happened to Peter—"suffered severe burns"—jibed with what he had told her at the restaurant. But she still felt extremely disturbed.

Then Katie returned to the list of search results and saw that there were other articles about the fire—six of them. She spent several minutes purchasing them and printing them out, and then read them in bed, in chronological order.

The fire had taken place in the middle of the night, while the family was asleep. Peter had tried to save the victims, but couldn't, and had suffered severe injuries himself, winding up in serious-but-stable condition. In the days afterward, he was hailed as a hero, but then doubts arose about the cause of the fire as information about the insurance policies was revealed. Investigators suspected that the fire had started when a halogen light in the living room accidentally ignited the drapes, but were questioning Peter anyway. After a brief investigation—according to the dates of the articles it had only lasted a couple of days—Peter was declared innocent of any wrongdoing.

Later, Katie was trying to fall asleep, but she kept stirring. So maybe Peter didn't set the fire that had killed his parents, but that didn't mean he wasn't psycho. What kind of person gets a job at a health club just to meet someone? What kind of nut buys an apartment for someone he hardly knows? What kind of lunatic proposes to someone he's gone on two dates with? And they weren't even really dates, not as far as she was concerned. For all she knew, Peter was so crazy, he'd killed Andy.

She had to get a grip, stop jumping to so many conclusions. Just because a guy was obsessed didn't mean he was a killer. But the thing that kept gnawing at her, that scared her most, was that she had been so oblivious. The way he'd gone overboard on their dates, how he always seemed so concerned about her, how he acted like he *knew* her, should've been indications that there was something seriously wrong with Peter Wells. Everything he did always seemed planned, like he'd been watching her for years, getting to know her from a distance. It was almost like he'd been stalking her.

Suddenly Katie sat up and turned on the light. The way her pulse was pounding, she was afraid she'd pass out or have a heart attack. She almost screamed for Susan to come into the room, but managed to control herself.

How could she have been so fucking blind? The other day, near the coffee cart outside the subway—the guy she'd seen in the sunglasses and the baseball cap. She'd been in denial about it since then, but not anymore. Peter had been watching her that day. She was sure of it.

PART THREE

25

Peter decided that, all in all, his second date with Katie had been a great success. Of course, it would've been nice if she'd said yes and accepted the ring and hadn't run away from him like he'd had the plague, but he had to focus on the positives. They'd strengthened their connection during dinner. He'd scored points by showing her his scar, increasing her respect for him. He didn't have a chance to kiss her, but he'd held her hand for a long time and she'd seemed very comfortable having skin-to-skin contact, even more so than on their first date. He imagined her, in her apartment, seriously regretting her behavior. It was only a matter of time until she called him to say that she'd made a huge mistake and to beg for a second chance. He wouldn't be cruel and make her squirm. Nope, that wasn't his style. He'd take her back right away.

The soaking tub had been installed and was functional. Peter luxuriated in the salted bath, breathing in the aroma of a scented candle. He had prepared a wicker basket of rose petals to sprinkle onto the water for his first bath with Katie. In her honor, he spread them around the tub.

He rested for a while with his eyes closed and then he turned on the LCD TV, which he'd installed above the tub, and played the DVD of the BBC version of *Pride and Prejudice*. Ah, was this the life, or what? As far as Peter was concerned, a better love story—hell, a better film—had never been made. It had always been hard to choose a favorite scene because the whole movie was so memorable. But if he had to pick one scene to watch again and again for the rest of his life, it would be the one where Elizabeth Bennett is standing alongside Mr. Darcy's sister, who's playing the piano, and Mr. Darcy gazes at Elizabeth longingly from across the room. God, that look of restrained, yet uncontrollable desire for a single woman was something that Peter had longed for since he could remember. Sometimes he'd practice "the Darcy look" in the mirror. It was hard to get it right by staring at himself, rather than at the object of his desire, but it got to the point where he could do it at will. It didn't seem forced, either. It was as if he were channeling Mr. Darcy. He'd used the look on Katie several times—at the gym and during their dates—and it had definitely worked its magic.

Sometimes Peter didn't bother with the rest of the DVD and played the piano scene again and again. But tonight, in the mood for a slow build, he started watching the film from the beginning. His cell phone was on a stool near the tub, but Katie wasn't calling. This didn't really concern him. These things needed to take their course. She might stew for a while longer, but eventually she'd realize how unusual it was to find true love, and she'd come back to him.

He remained in the tub until the scene at the Netherfield Ball, then put on his Ralph Lauren robe and continued watching the film on the larger screen in the living room. He couldn't take the suspense and he fast-forwarded to the piano scene. Wow, he'd never watched it on such a big screen, and it made "the look" even more romantic.

Entranced by the TV, Peter was making his own pained puppy-dog Darcy expression when he realized that he had an erection sticking up under his robe.

"Shit," he said. "Goddammit."

Without touching it, he went right into the bathroom and stood under a cold shower until it went down. His testicles hurt quite a bit because he hadn't had a nocturnal emission in at least a month or two.

The romantic mood had been officially killed. He busied himself, doing some straightening up and moving the living room furniture around. He was trying to make the apartment seem as homey as possible, but he knew his limitations as a decorator. He really didn't know what the hell he was doing and couldn't wait till the place had the benefit of a woman's touch.

Peter had his cell phone in the pocket of his robe. Every few minutes or so he checked it to see if Katie had called, but for some reason it hadn't rung. When it got to be past midnight, he knew he wouldn't hear from her until tomorrow. That was okay. She probably wanted to get in touch but figured it would be too late and she might wake him. For a while, he contemplated whether to just call her and get it over with. She'd probably thank him and tell him how great it was to hear his voice. But he talked himself out of it, deciding it would be much more romantic if she called him to apologize and confess her undying love.

He went to sleep, confident he'd hear from her first thing in the morning.

He didn't start getting concerned until noon when his cell phone still hadn't rung. It didn't make any sense to him. He called Verizon to see if there was something wrong with his service. Maybe he wasn't getting his messages—that occasionally happened—or there was some widespread outage. But the rep assured him that, as far as she could tell, there was no systemwide problem.

Peter needed to relax. He got into the bathtub, watched part of some movie on the Encore Love channel. He tried assuring himself that she just needed some more time and his phone would ring at any moment, but something seemed very wrong. It was taking too long; she should've come running back to him by now. Although he didn't see how it was possible, he feared that he'd misjudged the situation last night. Maybe it was more than another plot twist in their romance. Maybe she really was angry at him. Maybe she hadn't called him yet because she didn't want to call him. Maybe he would never hear from her again.

"Stop it, Peter," he said, and slapped the top of his head very hard. He was glad it hurt. He deserved to feel some pain for acting like such a fool. Why did he always have to imagine the worst? He was a smart guy—smart enough to know that nothing was ever as bad as it seemed. He reminded himself of the facts: They had fallen madly in love and were going to spend the rest of their lives together. That had to be the focus, not a doomsday scenario that had no basis in reality.

There was no reason to sit around. After all, he was her boyfriend now. He had a right to call her whenever he wanted to.

He tried her cell first and got her voice mail. He didn't bother leaving a message. Although he'd never called her at her office before, he'd found her work number when he was searching for information about her online and discovered a PR release she'd written. God, had that only been three months ago? It seemed like they'd been together for years.

"Mitchell Kushner's office. Can I help you?"

He went for a cool, relaxed tone. "Hey, what's up?"

Silence. Tears were probably swelling up. Her next words would be *I'm so sorry. I was such a fool. Please. You have to forgive me.*

But instead he got, "What do you want?"

Trying not to seem overly concerned, he said, "I just called to say hi, see what's up."

Another pause, a deep breath, then she said, "Stop calling me."

Why was she acting this way?

"Why? What's wrong?"

"I just don't want you to call me anymore, okay?"

"But I love you. I want to be with you."

"Stop it. Just stop it." Then, almost whispering, she said, "I'm sorry. I think you're a really nice guy, but it would be better if you stopped calling me, okay?"

"But why? I don't understand."

"I have to go."

"But—"

"Goodbye, Peter."

"Katie, wait. Katie? . . . Katie?"

She wasn't there.

He called back five times, but kept getting her voice mail. She probably had caller ID, was screening his calls. He didn't get it. Could this really be happening?

He had to talk to her again—right away. He could call from a pay phone and she might pick up, or he could go down to her office, wait outside for her after work. But it all seemed pointless. She sounded like she never wanted to see him again, ever, and if she saw him waiting for her in the office lobby, she'd probably freak and start screaming for security.

He had no idea why she suddenly seemed to hate him so much. He didn't know where he'd gone wrong.

Unless it had nothing to do with him.

Yeah, that had to be it, there had to be another guy. She had started seeing someone else, or maybe she had been seeing someone else all along, even while she was with Frat Boy. He struggled, trying to remember if she'd mentioned another guy. The only explanation he could think of was that she was screwing her boss.

She always went on about what a jerk he was, and how much she hated him, and it seemed like there was no way she'd ever be interested in him. But she talked about him a lot, and sometimes it seemed like she was even obsessed with him. Besides, in romances couples often sparred, acting like they had total disdain for each other, when they were actually fated to fall in love. What better example of that than Elizabeth and Darcy?

The more he thought about it, the more it made perfect sense. "Bitchell" was screwing her, violating Peter's future wife's beautiful body. If he was even kissing his bride-to-be, God help him, because at this point Peter wasn't letting anything stand in his way.

He called the detective, Hillary Morgan.

"Hello," she said. Her Jack Russell terrier was yapping in the background.

"It's Peter Wells." His tone was full-blown frantic and it wasn't a put-on. "I need you to go back to work immediately."

26

John Himoto finally got the big break he'd been waiting for.
He was at Chinatown East on Third Avenue, barely touching his shrimp
with snow peas and fried rice lunch special, going over his notes on the case,
trying to decide whether it was worth pursuing William Bahner, or it was
just another big dead end, when he got a call from Jeffrey Sykes, an officer in
his precinct.

"Hey, John, I think I got something for you."

"Yeah?" John said flatly, unimpressed. At this point it would take a lot
more than "I think I got something" to get a rise out of him.

"A bartender at the Big Easy said she saw the vic the night he was
killed," Sykes said.

"She saw him," John said, "or she thinks she saw him?"

"She says she saw him."

John, already standing up, his wallet out of his pocket, said, "Where are
you now?"

"I'm with her here at the bar. Where are you?"

John put a twenty on the table—the twelve-dollar tip would be the
waiter's biggest of the week—and headed toward the door.

"I'll be there in two minutes. Don't leave and don't let her leave."

"Thank you, sir!" the waiter shouted at John's back as he left.

The bar was so close by that John didn't bother driving there. He
walked down Ninety-second Street, then around the corner to the Big Easy.

It was a large, grungy, no-frills bar that catered to the same demograph-
ics as many Upper East Side bars. At night, it filled up with twenty-
something beer drinkers, but the daytime crowd was mostly middle-aged,

working-class men. Now, on a Monday afternoon, there were several construction-worker types at the bar, another guy playing Skee-Ball, and that was it.

Officer Sykes was waiting near the door.

"When you say two minutes you mean it," Sykes said.

"That her?" John said. The blond bartender was watching them from behind the bar.

"Yeah, her name's Mikala," Sykes said. "She said she'll talk to you."

"She's giving me that privilege, huh?" John said.

Sykes smiled and said, "You want me to stick around, boss?"

Boss. John liked that. Sykes was a smart kid, showing respect for his superiors. You wanted to move up in the force, you had to kiss some ass, get your nose nice and brown.

"That's okay," John said. "But, hey, good work. Thanks a lot."

"No problem, boss. Lemme know how it turns out."

"Will do."

John went over to the bar. Mikala was very attractive, definitely a wannabe actress, model type. She was blond, thin, and was wearing jeans and a cutoff T-shirt with the slogan STOP STARING right at the level of her breasts. Like a lot of waitresses and bartenders her age, she seemed to be on the dark side of thirty and had the hardened look of a woman who was sick of getting hit on by drunks and was frustrated that her career wasn't going the way she'd thought it would. She was probably already thinking about giving up and going back to wherever she came from. He noticed that her mouth was slightly downturned. He bet she'd smiled a lot more before she moved to New York and had all her dreams crushed.

John showed his badge and said, "How you doin', Mikala? I'm Detective Himoto, Nineteenth Precinct."

She was looking away, avoiding eye contact. "I told the cop everything I know already."

"Thank you," John said. "We appreciate that very much. But since I'm running the case, I'd appreciate it if you told me as well."

She rolled her eyes and then, in a very bored tone, said, "The guy came in here that night at, like, eleven thirty."

"Why do you remember him in particular?"

"He was fucking hitting on me, that's why."

"You get hit on a lot, I imagine."

"Yeah, that's true, I do, but he was more persistent than most guys. I brought him his beer and he was like, 'What's your name? Where're you from? Do I know you from somewhere?' Like he was trying every lame line he could think of. I was like, 'Look, I'm married, all right?' " She held up her left hand, showing a thick wedding band. "I call it my scumbag repellent. I'm not really married, but it keeps the pricks away, you know?"

John, taking notes, asked, "And you're almost certain the guy was Andrew Barnett?"

"I'm pretty sure he told me his name was Andy. But, look, like I told the other cop, I don't want my name in the paper about any of this."

"I'm a cop, not a reporter. Did he talk to anybody else?"

"Yeah, these two girls."

"Do you remember what they looked like?"

"One was pretty, had nice hair. Though I think he would've hit on anything with tits and a pulse. And maybe the pulse wasn't so important."

"What about the other girl?"

"I don't remember her."

"But you know there were two girls?"

"Look, I don't, like, memorize how my customers look. Sorry."

Thinking, *Man, what a bitch,* John asked, "How long was he talking to them?"

"I don't know. Not long—maybe ten, fifteen minutes. But then he tried to pick one of them up."

"How do you know?"

"Because he asked me for a fucking pen. Can you believe that? After I blew him off, he asks *me* for a pen? Like he thought I gave a shit and he was rubbing it in my face. I mean, I'm sorry the guy got killed, but he was a total jackass."

"Is there anything else you remember? Anything he said or did?"

"Why would I remember what some prick does?"

"So your answer's no."

Her eyes widened slightly and she said, "Wait, he did talk to some other guy."

"What other guy?"

"I don't know, and don't ask me what he looked like."

"What did he look like?"

Mikala almost smiled. "I really wasn't paying attention."

"Think. This could be extremely important. Was he tall, short . . . ?"

She shook her head in frustration for a few seconds. "I don't know, medium tall? Definitely not very tall. But I'm really just guessing."

"What was he wearing?"

"I don't know."

"Casual, well dressed, a guy on his way home from work?"

"I don't know."

"What about hair?"

"Dark, I think. And I think he had a goatee. Yeah, he definitely had a goatee."

"You ever seen him in here before?"

"No."

"How many other bartenders work here?"

"Five. Six, if you count Jake, one of the bouncers. But one, Dan, only works one day a week."

"You think they've seen this guy before? I mean, based on your description."

"I have no idea. Why don't you ask them?"

"I take it you never saw Barnett in here before, right?"

"I don't know, but it was the first time he ever hit on me, that's for sure. I never forget the real slimeballs."

"I'm gonna have an artist come down here, see if we can get a sketch of the guy you saw Barnett with."

"But I have no idea what he—"

"You remembered his hair and goatee—maybe you'll have more revelations. We're also going to have to talk to any other employees who were working that night. Was there a manager here?"

"Nicole."

"I'll need to speak to Nicole. And what about regulars? Were there any customers, steadies, who were here at the time?"

"No, I don't think so."

John looked around. "You don't have security cameras in here, do you?"

"No, but I know they're thinking about installing them."

"What about outside?"

She shook her head.

"Too bad," John said.

Mikala went back to work and John looked around the bar some more. If he'd gotten this lead the day after the murder, he might've been able to find a print, but now that a few days had gone by, finding any physical evidence in here would be highly unlikely.

He went outside and walked up and down the block, checking out the exteriors of each building for surveillance cameras. Unfortunately, the stores directly to the left and right didn't have any, but the apartment building on the next block had one. With any luck, it had recorded the dark-haired guy and Andrew Barnett passing by on the night of the murder.

John went into the building and got the number and contact name of the security firm responsible for the surveillance. He called right away and explained the situation to a customer service rep. The rep said he'd have one of the people in charge get in touch with him as soon as possible.

"I need to see that video immediately," John said. "I'll get a fucking court order if I have to."

"I'll do everything possible to expedite the situation," the guy said nervously.

"Do more than that," John said. "I'll give you an hour or we're coming down there."

The hard-ass routine worked. Five minutes later the head of security at the company called John and said the video would be at the precinct by five P.M.

Before the security guy got in touch, John had called in an order for a sketch artist to sit down with Mikala and come up with a composite of the possible suspect. For someone she'd had a casual interaction with, she could already recall more details about his appearance than the average person would've been able to. Hopefully, when she sat down with the artist, more details would emerge and they'd get a good sketch of what the guy looked like. Then they could get it in the papers and on the news and the case would quickly snowball toward a positive conclusion.

Next, John called Nicole, the bar's manager. It was a 718 number, meaning she could live in Brooklyn, Queens, Staten Island, or the Bronx. He didn't want to waste time traveling, so he questioned her over the phone. He explained the situation, but unfortunately she had no memory whatsoever of seeing Andrew Barnett, or the other guy, that evening. While he was on with her, his call waiting showed that Louis was calling. John ended the call with Nicole and said to Louis, "I was about to call you. We just got a big break."

"Yeah?" Louis said. "What's that?"

"I have a bartender who saw Barnett leave with a guy, probably within an hour of when he was killed. I think she can describe him, too."

"That's great," Louis said.

"I'm also gonna look at some surveill—"

"Listen," Louis cut him off. "I've got some bad news for you, man."

John knew what was coming. "What news?"

"You're off the case, John. Sorry, there's nothing I can do. This came down from up top, from the commissioner, and he has the mayor on his ass."

"But I'm telling you," John said, "I'm about to—"

"Come on, John, you know how it is. And it's not like I didn't give you any fucking warning. Where're you now?"

John shook his head, then said, "By the bar."

"Great," Louis said. "I'll tell Barasco from Manhattan North to meet you down there ASAP and you can fill him in on what's going on."

It had to be Nick Fucking Barasco. If there was one guy John didn't want to hand this golden case over to, it was him. Barasco had gotten all of the sexy murder cases lately, was a regular on the local news, and had gotten a rep as one of the top detectives in the NYPD. Normally John didn't have a problem with other people's success. Like most detectives on the force, Barasco was good at what he did or he wouldn't've been doing it. But Barasco was the type who let the success go right to his head. He always overdressed, in Armani and Hugo Boss, and walked with a goddamn strut like he thought he was a movie star. And he always treated John like shit. Although they'd met maybe a dozen times, whenever they saw each other Barasco always played dumb, saying, "Have we met?" The last time John had seen Barasco was just three weeks ago, at that funeral for that cop who was shot on Staten Island. At the chapel, John went up to him, just to bullshit and say hello, when Andrew Goldman, a city councilman came over. What did Barasco do? He blew John off in midconversation, actually turning his back on him, to talk to Goldman. John had decided that that was it, that he would never go out of his way to be civil to that prick again.

Now, here he was, about to hand him a case that had practically been solved.

Swallowing the last speck of his pride, John said, "Yeah, no problem, I'll wait here for Nick." Louis asked him for the address of the bar. John gave it to him, then Louis said, "Again, I'm real sorry about this, man. I know how much you wanted it."

"It's fine," John said, but even if he had the acting skills of Al Pacino, he wouldn't have been able to make that sound believable. "Really, it's no problem at all. I totally understand—I get it."

Then John clicked off and said, "Goddamn fuckin' bullshit."

He stood on the sidewalk, cursing for a while, probably sounding mentally disturbed. The most frustrating thing wasn't losing the case to Barasco; it was that Barasco would benefit from his work. It was like when you struggle to open a jar of peanut butter. You try and try and finally loosen it, and then somebody else comes over and says, "Let me try," and the cap comes right off.

John got a cup of coffee at a deli. He drank it on the sidewalk in front of the bar. When the coffee was gone, there was still no sign of Barasco. He started to wonder if the guy would even bother to show. Maybe he figured if John Himoto had a lead, it couldn't possibly be worth his while.

The artist arrived. John had him sit down with Mikala and start working on a sketch of the dark-haired guy, but there was still no sign of Barasco. John reported this to Louis, who told him that Barasco was on his way and to keep waiting.

Almost another hour went by, and then Barasco and another cocky, Italian-looking guy—probably his partner—came into the bar. The other guy was a real Prick Barasco in training, with his hair slicked back the same way, and wearing a similar, uncreased black designer suit. If they just had the sunglasses, they would've been the Men in Fucking Black.

As they entered the bar, they walked right past John and he had to say, "Hey, Nick," to get them to stop. Barasco squinted at John in a confused way.

Thinking, *Is this guy for real, or what?* John said, "Don't tell me you don't know who I am. It's John. John Himoto."

Nick smiled—he'd whitened the shit out of his teeth—and said, "Oh, yeah, right. How are ya? This is my partner, Tony Martinelli."

"Hey, man," Tony said, shaking John's hand.

"You remember me, don't you?" John asked Nick.

"Yeah, yeah, of course."

"We just saw each other at Santos's funeral."

Barasco's eyes were doing that annoying wandering thing they always did, looking around the room, acting like he was already losing interest in the conversation and was trying to find someone more interesting to talk to.

"Yeah, yeah, I know, I know," John said.

"Oh," John said. "Because you looked at me like you didn't know who I was, so I thought you might've forgotten."

"I didn't forget," Barasco said. "Santos's funeral. Yeah, right."

He was still acting like he was seeing John's face through a fog, the way you might barely remember the kid who sat in the seat in front of you in sixth grade when you meet him on the street thirty years later. John decided that Nick either had a severe head injury with massive memory loss and shouldn't be doing police work, or this whole forgetting thing was just a big act, a power trip that he pulled on everybody he considered beneath him.

"Sorry to bust in on your action like this," Barasco said, though it was obvious that he lived for moments like this. "But, hey, you know how it is."

"Yeah, I know how it is," John said.

"So Louis tells me you got something going on here, a lead or something?"

John would've loved to steer the asshole in the wrong direction—give him some bad info, set him on a wild goose chase. But he did the right thing, telling him everything he knew in great detail and giving him the names and numbers of all his contacts. Barasco kept saying things like "Yeah," "Uh-huh," and "I got it," but seemed to barely be listening. Martinelli was acting the same way, even though he had a pad out and was taking notes.

When John was through, Barasco said, "Thanks for holding down the fort for us, man," and walked away toward the bar. No handshake, no goodbye, no nothing.

John was glaring at Barasco's back, imagining running up behind him and sticking a knife into it, when he realized that Martinelli was standing there, choppers gleaming, with his hand extended, waiting to shake.

"Great meeting you, Jim," Martinelli said.

John gave the kid a long look, then turned and left the bar.

The walk from Second to Third Avenue, where John's car was parked, was uphill. John didn't know if he was in shittier shape than he'd thought or this fucking case had taken a toll on him physically, but three-quarters of the way up the block he had to stop and take a break. It took awhile to catch his breath and for his heart to stop pounding. He remembered during his last physical how the doctor had gotten a blood pressure reading of one sixty over ninety, even though John had been taking pressure pills for three years. The doctor had instructed John to lose weight and change his diet. John had done neither, and he hadn't been taking his medication regularly either. Having a heart attack now would be a fitting end to a very fucked-up day.

He recovered slowly, then took it easy the rest of the way. In his car, he felt better; well, he was confident he wasn't going to die—not yet anyway.

Driving downtown, there was a lot of traffic, especially approaching the Fifty-ninth Street Bridge, where it took five minutes to move one or two blocks. Occasionally he'd think about Barasco and Martinelli and shout a curse or bang the dash with his fist. He didn't know how he'd deal with it when he turned on the TV and saw those two cocksuckers shaking hands with the mayor, getting credit for *his* bust. To distract himself, he put on the radio to an oldies station. He loved sixties rock, but even "Wouldn't It Be Nice" didn't stop him from feeling like shit.

He pulled over and called his son.

"Hey, what's up?" Blake asked unenthusiastically.

"That's the hello I get?" John said.

"What's going on?"

"I was wondering if you wanted to get together. Maybe grab a cup of coffee."

"Now?" Blake asked.

"Yeah. Why not? I just thought it would be, you know . . . nice."

"But you never want to get together."

"That's not true. I've just had a lot on my plate lately."

"I saw you on the news the other night. How's that case going?"

John didn't want to get into it. "Fine. Look, can I come by or what?"

"I can't now," Blake said. "Mark and I are headed out."

"Okay," John said, wondering why he'd bothered. He wasn't gonna get any closer to his son. He might as well just deal with it.

"I'm sorry," Blake said. "If you'd called earlier—"

"That's fine," John said. "I'll call you tomorrow and we'll set something up. Take it easy, okay?"

John was relieved to get off the phone. The traffic was stop and go until he reached the bridge, but then he went at a steady clip the rest of the way to Queens.

He lived in Astoria, on Thirty-seventh near Steinway, in a two-bedroom apartment in a modest two-family brick house. He'd bought it after he married Geraldine and he'd lived in it for twenty-three years, six years alone. Very little had been updated, and it was in desperate need of a woman's touch.

He wasn't as tired as he should've been, and still didn't feel like being alone. He stripped to his boxers and T-shirt and then, after standing at the open fridge and putting away a couple of slices of two-day-old pizza with some Rolling Rock, he called the Asian Fantasy Escort Agency and arranged for Mary to come over in forty-five minutes.

John called escorts once in a while and had gotten Mary a few times. She was a young girl, probably twenty-two or twenty-three, from Taiwan. Obviously Mary wasn't her real name. She spoke English with a strong accent and had a naïve, just-off-the-boat kind of look. Although John had never dated an Asian girl—even in high school most of the girls he'd gone out with were Jewish or Italian—whenever he called an escort, he asked for an Asian girl. He bet a shrink would have a field day with that one.

Mary arrived wearing the same outfit she always wore—a black leather jacket over a skimpy red dress and matching pumps.

"Hey, how are you?" John said, and kissed her on the cheek. He was genuinely happy to see her.

"I'm doing great," she said. "How are you?"

She was very sweet and very pretty, with her long dark hair and beautiful smile—way too sweet and pretty to be a hooker. She'd once told John that she was a student at Queens College, but he knew that was bullshit.

"Eh, I'm all right," John said. "Had a rough couple days."

"So sorry to hear that," she said, meaning it. "Don't worry, everything going to be better now."

John took her coat. She had a thin, delicate body and had great posture, like she could've been a ballet dancer. He asked her if she wanted anything to drink and she said she'd have a glass of water. He brought the water from the kitchen and sat next to her on the couch.

They exchanged small talk for a few minutes. She asked him if he had any plans for the holidays. He lied and said he was going to spend a lot of time with his family. She said her family was planning to visit from out of town, but he knew she was lying, too.

As they talked, she started rubbing his leg. This was how it usually went. After a couple of minutes, she'd reach under his boxers and touch him there for a while, and then she'd do a strip tease. When she was naked, she'd give him a condom to put on and then she'd climb onto his lap. They'd talk dirty to each other, which would be fun for a while, but then, especially afterward, he'd feel like shit.

She was starting to move her left hand toward his lap when he said, "You know, I think I'll take a rain check for tonight."

She seemed confused.

"Not tonight," he said. "You can leave. Here." He opened his wallet and gave her the hundred and sixty for the visit plus his usual forty-dollar tip.

She didn't take the money. She seemed insulted, hurt, as if she were on a date and her boyfriend had turned her down.

"You sure you don't want me suck your very big beautiful cock?"

"No," John said, "I'm tired and not feeling too well."

She made a sad face, then said, "I suck your cock very gentle."

"Really, you should just go now." Then, as she was putting on her jacket, he said, "You know, you should think about quitting this shit."

She didn't seem to understand.

"I mean, get some other job," he added. "New job. New life."

"What wrong?" she said. "You don't like me no more?"

"Of course I like you, that's why I'm telling you this. You're beautiful, you're smart, you can probably do anything. I can help you get a job if you want. Do you want me to help you?"

John didn't know why he was saying all this, what he hoped to accomplish with this save one hooker, save the world crap.

"It's okay," she said. Then she kissed him on the cheek and said, "Call me again sometime, okay?"

She left and John was suddenly zonked, his lack of sleep the past few days catching up with him big-time. He didn't even have the energy to go into the bedroom. He lay on the couch, put on the TV for some background noise, and quickly fell asleep. It seemed like he'd been out for a long time, maybe several hours, when his cell phone rang, jarring him awake. He let the voice mail pick up, then whoever it was called again.

"Shit," he said, and went across the room to the console where he'd placed his phone. It was flashing KATIE PORTER. He'd given Barasco her number and he thought, *Let him do some fucking work,* and went back to the couch without picking up.

27

Katie sat at her desk, unable to focus. She wouldn't have even bothered coming in to work today, but Mitchell had an important meeting with clients from out of town and she had to help him prepare.

She was consumed by—who else?—Peter Wells. Last night, she'd barely slept, imagining that he'd killed Andy and his parents and that he would try to kill her next. At around midnight, she'd left a panicked message for Himoto, telling him that she might have some important information about a friend of hers and to call her back as soon as he could. So far she hadn't heard from him, and that was fine with her. He was a cop after all. If he didn't think it was worth following up on, it probably meant that he had better leads, or that he'd even solved the case. Hopefully, it would turn out she'd been exaggerating, scaring the hell out of herself for no reason. Peter was probably just an eccentric guy, not a killer, and meanwhile she was driving herself crazy. Bottom line, it was out of her hands now and she just wanted to forget the whole thing.

Shortly before noon, Mitchell came by her desk while he was on the way out to his meeting.

"Hey, just wanted to thank you for getting everything together for me today," he said. "I really appreciate it."

Wondering what was going on—why was Mitchell acting so nice?—Katie said, "It was no big deal."

"So how're you doing?" he said in a hushed, oddly concerned tone. "You okay?"

"Fine," she said cautiously. "I mean, I didn't sleep much, but . . ."

"Any news about the murder?"

At first Katie was lost, then it registered, and she said, "Oh, no. Not as of yesterday anyway."

"I can't imagine what this has been like for you," he said. "I mean, to have something like this happen. I've been fortunate"—he knocked on the desk—"I've had very little tragedy in my life. What I mean is, I've never lost someone I was very close to, who I cared about, especially not violently."

He seemed to have genuine concern for her, but she still didn't trust him.

"I wasn't going out with him for very long," she said. "I mean, not that it's been easy, because it definitely hasn't. But it's not like I lost my husband, or fiancé, or even a long-term boyfriend, you know? But thank you for saying that."

"Don't mention it." He looked at his watch, then said, "Shoot, I wish I didn't have to run; I would've loved to talk longer. I should be back at, what, around four thirty? If you want to pop into my office to talk or whatever, you can. I mean, I guess it would help you to talk about it, right?"

"That's really nice of you," Katie said.

"Or, wait, I have a better idea. What're you doing after work today?"

Katie hoped he wasn't getting at what she thought he was getting at.

"What do you mean?" she asked suspiciously.

"I was just thinking," he said, "maybe we could go out for a drink or, hell, even dinner. Nothing too fancy. Just someplace we could talk. I mean, I know you'd probably like to talk, just to get those feelings out there, and I'm a good listener. That's what people always say about me anyway."

He smiled widely, leaning over the desk to get closer to her. God, he was such a creep.

"Sorry, can't make it," she said, trying to restrain herself from saying, *You're such a fucking asshole.* "I have other plans."

"Well, that sucks," he said. "How about another night? I know I'm open Thursday and Friday nights this week."

"You know, I think I'm pretty booked up this week, but I'll let you know."

"Yeah, you do that. Would be great to have a little one-on-one time, just so you could, you know, get some things off your chest. I'm really looking forward to it."

One more wide, blinding smile, and then he was gone.

"Yuck," Katie whispered, feeling like she needed a shower.

Rather than going out to lunch like she usually did, Katie ordered in a Greek salad and spent her lunch hour online, job hunting. She just couldn't stomach working for Mitchell, that creep, any longer. She didn't care how quitting looked to prospective employers; her mental health was more important.

Some of the job descriptions she came across seemed promising. Over the next several days, she planned to fine-tune her résumé and then she'd start meeting with employment agencies. Her goal was to have a new job within a month.

Having—at least in her mind—settled her immediate employment future, everything suddenly seemed more manageable, including the Peter situation. If Himoto called back, she'd tell him what she knew and let him handle it. If he didn't call back, she'd do nothing.

It was always great not having Mitchell around. She spent her time fiddling with her résumé and exchanging e-mails with a few friends. Then, around two o'clock, Peter called, probably from an unlisted number, because the caller ID had flashed BLOCKED CALL.

At first, Katie panicked when she heard his voice, but when he started saying crazy things like he was in love with her, and wanted to be with her, she realized she was being ridiculous. He was just some lonely, pathetic loser who thought he could charm women and sweep them off their feet. She told him firmly that she wanted him to stop calling her and she was confident that he got the message.

After she hung up, she felt a little guilty for being so harsh with him, but she knew she'd done the right thing. She barely thought about him, until five o'clock, when she was leaving the building. She hesitated after exiting through the revolving doors, and took a close look around. Then, feeling ridiculous again for being so paranoid, she walked with the flow of people toward the subway.

On the way home, she decided to stop at Ichi RO on Second and Eighty-eighth for dinner. Normally, she was self-conscious about eating out alone, convinced everyone was staring at her, but this time she didn't feel at all awkward, saying to the waitress, "Table for one, please."

She felt good, healthy. What was that saying? You had to be comfortable with yourself before you could be comfortable with someone else? Well, that was going to be her new motto.

While she was midway through her spicy maki combo, her mother called.

"Hi, Mom."

"Where are you?"

"At sushi."

"Oh, sorry to disturb you. Are you with a friend?"

"No, I'm alone."

"Alone?" Her mother sounded all judgmental.

"Yep," Katie said confidently.

"Why didn't you go with a friend?"

"Mom, stop it. This is New York. It's no big deal here."

"I forgot, you're a big city girl now. So how're you doing?"

"Okay."

"Yeah? Did the police make any arrests yet?"

"Not yet . . . I mean, I didn't hear anything."

"Well, as long as you're okay. I worry about you."

"There's nothing to worry about, Mom. I'm fine."

"So what else is new? Have you been going to work?"

Usually she didn't like to reveal a lot of personal details about her life to her mother, knowing it would lead to a lot of prying and questioning. But she felt like telling her about Peter, just to see if she knew more about him and his past.

"Yeah, I've been going to work, but something strange is happening actually. Well, not really strange but . . . You remember Peter Wells?"

"Peter Wells, hmm. Why does that name sound familiar?"

"He was friends with Heather? . . . In high school?"

Silence for a few seconds then, "Oh, I remember Peter Wells. Very weird boy."

That word again—*weird*.

"Why do you say that?"

"Well, he was stalking Heather."

Katie started coughing. The hacking got worse as some wasabi burned the back of her throat.

"Are you okay?" her mother asked.

Katie sipped her water, then said, "Fine, wait," and coughed again. Then she said hoarsely, "What do you mean, stalking her?"

"You're too young to remember. You were how old, twelve? He was friends with her and then he wanted to be her boyfriend, but she wasn't interested. He kept following her around school and town, that kind of thing. If I'm remembering right, Dad even talked to his father about it."

"He did?"

"It was upsetting Heather. Anyway, Dad told his father that he wanted Peter to stay away from Heather and that was the end of it. Why? What about him?"

Still surprised by this revelation, Katie said, "Oh, I, um, I met him in New York."

"You met him? Where?"

Her mother suddenly sounded very concerned. Katie was embarrassed to admit she'd gotten so involved with Peter, that she'd actually gone on dates with him. She also knew that if she told her Mom that she thought Peter had been stalking her, and had bought her the apartment and the ring and gone overboard in so many ways, her parents would get all overprotective and insist on coming to the city and make a whole big production out of it.

So, deciding to downplay it, Katie said, "Oh, it's no big deal. He was just working at the health club where I work out. But he's not even working there anymore."

"Stay away from him, Katie."

"I just told you, he doesn't even work there anymore."

"You were talking to him?"

"Of course I was talking to him. I mean, just hello, how've you been, that kind of stuff. Don't worry."

"Good. Just stay away from him. I'm telling you, that boy's trouble."

Katie told her mother she wanted to finish her dinner and would call her later. She was relieved to get off the phone, but she'd lost her appetite. She managed a few more bites, then asked for the check.

On her way home, she called Himoto—just to make sure he'd gotten her previous message—but again she got his voice mail. This time she left a more detailed message, telling him that if he hadn't solved Andy's murder yet, there was a guy named Peter Wells she thought he should talk to.

A few minutes later, walking down her block toward her building, Katie felt uncomfortable, looking around a lot for Peter. Then she opened the outer door to her building and entered the vestibule, and full-blown panic set in when she saw the note with KATIE handwritten on it, wedged against the pane of glass of the inner door. She had no idea what Peter's handwriting looked like, but she was convinced he'd left the note. She wasn't sure what she should do. Should she open it? Or if it turned out that Peter was somehow involved in Andy's murder, would the note be evidence? Would she be better off calling the police and not touching it?

She stood there for a minute or so, thinking. Finally, she decided that the police would think she was insane if she called up about a note on her door.

She opened the folded piece of paper slowly, her hands trembling.

Hi Katie,

Sorry for the note. I really need to talk to you. Can you give me a call when you get this?
Thanks so much,
Will (Andy's roommate)
555-476-7284

It was a huge relief to see that the note was from anyone but Peter. She smiled and muttered, "Thank God."

In her apartment, she sat on the couch and dialed Will's number. She was still frazzled, trying to recover, when he picked up and said, "Hey, you got my note, huh?"

"Yeah, just now. What's up?"

"Sorry for that. I didn't have your number and you weren't listed."

"That's okay. What's going on?"

"That detective came to talk to me again and I, um, just wanted to talk about some stuff with you. What're you doing right now?"

"Nothing much."

"You want to meet for a drink? Someplace neighborhoody. Maybe Fetch on Third?"

The idea of a drink, of de-stressing, was very appealing.

"Yeah, that sounds cool," she said. "Can you give me, like, a half hour?"

"See you there."

Katie changed into jeans and a sweater, washed up, and put on a new face of makeup. Then, realizing it was getting late, she rushed out of the apartment to go meet Will.

She hadn't asked him what he wanted to meet about because she knew it either had to do with Himoto or Andy. She was looking forward to seeing him, though; it would be good to hang out with someone who had been going through some of the same stuff she'd been going through, who would be able to identify.

When she arrived she didn't see Will and thought he might not have gotten there yet.

"Hey, Katie."

Will was sitting at the bar off to the right. She'd forgotten how good-looking he was. He had nice dark skin, which seemed to be his natural tone, not a tan or tanning cream. The bone structure in his face was striking, and so were his muscular arms and shoulders and sincere greenish eyes that kind of matched the scrubs he was wearing. She wasn't sure of his nationality, but he looked like he had some Greek or Italian in him.

He asked Katie what she was having. She looked at his beer then said, "Gin and tonic. Sorry, I need something stronger."

Will ordered the drink, and then Katie told him how stressful the past few days had been for her and Will said it hadn't exactly been easy for him, either.

"That detective talked to me," Will said.

"Yeah, he said he was going to."

"For a *second* time. It really pissed me off. Not that he came to talk to me again—that's just him doing his job. But his whole attitude. He was acting like I was a suspect or something. I mean, maybe I'm just being paranoid, but that was sure as hell how it seemed."

"I wouldn't stress out about it," Katie said. "I don't think they really suspect you of doing anything. I think it was just because of what happened in your past."

He stared at her intensely, then said, "He *told* you?"

"Yeah. I'm sorry, I—"

"Now *that* really annoys the hell out of me. What's this guy doing, spreading shit everywhere about me, telling the whole fucking city?"

"I'm sure it's not like that."

"Yeah, but that's personal, you know? It's such bullshit. If he talks to people at work about that, at the hospital, I'll fucking kill him. Japanese cocksucker."

The racist comment surprised Katie—it seemed so out of character for him—but she understood why he was so upset.

"You have a right to be angry," she said.

"Damn right I do." His face was pink. "It was bad enough that the son of a bitch practically accused me of—" He realized he was talking too loud, looked around, and said, "That was bad enough. But now, knowing he's badmouthing me. Fuck, I was thinking of calling a lawyer anyway, but now I'm definitely going to."

The bartender brought Katie's gin and tonic. Katie reached toward her purse and Will said, "No, I got this," and paid. Then, after the bartender took the money, Will, seeming calmer, raised his glass and said, "To Andy."

"To Andy," Katie said and took a long sip of her drink.

"You know, the funeral's coming up on Friday," Will said.

"No, I didn't know that."

"Me and a couple of roommates are heading down. You wanna road-trip with us you're welcome to."

Katie liked Will a lot, but driving in a car with a bunch of frat boys to the funeral of a guy who'd date-raped her wasn't exactly appealing.

"Sorry, I wish I could," she said, "but it's been so crazy at work lately."

"That's cool," Will said. "It was hard for me to get the time off at the hospital, but I traded shifts. I'll probably be gone twenty-four hours, in the car ten, and then go right into a twenty-four hour shift when I get back. Welcome to my life."

They sipped their drinks. Katie's must've been strong because she already felt buzzed. They talked about Andy some more, about how sad it was for his family, and then Will asked her about her job. As she explained what she did every day, and how boring it was, and how she still wasn't sure what she wanted to do with her life, he hung on every word she said, asking a lot of questions. Several times she noticed how good-looking he was and hoped she wasn't blushing. She wished she'd met him last month and not Andy. If she had dated him she wouldn't have set him up with Amanda and she wouldn't have gotten involved with Andy or Peter and everything would've been so different.

They finished their drinks and ordered another round. Will went to the bathroom and Katie noticed that he had a really nice butt. When he returned, he smiled and put an arm around her for a few seconds—but not in a way that grossed her out and made her think that he was pawing at her. He was *so* not like Andy.

"I know Andy liked you a lot," he said.

Freaked out for a second because she felt like he was reading her mind, she said, "He did?"

"Yeah, he was always talking about you. He really thought you were great."

"That's nice to hear," Katie said, and it did make her feel a little better about things.

"But I have to admit, I was kind of jealous."

Will seemed to be blushing a little himself, looking down at his beer.

"Jealous?" Katie asked. "What did you have to be jealous of?"

"What do you think? When we went on that double date I couldn't stop looking at you. Couldn't you tell?"

"No. I mean, I know we looked at each other a few times."

"I guess I did a good job of hiding it. Maybe I shouldn't've gone to med school. Maybe I should've been an actor."

Katie laughed. Then she looked at him and he was looking back at her—but not at her, at her lips—and then they were kissing. He was a great kisser. His tongue was gentle and his lips were soft and she didn't want to stop.

But then it hit her what they were doing and she pulled back and said, "Wait, we can't do this."

"Why can't we?"

"What do you mean? Because you're with Amanda."

"What? Not at all. I mean, we had that one night together, but it never, like, progressed."

Katie remembered Amanda had said she hadn't heard from him in a few days, but Katie still thought of them as being together.

"I don't know, I feel weird," Katie said.

"It's not weird at all."

He kissed her again. It felt just as good. Even better.

She pulled away, then said, "I can't do this," and stood up and started putting her coat on.

"You don't have to go," he said.

"Sorry, I just need some time to myself right now," she said. "I mean, after what happened to Andy and other stuff that's been going on."

He reached out, held her hand and said, "We don't have to start anything now. We can take it slow, as slow as you want to. I mean, I didn't invite you out tonight thinking anything would happen with us. That wasn't my intention at all."

Katie was looking away, suddenly distracted. The woman with the short straight hair standing near the door at the front of the bar—Katie was positive she'd seen her before, outside her office building when she was looking around for Peter. Now, when the woman saw Katie noticing her, she looked away immediately.

"Fuck," Katie said.

"What is it?" Will asked.

"That woman over there. I think she's following me."

"What woman?"

Katie looked over and the woman was gone.

"Shit," Katie said. "I definitely saw her. I mean, I *know* I saw her."

"Where did you see her?"

Katie realized Will was still holding her hand, and she yanked hers away.

"Why would she be following me?" Katie said to herself. "What the hell's going on?"

"Maybe you made a mistake," Will said.

"I'm not making a mistake," she said, and she rushed out of the bar. She looked in both directions but didn't see her anywhere.

Will came out and said, "Hey, is everything okay?"

He seemed concerned, as if she were losing it, and maybe she was. She suddenly felt very drunk.

"I can't believe this is happening to me,"

"Just relax," Will said, putting an arm around her. "Everything's going to be okay."

She moved away and said, "Stop touching me," then, thinking that probably sounded too harsh, said, "I really just have to go home now. Thanks for the drink."

She left, hoping Will didn't come after her, offering to walk her home. He didn't.

Heading down the side street, she kept looking around to see if the woman was following her. She was beginning to wonder if she hadn't seen the woman in front of her building, if she was just having a big freak-out attack over nothing.

No, she was positive she'd seen the woman earlier. She'd been right there near the entrance to her office building. For all Katie knew, the woman had murdered Andy. Maybe she was some crazy, jealous ex-girlfriend.

Katie called Himoto again, expecting to have to leave another message, but this time he picked up.

"I'm sorry I didn't get back to you right away," he said.

"I need to talk to you," Katie said.

"Yeah, listen, the reason I—"

"There's some stuff I didn't tell you that I have to tell you. There's this guy, Peter Wells, I met at the health club where I work out, and he probably doesn't have anything to do with anything, but I still think you should check him out because he's been getting very obsessed, and now I think there's a woman following me."

"Can you slow down?"

Katie was aware that she'd been talking very fast, but she couldn't stop herself.

"I'm really nervous right now," she said. "I'm positive this woman is following me. I saw her outside my office and then she was in this bar I was just at. And I think this guy Peter is following me, too. Or at least he was following me. I'm telling you, he got very obsessive and—"

"Okay, relax," Himoto said. "You really need to calm down."

"I can't calm down."

"You have to."

Katie stopped walking. She was at the corner of Ninety-second and Second.

"Now, look," Himoto said. "I was starting to tell you, I was taken off the case."

"*What?*" This seemed like horrible news to Katie, like yet another part of her life was falling apart.

"Calm down, okay? There's a new lead detective on the case, his name's Nick Barasco. I already told him about you and that you called. I'm actually surprised he didn't get in touch with you already. It sounds like he should definitely look into whatever you're talking about. Did this guy you mention . . . Peter Wells was it?"

"Yeah."

"Did he know Andrew Barnett?"

"No. I mean, I don't think so but—"

"Does he happen to have dark hair?"

"No. His hair's blond."

"Okay, look, this is definitely something we should look into, whatever it is. I'll throw Nick another call and give him your number again. Do you have a pen?"

"What?" She'd heard, but she was still frazzled. "Oh, yeah, I think so."

"Let me give you Nick's number. If you don't hear from him, you can call him yourself. You ready?"

Himoto gave Katie the number and she scribbled it onto the back of an ATM receipt.

"You just take care of yourself," Himoto said. "We'll take care of everything else, okay?"

Safe in her apartment, Katie tried to take Himoto's advice, but it didn't work. Her mind kept churning, inventing worst-case scenarios. In the worst of the worst, she imagined that the woman would be waiting for her when she left for work in the morning; the woman would have a gun and shoot her in the head. And when she wasn't thinking about ways she would end up dead, she was feeling guilty as hell for kissing a guy Amanda was into. She hoped Will wouldn't go and tell her. She didn't see why he would, but guys were such dicks, nothing was beneath them. She wished she hadn't gone out to meet him. He seemed like a nice guy, but he was probably a scammer, just like Andy. Wearing his scrubs, feeding her that crap, *I didn't invite you out here thinking anything would happen.* Yeah, right. He didn't ask her out to talk—he asked her out because he was horny and wanted to get his rocks off. What a prick.

And what was the deal with that new detective, Nick What's His Face? Why the hell wasn't he calling her? She'd been dating the victim after all.

Sick of waiting, Katie called and got his voice mail. She left a message, telling him to call her back right away, that it was fucking urgent, and that she would have her phone on and in bed with her all night.

28

"Holy shit, I know that guy," Peter said.

He was at Hillary Morgan's apartment, sitting next to her at the desk at her home office, viewing a slide show of digital images on the LCD monitor. The photos showed Katie sitting at a bar next to a guy in doctor's scrubs. In some of the shots Katie was smiling; in others she had a more serious expression. The one that got to Peter most, though, the one that made him sick with rage, was the one where they were kissing.

"Who is he?" Hillary asked.

"I don't know-him know him. I mean, I've seen him."

"Where?"

It was when he'd followed Katie and Frat Boy on that double date. He was the other Frat Boy who'd been out with the other girl.

But realizing there was no point in giving Hillary too much information, he said, "I just saw them together once, I think. At a party or something."

"I'm really sorry," she said. "It's always difficult to find out a loved one has been unfaithful."

Peter hated the way she was trying to soothe him, like she thought he needed a mommy to tell him everything would be okay.

"Did they leave together?" he asked.

"I'm not sure," she said.

The slide show was repeating, showing the worst picture of all—Katie with her tongue halfway down Scrub Boy's throat.

"Why not?" Peter asked. "I mean, you were there, weren't you?"

"There's something else you should know."

Hillary had an ominous tone, but Peter still couldn't shift his gaze away from the slide show.

"I was using a concealed camera," Hillary went on. "She had no idea I was taking the pictures, and neither did the guy she was with, but . . . but she saw me."

Now Peter looked at Hillary and said, "What did she do?"

"I don't know. I got out of there quickly—hopped in a cab. There was no confrontation or anything like that."

"So she saw you. You were just some woman in the bar. What difference does that make?"

"No, she looked at me in a knowing-type way, like she recognized me. I think she must've seen me earlier in front of her office building."

"Whatever," Peter said. "I guess your job's done anyway. Do me a favor—delete all the picture files you have—the original images on your camera and anyplace else you might have stored them."

"Don't you want copies?"

"No." He was nearly yelling. Calmer, he said, "I don't want any copies. I want these pictures to be gone forever. I don't want them stored on your hard drive, and I don't want them on CDs or thumb drives. I want them erased, wiped out forever. Do you understand what I'm saying?"

"Yes."

He wasn't sure, but he thought she seemed frightened. He was probably just imagining it.

"You didn't print out any copies of the pictures?" he asked.

"No," she said.

"Good."

He paid her what he owed and left the apartment. In the cab, going across town, Peter was preoccupied, thinking about Scrub Boy, about what a user, what a total opportunistic pig he was. His friend who'd been dating Katie had been killed and what did he do? Within a week, he ditched his own girlfriend and swooped in and made the moves on Katie. Scrub Boy was even lower and more repulsive than Frat Boy.

When the cab let Peter out in front of his brownstone, he noticed the cops right away. They were standing on the sidewalk and both had slicked-back hair and were wearing dark suits and were chewing on gum. Even in plainclothes their whole cocky attitude screamed: We're cops! But Peter wasn't at all concerned. He knew they had nothing on him.

As Peter approached, the older one came over to him and said, "Peter Wells?"

"Yep," Peter said, trying to sound as confused as anyone would feel when a stranger approaches him on the street and knows his name.

The man flashed a badge, then said, "Detective Nick Barasco, Homicide. Mind if we have a word with you?"

Jesus, this guy was so into himself, he reeked of it, and his partner seemed the same way. They were so fake, so see-through. But Peter knew exactly how to talk to shallow, egomaniacal guys like these. It was time for some good ol' male bonding.

"Yeah," Peter said, "what's it about?"

"We just spoke to an acquaintance of yours named Katie Porter. She told us where you live."

"Is Katie okay?" Man, he was good. Oscar caliber.

"Yeah, she's fine. You know of course that the guy she was dating was killed last week."

"I know. It's terrible."

"She said you guys went out a couple of times."

"Yeah, it's true, we've been dating."

Suddenly very serious, as if he'd hit on something, Barasco said, "According to her, you're not boyfriend and girlfriend."

"We weren't . . . I mean, aren't. We went on a couple of dates, yeah, but . . . I mean, you guys saw her, right? Can you blame me?"

The detectives looked at each other, smiling. They were three dudes hanging out, shooting the shit in a locker room. They might as well have been slapping each other's asses.

"Yeah, she is a pretty good-looking girl," the younger guy said.

"I rest my case," Peter said. "By the way, what's your name?"

"Sorry. Tony Martinelli."

"Nice to meet you, bro."

The "bro" was perfect.

"Katie said you were getting pretty serious about her," Barasco said, all businesslike, as if trying to keep the conversation focused. "She said you bought an apartment for the two of you to live in."

Peter smiled in a purposefully cocky way, then said, "I just told her, to try to impress her, you know what I mean? Of course, I didn't buy the apartment for the two of us. You think I'm crazy or something?" He laughed. "But she wasn't the first girl I fed that line to and she won't be the last."

Martinelli smiled, appreciating Peter's strategy for luring in women, maybe thinking that he'd have to remember to use the buying-an-apartment line himself sometime.

"She also said you proposed to her," Barasco said.

"Her and many," Peter said. "Her and many."

The cops laughed. Peter was scoring major points now.

Then, suddenly getting serious again, Barasco said, "Can I ask you where you were the night Andrew Barnett was killed?"

Peter knew it would come off poorly if the day was too fresh in his mind so he said, "When was that again?"

"Last Thursday evening. But you can start with where you were in the afternoon."

Peter waited a few more seconds, then said, "Yeah, I remember now, because Katie called me the next day and I went over to be with her. I walked home from work in the afternoon—I was working at a health club uptown—"

"The Metro Sports Club," Barasco said.

"That's right," Peter said. "I hung out in the park for a while, then I think I grabbed a Subway for dinner. No, it was a slice of pizza, that's right, and then I got to my hotel room at around seven o'clock and stayed there the rest of the night."

"Your hotel room?" Barasco asked.

"Yeah, I was staying at the Ramada on Lex. Renovations on my apartment weren't complete yet."

"Looks like a nice place you got there," Barasco said, looking at the building.

"Yeah, it's really nice," Peter said.

"So about the health club. Katie said you started working there just so you could meet her?"

"No," Peter said, as if he thought this was ridiculous. "I never said that."

"She said you did."

"Hmm, there must be some misunderstanding or something. I worked there, thinking I'd become a fitness trainer. I ran into her by accident. But, no, I didn't start working there just so I could meet her. I mean, I like her, but I don't like her that much."

Martinelli smiled, locker room style.

"But you don't work there any longer," Barasco said. "Is that right?"

"Yeah, I quit just the other day. I decided it wasn't for me."

"We understand you're independently wealthy."

"Wealthy's stretching it, but I'm doing okay."

"Can I ask where your money came from?"

"My parents were killed when I was twenty-two. I collected an insurance policy."

"I'm sorry to hear that. How'd it happen?"

"There was a fire at my house upstate."

"Jesus. So that must've been quite a policy to buy this place. I mean, the way the real estate market is now, this place must've cost you a pretty penny."

"The insurance policy was pretty significant, and I made some good investments, in the stock market, real estate, stuff like that."

"Man, I should get you to manage my money," Barasco said. "The funds I invest in just seem to go right down the fuckin' toilet."

"Tell me about it," Martinelli said.

"But there's one thing I don't get," Barasco said to Peter. "If you've got all this money, why'd you have to work at a health club?"

"Because I'm a moron?" Peter stayed deadpan for a couple of seconds for comic effect, then grinned. "No, seriously, I'm not exactly rolling in dough. This place did cost me a lot and there are a lot of expenses for renovating, decorating, et cetera. But I worked at the health club because I thought I wanted to become a personal trainer. It's always been a dream of mine, but now I'm not exactly sure what I'm gonna do careerwise . . . Is this gonna go on much longer? Sorry, but I really have to go in and use the john."

Barasco and Martinelli looked at each other, then Barasco said, "That should do for now. Oh, one last thing—did anybody happen to see you at the Ramada the other night? Somebody who could vouch for your story?"

"I don't get it," Peter said. "You don't believe me?"

"Don't worry, it's routine," Barasco said. "We're asking everybody the same questions."

Peter squinted and wrinkled his forehead, as if thinking deeply, then said, "There's this guy Hector at the desk. He was working that night, I think. He might remember seeing me."

"Great," Barasco said. "We'll be back in touch."

A couple of minutes later, in his apartment, Peter couldn't resist laughing out loud. Were the cops a bunch of total morons or what? It was obvious to Peter that the detectives weren't taking him seriously as a suspect; otherwise there was no way in hell they would have let him off the hook so easily. The only reason they'd questioned him at all was because he had started dating Katie. They were probably talking to every acquaintance of Katie's and Frat Boy's, fishing for straws. By now it figured that they'd also gotten a description from somebody at that bar that night of the "guy with dark hair and a goatee" who was talking to Frat Boy. Since Peter didn't fit that description there was no reason for the cops to investigate him too deeply.

When they went to the Ramada Inn, Hector, in all likelihood, wouldn't remember exactly what time Peter returned to the hotel that night, but he would give the detectives a rave review of Peter's character. He'd tell them that Peter Wells was a great guy, that there was no way that he would ever hurt anybody. Yeah, the cops were going to get nowhere fast all right.

Then Peter realized that he could be losing valuable time. After peeking out the window and making sure that the detectives were nowhere in sight, he put on his Yankees cap and a pair of sunglasses and grabbed a pair of latex gloves. Moments later, he was outside, heading toward the subway.

When he arrived at the Ninety-sixth Street station, he bought a copy of the *New York Post* at the kiosk, and then headed toward the building where he had seen Frat Boy and Scrub Boy return to after their double date.

There was a bench alongside the apartment building on Ninety-fifth and Third. He looked around carefully, didn't spot any security cameras, so he sat, with the open *Post* on his lap, watching the light flow of people walking to and from the building. He hoped that since Frat Boy had used this entrance, Scrub Boy used it as well. If he was wrong and Scrub Boy used a different entrance, like maybe one around the corner on Ninety-sixth Street, then Peter would be screwed.

Peter wished he had another option, but he knew he had no choice but to wait. The only other way he could find Scrub Boy would be to follow Katie around until she met him again. But he knew it would be too risky to be near Katie, even in a disguise. They were at a delicate stage in their relationship. He needed to win her back, not scare her off. Besides, what good would it do to find Scrub Boy when he was with Katie? He needed to get him someplace alone, someplace where he could kill him with no chance of getting caught.

He waited the rest of the morning and into the afternoon. He was watching for Scrub Boy, but he was also looking out for any cops, especially Barasco or Martinelli. It was possible that they could stop at the building to interview Scrub Boy, or one of his roommates—Katie had mentioned that Frat Boy had lived with several guys—and Peter knew it would be very difficult to explain why he was hanging out in front of the building.

The rest of the afternoon, Peter peered through the sunglasses, occasionally flipping pages of the newspaper, watching every person who passed by. It was exhausting work, but he knew he couldn't let up. Occasionally, he stood to stretch, but otherwise he didn't leave his position.

After six o'clock, people—mostly anal-retentive-looking twenty-somethings—started returning from work in droves. Peter hoped that Scrub Boy had a normal work schedule and would be among them. Maybe Peter wouldn't have an opportunity to get rid of him today, but at least it would help him plan for next time.

Peter was so focused on the people heading toward the building that he almost missed Scrub Boy walking in the other direction. He saw him from the back, as he was waiting to cross Third Avenue. He was wearing scrubs, of course, and looked as disgustingly arrogant as he had on the double date and in the pictures Hillary Morgan had taken.

Casually, Peter got up and went to the south side of East Ninety-fifth Street, and then waited to cross the avenue at the opposite corner. He was going to follow Scrub Boy wherever he went, but he knew he couldn't follow directly behind him and be seen by some building's security camera. He wasn't an idiot after all.

The light changed and they crossed Third Avenue, Peter slowing to let Scrub Boy get about ten yards ahead of him. As they approached Lexington, Peter hesitated again, in case Scrub Boy crossed in his direction, but instead he made a right and headed toward the subway at Ninety-sixth Street. Peter crossed to the opposite side of Lexington and continued to follow. He assumed that Scrub Boy was planning to take the train downtown. Peter didn't like that—too many people riding the trains at this time of day, too hard to kill somebody. Besides, in a subway station there could be cameras anywhere. Peter thought, *Don't go to the subway, don't go to the subway, don't go to the subway,* and, sure enough, Scrub Boy passed the subway entrance and crossed Ninety-sixth Street, continuing uptown toward Spanish Harlem.

At Ninety-seventh Street, Scrub Boy crossed Lexington and continued west. Peter continued to follow him on the opposite side of the street. It was a fairly quiet block, not too many people around. There were no stores or large apartment complexes and Peter looked around carefully, but didn't notice any security cameras. If it wasn't still light outside, he might've been able to do it right there.

They crossed Park Avenue and turned north onto Madison and then Peter saw Mount Sinai Hospital, the large buildings occupying several blocks, and realized that was where Scrub Boy was headed. He also knew that he probably wouldn't have a chance to get rid of the skinny-necked fucker today. He couldn't help feeling a letdown, the way you might psych yourself up about going out to some great party only to find out that the party's been canceled.

Scrub Boy crossed to the west side of Madison and continued uptown, alongside the hospital. Peter followed on the east side of the street. Near one of the entrances, the asshole spotted someone he knew, another guy his age in scrubs, and they shook hands and stopped to talk. Peter stopped as well.

Scrub Boy and the other doctor had a short conversation, smiling, then they parted and Scrub Boy continued uptown. At around One Hundredth Street, he entered the building through a large revolving door. Peter watched from across the street, trying to decide what to do next.

He knew that following Scrub Boy into the hospital was out. Too many security cameras, too many people around. But that didn't mean he couldn't stick around, to see if an opportunity came up to do it somewhere else. It seemed unlikely, but he had nothing to lose.

Peter knew that people were creatures of habit; they stuck to routines. Maybe the predictability gave them comfort or something. Katie, for example, always took the same route to work every day. On their date in the park, she'd even told Peter that sometimes she felt like "such a rat." Peter had seen the same ratlike qualities in other people. Stuff like that had always fascinated him. If he'd gone to college he probably would've majored in psychology, studied human behavior. Not to become a psychologist—he had no interest in helping people—but to learn as much as he could about other people's habits. While the hospital probably had many exits and Scrub Boy could take any one of them, Peter hoped that he was a rat and would exit the building the way he'd gone in. If he did, he'd probably retrace his steps home. Peter would have to be careful on the major streets, but he was confident that on Ninety-seventh Street, between Park and Madison, there were no security cameras and he could strangle Scrub Boy without being seen.

Peter knew he was taking a big risk. Doctors sometimes worked twenty-four-hour shifts, or longer, so, for all he knew, he would have to wait until tomorrow night to have a chance to kill the bastard. And if the guy didn't stick to a routine, exited the hospital some other way, all the waiting could be pointless.

It didn't help that Peter already had to take a leak. The street was too busy to go between parked cars, and the last thing he needed was a cop noticing, or someone seeing him peeing and reporting it to a cop. But there was no way he was going to leave the area now. He didn't care if he had to hold it in all night and all of tomorrow; hell, even getting a bladder infection or some minor kidney damage would be better than missing this chance.

Peter stood near a bus stop, holding the open *Post*, pretending to read it, but he was really watching the revolving doors. Casually, he inspected the area and was confident that there were no security cameras in the vicinity. He didn't want anyone to notice him loitering in one spot, so he alternated—strolling half a block in one direction, then back in the other—while continually, casually, looking out for Scrub Boy.

As it got dark, pedestrian traffic lessened. This was great because there was much less chance of being noticed and he was able to spend most of his time directly opposite the hospital entrance. He was thinking, *Scrub Boy appear, Scrub Boy appear, Scrub Boy appear,* but it didn't work this time.

The hours went by. Peter's feet ached, he was starving, and he had to piss like hell, but the idea of giving up didn't even occur to him. Then, at around ten o'clock, it started getting windy and Peter remembered that the weather forecast had been for rain, heavy at times, tonight into tomorrow morning. At around eleven, the storm arrived. It was raw, nasty, windswept rain, and Peter quickly became soaked. The rain had a couple of major upsides, though. Figuring he was wet anyway, so what difference did it make, he peed his pants. It was a huge relief. Also, by tilting his head back and sticking out his tongue he was able to drink enough water to quench his thirst. Now he was confident he could easily last another twenty-four hours or longer if he had to.

He didn't have to.

At about eleven thirty, Scrub Boy left the building. He headed downtown along the west side of Madison Avenue, holding an umbrella against the wind and rain. Peter followed along the other side of the street. As they approached the corner of East Ninety-eighth Street, Peter slowed, expecting Scrub Boy to cross at the same corner he'd crossed at earlier. He did, just like a rat in a maze going after a piece of cheese. As Scrub Boy crossed to his side of the street, Peter crossed to the other side to avoid any stores with security cameras. At the next corner, Ninety-seventh Street, Peter expected the asshole to turn left, and turn left he did. Peter crossed the street and followed him, again sticking to the opposite side of the street.

Between Madison and Park, the street was empty—probably even emptier than usual, thanks to the rain—but there were many tenements and Peter felt it would be best not to strike until Scrub Boy reached the other side of Park Avenue, a darker block where there were fewer residences.

But when they reached Park Peter thought he might've blown his best opportunity. The pedestrian-crossing light on Park was red. Rather than waiting, Scrub Boy started to turn right and Peter feared he would go to the much busier Ninety-sixth Street, and the chance to kill him would be gone. But before he took two steps, Peter thought *Rat, turn back, Rat, turn back*— in his desperation, he almost said it out loud—and, like magic, Scrub Boy decided not to head to Ninety-sixth, and instead turned back and jaywalked across the avenue. Remaining on the other side of the street, Peter followed.

As Scrub Boy headed toward Lex, Peter knew it was nearing time to strike. Confident from his earlier observation that there were no security cameras in this area, Peter crossed to the south side of Ninety-seventh Street and followed about twenty yards directly behind him. The spattering of rain against the pavement was loud enough so that he didn't notice Peter. And if he did happen to turn around, what would he see? A very normal, non-threatening guy, walking home in the rain. He would have no reason at all to be alarmed.

Midway along the block, Peter increased his pace, while staying light on his feet, making as little noise as possible. He was gaining ground fast now, the distance between his hands and Scrub Boy's neck decreasing with his every stride. As Peter put on the latex gloves, he imagined that Scrub Boy was thinking about Katie, about how he couldn't wait to see her again. He was probably planning to call her when he got home, see if he could arrange a late-night booty call. Maybe he was hoping she was lonely, vulnerable because of what had happened to Frat Boy, and that he could use that to his advantage. Not because he liked her or wanted to get to know her better or even because he thought she was particularly pretty. No, the last thing he cared about was her, or about her feelings. He wasn't even thinking about making love to her. No, love had no meaning at all to that prick. He didn't want to love her, he wanted to fuck her, jam his dick into her as far as he could, pound against her body so hard that it would make her wail in pain. All guys like him were the same; they didn't know the first thing about love. It was all about hate, about pain. Guys like him didn't deserve to live. What was one less dick bag in the world anyway?

Peter was several feet away from Scrub Boy when he noticed the group of kids up ahead near Lexington. There seemed to be about five or six of them, but they were far away and seemed distracted, talking amongst themselves. If Peter had time to process the threat of the kids on the corner, he probably would have decided against attacking Scrub Boy right then. He would've waited for another chance, even for another day. But it was too late to reconsider. He was beyond the point of no return, lunging forward, grabbing the skinny fuck's neck.

He was glad that it was a thin neck, thinner than Frat Boy's, and easier to get his hands around. Still, the wetness from the rain made it difficult to get a firm grip, and as the rat reacted instinctively, dropping the umbrella, trying to pry his attacker's hands away, Peter was afraid he would scream and that the kids on the corner or maybe someone else, in one of the nearby apartment buildings or tenements, would hear something and call the cops. To prevent this, Peter let go of Scrub Boy's neck altogether and then, moving quickly, wrapped his arms around his midsection, tackled him to the ground like a linebacker taking down a running back, and rolled together with him off the curb into a space between two parked cars. Scrub Boy managed to scream a couple of times, but even if someone heard it wouldn't matter. They were out of view now, between the cars, and, besides, what was a little screaming in New York City? In New York, screaming was normal background noise, as normal as honking horns and car alarms.

But Peter knew he had to move ultrafast now. Maybe a couple of screams would go unnoticed, but if the screaming was loud and persistent enough, someone could become alarmed. Peter managed to get his hands around Scrub Boy's neck, but the son of a bitch was a fighter. He kept wriggling and twisting and fighting and managed to break away from Peter's grip long enough to scream, "Help me! Help!"

Peter couldn't risk any more of this. The screaming was hoarse and probably wasn't carrying very far, but if Scrub Boy was able to belt out a few more "helps" the kids at the corner or someone else might hear. There was no way in hell Peter was going to let that happen. The big thing Peter had in his favor was that he was much stronger than Scrub Boy. They were probably a similar size and weight, but in muscle mass there was no comparison. The fucker was grabbing Peter's forearms, trying to free himself, but Peter was able to overpower him. But then, instead of trying to strangle him, Peter grabbed his head and started banging it against the gutter again and again. It made a surprisingly hollow sound, reminding Peter of the time in Mexico that he tried to open a coconut by cracking it against a rock. It shut the rat up, though; that was the important thing. It was also a much easier way to kill someone this way than strangulation. Within thirty seconds Scrub Boy's eyes closed as he lost consciousness, and after another thirty seconds he seemed to be dead. Just to make sure, Peter banged the head for another minute or so.

It was an efficient way to kill somebody all right, but it had a couple of minuses. The first was, it was exhausting. Peter considered himself to be in excellent shape and it had still taken a lot out of him. Kneeling over the body like in the woman-on-top sex position, Peter's heart was going the way it did when he used level 20 on the Life Fitness machine at the gym. The other minus was the blood. There was a lot of it—well, enough to create a nuisance. Peter had been aware of it while he was banging Scrub Boy's head and knew some of it might wind up on his clothes. He'd have to be careful about getting rid of any evidence, and make sure not to leave any of it in his apartment. Still, none of the negatives came close to overwhelming the positives—Scrub Boy was dead, the path to Katie's heart was clear once again.

Peter got up slowly, peeked over the car. The kids were gone; no one else was around. As carefully as he could, he took off the gloves and put them in his jeans pocket. He'd have to get rid of all his clothes as a precaution, but there wasn't as much blood on the gloves as he'd feared. In case the kids were around the corner on Lex, Peter walked to Park Avenue at a normal pace, and then headed downtown. He planned to avoid eye contact with anyone he passed in the vicinity, but the sidewalks were empty. Everything was going his way and it felt so good.

29

Katie's roommate, Susan, was spending the night at her boyfriend Tom's and Katie, alone in the apartment, was terrified. She had to check several times to make sure the locks were bolted and that the chain was on. But every noise she heard outside, in the hallway or on the stairs, scared the shit out of her.

Earlier, before she went to work, the two detectives had finally gotten in touch, and she went into work later so she could talk to them at her apartment. She'd told them all she knew about Peter and about the woman who'd been outside her office and at the bar, but this didn't calm her down; actually it had made things worse. She felt like they hadn't taken her seriously, like they thought she was just some ditzy, paranoid country girl in the city, and wasn't it cute that she thought some guy was out to get her? She feared that the detectives would go talk to Peter and then Peter would get so angry at her that he would come over to her place and try to kill her. She was also afraid of that woman from the bar. Maybe she knew Peter, was a crazy friend of his or something. Maybe he'd even killed Andy and was planning to come after Katie next.

Katie tried to distract herself by reading and going on eBay, but she couldn't stop obsessing. She turned on the TV, figuring a movie would help her relax. One of the first movies she flipped to was *Scream 2,* during one of the gruesome murder scenes. She turned quickly to something else, not only because of the mood she was in, but because she just couldn't deal with horror movies. When she was growing up, it was different. She and Heather were horror fanatics. Whenever their parents went out at night, they would turn out all the lights and watch horror movies, scaring the crap out of themselves. Back then, it was fun to get scared; it was exciting. But since Heather died,

Katie hadn't been able to watch movies with excessive violence. Life was disturbing enough.

She watched the Food Network for a while, then *House Hunters* on HGTV—that was more like it. During a commercial, she surfed the movie channels, stopping on *Sense and Sensibility*. She started watching it, then remembered how, that night at the French restaurant, Peter had mentioned that he loved all of the Jane Austen movies, especially some British TV version of *Pride and Prejudice*. She'd told him she'd only seen the one with Keira Knightly, and he went on about how much better the other one was and how they'd have to watch it together sometime.

Suddenly feeling nauseous, Katie turned the channel. Thanks to Peter Wells, she'd never be able to enjoy a fucking Jane Austen movie ever again.

She started watching some of *Wedding Crashers*, figuring laughing would be a good thing for her, when she heard creaking footsteps outside in the hallway. She was convinced it was Peter coming to kill her. He'd somehow managed to get into the building and now was going to break down the door or chop through it with an axe like Jack Nicholson in *The Shining*.

She went to the phone and dialed 911. The operator picked up and Katie screamed, "There's someone breaking into my apartment!"

"Is the person in your apartment right now?" the operator asked.

"No. He's—" Then Katie heard the laughter in the hallway—female laughter. It was her neighbor, what's-her-face with the red hair, talking to a friend. Feeling like a total idiot, Katie said to the operator, "Sorry, I . . . I made a mistake."

"Is there someone in your apartment or not, ma'am?"

"No, there isn't. Sorry."

She hung up quickly.

This was crazy—she had to get a grip. After checking the locks, she returned to the couch. TV wasn't helping. She didn't know how the hell she was going to fall asleep tonight. Though she didn't smoke, she craved a cigarette. She needed to fucking relax somehow. She opened the fridge, found an old bottle of wine in the back. No glasses were clean, so she poured some into a mug. It tasted more like vinegar than merlot, but it calmed her a little bit.

It was starting to rain, the drops splattering hard against the window. Rainy nights were very horror movie–like. The farmhouse in the middle of nowhere, the power cut off, the killer outside . . .

"Stop it!" Katie screamed. "Just fucking stop it!"

She gulped more merlot and reminded herself that she'd done everything she could and that the police would protect her. Besides, this wasn't a farmhouse in the middle of nowhere—this was an apartment building in the middle of Manhattan. She had neighbors a few feet away, right behind the thin walls. Nobody was going to hurt her here.

But she wasn't buying any of this crap. She felt completely alone in the world, more alone than she'd ever felt in her entire life. How had this happened? A couple of weeks ago everything had seemed so great—she was going out with Andy, adjusting to life in the city, and now everything was shit. She had no boyfriend, no close friends. She knew her relationship with Amanda would be ruined forever. How could she ever face her after making out with Will, a guy Amanda was so into? Katie couldn't believe she'd done that. What the hell was wrong with her?

She wanted to be home, in Lenox, in her old bedroom. In her closet there, she still had her old stuffed animals, and she wanted to take out Snoopy and Clifford and curl up with them, the way she did when she was a kid whenever she was sad. She knew if she called her parents and told them what was going on, they'd freak and come to New York immediately to get her.

But Katie didn't want to call home. Her mother would just get on her case, blaming her for getting involved with Peter Wells, and her father would be his usual distant, unsupportive self. Besides, calling her mommy and daddy would just make her feel like a big fat baby.

It was past midnight. Katie knew she had to try to get some sleep or she would be a wreck tomorrow at work. The rain was still coming down hard and there were occasional rumblings of thunder. She dimmed the light, but didn't turn it down completely. She was so anxious, she didn't know how she'd ever fall asleep. She kept thinking about Peter, replaying just about every conversation she'd ever had with him, as if the repetition would reveal some hidden truth. But it didn't do anything except increase her anxiety. One thing that was really stressing her out was what her mother had told her, about how Peter had stalked Heather in high school. Katie was still amazed by how little she remembered from that period of her life, how it all seemed to have taken place in a fog. Maybe she'd blocked it out because the memories of Heather were too painful, the same way she rarely thought about her sister's suicide and the weeks afterward. That had been the darkest period of Katie's life by far. It had been terrifying to see her parents lose control that way, wailing uncontrollably. The whole family met with a grief counselor, but it didn't seem to help. They were beyond grief, unreachable.

Katie cried a lot, too, during that period, but most of the time she was just numb. Now, in bed, Katie shuddered as she let the horrible memories back in. She pictured her sister with an insane, wide-eyed expression, leaping off the roof of the dorm and splattering on the concrete. One thing Katie never understood at the time, and which still baffled her, was what the hell had happened to make Heather want to do that to herself? Yeah, she'd suffered from depression during her freshman year and hadn't been taking her Prozac, but lots of people in the world were depressed and most of them didn't jump off buildings. When Heather was living at home, she'd suffered from typical teenage angst, had a period of anorexia, rebelled during her senior year of high school, and started cutting and hanging out with the druggie crowd. But she never had any major problems, or at least didn't seem to have any. Then when she started at UMass everything seemed normal. She didn't have any serious adjustment issues; why would she have? The UMass campus at Amherst was only about an hour's drive from Lenox, and she frequently came home on weekends. She seemed to have a lot of friends and was doing well in her classes. She'd never been the straight-A type, but she was getting mostly B's and wasn't failing any classes. But somehow, despite all this, she hated herself so much that she decided to end her life.

There had been no doubt that she jumped and wasn't pushed. The police did a full investigation and a witness—a maintenance worker—had seen her go up to the roof alone, and a few students who were up there sunbathing had seen her jump. Her friends had claimed that she'd been very agitated during the week before the suicide and the police speculated that academic pressure might've caused her to jump. But this had never made much sense to Katie. It had been finals week, and every student on campus, especially freshmen who were taking year-end exams for the first time, had been under pressure. Heather had never been the type to freak out about academics. She was laid-back, a vegetarian, listened to the Grateful Dead. She might've been nervous about her exams, but Katie was positive that something like that alone wouldn't make her kill herself.

Katie remembered the police and school counselors suggesting other possible causes for Heather's distress, including that some crisis they weren't aware of had led to a psychotic breakdown. For years, Katie had wondered what that crisis could have been. Heather hadn't been getting along with a roommate, but that didn't seem like a big enough deal. A guy she knew had died, and she'd been upset about it, but that didn't mean . . .

Katie sat up in bed, afraid she would hyperventilate if she sat still; then she rushed into the living room and started pacing. She had to relax, get a grip.

A guy she knew had died and she'd been upset about it.

This had never seemed significant to Katie before, maybe because she was fourteen when Heather had died, and the idea of "a guy she knew" dying being enough to cause a suicide didn't really add up. But "a guy she knew" was only how her parents had described the relationship to her. What if it had actually been more serious than that? If she'd been so upset about some guy dying, it figured that the guy probably wasn't a casual friend. Parents were so lost about those sorts of things. The guy had probably been someone she'd hooked up with, or even had fallen in love with. Girls in college don't exactly report home to their parents every time they start having sex with a guy—God knows Katie never had.

If the guy who'd died had been a boyfriend of Heather's, that changed things dramatically. Maybe Heather's death had been indisputably a suicide, but what about the guy's? Katie remembered the cause of the guy's death—he'd fallen off the roof of his frat house while drinking during a frat party. The police at the time had even pointed out that Heather may have decided to jump to mimic the way the guy had died, and Katie vaguely remembered the cops stating some psychological mumbo jumbo about how suicide victims often choose their cause of death by mimicking another recent dramatic death, maybe because they're striving for the same type of attention. As a fourteen-year-old Katie had questioned that logic, but now it seemed to hold more weight. Maybe Heather really loved this guy and wanted to die the way he'd died.

But, the catch was, what if the guy hadn't fallen? What if someone had pushed him? Someone like Peter Wells.

Katie continued pacing frantically, wondering, What if Peter couldn't get over Heather when she went away to college? Maybe he started stalking her on campus. If he did, it figured Heather wouldn't want to worry her parents by telling them about it. She might've feared that they'd get overprotective of their freshman daughter and make a big deal about it. She also might've figured that Peter was harmless and that she could handle the situation herself. But this had turned out to be a huge mistake. Peter continued stalking her and then he saw her, hooking up with this other guy. He got insanely jealous and killed him, pushing him off the roof at that frat party. It all seemed to fit. Maybe this was what Peter did—he got obsessed with girls and killed their boyfriends, just like he'd killed Andy.

Katie was going to call 911 again, but stopped herself. She felt out of control, a little crazed. In the state she was in, who would believe her? Those detectives hadn't exactly taken her seriously about Peter being involved in Andy's murder, so why would they care when she told them her new theory about how Peter had killed Heather's boyfriend?

A few minutes went by and Katie was glad she hadn't made the call. Now that she had a little distance she realized how far-fetched the whole thing would have sounded. She had some imagination all right, the way she could always imagine worst-case scenarios so vividly.

She got back into bed. After a while, she managed to fall asleep, but then a noise jolted her awake. She didn't know what time it was, but there was some light outside, coming through her window, and the rain had stopped. She heard the noise again, someone jiggling the front door. Thinking *It has to be Peter,* she locked herself in the bedroom, and then heard the front door opening.

"Who's there?" she shouted.

No answer. Just footsteps, coming closer.

"I said who the fuck's there?"

"Katie?"

Shit, it was Susan.

Katie opened the door and said angrily, "What the hell's wrong with you? Why didn't you answer me when I said who's there?"

"I did. What's wrong with you? Why're you yelling at me?"

"You didn't answer. You just barged in here, scaring the shit out of me."

"I just walked into my own apartment. Why're you acting this way?"

"I thought you were Peter."

"Who?"

Katie was still delirious, confused, her heart beating madly.

"Peter Wells, that guy I grew up with in Massachusetts."

"Why would you think I'm him?"

"This is getting out of control. I have to tell the police. I can at least tell them, right? Let them decide what to do, right?"

"You sure you don't want to get back to sleep?"

Katie went to her room, found the business card Detective Barasco had given her, and got his voice mail. Not surprising, considering it was, what— she looked at her clock—seven thirty in the morning?

She started leaving a message, "Hi, this is Katie Port—" and then hung up, figuring it was stupid to call when there was no way they'd take her seriously. But she needed to tell someone, someone who'd at least listen to her.

She had Detective Himoto's number programmed into her cell. She scrolled to the number and clicked send.

"John Himoto."

She was surprised he'd picked up, especially at this time of day.

"This is Katie Porter."

"Yes, I know that."

"Look, I remembered something else about this guy Peter Wells. Well, I didn't *remember* something, but it's something I think you guys should know—"

"Did those detectives get in touch with you?"

"Yeah, I met with them yesterday—"

"Then you should really be in touch with them now. Did you tell them what you told me the other night?"

"Yeah, but—"

"And?"

"They said they'd look into it, but I don't think they took me seriously."

"Trust me, they took you seriously. If there was anything about that guy . . . Peter?"

"Yeah."

"If there was anything there, they'd take care of it; trust me on that. Did they say they were gonna talk to him?"

"Yes."

"Then it's taken care of."

"But I think he might've killed my sister's boyfriend, too."

Himoto didn't answer right away—Katie heard static. Then he said, "What makes you think that?"

"Because my sister committed suicide in college and Peter was stalking her, too, only I didn't know he was stalking her until the other day when my mother told me he was. Then I got to thinking, last night when I couldn't sleep, about when Heather, that's my sister, killed herself and I remembered that a friend of hers had been killed, he fell off a roof, and she was extremely upset about it. It hit me that the guy wasn't just a friend, he was a boyfriend, and Peter might've killed him, like he killed Andy. I mean, if he killed Andy. Does this make sense? D'you understand what I'm saying?"

Katie was aware of how she'd been talking a mile a minute, probably sounding like a nut.

"Yes, I understand what you're saying, but you shouldn't be telling me about this. You should be telling this to Detective Barasco."

"But he doesn't listen to me. You listen to me. Can't you do something? Just check him out? Do some investigating or something?"

"Miss Porter, this is not my case anymore. I can't be any clearer about that."

"I understand that but—"

"Look, I'm driving into the city now. I can't have this conversation."

"You think I'm crazy, don't you? You think I'm just making up stories?"

"I don't think that at all," Himoto said. "It sounds like this is something you should definitely run by Detective Barasco. Why don't you throw him another call?"

Katie felt defeated, helpless.

"I did. I got his voice mail."

"Leave him a message, he'll get back to you."

"But—"

"Look, I really have to go now. Relax. Everything's going to be okay. This is the NYPD, the greatest police force in the world. You don't have to worry so much, okay?"

Starting to cry, Katie managed, "Okay."

She ended the call, took awhile to get hold of herself. Then she left a message for Barasco. She had no idea what she was supposed to do next. Just sit and wait for him to get around to calling her back? She didn't feel like going in to work today and she didn't see why she had to. Other people in the office called in sick when they had hangovers and PMS. Meanwhile, a guy she'd been dating had been killed and another guy she dated had been stalking her and her sister and might have killed their boyfriends and, oh yeah, set his house on fire and killed his parents. If this didn't entitle her to one goddamn mental health day, what did?

Susan was in the shower. Katie went into the kitchen and made coffee—out of habit, not because she needed the caffeine. She was plenty edgy and wide awake without it.

Katie was on the couch, sipping a cup of Folgers Vanilla, when Susan came out of the bathroom, wrapped in a towel.

"You sure everything's okay?" Susan asked.

"Yeah, fine," Katie lied. "Sorry I freaked like that before."

"I was worried about you."

"You going in to work today?"

Katie was hoping she wasn't.

"Yeah, I just didn't have a change of clothes at Tom's so I wanted to come back home to shower. Why? You're not going?"

"No, I just need a day to unwind, you know?"

"Yeah, you should really do that. Go get a mani-pedi, go shopping. That'll make you feel a lot better."

Katie liked Susan, she was a good person, but her advice in a crisis situation was worthless. Did she really think that getting her toenails polished would solve anything?

But Katie still felt a lot more comfortable with Susan around. When Susan left for work, Katie started to become paranoid again. It wasn't as bad as last night, but she kept checking the locks, imagining every noise she heard was Peter breaking in.

And what was taking Barasco so long? Why couldn't he at least have the decency to get back to her?

At ten o'clock, Katie called him again and got his voice mail. Pissed off, she didn't bother leaving a message. This was ridiculous. She felt like she had important information and no one from the police was even paying attention to her.

She heard drilling downstairs; the maintenance people were probably doing work in that vacant apartment on the second floor. That made Katie feel a little safer, for now anyway. Then she had an idea.

She dressed quickly, putting on some sweats, and then went to the front door. She heard the drilling, as well as some chatter from the workers, and figured they'd hear her if she screamed. *Might as well get it over with,* she decided, and opened the door quickly and went out into the hallway. She seriously expected Peter to be there, to grab her and try to force her into the apartment, but he wasn't. She fumbled with the key, then locked the door and raced downstairs as if the building were on fire.

On Ninety-second Street, in broad daylight, she figured she was safe. He wasn't just going to jump out and kill her anyway. Still, she jogged to the corner, not feeling truly safe until she reached very busy Second Avenue. She was able to hail a cab quickly and told the driver to take her to Sixty-seventh Street, between Third and Lex, the address of the Nineteenth Precinct on the business card Detective Himoto had given her.

When she arrived, she told the woman at reception that she needed to speak to Detective Himoto right away.

"Does he know what this is about?" the woman asked.

"Just tell him Katie Porter's here."

"Have a seat please," the woman said, but Katie couldn't sit. She started pacing.

After several minutes Himoto came out to the waiting area and Katie rushed over to meet him.

"I'm sorry I came here," Katie said, "but I feel like that other guy, Detective Barasco's totally blowing me off and—"

"There's been a new development," Himoto said.

"What development?"

"Come with me."

Katie followed Himoto through the precinct. His expression had been poker-faced, hard to read, but she hoped that "a new development" meant good news. Maybe they had arrested Peter, or there had been some other break. Maybe that woman from the bar had been arrested.

They went into his office and he told her to sit down.

She sat, then said, "So what's the development? Did you arrest somebody?"

"I'm afraid not," Himoto said, sitting in his chair on the opposite side of the desk from her. "I'm afraid there's been another murder."

Katie was confused. Another murder? Someone else had been killed, so they weren't even looking for Andy's killer anymore?

"I don't get it," she said. "How is another murder a development? What does that have to do with Andy?"

"We think it's related to Andy's murder. Actually, we're positive it is."

Still not getting it, Katie said, "I really just need to sit down with somebody, somebody who'll listen to me and let me tell him what's going on. Because that Barasco guy won't even return my calls. Can I just tell you about Peter Wells?"

"I'm trying to explain to you, Katie," Himoto said, talking slowly, in a scolding principal-like way. "Detective Barasco is extremely busy this morning, though I'm sure he'll be in touch with you as soon as possible. This other victim . . . he was one of Andrew Barnett's roommates."

It was starting to hit Katie now. It was hard to get the words out, but she managed, "W-w-wha . . . what . . . what do you mean?"

"It happened last night, on Ninety-seventh Street. He was on his way home from work at Mount Sinai Hospital when he was attacked."

This isn't happening, Katie thought.

"Who w-w-was it?" Katie asked. "W-w-what was his name?"

"William Bahner," Himoto said.

Katie lost it. Himoto tried to console her, but for a while, maybe five or ten minutes, she was a total mess. Gradually, she was able to calm down. Well, calm down enough to get out, "It was him. It had to've been him."

"I take it you knew William Bahner very well," Himoto said.

"He saw us. He must've seen us, right? It's the only thing that makes sense."

Katie wasn't really talking to Himoto. She was talking to no one, thinking out loud.

"Who saw you?"

"But he wasn't there. That woman was there. Maybe the woman did it. Maybe it had nothing to do with him."

"When was the last time you saw William Bahner?"

Now Katie looked at Himoto, as if she'd forgotten he was in the room. "I told you, I was with him the other night, the night that woman saw us at the bar."

"I was unaware you were with William Bahner that night."

"She saw us. The woman saw us, don't you get it? It was her, or maybe she was working with Peter Wells. Maybe she's, like, a friend of his or something."

"Why would he have a friend follow you?"

"Because he's obsessed with me! He was obsessed with my sister, too, and I think he might've killed her boyfriend. I've been trying to tell you guys this, but you won't fucking listen to me."

"I'm listening now, okay? So calm down, okay? You have to try to calm down. Getting hysterical right now won't accomplish anything. Can you calm down? You think you can do that for me?"

"I'm calm," Katie said. "I'm very fucking calm. Now what the fuck're you gonna do?"

"I need you to explain to me, calmly, what happened at the bar the other night."

"I was out with Will and I saw that woman with the short hair, the same one I'd seen outside my office building."

"And you don't think this could've been coincidental."

"I work on Lexington, in the fifties. This was on, like, Ninety-second Street, the same day, like an hour or two later. No, it was not coincidental."

"Okay, so you saw the same woman. So what makes you think she has anything to do with William Bahner's murder?"

"Because she saw us, don't you get it? She saw us together."

"Together?"

Katie realized it wouldn't sound great, admitting she'd made out with Andy's roommate less than a week after Andy had been killed, but she knew she had no choice but to fess up.

"We kissed, all right?" she said. "But it's not what you think, okay? I had a couple of drinks and I was vulnerable or whatever and I kissed him. It was a stupid thing to do, I know, but I did it and the woman saw us. Then, when she saw me noticing her, she ran out of there."

"So you think the woman was so upset that you kissed Bahner that she went ahead and killed him."

"I still can't believe he's dead. I just can't believe it."

"You think jealousy could've been the motive?"

"I have no idea . . . Maybe."

"You think she was an ex-girlfriend of his?"

Katie thought about it, then said, "No."

"How can you be sure?"

"She was older. Like in her thirties."

"Guys like older women."

"No, there's no way. He was facing her at the bar. He would've recognized her."

"Okay, so let's get back to this Peter Wells. What do you think he has to do with this woman?"

"I don't know, okay?" The questioning was getting frustrating. "Maybe she knows him."

"So he has a friend of his follow you, report back that you kissed some guy, and he gets so jealous he goes out and kills him."

"I think Peter's crazy. He doesn't seem that way when you talk to him. I mean, he has a lot of charm and everything, always seems to say the right things. But the things he says and does—when you think about them, they all add up. I mean, he asked me to marry him. He bought a fucking apartment for me. And this is a guy I've known, what, a week? I mean, I knew him before then, but he bought me a goddamn ring. Oh, and he said he got this job at the health club I work out at just so he can meet me. I think he was following me around places, to work and wherever, and then my mom told me he was stalking my sister. When I heard that, I freaked. I remembered that stuff I told you over the phone, about how a guy she knew—probably her boyfriend—died in college, and I wondered if he could've had something to do with it. I mean, our boyfriends, guys we're with, keep getting killed. You can't tell me this is all a fucking coincidence . . . Oh, and then there's the stuff about the fire."

"Fire?" Himoto asked.

Katie reached into her pocketbook and took out the articles she'd printed from the Internet and dropped them on Himoto's desk.

"There was a fire," she said, "at his house near Albany, where he moved with his family. His parents were killed and he cashed in some huge insurance policy. The police up there investigated. They thought it might've been arson."

"But they concluded that it wasn't arson."

"Don't you fucking get it?" Katie said. "It all adds up. I mean, you wanna talk about coincidences? And now Will's dead. You have to do something before he kills me, too."

"Nobody's gonna kill you," Himoto said. "We're gonna look into every aspect of this. No stone will be left unturned."

Sick of Himoto and his goddamn cliché-speak, Katie said, "When exactly will these stones be turned? Barasco hasn't gotten off his ass—he won't even call me."

"I talked to him briefly before you arrived. He's currently talking to William's roommates."

"What about Peter?"

"I'm sure he's going to explore that angle fully as well. He probably has another detective looking into it right now."

"But you have to call him to make—"

"Will you let me finish?" He glared at her then said, "I'm going to impress on Detective Barasco that he should talk to you again as soon as possible. But right now he's talking to Barnett and Bahner's roommates, and if I was in his shoes I'd be focusing on the same thing. Two roommates are dead, four are alive, you talk to the living ones. Maybe there was some dispute we don't know about. Maybe there was something going on with a girl."

"Yeah, me," Katie said.

"Look, I agree with you, that what you're saying about this guy Peter should be a cause for alarm. He sounds like he could be a potentially dangerous guy. But there are other factors in this case you have to be aware of. We have a credible witness who saw Andrew talking with a dark-haired guy at a bar on Second Avenue before he was killed."

"I know. Barasco told me about that yesterday."

"This seems to be the best lead so far because it's likely that Andrew and this guy left the bar together. By the way, is there a chance that Andrew was bisexual?"

"No. I really doubt that. He was really into girls. Too into them."

"Because that's a possibility we have to explore as well. That Andrew went to the park with his killer with the intention of having a sexual encounter. Strangulation is often associated with crimes of passion."

"Was Will strangled?"

"No, he died from severe head injuries."

Imagining the scene, how violent the killing must've been, Katie cringed.

"The other thing you have to remember is I had my suspicions about William Bahner from the beginning," Himoto continued. "Not that he necessarily had any direct involvement in Andrew Barnett's murder, but that he was holding back, not being entirely truthful. Maybe something was going on we don't know about yet. Maybe Bahner knew who killed Barnett, was going to blow the whistle, so this other guy killed Bahner. I could sit here all day making up theories, but we don't know which have credence and which don't until we start checking each one out."

"Did Barasco say anything to you about Peter?" Katie asked impatiently. "Did he even ask him about Andy? Does he know where Peter was the night Andy was killed?"

"I'm sure that was all covered."

"He didn't mention Peter, did he? You don't even know if he talked to him."

"I didn't ask him about that. It's not my case anymore and, frankly, it's up to him who he talks to and who he doesn't talk to."

"So there's a chance he didn't talk to him at all."

"I didn't say—"

"Call him right now."

"I'm not going to do that."

"You want Peter to go ahead and kill somebody else? Maybe even me?"

"I'm not gonna explain this again to you."

"He's gonna kill again. I'm telling you he will."

"You're jumping to a lot of conclusions," Himoto said. "Should we talk to Peter Wells? Yes, absolutely. Will we talk to him? Yes, absolutely. But the fact remains that he doesn't fit the description of the primary suspect. You said he has blond hair, right?"

"Dirty blond."

"The suspect we're looking for from the bar has dark hair and a goatee. So that's where our focus is—"

"What did you just say?"

Katie was suddenly so tense she was actually shaking.

"I said Peter doesn't fit the description of—"

"Peter had a goatee. He shaved it. Oh, my God, he shaved it last week, I think the day after Andy was killed! Yeah, he definitely did, because that was the night I called him to come over. I'd just talked to you and I was scared and he came over and he didn't have his goatee."

"But the suspect has dark hair."

"Maybe they made a mistake. Maybe it was just dark in the bar. Or maybe he dyed his hair or was wearing a wig or something. It's him, don't you get it now? It's him. Every piece fits. It has to be him."

"Are you sure he shaved his goatee last Friday?"

"I'm positive! Oh, my God, it really was him. You're gonna do something now, right? You're not gonna just sit here and let him get away with this."

"We're not gonna let anybody get away with anything," Himoto said.

"You promise you'll talk to him?"

"I guarantee it."

Starting to relax a little, feeling like she'd finally gotten through to him, Katie said, "So what am I supposed to do in the meantime?"

"I'd advise you to try to stay calm, go about your regular routine. You going to work today?"

"I couldn't deal with work."

"So why don't you stay home?"

"I'm too scared to be in that apartment. He knows where I live. I'm afraid he's gonna come over, try to break in."

"If he shows up at your apartment and is attempting forced entry, you keep your door locked and you call nine-one-one."

Katie was shaking her head, starting to cry.

"I'm too scared . . . I'm just too scared . . ."

Himoto let out a heavy breath, looked at his watch. "I'll tell you what I'll do. I'll drive you back to your apartment, okay? Make sure you're okay there. Is there a friend you can call to come over?"

Now that Will was dead, Katie realized she really didn't have a rift with Amanda anymore.

"Maybe," she said.

"Then maybe you should call her. It might be good for you to be with someone today. Meanwhile we'll do our thing here, okay?"

Tears dripping down her cheeks, Katie nodded slowly.

Katie and Himoto left the precinct together and went to his car, which was parked right out in front. Before she got in, she had to wait as he picked up some garbage off the front passenger seat and the floor in front of it and tossed it into the back of the car.

He was playing some oldies station, music from the sixties or something. He did his best to make small talk with her, asking her what she did for a living and how long she'd been living in the city, but she wasn't exactly in a chatty mood. She was distracted, upset, and gave mostly one-word answers.

Then, staring out the window, she remembered something.

"He wasn't surprised," she suddenly said, turning toward Himoto, interrupting whatever he was talking about.

"Who wasn't surprised?" he asked.

"Peter," she said. "At this restaurant we were at, when I told him you didn't have the right guy, that the murder case was still open. He wasn't surprised at all. I didn't think anything of it at the time, but he was, like, totally calm about it. Almost *too* calm, you know?"

The ride only took several minutes. Himoto pulled in front of her building, saw she was hesitant to get out alone, and said, "I'll walk you up."

Katie felt safe with Himoto, but didn't know how she'd handle being alone again.

"Maybe I should have my parents come pick me up later," Katie said, "take me to Massachusetts."

"That might not be a bad idea," Himoto said. "It might be good to get away from the situation for a little while, clear your head, be with your family. But make sure you have your cell with you, just in case we need to be in touch."

Katie opened the door to the apartment. She didn't hear the maintenance people working downstairs anymore.

"This is gonna sound crazy," Katie said. "But can you just come in with me, make sure he's not in here . . . I know it's ridiculous . . ."

"It's not ridiculous," Himoto said.

Katie remained in the living room, as Himoto went around checking every room.

"Coast is clear," he said when he returned.

"Did you check the closets?" Katie asked.

"Checked the closets and looked inside the shower."

"I guess I've seen too many horror movies," Katie said, as if she were making a joke.

At the door, Himoto said, "I promise you, everything's going to be okay."

"I know it will," Katie said, though she couldn't have been telling a bigger lie.

30

Wearing his silk robe, Peter relaxed on the couch, sipping a tall glass of San Pellegrino with a wedge of lime. He wasn't surprised to see that the killing of Scrub Boy was a major story on the TV news. Murdered white people always got a lot of attention from the media, and the fact that the dead guy was a doctor, or training to be one, and that his roommate had been killed less than a week earlier, made the story even more newsworthy.

But the best news of all was that the police were as clueless as ever. Because Frat Boy and Scrub Boy had been roommates, the cops were looking for some connection with the other roommates. That dead end would keep them busy for a while, Peter thought, smiling. Then he had a really good laugh when the police sketch of the prime suspect in the case was shown on the screen. The dark-haired guy with the goatee looked nothing like Peter, didn't even have the same general facial features or bone structure. The picture made it seem like the killer was some big, fat, insane-looking Latino guy.

Peter's only real concern had to do with Hillary Morgan, the detective. Would she realize that Scrub Boy was the same guy she'd photographed with Katie? Yeah, the murder was getting major coverage, but it wasn't like everyone in New York was going to pay attention to the story. Maybe she wasn't the type of person who even followed the local news. And even if she did hear about the murder, would she take a very close look at a photo of Scrub Boy in the paper or on TV? Besides, she was a licensed PI, and Peter figured that PI's must have some kind of client privilege or something. Unless the cops came after them with court orders, they probably kept their mouths shut.

Peter was ninety-nine percent certain that he had nothing to worry about with Hillary, and he was even more confident that his other tracks had been covered. Last night, he had walked all the way home from the Upper East Side. The walk had taken him about an hour, but it was safer than risking the possibility of being seen with bloodstains, or possibly getting blood on the backseat of a cab. In his apartment, he carefully placed the jacket with blood on the sleeves in a plastic bag. Although he didn't see blood on any other clothing, just in case, he added the shirt and jeans he'd worn. Then he walked downtown to the East Village and deposited the bag in a garbage can in front of a tenement. Since the garbage can was about a hundred blocks away from where he'd killed Scrub Boy, there was no way the cops would be searching for evidence there. Within a day or two, the bag would be on its way to becoming landfill, if it wasn't already.

Killing people and getting away with it was so easy. You had to be a total moron to get caught.

Peter figured that Katie would be in touch with him at some point today. She'd hear that Scrub Boy had been killed, and she'd rush to Peter for support, the same way she'd come running to him after Frat Boy's death. And this time when she came to him she'd stay with him for good, because that was the way it worked with romances. The obstacles were all gone. Boy got girl, boy lost girl, and now it was time for girl to realize the huge mistake she'd made and rush back into boy's arms.

But then Peter wondered why he was sitting around, waiting. Didn't Richard Gere go back to Julia Roberts in *Pretty Woman*? Didn't Bill Pullman go back to Sandra Bullock in *While You Were Sleeping*?

He decided, to hell with it. If he didn't hear from her soon, he'd crawl back to her, swallow his pride. He'd tell her he was sorry for being so open about his emotions, and for proposing to her so quickly. If admitting to a couple of things he wasn't really guilty of was what it took to win Katie back forever, then so be it.

John Himoto left Katie Porter's apartment and went downtown to Christina's, an Italian restaurant on Second Avenue near Thirty-third Street, to meet his son for lunch.

When John arrived, Blake was seated at a table off to the right. Blake looked as flaming as ever, with goddamn streaks in his hair and the designer clothes and the way he was sitting with one leg crossed over the other. As hard as John tried to be open-minded, he couldn't pull it off. Over the years he'd had many talks with Blake, telling him things like, "It's your life, you can do whatever you want," and "As long as you're happy, I'm happy," but neither of them ever really believed it.

They hugged hello—it was a loose, awkward hug—and then John asked, "Been waiting long?"

Blake said, "No," and John said, "Good."

From there, things went downhill. John felt like people in the restaurant were watching, and thought he saw the bartender look over in a smug way, as if thinking, *I'm sure glad my kid ain't a flamethrower*. The waiter took their orders—ziti for John and a freaking salad for Blake—and then there was more awkward silence. When John's cell rang he said, "I gotta take this," without checking the caller ID. He was just glad to have an excuse to get away.

Heading outside, John checked the display and saw the call was from Nick Barasco. John had called him from his car on the way downtown.

In front of the restaurant, John flipped his phone open, said, "Hey, thanks for getting back to me."

"No problem," Barasco said, but he sounded annoyed. "What's up?"

"I had a talk with Katie Porter."

There was a long pause—John thought the call might've been lost—then Barasco said, "The girl Barnett was dating."

"That's right."

"Why were you talking to her?"

John let out a deep breath then said, "She came into the precinct this morning. She was very upset."

"Look, I'm busy," Barasco said. "What the hell's this about?"

"She thinks this guy Peter Wells was stalking her sister."

"Yeah, I know, she told me all about that yesterday."

"Did she tell you she thinks he might've killed her sister's boyfriend? She also thinks he might've altered his appearance on the night of Andrew Barnett's murder."

"Look, we talked to the Wells guy yesterday and there wasn't much to go on. He says he was in his hotel room at the time of the murder, and the guy who works at the desk says he doesn't remember Peter going out."

"So the alibi isn't airtight."

"Is this why you called me?"

"She says she was with William Bahner the other night, the night before he was killed, so I think this should be looked into, that's all."

"If she was with Bahner, that's a good reason to talk to her again. But that has nothing to do with Peter Wells."

"I just wanted to express my concern that—"

"Your concern has been expressed—thanks so much. From now I'd suggest you let me handle my own case, you think you can do that? I think my track record speaks for itself, don't you? Oh, and FYI, I had a call from Katie Porter this morning, so I don't know why you're even wasting your time."

"Yeah, you're right," John said, "I am wasting my fucking time." He closed the phone so hard he could've broken it then said, "Goddamn asshole," louder than he'd intended, and the woman sitting outside, having lunch with her young daughter, gave him a nasty look.

"Sorry," John muttered, and went back into the restaurant.

He rejoined his son, who was sitting with his arms crossed, looking pissed off. Now John had to deal with this shit? He did his best to have a pleasant time, but his son's pissy attitude and the leftover anger from the conversation with Barasco was like a potent stress cocktail. John kept replaying snippets, especially that last beaut, *I think my track record speaks for itself.* He couldn't imagine what his blood pressure was right now. One seventy over one hundred? Higher?

Their meals arrived and John started eating quickly, double-biting. He was trying to hold a conversation with his son, asking him questions about his job as a social worker at a middle school in lower Manhattan, but it was useless. They had zero to say to each other and things weren't going to get any better.

John finished his ziti, then Blake asked, "Should we get the check?" even though he'd barely touched his salad.

"I'm ready if you are," John said.

As John paid the bill, Blake put on his jacket and went outside. When John left, he saw Blake waiting for him on the sidewalk.

"Well, this was a lot of fun," John said.

"Yeah," Blake said. "It was a blast."

John couldn't think of anything else to say. He moved forward, as if to hug his son goodbye, but couldn't go through with it and shook his hand instead.

Driving uptown, John felt like shit, and there wasn't a damn thing he could do about it.

Or was there?

He could do a little poking around on his own, see what he could find out about this Peter Wells guy. Working on another detective's case was a big no-no, but what the hell did he have to lose? He was already one of the least-respected detectives in the whole city; what was one more blotch on his record?

Near Forty-second Street, a cabbie tried to cut John off.

"Yeah, right," John said, and he hit the gas and gave the fucker the finger as he sped away.

31

Trying to stay as calm as possible, Katie called her parents.

"Mom."

"What is it?" Her mother was already concerned. That was the freaky thing about mothers; they always *knew*. "What's wrong?"

Katie explained that she was in "a bad situation" and that she needed to go home to Lenox right away.

"What is it? What happened?"

Katie wanted to keep things vague. The last thing she wanted was to panic her parents and cause them to get into an accident on the way to the city to pick her up.

"It's no big deal," she said, trying not to let her voice waver. "I just think it would be a good idea to, like, get away for a while."

"Tell me what's going on right now, Katie."

"Nothing's going on." She didn't know how much longer she could keep this up. "Really, you guys don't have to worry about anything or—"

"Does it have to do with the murder? Did something happen with the police?"

"No, it's nothing like that."

"I can hear it in your voice. You're lying."

"I am not lying. I'm telling you the truth."

She wasn't even fooling herself.

"You're scaring me, Katie."

"I'm telling you, it's okay. I'm not in any danger."

"Where are you?"

"Home. In my apartment."

"Who's there with you?"

"No one."

"Oh my God."

"Mom, don't panic—"

"Dad's not home. He's in Pittsfield, showing a house. I'm gonna call him right now. As soon as he comes home we're coming to get you."

"Okay, but don't, like, get him excited or anything."

"Did somebody hurt you?"

Thinking about the date rape, Katie felt like she was about to cry. She managed to say, "No, I'm just scared, that's all."

"Scared of what?"

"Nothing . . . Just the whole situation. I want to come home."

"I still feel like there's something you're not telling me."

"I'm telling you everything. I'm just scared. I'm really, really scared."

She started crying, feeling like a total baby. So much for Miss Independent.

"This is crazy," her mother said. "You should've let us pick you up the other day. I can't believe we listened to you."

Sobbing, Katie said, "I'm sorry, Mommy."

Mommy? God, did she really say, *Mommy?*

"Look, I have to go so I can call your father. I'll wait outside and just get in the car with him when he comes by so we don't waste any time. We'll be there in three hours, maybe less. We'll call you from the road."

"Drive carefully," Katie said.

She checked to make sure the locks were bolted and that the chain was on, then she showered. The hot water was relaxing until she started thinking about *Psycho* and got out quickly, rinsing the rest of the shampoo out of her hair in the sink.

After she got dressed, she packed a suitcase with stuff she might need for three or four days. She didn't care if Mitchell fired her for taking off work; maybe it was time to move on anyway.

She was hungry and prepared a bowl of Special K and strawberry yogurt and ate it in front of the TV. She flipped around, watching midday talk shows, with the volume on very loud. Around noon, her mother called. She said she was in the car with Katie's father and that they were on their way to the city. Katie—much calmer than before—assured her mother that everything was fine and there was no need to rush.

While she was finishing the conversation with her mom, a call came in on the other line from Detective Barasco. Katie was surprised—she had somehow expected that Barasco would completely blow her off. But Barasco seemed very eager to talk, saying he was in the neighborhood and asking if he could come up immediately.

Several minutes later, Barasco and Martinelli arrived. They seemed very hurried and serious and started questioning her as soon as they walked in. She didn't get any of that *they-think-I'm-a-ditz* vibe she'd gotten yesterday. It was all business.

They told her that they spoke with Peter yesterday and wanted to know if Peter knew William Bahner, or ever talked to him.

"I have no idea," Katie said. "I mean, he never mentioned him."

"Do you have any idea where Peter was last night?" Barasco asked.

"No, none," Katie said. "The last time I saw Peter was Monday night, when I left the apartment—the apartment he bought for me." She rolled her eyes. The questioning about Peter didn't upset her at all; actually, it was comforting to know that Peter was being taken seriously as a suspect, that the police were finally doing something.

"What about you?" Barasco asked. "How well did you know William Bahner?"

"I didn't know him very well. But, like I told Detective Himoto, I was with Will two nights ago."

Barasco wanted to know everything Katie knew about William Bahner. She told him about the double date with Andy, and how her friend Amanda had "kind of hooked up" with Will. Then she told them how two nights ago she came home and saw the note on her door from Will and went to meet him at Fetch on Third Avenue.

"What did he want to meet with you about?" Barasco asked.

"Just to talk about Andy, about what happened to him, and about maybe going to the funeral and stuff like that. Oh, and he was pissed off that Himoto had questioned him about assaulting that kid in high school. He didn't want that getting out, you know, around the hospital."

"Was there anything else?"

Katie was uncomfortable mentioning that she'd kissed Will, but she didn't see how she could avoid it. "Not really. We had a couple of drinks, and then he started kissing me." She thought she saw Martinelli smile, as if thinking, *Kissing her friend's boyfriend, what a slut.* "I wasn't into it at all," she said quickly, "and I told him so, and then I noticed a woman standing there. And I remembered I saw the same woman outside my office, when I was leaving work."

"What did she look like?" Barasco asked.

Katie described her.

"Had you ever seen this woman before?"

"You mean before I saw her outside my office? No. Never. At least I don't think so."

"Are you sure you saw the woman outside your office?"

"Yes, I'm positive," Katie said. "I took a really close look around because I was afraid Peter was following me, I mean after the scene at that apartment the night before and everything. Why? Do you think the woman could've—"

"Highly unlikely, given the way Bahner's head had been bashed in. Unless she was a bodybuilder, but you say she had a slim build, right?"

"Yeah, but Peter's really strong. He's not a bodybuilder, but he works out. He has really ripped muscles."

"Peter Wells had an alibi for the night of Andrew Barnett's murder."

"What about for last night?"

"We don't know yet. Do you have any idea who this could be?"

Martinelli showed her a police sketch of a stocky, dark-haired guy with a goatee.

"That could be Peter," she said. "I mean, it looks like his eyes and cheekbones."

"You think he could've changed his appearance?"

"He shaved his goatee, right after Andy was killed," Katie said. "I told Detective Himoto this already—I mean, the timing works out. Peter could've dyed his hair darker and dyed his goatee, too. And how about how he might've pushed my sister's boyfriend off a roof in college?"

Talking very quickly, she explained how her sister had been distraught because a guy friend of hers had died, and how Peter could've killed him, and how Peter might've seen her with Will, or the woman had told him she had been with Will, and then Peter could've killed Will. She was aware of how the more she talked, the more bizarre and less credible she probably sounded.

Finally, Barasco cut her off midsentence and said, "We appreciate all the information. Please just stay available in case we need to talk to you again."

Katie didn't want to mention that she was planning to go up to Massachusetts. She was afraid they'd want her to stay in town and there was no way she was doing that. It didn't seem to matter anyway—since they could always call her on her cell if they had any more questions.

Although Katie was less than convinced that Barasco and Martinelli believed her theory about her sister's boyfriend, she was confident that they would at least talk to Peter again to see if he had an alibi for last night. She was glad that things finally seemed to be under control.

She watched some more TV and nibbled on the only food she could find in the fridge—a couple of rice cakes and half a thing of cottage cheese. Her parents called from the road again and she was able to communicate to them, much more convincingly, that she was fine and there was no reason to panic. When she got off the phone with her parents, she considered calling Amanda at work, just to have someone to chat with. But as she started to dial, she reconsidered and clicked off. Amanda probably hadn't even heard about Will's death yet or she would've called, and Katie didn't want to be the one to have to break the news.

But before Katie could put the phone down on the coffee table, it started to ring. Figuring it was her parents calling back, she was about to flip open the phone, but stopped just in time when she saw PETER flashing.

"Fuck," she said.

There was no way she was picking up. She let the phone ring six times and then it stopped. She hoped he wouldn't leave a message, but then heard the beeping sound, announcing that she had received a new voice mail. She wasn't sure what to do. She wanted to ignore it, or delete it—the last thing she needed was to hear that creep's voice—but decided that could be a big mistake. It could be evidence; the police might need to hear it. She deliberated for several more minutes, then decided to stop being such a wimp and she called in for the message:

"Hey, Katie, it's me, Peter. I just wanted you to know, I've been thinking about you a lot. But I bet you already knew that, right?" He laughed. "But, seriously, Katie, I just want you to know I feel bad about everything that happened the other day. I know I come on too strong sometimes, and I didn't want to frighten you off or anything. I mean, I obviously don't want to do that . . . But I want you to know I meant everything I said and I really want to talk to you . . . Also, I just saw on the news what happened to your friend Andy's friend. That sucks so bad. I can't imagine what you're going through and I'd love to help you through it any way I can. So you can give me a call back today anytime. Cool? . . . Can't wait to hear your voice."

Katie was disgusted. Peter sounded so gross, so totally icky on the phone, she couldn't believe she'd ever been attracted to him, that she'd thought he was charming. How could she have fallen for that bullshit? It must've been because she was rebounding from Andy. Otherwise, there was no way she would've been interested in a fucking weirdo like him.

She was deciding what to do, if she should tell Barasco that Peter had called or just forget about the whole thing, when the cell rang, flashing PE-TER again.

"The fuck's wrong with you!" she screamed at the phone.

She let the voice mail pick up again, waited, then angrily called in for the message:

"Hey, Katie, it's me again . . . um, Peter. Just occurred to me, maybe we could get together today sometime, maybe just for coffee or something just to talk. Or maybe we can go to dinner? I can make a reservation someplace special. So if you're up for it just—"

Unable to bear any more, Katie ended the call and turned the phone off.

She was terrified, back to how she'd been last night and this morning. Somehow she managed to calm down, convincing herself that she was probably panicking for no reason. She reminded herself that the police were on top of things now. They knew everything about Peter's past and there was no way he could hurt her.

From the landline phone, Katie called Barasco and got his voice mail. She explained that Peter had left two messages and summarized them. She said she was very concerned and to call her back as soon as possible.

When she hung up, the phone started ringing and Peter's cell number was flashing on the display.

"Fucking stop it," she said, and pulled the cord out of the jack. She gave herself a pep talk—*You're blowing things out of proportion . . . He didn't threaten you . . . You told the police.* She was starting to relax a little when the intercom buzzed. It was as if somebody were listening to her thoughts and trying to do everything possible to scare the crap out of her. A rational voice in her head told her that it was probably Barasco coming back to ask her a few more questions. The irrational voice said it was Peter coming to chop her into pieces.

The intercom buzzed again, this time longer, steadier, more impatiently.

"Fuck you!" Katie shouted, and checked the locks again.

Then there was another buzz, even longer this time. She didn't hear any construction going on in the apartment downstairs. It was like she was in the building all alone. She was kidding herself, thinking it was Barasco. Barasco would've called to say he was coming over, and Himoto had her landline number as well. It could be a delivery guy, from UPS or wherever. Those guys buzzed whenever packages arrived, but they didn't buzz again and again like maniacs.

When the intercom buzzed for the fourth time, Katie decided it had to be Peter. Who else could it be? She considered talking to whoever it was on the intercom, and if it was Peter telling him to leave her the fuck alone. But that would only incite him and that was the last thing she wanted to do. It would be a much better idea to ignore the whole thing, pretend she wasn't home.

Then, as the intercom buzzed steadily, for what seemed like twenty seconds, Katie thought, *He knows I'm here.* She went to the phone, dialed 911, and explained to the operator that someone was trying to break into her building. Katie was so frantic she needed to repeat herself several times. The operator took her address and said someone would come by immediately to check out the situation.

The bell rang once more and then there was a long silence. It seemed to last two or three minutes. Katie hoped this meant that Peter had given up. She tried not to think about another possibility, that he had buzzed other apartments and someone had let him into the building. Terrified, Katie listened with her ear against the door, but didn't hear any footsteps on the stairwell. If he did come up and tried to break in, she had no idea how she'd defend herself.

Still listening closely, she heard a sudden loud noise that shook the door. Assuming it was Peter banging, trying to get in, she screamed, and then a woman in the hallway said, "Are you okay in there?"

It was one of her neighbors. She was on her way out and had slammed her door.

Recovering from the near heart attack, Katie said, "Yeah . . . everything's fine."

It was quiet for a few seconds—Katie imagined the neighbor staring, puzzled, at the door to Katie's apartment—and then the footsteps headed downstairs.

Katie continued to get hold of herself then realized the huge mistake she'd made. She shouldn't have let her neighbor leave. She should've told her what was going on, that someone was trying to get into the building, someone who might want to kill her. The woman could've stayed with her until the police arrived. But now the woman was going to open the door to the vestibule and Peter could be down there, waiting for someone to leave so he could get in.

Listening with her ear against the door again, Katie's worst nightmare came true. She heard heavy footsteps on the stairs, and they were getting louder and louder.

32

When John Himoto arrived in his office at the Nineteenth Precinct, he read the printouts Katie had left about the fire near Albany that had killed Peter Wells's parents. There was a mention in the article of a Detective Sgt. Jeff Franklin from the Colonie Police Department. Although the fire had been six years ago, John called the department in Albany in the hope that Detective Franklin was still working there. It turned out he was—he'd been promoted to police chief—but unfortunately he was on vacation this week.

"Is there anyone else I can talk to who has knowledge of the case?" John asked.

John was put on hold, for so long he thought he'd been forgotten, and then the woman came back on and said she wasn't sure who John should speak to, but would have someone get in touch with him as soon as possible. About two hours later, a Detective Litsky called and said, "Jeff's on vacation this week—Club Med, Cancún. Meanwhile, I can't remember the last time I saw the ocean. But do I sound jealous?"

Impatient with the small talk, John said, "Do you know anything about the fire in Colonie that killed Eleanor and Charles Wells?"

"Oh, yeah. Actually, I was one of the first officers on the scene that day. I made detective since then."

"Do you remember Peter Wells?"

"Yeah, I remember him. We thought he did it."

"Why's that?"

"There was just something off about the guy. He was too cool, you know what I mean?"

"Could he have been in shock?"

"Maybe . . . Maybe not. That was the thing about the guy—it was hard to tell. He was the type of guy you talked to and came away not knowing what the hell to think."

"But you never brought charges."

"We had no hard evidence and no witnesses—well, other than Peter Wells. The fire was ruled accidental, caused by a halogen lamp igniting curtains in the living room. The house was wood, went up like a matchbox."

"How was Wells able to escape?"

"He wasn't drunk, that's how. The victims had been drinking and had passed out cold. Wells said he tried to get to them, but couldn't. The big hero, or would-be hero. Yeah, he had all the bases covered all right."

"And I understand they each had a one-million-dollar insurance policy, right?"

"Yep, that was the suspected motive. But 'suspected' was the key word. I remember Jeff thought he did it, but Arson concluded it was an accident, and the insurance investigators must've felt the same way. So that was it—we had nothing to go on. Why? You think he has involvement in something downstate?"

"It's starting to look that way," John said.

He thanked Litsky for his time and immediately made another call—to Information in Massachusetts. He got the number for the Amherst Police Department, and after talking to several people there he found out that a Detective Merker had handled the Heather Porter suicide investigation. John left a message for Merker, and about an hour later Merker, who sounded like he was in his fifties or sixties, returned the call.

Merker remembered the case clearly, said it was a very sad day.

"Any chance it wasn't a suicide?" John asked.

"No chance at all," Merker said. "A few people saw her jump. They were sunbathing on the dorm roof."

"Do you remember something about a boyfriend of hers being killed?"

"A boyfriend?"

"Yeah. Maybe someone she was dating who had been killed, who she was distraught over."

Merker thought about it, then said, "Nope, don't remember anything like—Wait a second now. Yep, yep, it's starting to ring a bell. It was unclear if it was a boyfriend of hers, or just some guy she . . . what do they say? Oh, yeah, 'hooked up with.' I forget his name but, yeah, I remember her friends saying that was one of the things she was upset about, that could've caused her to jump."

"What about the friend? How did he die?"

"Fell off a roof, if I remember correctly. He was drunk at the time, at a frat party. Believe it or not, that happens quite often at college campuses around here. Actually, that's why we thought Heather Porter might've jumped, to check out the same way her boyfriend died. Seemed to make some sense anyway. Of course, we had no way of knowing—"

"I'm sorry," John said. "You said he was drunk?"

John remembered what Detective Litsky had said, about how Peter Wells's parents had been intoxicated.

"Oh, yeah, he was drunk all right," Merker said. "I think totally shit-faced is the term *du jour*. There was a frat party going on, and he'd been drinking all night."

"Any chance of foul play?"

"We looked into it, sure. I think there was a witness or two, I don't really remember. But we concluded it was an accident—just another drunk kid taking the Budweiser dive. That's what we call it up here."

John thanked Merker for his time, then called Barasco, mildly surprised that the schmuck bothered picking up.

"What now?" Barasco asked.

"You talk to Peter Wells yet?"

"Hey, didn't I tell you to stay out of my case?"

"Cut the shit, all right? I just talked to a couple of cops upstate—this guy could be dangerous. Have you brought him in yet or what?"

"Not yet," Barasco said.

"Why not?"

"Because we can't locate him, that's why. He isn't answering his cell phone and he hasn't been home all day."

33

The footsteps on the stairs were getting louder. Katie, listening at the door, was immobilized for a few moments, unable to think clearly or do anything, then she darted into the bathroom and locked herself in. She sat on the closed toilet and waited, praying.

There were a couple of loud knocks on the front door.

"Leave me the fuck alone!" she screamed, realizing a moment later that was the worst thing she could've done. It would've been better to stay silent, make him think she wasn't home.

"Hello? Are you able to come to the door?"

It wasn't Peter. The guy sounded official, like a cop.

Katie left the bathroom, then said, "Who's there?"

"Police."

Relieved, muttering, "Thank God," Katie looked through the peephole, then opened the door and saw two cops there—a black guy and a white woman.

"Katie Porter?" the guy asked.

"Yes," Katie said. "Come in, please come in."

The cops entered the apartment, then Katie said, "Thanks so much for coming over. I was afraid it was him."

"Who's him?" the woman asked.

Katie explained what was going on with Peter, and how she'd spoken to the detectives about the two murders.

"There was no one in the vestibule when we arrived," the male cop said.

"Well, he was there before you came," Katie said. "He was ringing the bell for, like, fifteen minutes."

She knew she was exaggerating, but so what?

"How do you know it was him?" the woman asked.

"It had to be him. He was just calling me and then the bell started ringing."

"Maybe it was a delivery guy or something," the man said.

"I thought of that, but I'm not expecting any deliveries. I'm telling you, it was Peter."

"We'll see if anyone's down there when we leave," the man said.

"Can't you stay here?" Katie said. "My parents are gonna be here soon, in like an hour or two, but can you stay till they get here?"

"I'm afraid we can't. If anyone starts ringing your bell again and you become alarmed you can call us again and report it. We have officers in this area all the time and we can be here in five minutes."

"Or we can take you someplace if you like," the woman said.

Katie considered this, but she didn't want to leave. She was afraid if she was out somewhere in public Peter would come up to her and strangle her, or bash her head in.

"I'm not going anywhere," she said.

The cops could probably tell how frightened she was because the guy said, "It seems like you have a very secure apartment here. I see you've got a Medeco lock. You can call the detectives you spoke to just to let them know you're concerned but as of right now we don't see anything that alarms us. The front door downstairs seems very functional and secure. I would just try to relax until your parents get here."

"Will you check to make sure he's not in the building? Maybe he's hiding in the stairwell or something."

"Yes, we'll absolutely make sure he's not on the premises," the woman said.

Katie waited with the door open while the cops checked the stairwell, including going all the way up to the roof. They returned and told Katie that everything looked good and that the roof entrance was locked so no one could've gotten in. They advised her to wait in her apartment with the door bolted and chained until her parents came, and then they left.

It took Katie awhile to get a grip again, but she eventually did. For all she knew, it had been a delivery person ringing the bell after all. She wasn't convinced, but she felt more relaxed when she heard the construction resuming downstairs. At least there were people in the building nearby if she needed help.

She connected the landline and called her parents. They said they were approaching Sheffeld, Connecticut, which meant they wouldn't be in the city for at least another hour and a half. She assured them that she was fine and to drive safely, that was the most important thing. After she hung up, she disconnected the phone again.

She was going to turn the TV back on, but decided it would be best to keep the apartment silent, so if Peter somehow got into the building he would think there was no one home and leave. She kept the lights off as well in case he bent down and tried to look through the crack under the door.

Time crawled, but as a half hour, then an hour went by, and the doorbell didn't ring, Katie started to wonder if she'd overreacted. Maybe she'd been jumping to a lot of conclusions and the murders had nothing to do with Peter. Like Himoto had said, two roommates had been killed—it made sense that one of the other roommates was somehow involved.

Then, at around three-fifteen, she connected the phone again and called her parents to find out where they were. They were in the Bronx, about twenty minutes away, and said that when they arrived they would double-park in front of the building and take turns coming up to use the bathroom. Katie asked them to call her landline from the vestibule rather than buzzing her apartment. Her mother asked why they needed to do this.

Thinking fast, Katie said, "Oh, the buzzer just freaks out sometimes, that's all."

The twenty minutes seemed to take about an hour, but then the landline finally rang and Katie saw her mom's number flashing.

Katie answered the phone and said, "Are you here?"

"I'm downstairs."

"Come on up," Katie practically screamed because she was so excited.

She buzzed her mom in, and when she saw her, she felt like it was that time at sleepaway camp when she was ten years old and very homesick. When her parents came to pick her up, she felt like her misery had finally ended.

Hugging her mom so tight she was probably hurting her, she said, "God, you have no idea how good it is to see you."

Katie was starting to cry and her mother said, "You have to tell me what's going on."

"I will in the car," Katie said. "I just want to go home."

After her mom used the bathroom, her father came up to use it. Katie didn't usually express a lot of emotion with her father, but she gave him a long hug and she could tell her father was very worried about her. She realized that, in some way, this whole situation must've been digging up awful memories for her parents. They'd already lost one daughter and they didn't want to lose another.

Her father went to the bathroom and then picked up Katie's suitcase and said, "Let's get a move on. I don't want to have to drive in the dark."

Katie had no idea how long she would stay in Massachusetts, but as she left, she felt like she was going on a long trip, that she wouldn't be seeing her apartment again for a very long time.

34

Peter was buzzing Katie's apartment, wondering what the hell her problem was. He knew she was home because when he'd called her office the receptionist told him she'd called in sick today. He doubted she was actually sick. He figured she was just upset about Scrub Boy and was taking a personal day. Figuring it would be rude to just show up, he'd called her cell a few times, left a couple of messages, but then she'd turned it off. He knew she'd turned it off because at first her voice mail was picking up after six rings, and then it started picking up without ringing at all. He started calling her home phone and it kept ringing and ringing, meaning she'd either disconnected it or was screening calls. Now, to add insult to injury, she wasn't answering her buzzer, trying to make him think she wasn't home. Peter had no idea what he'd done to make her so upset but he knew he had to talk to her immediately, to straighten things out.

He rang the buzzer again, then he went outside, trying to decide what to do next. His timing turned out to be perfect because when he noticed the police car coming slowly down the block, he had a chance to slip away casually. When he got close to the corner of First Avenue, he ducked between two parked cars and then snuck a peek and saw the two cops getting out of the car and heading into Katie's building.

Was it possible that Katie had actually called the cops on him? He had to give her the benefit of the doubt—maybe the police were going to another apartment. But it was hard to convince himself of that one. It was *like* Katie to panic because of a couple of harmless phone calls. She obviously had gotten it into her head, for whatever reason, that he was a bad person. How or why she'd gotten this idea into her head completely baffled him, but just because she was a little unstable right now, he wasn't going to hold it against her. Maybe she had some kind of anxiety disorder. When he had a chance to talk to her, and she was in a different mind-set, he would do his best to get her the help she needed.

After about twenty minutes or so the cops finally left the building. Peter remained out of view between the cars until the cops drove away. He desperately wanted to go back to the building and start ringing Katie's buzzer again, to try to convince her to let him up or figure out some way to get into the building. He knew if she heard his voice and understood how sincere and harmless he was, she would let him up and they'd kiss, long and romantically, and everything would be okay. But he was afraid that, in her present state, he wouldn't have a chance to get through to her. She'd panic again and call the cops and that was the last thing Peter needed—having to answer more ridiculous questions from incompetent detectives.

So Peter decided the best thing to do was wait. She would have to leave her apartment at some point, even if it was just to go to the grocery store, or for a slice of pizza, or to Starbucks. When she saw Peter she would realize instantly how much he meant to her. Seeing him was the key. He wouldn't have to say anything. She would just know.

Waiting was getting easy for Peter; he had gotten used to it. He stayed where he was, toward the end of the block, but continued watching Katie's building. A couple of times the doors opened, and Peter's heart started pounding as he expected to see Katie's beautiful face, but each time he was disappointed when someone else appeared. Then, at around three thirty, a blue Volvo pulled in front of the building and double-parked. An older woman got out of the car. At first, she looked like no one, a stranger, then Peter realized it was Katie's mother.

He hadn't seen Mrs. Porter in about nine years, and she'd changed a lot. Her hair looked much grayer, and she'd put on some weight. But she still had that Porter look. It reminded Peter of Heather Porter, and of why he was so attracted to Katie.

Several minutes later Mrs. Porter returned to the car. Then Mr. Porter got out and headed up the stoop. He'd aged well, looked almost exactly the same. Peter had never liked him, though. He knew Mr. Porter was the reason why Heather used to always hit him with that "I just want to be friends" crap. Mr. Porter was putting ideas into his daughters' heads.

Mr. Porter left the apartment, carrying a suitcase, and Katie followed. She looked around in every direction and Peter ducked out of view. When he looked again, he saw them driving away. He was positive they were going home to Lenox. Where else would they be going?

This was like a total fucking nightmare. He was furious with himself for not going up to her apartment to persuade her to take him back while he had the chance. He was also angry at Katie—this running-away bullshit was insulting as hell. It was getting harder and harder to cut her slack, to believe that she actually cared about him and wanted a future with him. He could have been misjudging everything.

He had seen before how easily love could turn to hate. It had happened with his mother. One day, she was the greatest woman in the world; the next he couldn't stand the sight of her and knew he couldn't be happy until she was dead. He hadn't expected such a dramatic turn to happen with Katie, but he couldn't deny it, either.

Then Peter sprang into action. Katie's leaving New York altered the situation, but it didn't change it permanently. Or at least it didn't have to.

Peter searched the Web on his cell phone for a rental car place. He found the closest one, a Budget on First Avenue and Ninety-fifth Street. He rented a Ford Taurus and in twenty minutes he was heading through the Park on Ninety-sixth Street toward the West Side.

He had a great plan, but in order for the plan to work he had to beat the Porters to their house in Massachusetts; he had to be waiting there for them when they arrived. He knew the fastest route was to take the Taconic Expressway. He had no way of knowing if the Porters would take the Taconic or not, but he figured if they did, they'd probably stop someplace to eat and use the bathroom. There was also a chance they would take a different, slower route. Route 22 to Route 7 was technically more direct, but the roads wound through small New York and Connecticut towns. If they went that way, Peter would beat them easily.

Peter was convinced that, one way or another, he would get to the house before they did. He was careful, though, to avoid getting pulled over for speeding. As badly as he wanted to floor it, he drove at the speed limit. He kept a lookout for the Porters, in case he passed them, but he didn't see them. This worried him a little. He hoped it meant that he had simply missed them on the road, or that they'd taken a different route, not that they were traveling faster than he was.

His tension remained high until he arrived in Lenox and approached the Porters' two-story Colonial house on East Street and didn't see their car parked in front. He drove up the road a bit, past the house, and parked the car in the lot at the middle school. The school didn't exactly bring back fond memories. He had been tormented as a teenager; those assholes had made his life hell. But there was no use thinking about the past, letting that negativity seep in. He reminded himself of an article he'd read somewhere about how the body's cells changed every seven years. That meant that the unhappy teenager in his memories wasn't even him.

He walked back to the Porters' house. Okay, now it was a matter of finding a way inside. It was dark out, nearly pitch-black. The cool, crisp mountain air reminded him of how much he missed the country. Maybe he could convince Katie to leave the city, move upstate. Maybe she was getting tired of the whole city thing; maybe she wanted to return to her roots. He could see it clearly—he and Katie hiking in the woods, getting into bike riding and winter sports.

As he approached along the driveway, he hesitated, remembering that the Porters used to have a German shepherd. Peter wasn't good with dogs; he sucked with them, actually. When he was a kid, he was chased by a big black dog on the way home from school one day, and it seemed like dogs had hated him ever since. Trying to make as little noise as possible, he went alongside the house, toward the backyard. He figured they didn't have a dog anymore—maybe the mutt had died—or it would've been making a racket.

He looked around, trying to find a way in. It wasn't difficult. In Lenox a lot of people still left their doors unlocked, and the only people who had alarm systems were "summer people" who were fearful of break-ins when they closed up their houses for the winter. Toward the back of the house, Peter found a window that was partway open. He opened it all the way, pushed up the screen and voilà; he lifted himself up and over, and he was inside.

But, a moment later, he heard the clatter of clawed feet approaching on the hardwood floor. He panicked, was about to scream. Then his whole body relaxed when a fluffy tabby entered the room and came over and sniffed him a few times and started rubbing its head against his pants leg. He and cats had always gotten along beautifully. He bent down, petted the cat, and said, "Thatta, girl, thatta, girl," and the Tabby started purring, snuggling up against him.

35

Riding in the backseat of her parents' car, Katie was finally able to get hold of herself. Calling her mom and dad and leaving New York had definitely been the right move. If she had had to stay in the city any longer she would've lost her mind.

In the car, she told her parents, in general, what had been going on with Peter since Andy had been killed. But still not wanting to get them all freaked out, she downplayed most of it, saying things like "he kept buying me stuff" and "he got kind of clingy," instead of telling them the truth, that he had been stalking her and harassing her, and had bought her an apartment and a ring, and, oh yeah, might have even murdered a couple of her friends. She also didn't tell them anything about the connections she'd made between Peter and Heather's suicide, knowing that would be way too much for them to handle.

Her mother, of course, couldn't restrain herself from getting jabs in, like "I told you to stay away from Peter Wells," and "Next time maybe you'll listen to your mother." Katie didn't want to get into it and gave in, saying, "I know, you were obviously right, Mom."

At a Burger King in Pawling, they stopped for some dinner to take away and to use the bathroom. Katie couldn't help feeling like a kid, in the backseat of her parents' car, eating a Whopper with cheese and sipping a chocolate milkshake. But the childlike thing was comforting; it was starting to grow on her. The familiarity of her parents' bickering and the staticky radio—her dad refused to go twenty-first century and subscribe to satellite—brought her back to a time in her life when everything was simple, when she didn't have serious worries about anything. For short periods, she even managed to forget all about Peter and what had happened to Andy and Will.

When they crossed the Massachusetts border it was around seven o'clock, past sunset. After a deer darted across the road about twenty yards in front of them, her mother insisted that her father drive slower the rest of the way and they did, going about thirty miles per hour until they reached the less windy Route 7.

They arrived at the house in Lenox at a little before eight o'clock. They parked in the driveway and then Katie got out of the car first and walked to the backyard, away from the porch light. Then, in pitch-darkness, she tilted her head back and looked up at the sky. She'd missed seeing so many stars. In Manhattan, on a clear night, you could see about three or four of the brightest stars, and that was it. If she ever moved back to the country, she promised herself that she'd look at the stars every night, not take little things like that for granted.

Her parents had gone into the house. Katie remained in the backyard for a while longer, enjoying the aloneness, then she strolled back to the front of the house, kicking up gravel in the driveway like a kid.

In the house, her mom, in the kitchen, unloading the dishwasher, said, "There's leftover salad and chicken from last night."

"That's okay, Ma. The Burger King filled me up."

"How about some ice cream or cookies?"

Katie thought about the weight she'd put on lately—three pounds, according to the last time she'd weighed herself—and she felt like she'd put on more since then. But the idea of sitting in front of the TV at her parents' house, stuffing her face, appealed to her in a cozy way, and after everything she'd been through lately she deserved to treat herself. Besides, she wasn't dating anyone and didn't plan to for a long time, so what difference did it make if she gained a little more weight?

"Okay, I'll have a couple of cookies, but just a couple."

A half hour later, she was sitting cross-legged on the couch, watching some dumb movie on Lifetime, the bag of double-stuffed Oreos about one-third eaten. Sitting on the chair next to her, her mom was eating Ben & Jerry's Cherry Garcia straight from the container. Her dad stayed up for a while, reading on the screened-in porch, but at around ten o'clock he went upstairs. When the Lifetime movie ended, her mom said good night, first telling her how great it was to have her home and kissing her two times on the top of her head.

Katie remained in the living room, watching TV and eating Oreos. She finally hit her nausea threshold as the calorie guilt set in. She'd have to go bike riding tomorrow to make up for it.

At around eleven, she crashed from the sugar high and was suddenly exhausted. She shut off all the lights downstairs and went upstairs to her bedroom.

John Himoto was calling Katie's home number, still getting no answer. Her voice mail was picking up right away on her cell so she'd probably turned it off. Finally he decided to stop fucking around and he got in his car and went to her apartment.

She wasn't home—or she wasn't answering the buzzer. He didn't like this at all. Barasco had spoken to her around noon and she hadn't mentioned anything to him about going to her parents' in Massachusetts or anywhere else. John waited, hoping she was just out shopping or something.

A half hour, then forty-five minutes went by. John called Barasco again, couldn't reach him, but got through to his partner, Martinelli.

"Any word on Peter Wells?"

"*Nada,*" Martinelli said.

"Shit," John said. "What about Katie Porter?"

"The girl? What about her?"

"Where the hell is she?"

"Home, I guess," Martinelli said.

"Yeah, well, I'm at her home and she's not here, so guess again."

"Look," Martinelli said, "I'm real busy right now and—"

"Listen to me," John said. "I have reason to believe that Katie Porter is in serious danger, and we have to do everything we can to make sure that Peter Wells doesn't come into contact with her."

"We're doing everything we can."

"Yeah, everything except finding him."

"I don't know what you want me to tell you," Martinelli said.

"Did Katie tell you anything about leaving town?"

"Nick told her to stay in the city and she said she would. Look, I gotta go. If Nick even knew I was talking to you, he'd be pissed off as all hell."

"Yeah, like I give a shit," John said and clicked off.

He tried Katie's numbers again and still couldn't get through. Okay, he had to think, put himself in her place. She was scared so she might have panicked—maybe she didn't leave town, but she could've gone to stay with a friend. Taking a shot, John called Katie's friend Amanda, the girl he'd met with the other day. Unfortunately Amanda claimed she had no idea where Katie was, and John believed her.

He decided there was nothing he could do now except stick around and wait. She could have gone to a movie or out to dinner. He had to hope anyway.

He sat on the stoop, waiting for her to come home, occasionally calling her numbers and not getting through. It was frustrating, but he didn't know what else to do. He kept thinking about what he'd told Katie when he'd seen her last—*I promise you, everything's going to be okay.* If something happened to her, he knew those words would haunt him for the rest of his life.

At ten o'clock, there was still no sign of her. He called Barasco again—the fuck wouldn't pick up—and he couldn't get through to Martinelli, either. At eleven thirty, John was still sitting on the stoop when Katie's roommate and a guy, probably her boyfriend, arrived.

John stood right away and said, "Excuse me, you live with Katie Porter, right? Your name's Sharon, right?"

"Susan. What happened? What's wrong?"

"Is Katie okay?" the guy asked.

"I don't know," John said.

"What do you mean?" Susan said. "Where is she?"

"I don't know, and it's extremely important that I find her right away. Did she tell you she was going anywhere?"

"No, but why is—"

"I don't have time to explain. Can we go upstairs? Maybe she left a note or something."

John went up with them to the apartment. Sure enough, there was a note on the dining table.

> Hey, my parents picked me up and I'm going home. I'll call
> you, Katie.

"Goddammit," John said, feeling like he'd wasted the past three hours. Hoping it wasn't too late, he said to Susan, "Where do her parents live?"

"Katie's parents?" Susan asked.

"Yes." John wanted to grab her, shake the words out of her.

"They live in, um, Massachusetts."

"I know that. But where?"

"I don't know."

"Think."

"I am thinking. I don't know. She never told me."

"Does she have an address book?"

"I'm not sure."

John went into Katie's room, started looking around, checking drawers, but couldn't find an address book. Maybe she had the address or phone number on her computer somewhere or maybe he could find the info online, or by contacting her work or college, but that could take hours and he didn't have hours. Hell, he might not even have minutes.

Then he had an idea.

He went out to the living room and said to Susan, "Does your phone have a log?"

"A what?"

"Does it log calls? Does it keep a list of last calls, calls made . . ."

"Oh, yeah, of course."

"Check it right now."

Susan checked the incoming numbers and saw there was a recent call from a 413 area code. John dialed the number. It rang four times, then a woman answered.

"Mrs. Porter?"

"Yes?" She sounded suspicious.

"Himoto, NYPD. Is your daughter Katie with you?"

"Yes, she's here."

"Thank God," John said.

"What's this about? What's going on?"

"Just listen to me," John said. "Call the police right now, dial nine-one-one. Tell them that you think someone's breaking into your house."

"But no one's breaking in."

"Doesn't matter—that'll get 'em over there immediately. Then have them stay with you until you hear from me. Or, even better, have them call me, or you call me as soon as they arrive. I'll give you my number, okay?"

"It's the police," Mrs. Porter said to someone.

Then John heard a man's muffled voice, probably Katie's father's, but he couldn't make out what the guy was saying.

"The New York police," Mrs. Porter said to the guy. "He won't say."

"Mrs. Porter, are you there?" John said.

"Yes," she said.

"Don't waste any more time. Call nine-one-one immediately, okay? Or have your husband call from another line."

"Oh, okay," she said, sounding frazzled. "But maybe I should wake Katie up and tell her."

"I thought Katie was with you," John said.

"She's with us in the house, but she's sleeping," Mrs. Porter said. "We were sleeping, too, till you called."

"Go wake her up right now," John said. "Then all of you stay together until the police get there and make sure the doors are locked."

"You're scaring me."

"Just go," John said, nearly screaming.

It got quiet on the line for ten, twenty seconds, maybe longer. Then he heard Mrs. Porter calling, "Katie? . . . Katie?" Then louder, "Katie? . . . Katie?!"

A few seconds later she got back on and said, "She's not here!"

"Are you sure?" John said. "Did you—"

"She's not in her room, she's not anywhere. Oh my God, she's gone!"

36

Katie washed up, then went into her bedroom, closed the door, and put on her comfy PJs. Her room was still decorated the way it had been in high school, with the same pink girly furniture and, of course, a big Backstreet Boys poster above her bed.

In a suddenly nostalgic mood, she started searching the CD rack for her *Backstreet's Back* CD. She stopped searching when she thought she heard something behind her, in the closet. She stared at the closet door, then half smiled, remembering the times she and Heather would be home alone and scare the crap out of each other with ghost stories. Knowing the noise she'd heard was either the house settling or something shifting by itself, she resumed searching for the CD. Finally she found it—it had been misplaced in a Creed CD case—and put it in the stereo.

As the Backstreet Boys started crooning she was instantly transported back to ninth grade, when she was convinced that she was going to marry Nick Carter someday and have his babies. She wanted to crank the song, but didn't want to wake her parents, so she put on a headset and then upped the volume. She lay in bed with her eyes closed, singing along, but not too loud.

When the song ended, she lowered the volume and dimmed the light.

The next time she opened her eyes Peter Wells was looking down at her. Before she could process what was happening, his hand came down over her face and he said something. She couldn't hear what he'd said with the music going. Then she saw that in his other hand he was holding a large knife.

She tried to scream, but he was pressing his hand down over her mouth so hard it hurt. Then, with the hand holding the knife, he managed to lift the headset off her ears and he whispered, "I won't hurt you. I swear to God, I won't hurt you."

She was trembling, thinking, *This can't possibly be happening. This has to be a fucking nightmare.*

"Just relax," he said. "Calm down. It'll be okay, I promise. I didn't want to do it this way, I really didn't. But what choice did I have? You wouldn't take my calls, you wouldn't answer the door, and then you ran away up here. This isn't the way it was supposed to happen. You were supposed to stay in New York and fall in love with me there. But you know what? I'm not angry at you."

Katie was looking at the knife, only an inch or two away from her throat. She recognized it; it was from the kitchen downstairs. Then she thought about her parents. She was pretty sure that the TV had been on in their room before, but maybe Peter had tied them up or even killed them.

Warm tears were dripping down the sides of her face.

"Remember that day in the park," Peter said, "when we were watching the ducks? I was thinking about that before, how beautiful you looked that day. I knew right then that what we had was real, that it would last. When did you know?" He stared at her, as if waiting for her to answer. Then, realizing his hand was still covering her mouth, he said, "It's okay, we'll have plenty of time to discuss all of that stuff. But I wanted to ask you about our first kiss. Wasn't it perfect? Not the one on the blanket, the one in the carriage in the park. I consider that our first kiss, don't you?"

God, Katie couldn't believe that she'd actually kissed this fucking lunatic.

"Okay, this is what's going to happen next," he said. "We're going to leave the house. I'm going to take you someplace. I can't tell you where yet, but trust me, it'll be very romantic, I know you'll love it. I have a car parked across the road. We'll leave the house together, quietly, and walk to the car. I can trust you, right? I mean, you won't panic and scream or anything, right?"

Katie nodded weakly.

"Good," Peter said. "Because I know I've done some things lately that made you panic and I'm really sorry for that. I came on too strong. I think I almost blew it when I showed you the apartment. I should've built up to it gradually, maybe waited another week or two before I unveiled it. And the ring and the proposal—that was too much, too fast, too. Damn, I hate it when I get impulsive like that. Oh well, can't undo the past, right? But it's okay now because we're together, that's the important thing. As long as we have each other, we don't need anything else. Besides, I'm going to propose to you again—in the right way, at the right time. But we'll work out all the details, let's just get out of here, okay? The thing is, we don't want to wake up your parents. That's why I have to keep the knife on you, just in case you panic. I know you don't want to panic, that you want to leave here with me calmly, but you might freak out and not be able to control yourself, and I can't have your parents waking up and causing a whole scene, right?"

She knew he was lying. He'd already killed her parents like he'd killed Andy and Will and Heather's boyfriend. He'd probably hacked them to death in bed with the knife.

"Right?" he said again.

Katie managed to nod, but couldn't hold back the tears.

"Stop crying," he said. "There's no reason to . . . Oh, wait, I get it, they're tears of joy, right? You're so happy to see me, you're crying. I know, I'm happy, too. I'm so glad I came here to get you. I want to kiss you, but I'm going to have to let go of your mouth. You won't start to scream, will you? Because if you do, your parents will wake up and that wouldn't be a good thing. Okay, I'm going to move my hand away. Ready?"

He lifted his hand. Her lips were trembling as if she'd just come out of a freezing swimming pool.

"So beautiful," he said.

He looked at her for a few moments with a contented half smile, like a proud father admiring his baby in a crib, and then he closed in slowly toward her to kiss her. Instinctively, she started to jerk away, but stopped herself, knowing that avoiding the kiss would offend him. She had to do what he wanted—for now anyway.

Kissing him, feeling his moist lips, and the sickeningly warm breath from his nostrils, was the worst experience of her life. It was worse than being date-raped. After several seconds he tried to work his tongue into her mouth and she had to let him. It took all her strength and concentration not to vomit in his face.

Finally the kiss ended.

"Perfect," Peter said. "Just like in the park."

Katie wanted to spit at him, the fucking bastard.

"Okay, you can get up now," he said. "Get dressed, put on some shoes. I noticed you didn't unpack yet, so you can just take the suitcase with you—that'll be perfect. Tomorrow you can call your parents and explain that you took an early bus back to the city."

She was starting to believe that he hadn't killed her parents after all. She remembered hearing the noise in her closet before—Peter could have been hiding there all along and her parents were in bed asleep, unharmed.

"Get up slowly," he said.

She did as she was told, then put on the clothes she had worn earlier—jeans, a sweatshirt, and, luckily, running sneakers. The sneakers were key. If she had a chance to escape and had to run, she'd be ready. She was also glad that she had her cell phone in her jeans pocket. It was turned off but if she needed it later, it would be there.

When she was through getting dressed, Peter said, "Wait," and turned off the stereo, then took another look around. Katie had no idea what he was checking for, but then he said, "OK, let's go. But walk as quietly as you can, and don't say a word till we get to the car."

Katie left the room ahead of him. He was still holding the knife and she knew that if her parents heard a noise and woke up, or just happened to leave their bedroom to go to the bathroom, Peter would kill them both.

Trying to walk as quietly as possible, wincing each time the floorboards creaked, she headed toward the stairs. Then she and Peter both stopped when they heard a noise from the direction of her parents' bedroom. She looked at Peter, and if she had any remaining questions about him, what he was capable of, they were answered right then. She saw his hate, his rage, his total disregard for human life. He was a cold-blooded murderer, a monster who killed people with his bare hands. It was so clear, she couldn't believe she'd been so oblivious for so long.

Katie knew that if her father's prostate was acting up and he left the bedroom to go pee, Peter would kill him. Then he'd kill her mother, too. People's lives didn't mean anything to this fucking psycho.

Katie and Peter continued to stand perfectly still, staring at the door. But then, as the seconds went by, it became increasingly clear to Katie that the sound they'd heard was probably her mother or father shifting in bed and that neither of them was going to leave the bedroom. Finally Peter nudged Katie and they continued toward the stairwell.

They went outside and headed away from the porch light into the darkness. She wanted to ask him where they were going, but remembered he'd instructed her to not say a word till they got to the car and she didn't want to do anything to upset him. It crossed her mind that maybe she'd misjudged him, that he was only angry at her for running away from the city, and he wasn't going to take her into the woods and cut her throat open.

As they neared East Street, he let go of her hand and dug into his pocket—she heard keys jiggling. Then he turned on a small flashlight-type thing; it didn't cast much light, but in the total darkness it was enough to at least see the ground in front of them. She still wanted to know where the hell he was taking her, but she felt a little more hopeful now because they were on a road. Although cars only occasionally came by, especially at night, maybe if she got lucky, someone would come by and see them, maybe notice the knife in Peter's hand and call the cops. Or maybe Katie could try to flag the car down, get it to stop. But no cars were coming, and there was almost total silence except for the sounds of crickets and Peter and Katie's crunchy footsteps.

They turned into the parking lot of the Lenox Middle School and approached the only car there. As they got closer, the light from the key chain shone on the New York license plate: RBP*9FL. She memorized it, just in case.

He opened the driver's-side door and said, "Get in."

Katie hesitated, wondering if this was a bad idea, if she should just make a run for it. She was wearing her sneakers; she worked out, was in shape. But Peter was wearing sneakers, too, and he also worked out, and could probably outrun her. Besides, where would she go? Home, so he could follow her and kill her parents? Her other option was to start screaming, but she wasn't sure anyone would hear her, and Peter would definitely lose it. No, she had to keep playing along until a better opportunity came up.

She got into the car and he got in after her.

"If I put the knife down, you won't freak, right? I mean I can trust you, can't I?"

"Of course you can trust me," she said.

She thought she'd delivered this perfectly, with no hesitation.

"Great," he said, and he rested the knife on the floor, next to the brake pedal.

He started the car and looked in the rearview as they backed up.

"I didn't get a chance to thank you yet," she said.

He waited till the car was in drive and they were heading toward the road before saying, "Thank me for what?"

"For rescuing me from my parents."

"You mean you're not angry?"

"Why would I be angry? I mean, okay, the knife was a little overboard, but I understand why you did it. You wanted to get me away and you didn't know how else to do it. I just wish it could've been easier."

They turned left and were approaching Housatonic Street.

"In what way?" he asked.

"I wish you didn't have to come get me. I wish things had worked out differently in New York. I wish a lot of things."

Katie thought she was doing a good job. Her voice was steady, not trembling at all.

They turned left on Housatonic Street, heading toward Route 7. Was he planning to go to New York, back to his apartment? She hoped so. It would be good to be in a populated place, where there were people around who could help her. She'd been so safe in Manhattan and hadn't even realized it.

"It's great you feel that way," he said, but he didn't seem very excited.

At the light at Route 7 they turned right. Fuck, they weren't heading toward Manhattan. They were going north to Pittsfield, Vermont, freaking Canada.

"So, where are we going?"

She tried to get a playful, even naughty tone in her voice, as if she thought it was exciting to be dragged out of bed at knifepoint and taken to an unknown location. Like she had a kidnapping fetish or something.

"I told you, it's a surprise," he said.

"Come on, you can tell me," she said. "I'm gonna see it soon anyway."

"It's a surprise," he said again, and she knew that pressing was useless; he wouldn't budge.

She didn't like this at all. She worried that she'd made a huge mistake, leaving the house. Maybe he wouldn't have killed her parents. She and her mom and dad would've outnumbered him anyway. Her dad was in his fifties, but he was in pretty good shape. Maybe they could've overpowered Peter, restrained him till the police arrived. But now it was one against one and she'd have zero chance.

Keeping the lovey-dovey bullshit going, figuring it was still her best shot to save herself, she said, "It's so good to see you, to be next to you again."

"I feel the same way," he said. "Just smelling your perfume is so great."

Could he be any ickier?

"I'm so glad you're not mad at me," she said. "I only freaked out that way this morning because of my parents. They wouldn't let me answer the phone or the door and then they made me come up here. I was hoping you'd call and I could convince you to come get me. Then I opened my eyes and you were there. It was like a dream come true."

"Wow. You don't know how good it feels to hear you say that. I mean, I was hoping you'd say that, but things rarely go the way you imagine they will."

"It doesn't have to be that way." She touched his right leg, and started to massage it gently. It was disgusting the hell out of her, but she had to make this look good. "I think if you want something bad enough, you can get it. I forget what it's called, creative something?"

"Creative visualization."

"Yeah, that's it. All you have to do is visualize what you want and it comes true. I do it all the time."

"Does it work?"

"Sometimes. Most of the time, actually. It depends how well I can picture it. I mean, how hard I concentrate, you know?"

Katie was proud of herself, able to sound so calm, when she was such a mess inside.

"Well, I've concentrated very hard on you," Peter said.

"And see?" Katie said. "It worked. Here I am."

"What about the other night? You're not mad at me for proposing, for showing you the apartment?"

"I'm really sorry I freaked about all that. I guess it all just took me by surprise, you know, and I just, like, reacted."

"Did you ever get evaluated for an anxiety disorder?"

She couldn't believe it—this maniac was playing shrink with her. Was he for real?

"No," she said pseudonaively. "Should I?"

"I think it would be a good idea. You seem to get very anxious sometimes and it affects your behavior. I'll show you some techniques—you should definitely learn how to meditate—and there're some great books you can buy. You should also look into holistic stuff—herbs, Saint-John's-wort, stuff like that. There're other things you can do. When I was living in Mexico, I met this guy who was into homeopathic medicine. Way it works is you need to be analyzed, figure out what your own personal cure-all is. Mine is sulfur, but for you it could be ignatia, belladonna, or whatever."

"Wow, that would be great," she said. "Thanks."

Casually, so he wouldn't notice, she maneuvered in her seat slightly and reached into her back pocket and started removing her cell phone.

"So how did you know I'd be at my parents' house?" she asked.

She was just trying to keep the conversation going, get him distracted. Meanwhile, as he explained that it was "just a lucky guess" and how he'd rented the car and driven up, she managed to remove the phone. She had once read a newspaper article about a woman who'd been kidnapped and called someone on her cell phone while in the kidnapper's car. She made a reference to where she was, what road they were on, and the person on the other end got wind of what was happening and called the cops.

Katie's big problem was that her phone was off. After she flipped it open, she'd have to feel around for the power button—she thought it was on the right side, but she wasn't sure. Then, when she found it and turned the phone on, a booting up tone would sound, and she'd have to figure out some way for Peter to not hear it. Finally, if she got the phone on, she'd have to try to make a call. She knew if she pressed SEND twice, she'd call the last number she'd dialed, her mother's cell phone. But her mother probably didn't have her phone on. She always had the stupid thing off, and her father was always yelling at her about it. Katie would have to scroll down, past her mother's number, to previous numbers she'd called, and hopefully contact Detective Himoto, or that other guy, Barasco.

As Katie kept the conversation going, saying banal things like, "How long did it take you to drive up?" and "I wonder if you drove past us," she flipped open the phone, pressed the button she thought was power, and slid the phone under her butt, to smother the booting-up tone.

"What're you doing?"

Katie froze. Totally tongue-tied, she couldn't think of any way out.

With the phone under her butt, she said, "What do you mean?" hoping he hadn't noticed what she was doing.

"Give me the phone," he said.

Fuck, she didn't know how he'd caught on; she'd been so careful.

"The phone?" she said.

"Just give it to me."

"I wasn't—"

"Give it to me right now."

She removed it from under her, and said, "I wasn't doing anything."

He reached over and snatched it.

"What's the big deal?" She was trying to downplay it, stay playful, but it was hard to keep the act going.

"Who were you calling?" Peter asked.

"I wasn't calling anybody."

"Were you calling the cops?"

"No."

"Bullshit."

He was shaking his head. She noticed they were speeding, doing about sixty on the winding road. Hopefully they'd pass a police car, get pulled over.

"You know," he said, "I don't know what it is. I'm so nice to you. I give you things, I take you to great meals, I treat you like a goddamn princess. And this is the thanks I get? This is what you do to me?"

"I didn't do anything."

"It's like you're a fake person; you don't give a shit about anything. You tell me all these things. I try to help you, I try to take care of you. But it's like you don't really love me, do you? You really fucking don't."

"What do you mean? Of course I—"

"You think I'm a fuckin' idiot? Huh? You think I'm a total fuckin' moron? You think I don't know what true love is? I watch *Pride and Prejudice,* all right? I know what fucking love is, and I know when somebody's full of shit!"

God, he sounded totally unstable now, like he could snap at any moment.

"See?" he said. "You're not even denying it. This is all total fucking bullshit!"

Trying to stay calm, but not doing a very good job of it, she said, "I can understand why you're upset, but it's not true. I do love—"

"Shut up, you stupid fucking bitch!" he screamed so loud it actually hurt her eardrums. His eyes shifted toward her for a moment, looking away from the road, right at her, and she knew she'd miscalculated this situation big-time. She wasn't special to him at all. She was as meaningless as any other person.

"Admit it," he said. "You fucked both those guys, didn't you? They had their scummy cocks in your mouth, didn't they?"

"That's not true," she said.

"Bullshit! I saw the pictures! He had his tongue down your fucking throat. I know you had his cock in there, too!"

Katie was thinking, *Pictures? What pictures?*

Then she noticed Peter was reaching down to his left for something. A moment later he was holding the knife.

"It wasn't supposed to end like this," Peter said. "Creative visualization is bullshit. I visualized the ending. I visualized it a million fucking times and it didn't go like this."

"P-p-please," Katie stammered. "Just put the knife down. You're wrong. I'll show you how wrong you are. Just put the knife down."

"It's too late," he said. "Everything's too fucked up now."

Peter waved the knife, the blade inches away from her neck, and she grabbed his forearm. She had to get the knife; it was her only chance. But it was hopeless—he was too strong. He jerked his arm back and she let go, and then the car swerved. They were going very fast downhill, around a bend, and the brakes screeched as they went off the road, onto the shoulder. Then they were tumbling, the car upside down, and Katie's head crashed against something.

When she opened her eyes she didn't know what was happening. She was confused, dizzy; her head hurt like hell and her left arm killed, too. She couldn't move at all and it took her a few seconds to realize why. The air bag had deployed and she was wedged between the bag and the seat. There were flames coming from the car's front end, which was mangled. The car was on its left, so Katie, on the passenger side, was suspended several feet off the ground.

Katie was starting to struggle to free herself and get out of the car, then she looked to her left, or really down, and saw, in the flickering light from the flames, that the driver's air bag had also deployed, but the damage was much worse on Peter's side. The door was pushed in and mangled and he seemed to be wedged in worse than she was. There was blood on his face and he seemed dead or unconscious.

Then Katie smelled gasoline and feared the car might explode. She searched around for the door handle. Finally she found it, but the door wouldn't open. She continued trying, with no luck, and thought this was it, she was going to die. She yanked and pulled the handle several more times, but it wouldn't budge, and then she tried the window switch. She did this out of total desperation—she didn't think there was any way it would possibly work, but remarkably the electrical system in the car was still functioning and the window opened all the way.

Now all she had to do was free herself. As she was undoing the seat belt, she saw why her arm hurt so much. Two jagged bones were jutting through the skin below the elbow. Using her other arm, her right one, she was able to wriggle her body enough to create some room between herself and the air bag and was able to inch her way toward the window. But the flames seemed to be getting more intense and she didn't think she'd be able to make it out.

She was dazed, disoriented. She had no idea if she had been struggling to make it through the window for one minute or ten minutes, but she was finally able to hoist herself and, by grabbing onto the roof of the car with her good hand, she made it partway out.

"Wait."

She looked back over her shoulder and saw Peter. His eyes were starting to open.

"Help me," he said weakly. "Please . . . p-please . . . help me . . ."

Katie's instinct was to go back, try to save him. He would die if she didn't, and she couldn't let another human being die.

The pain in her arm was nearly unbearable; it was hard to think straight. She started to go back toward Peter, when she thought about the people he'd killed—Andy, Will, and God knew who else. She didn't know if Peter really had killed Heather's boyfriend, but he probably had. And what about his own parents?

"I'm sorry," Peter said. "I'm so, so sorry. I didn't mean anything I said before . . . I was just angry because . . . because you hurt me . . . but I won't hurt you . . . I promise I won't."

He held out his hand toward her. She was about to grab it when her better sense returned and she thought, *He's so full of shit.* She started to pull her arm back when Peter lunged toward her, grabbed her wrist, and pulled her toward him.

"Where the fuck were you going?"

He didn't sound so weak anymore.

"Noplace. I was just g-gonna help you."

"Bullshit. You were gonna leave me here."

"I wasn't—"

"Stop bullshitting me!"

In his other hand, he was holding the knife.

"I'll help you," she said. "Just let me go."

"You think I'm a total idiot? If I let you go, you're gonna run out of here and let me die."

"I won't. I swear."

"How could you do that to me? How could you just leave me?"

He was crying.

"Please," she said, "just let me go. I'll get us both out of here, I prom—"

He swiped at her right arm, the one that wasn't broken. The blade tore through her sweatshirt, into her skin.

"I didn't want to do this to you," Peter said.

Peter swiped at her arm again, higher up this time, closer to her shoulder. She made no attempt to stop him; she didn't even flinch.

"Maybe it's better this way," he said. "We can die together, like Romeo and Juliet. It would be tragic, but romantic. Yeah, I kind of like that."

"Please, don't," she said.

"I have to," he said. "Don't you get it?"

He would kill her now. He would come at her with the knife again and this time he'd slash her throat.

But when his arm moved she grabbed it with her right hand and held it back. She was surprised she was able to do this, especially with the gashes.

She continued to hold his arm back, as the blade remained poised, ready to go into her neck the instant she stopped fighting.

"Give up," he said. "Dying doesn't hurt. Trust me."

"Fuck you," she said.

She continued struggling, but he was too strong. Even in his awkward position, it was getting harder and harder to hold him back. In the light from the flames, she saw the blade, getting closer and closer to her neck. Then she leaned in and bit his face as hard as she could. He screamed in her ear and there was blood in her mouth and she kept biting, knowing this was her only chance. He tried to push her away, but her teeth remained clenched and then she felt the knife drop onto the seat. She went for it right away, releasing her bite. He was in shock and couldn't defend himself as she drove the blade into his neck. She kept removing it and sticking it in again, and then she totally lost it and started slashing his face. Even when it was clear that he was dead, she continued to attack him, wanting to cut him to shreds.

Finally she stopped, staring at the bloody mess. Then the strong gasoline odor and the flames reminded her she needed to get the fuck away. She managed to hoist herself out and then she fell to the ground. She got up and started running as fast as she could, away from the burning car, into the darkness. Then she heard the explosion, looked back and saw the red fireball and all the smoke. She was exhausted, in agonizing pain, and very disoriented. She ran along a grassy area, then she saw headlights to her left, and veered in that direction.

She screamed and waved, but no cars stopped; none even slowed. Staying on the shoulder, she continued running and shouting for help.

Eventually, she reached a house. She banged on the door. A girl, a teenager, answered. Katie fell onto the floor, clinging to the girl's legs and sobbing.

37

John Himoto felt a tug on his line and the guy next to him said, "Looks like you got a big one."

It felt big all right. When he was reeling it in, he had to give it some slack to run with, and the way his whole rod was bent, it seemed like he was going to pull in a twenty- or thirty-pounder. Everybody on his side of the boat was looking over, watching, and the guy with the net was waiting, ready to scoop up the sucker as soon as John lifted it out of the water.

John, sweating and breathing very hard, was finally able to reel the fish in at a good clip. And, yeah, it was a biggee—a striped bass that looked about three feet long. People were applauding, and it was by far John's biggest catch ever.

Too bad it wasn't his catch.

As the guy was taking the fish out of the net, John noticed that his line was tangled with another line that seemed to be attached to a rod on the other side of the boat. When the lines were untangled it was discovered that the other guy's hook was in the fish's mouth, not John's.

The other guy, who was out fishing with his young son, was cool about it. He suggested that he and John cut the fish in half, split it fifty-fifty, but John didn't think that was right.

"No, it's yours," he said. "It was on your line."

"You sure?" the guy said.

"Positive," John said. "Enjoy it. Take some pictures with your kid, knock yourself out."

John caught a decent-size fluke later on in the morning, and that was good enough for him. He went home, fired up the grill in the backyard, and cooked up the fish with some salty vinegar fries. The Yankees were playing the Indians and he kicked back and listened to the game on the radio as he ate lunch with a couple of ice-cold brews.

It had been five months since John had walked away from his job, and he didn't miss it at all. When he packed it in, he'd thought there was a good chance he'd regret the decision. Louis had told him, "You'll be on your hands and knees, begging me to take you back, you'll see," and John had known a lot of cops who'd had trouble moving on. They missed the constant action, the buzz of being on the force. But, so far, John had been very content to spend his days fishing, going to the racetrack, or just hanging out at home, doing absolutely nothing.

Of course, once in a while, John had a rough time. It was usually in the middle of the night, after he woke up from a nightmare. He'd think about a case from the past that had slipped through his fingers, and he'd obsess about all the would'ves, could'ves, and should'ves. The one he thought about often, probably because it had been the most recent, was the Peter Wells case. He beat himself up pretty good about how, if one or two things had broken differently, he could've caught on sooner and prevented the death of William Bahner.

But John tried not to let the negativity affect him too much. Every detective fucked up from time to time and every detective knew that the trick to maintaining your sanity was to not let your failures haunt you. At some point, you had to put it all behind you, move on, forget about the past, and that was exactly what John intended to do.

A s Katie approached the north entrance to the Central Park Sheep Meadow, she spotted Amanda, waiting, reading a copy of *Time Out New York*. She hadn't seen her in about six months and she couldn't believe how amazing she looked. She was wearing tight jeans and a tight black V-neck top. She seemed to have lost about ten pounds and her hair looked great, too. She was growing it out, and it looked full and shiny in the bright sunshine.

Amanda saw Katie coming toward her and smiled widely. After they hugged and kissed each other on their cheeks, Katie stood back and said, "Wow, look at you. You look amazing."

"Thanks," Amanda said. "So do you."

"Please," Katie said, knowing Amanda was just trying to be nice, returning the compliment. Katie had put on about ten pounds, and she knew it showed because none of her old jeans fit anymore.

"I'm serious," Amanda said, keeping the fake, yet socially appropriate, sincerity going. "Have you been dieting?"

"No, actually, I've been gaining weight, but who cares? I can't remember the last time I weighed myself. You look incredible, though. I love your hair."

It was the first beautiful day of spring and the Sheep Meadow was jam-packed. Guys with their shirts off were tossing footballs and Frisbees, and girls were lying on blankets, reading or just hanging out with their friends. Katie and Amanda found a spot in the shade and sat down on a picnic blanket that Amanda had brought.

"So I want to hear everything about this new guy," Katie said. "You said his name's Steve, right?"

Amanda had e-mailed Katie and talked to her on the phone, going on about her new boyfriend and what a great guy he was. They'd met at a party, had been seeing each other for almost three months, and were talking about moving in together.

"He's incredible," Amanda said. "He's smart, he's generous, he's supportive, he's interesting, he has a great career . . . He's the real deal."

"What does he do again?"

"Lawyer—well, tax attorney. I know, it sounds dull, but he's not that way at all. If you saw him you'd never guess he was a lawyer. You'd think professor, journalist, something like that. He's really down to earth, loves just staying home, watching TV, going to movies. He's a really good skier. In the winter we went up to Vermont a few times and next year we're gonna go to Colorado."

"That sounds great," Katie said. "I'm really happy for you."

"Thanks," Amanda said. "So tell me about you. What've you been doing? What's going on? You look great; how're you feeling?"

"Pretty good, actually," Katie said. "Knock on picnic blanket." She laughed, then said, "I'm almost done with physical therapy."

"Congratulations," Amanda said.

"Thank you," Katie said. "Yeah, I'm feeling pretty much back to normal, believe it or not. I still get some pain in my arm sometimes, but I can live with it. Lemme see, what else? I've been seeing someone, a therapist, and, I have to admit, it's been helping a lot."

"That's great," Amanda said. "In college, after I was date-raped, I didn't talk to anybody about it for way too long. And I know some people who've been through some really traumatic shit, but not nearly as traumatic as what you went through. I mean, like, car accidents, muggings, things like that.

They didn't get help, and it really screwed them up, so, yeah, it's great that you're seeing somebody."

"What else?" Katie said. "I don't know, things have been pretty boring, I guess. I've been really into my job."

"Do you still have that horrible boss?"

"No, Mitchell left, thank God. I have a new boss, Jenny, and she's great. We're friends—not friends friends, but we go to lunch sometimes, go out for drinks, stuff like that. I really like her a lot."

"It's great you have a boss you get along with."

"I know, it makes a big difference. Coming home every day, pissed off at the world, starts to have an effect on you after a while. It seems like you're dealing with everything, but you're really not, and before you know it, things start blowing up in your face."

Katie made a mental note to discuss this issue with her therapist at her next appointment.

"Have you been seeing anybody?" Amanda asked.

"No, not really," Katie said. "There was one guy. Remember Dave, that guy I went out with senior year?"

"Oh, right, where's he now?"

"He's going to grad school in Florida. Anyway, he was in the city a couple of months ago and he called me. We went out and kind of, like, hooked up one night, but that's it."

"Hey, there's nothing wrong with old-boyfriend sex," Amanda said. "God knows I've been there, done that. But Steve has a lot of very cute friends. If you want me to—"

"Thanks," Katie said. "That's nice of you, but I'm just not into a relationship right now."

"It doesn't have to be a relationship."

"I know, I'm just not ready for anything. In a few months I'm sure I'll be back out there and be a dating machine again, but right now I'm just focusing on my job and getting my life back together."

"So I guess you don't care that that very cute guy's been checking you out."

Katie turned to look in the direction Amanda was looking and saw a guy with wavy blond hair sitting on the lawn on the other side of the tree. He was a surfer-dude type, but very good-looking, like he could have been a model or an actor. He smiled at Katie, but she looked away quickly, back toward Amanda, and said, "Yeah, he is kind of cute."

"Kind of?" Amanda said. "The guy could be an underwear model. I saw him with his shirt off before, and it was washboard city."

"He's probably gay."

"A gay guy wouldn't be staring at you the way he's been staring. Should I tell him to come over?"

"No, really, I'm just not into it right now," Katie said. "But thanks for looking out for me. That's really sweet of you."

Katie and Amanda hung out for about an hour, and did some more catching up. Then Amanda said she had to go, to get ready to meet Steve for dinner, and Katie walked her back out to the path.

"It was really great seeing you," Katie said.

"Yeah," Amanda said. "We have to hang out more often. I know—you want to go to a movie next week?"

"That sounds awesome," Katie said.

They agreed to talk sometime during the week. A few minutes later, Katie, wearing sunglasses and her iPod, listening to the new Pink download, was walking back toward the East Side. It had been great to see Amanda again, but now she was looking forward to returning to her apartment, changing into some comfy clothes and catching up on some work. Or maybe she'd blow off the work, and order in some food—she was in the mood for Indian. Then she'd get into her comfy PJs and watch TV or read a good book.

At the bottom of the hill, she was waiting at a crosswalk for bicycles to pass so she could continue toward the East Side, when she turned to her right and noticed the blond guy Amanda had pointed out before. He was looking right at her, and she got a vibe that he'd been staring at her for several seconds, waiting for her to look in his direction. He smiled and she turned away, conscious that she wasn't smiling or giving him any indication that she was interested.

There was a break in the bike traffic and Katie walked quickly across the road where all the skaters hung out, and then continued along the path and, veering right, passed the Bandshell. At one point, she looked back over her shoulder and felt a jolt in her stomach when she saw that the blond guy was following her. He could've just happened to have been walking in the same direction, but she didn't think so. They had passed several paths and he could've headed in a lot of different directions, so the odds seemed slim that he just happened to be going the same way as her. He was also only about ten yards behind her, which was weird, because since she had spotted him on the road she had increased her pace and was walking at about a jogging speed.

Her pulse was pounding and it wasn't only because she had started walking even faster. She couldn't believe she'd let this happen. She'd had a feeling about this guy, got bad vibes, whatever you wanted to call it, and yet she'd stupidly walked to a fairly unpopulated part of the park. Yeah, it was unlikely that he'd try to assault her in broad daylight, but she could've easily avoided the situation by cutting over toward Bethesda Fountain, where there were tons of people, when she'd had the chance. Now all she could do was try to get away.

When she reached the next path, she continued straight, toward the east side, hoping that he'd turn right. But she didn't even have to turn her head to know he was still following her. Although she was walking at an even quicker pace, he seemed to have gained ground because the sounds of his footsteps and kicked-up bits of gravel seemed to be getting louder. He was probably still at least ten yards behind her, but there was no doubt in her mind now what was happening. He was going to continue behind her, hoping she'd head into a semisecluded area. If she didn't, and left the park, he'd follow her home. Maybe he wouldn't try something today, but he would find out where she lived and then, some other night, when it was late, and she was alone, he'd follow her into her vestibule and rape and murder her.

Like hell he would.

She crossed the park's East Drive and went along the path toward the exit to Fifth Avenue. Of course he was still tailing her. She acted oblivious, but then, moving fast, she reached into her purse, turned, and rushed up to him. She grabbed his arm, squeezing it as hard as she could, and said, "Stay the fuck away from me, you fucking scumbag."

"What the hell?" the guy said, stunned. Yeah, he was stunned all right. He was probably used to following girls all the way back to their apartments and attacking them. No one had ever turned the tables on him before.

"What's wrong with you?" he said. "I was just walking."

He sounded so innocent.

From her purse, she removed a small canister of pepper spray.

"You want me to burn your fucking eyes out?" she said. "Huh? That what you want?"

He held his crossed hands up in front of his face like a big coward and said, "What're you, crazy or something?"

"You think I won't do it, huh? You think I won't?"

"Jesus Christ," he said, and he turned and ran away.

"Stalking bastard!" Katie screamed after him.

She waited until he was out of sight, then she continued on her way out of the park, the pepper spray still in her hand. She doubted he'd have the balls to show his face again. If he did, God help him.